CW00495282

Other Works by Rachel Rener:

The Gilded Blood Series

I. Inked
II. Jinxed
III. Linked
IV. Synced

The Lightning Conjurer Series

I. The Awakening
II. The Enlightening
III. The Christening
IV. The Reckoning

The Girl Who Talks to Ashes

The Little Morsel

The Precipice of Sin

(As part of the *From the Shadows* Anthology)

Autographed Books Available at
~ www.RachelRener.com ~

Table of Contents

Common Blood Types and Their Magical Classes........... 6
The Fae Realm 8
Linked Recap... 10
Radioactive Spiders 16
Hard Knock Life 26
Wisp Repellant... 39
Follow the Yellow Lit Road.. 49
A Clean Slate.. 57
Family Reunion 66
La Petite Mort 73
A Cold Awakening... 88
Into the Woods... 99
Scorched Earth 112
A Rare Bird... 127
Jewish American Princess.. 138
With Friends Like These 147
Blood for Blood.. 158
Uninvited Guests 174
A Chilly Disposition... 190
Blood is Thicker Than Water 204
Scream Queens 216
The Third Realm 229
Suppressive Fire.. 238
Running Up That Hill... 249
Brother in Arms.. 273
Fire and Ice 287

DARKNESS AND LIGHT 296
AMENDS 310
FIFTY SHADES OF GOLD 326
EPILOGUE 344
GENEALOGY 377
NOTE FROM THE AUTHOR 379
GLOSSARY FOR THE GOYIM 380
JÍNI KELÍMI'NAZ / ELVISH DICTIONARY 384
CHEAT SHEET FOR ASPIRING RUNEMASTERS 388
THE LIGHTNING CONJURER SERIES 392
THE GIRL WHO TALKS TO ASHES 393
THE LITTLE MORSEL 394
FROM THE SHADOWS 395
ACKNOWLEDGEMENTS 396
ABOUT THE AUTHOR 399

COMMON BLOOD TYPES AND THEIR MAGICAL CLASSES

Blood Type	Magical Class*	Commonality	Brief Description of Abilities
O-	Benefactor (Universal)	Rare 6.6%	*Has unlimited capacity to create magic/incarnates with the support of a catalyst, but with limited control of creations. Catalysts include: magical pigments, enchanted talismans, wands, conduits, or any other artifact that has been Endowed with magic.*
O+	Benefactor (Limited)	Common 37.4%	*Has limited capacity to create magic/incarnates with one or more catalysts. Limited Benefactors are unable to control even their own magical creations without the help of an amiable Manipulator.*
A-	Extractor (Universal)	Rare 6.3%	*Has unlimited capacity to harness magic from objects, ingredients, or other fae, thereby rendering their target magically-bereft. The extracted magic can then be stored or temporarily mimicked by the Extractor.*
A+	Extractor (Limited)	Common 35.7%	*Has limited capacity to separate magic from ingredients or objects, often rendering them weaker, though not entirely inert. Harnessed magic cannot be repurposed or channeled without the cooperation of an Endower.*
B-	Endower (Universal)	Very Rare 1.5%	*Has unlimited capacity to channel, bestow, and sometimes restore extracted magic into another item or conduit for indefinite use. Powerful Endowers of the past created ancient talismans that are still used to catalyze magic today.*

B+	Endower (Limited)	Rare 8.5%	*Has limited capacity to repurpose magic obtained by Extractors into another artifact, though the Endower will not be able to rechannel the magic without the help of a willing Benefactor.*
AB-	Manipulator (Universal)	Very Rare 0.6%	*Has unlimited capacity to seize control of magical creations and incarnates through a talisman, catalyst, or conduit – even the creations of others. However, their capacity to create magic is extremely limited.*
AB+	Manipulator (Limited)	Rare 3.4%	*Has limited capacity to control magical creations; wholly unable to spark magic or bring incarnates to life without the assistance of a Benefactor.*
Varies	Argent ∝	Extremely Rare <0.00001	*Argent a.k.a. "silver" blooded describes a fae of mixed heritage, whose bloodline is so diversely rich in magic that they can perform up to three types of channeling. This is most common in fae of interspecies heritages, occurring in only 1 in 100,000 [live] fae births.*
Rhnull	Gilded ∞	Extraordinarily Rare <0.0000005%	*Only 1 in 2 million fae (and 1 in 6 million humans) carry Rh-null blood, meaning their blood cells contain no magic-inhibiting properties that human scientists refer to as antigens. All known fae carriers were exterminated or lost in the Blood Wars. On Earth, fewer than 50 humans have the extremely rare condition. To date, only one living fae descendant has "gold blood," thus allowing them to spark, extract, endow, and control magic.*

* MAGICAL CLASS APPLIES ONLY TO FAE BORN UNDER THE POWER OF THE CERULEAN SUN. HUMANS WITH THE SAME BLOOD TYPES ONLY HAVE MAGICAL ABILITY IF THEY ARE DESCENDANTS OF FAE LINEAGES. EVEN THEN, THEIR MAGICAL POTENTIAL IS SIGNIFICANTLY DAMPENED WITH EVERY GENERATION THE FAE ANCESTOR HAS BEEN REMOVED.

THE FAE REALM

MAP OF THE MAIN CONTINENT

Part 1 & 2

LINKED RECAP

Hi, everybody! Talia here.

Do you ever walk into a room and then immediately forget why you walked in there? Yeah, me too. I can't even remember what I ate for breakfast, let alone what happened in some book I read three months ago. Don't these authors realize that a month in book-release time is equivalent to, like, an *eon* for those of us with limited memory cells?

Someone seriously needs to take these writers down a peg.

Anyway, because so many of us are in the same forgetful boat, I have munificently volunteered to create a handy dandy synopsis of all the outrageous shit that has brought us to the 4th and final book in the Gilded Blood Series. Yeah, I know, I can't believe it either! It seriously feels like only a week has gone by since the events of the first book (which, in hindsight, might actually be accurate).

...Wait, where was I? Oh, right!

~ALL THE [IMPORTANT] SHIT THAT'S HAPPENED~

So, first of all, we have some important names to remember:

- There's me, **Talia Kestenbaum**, twenty-five-year-old art school dropout, tattoo artist, and Runemaster-in-Training. Oh yeah, and I'm also the daughter of my half-banshee, half-Jewish mother, **Dee Dee**, and my half-harpy, half-??? father, **Howard**. People are telling me the "???" might be elven, but I seriously doubt that. So, for simplicity's sake, just think of me as a Jewish-Harpy-Banshee mutt. Which is probably how I came to possess extremely coveted "gold" blood (throwing a rusty wrench into the elves' egotistical *pure blood* mishegas), which unlocks all forms of magic across two realms. Yay, me.

- My boss-turned-boyfriend Zayn (a.k.a. **Zæynek al'Bâra-mahd**, the uncrowned king of the Summer Court), who also happens to come from an interesting mixed bloodline – i.e., incubus and elven. He's decided to take up a new hobby of reclaiming the Summer Court, mostly because he's tired of Sol strong-arming the Fae Realm into bloody subservientness, but also because, like me, he's got a bit of a martyr complex. His mother was the late **Queen Jaína**, who was married to the Unseelie-banishing, war-mongering douchebag, **King Saedis**.

- Zayn's familiar, **Hibiscus** (a.k.a. '**Biscuit**,') sacrificed himself to save my life alllll the way back in book one. But my blood, tears, and fervent wish to bring him back imbued him with a piece of my soul, effectively making him my and Zayn's "soul-baby," as well as the link that connects us spiritually.

- **Sol** (who, like Cher, is apparently too cool for a last name), the vicious fae mob boss who single-handedly brought down both the Summer and elusive Winter Court with his ruthless Unseelie army, slaughtered the royal family (including Zayn's mother, stepfather, and three half-siblings), enslaved Zayn for fifty years (until I came along and freed him, yay!), and then slapped an ugly, spider-shaped Requisition Rune (a.k.a. his poisonous incubus claim) on my shoulder right before I nearly killed him. Because he's still pretty upset about that last part, he's doing everything he can to **a)** recapture me for my highly-coveted blood, and **b)** make sure Zayn doesn't successfully mount a revolution.

(Whew, that was a hard one! Don't worry, it gets easier from here.)

There's also:

- **Calus**, the sniveling, vile, face-stealing son-of-a-boggart who calls himself a Runemaster but was really a Death-Magic-exploiting schmuck who, thankfully, found himself on the wrong end of Sol's temper, thus earning himself a broken neck. ☠

- Korinne – a.k.a. **Kor'ínthe al'Rahími**, my new elven bestie – who was also an enslaved Runemaster until I freed her. After **Lanmè**, my other [mermaid queen] bestie, helped us escape Sol's goons by drowning several dozen of them with the assistance of her sisters (mermaids aren't fond of having their hides turned into upholstery, go figure) Korinne returned to her kin in the southern elven territory. Unfortunately, their sanctuary was just attacked by Sol's strung-out, drug-addicted vampires and various other demons and sundry that he Manipulated to his cause. Together, Ko-Ko, Zayn, and I managed to get most of the elves out of there via boats, which we sailed across the ocean to the Western Wastes – meeting another lovely mermaid named **Oralay** on the way.

- Among the three hundred elves we saved, there's **Safir**, Korinne's close friend and Captain of the elven army (who was almost eaten by a sand serpent till I bullied him into horking her up), **Éyrel**, an affable teenage elf who's twice my age in Terran years, and his father, **Tanak**, one of the elven officers. They're all really nice. We love the elves, even if they have a slight superiority complex (particularly toward Unseelies).

- Speaking of which, **Unseelies** are the "bad" fae who usually aren't really bad – banshees, incubi, glaistigs and the like. **Seelies** are the "good" fae who are supposedly more powerful and pure-of-heart – elves, pixies, Blue Fairies from Pinocchio and what-have-you. But Zayn and I are trying to make everyone understand that Seelie or Unseelie, the only thing that truly matters is not being a massive schmuck.

As for **important plot points**, there's just three more things to keep in mind: **One**, I have a stupid Requisition Rune on my shoulder that'll kill me if I touch anyone other than Sol. I'm also getting some weird sensations from it, almost as though I can feel Sol's moods – *ugh*. (And if you think *I'm* unhappy about it, you should see Zayn.) **Two**, after discovering the Waypoint in the Western Wastes had been smashed to smithereens, Zayn, the elves, and I decided to take a shortcut through the mountains in order to reach the Summer Palace before Sol and his army. But even then, it's gonna be tight. Unfortunately, that brings us to point **Three**: Upon learning that we couldn't quickly portal to the palace, Zayn and I realized that one of us would have to run ahead and warn my mom, **Lamswyth** (a lusty-yet-loyal satyr who was once the king's advisor), and the other elven refugees about Sol's impending arrival. So, Zayn and **Mavros** (Sol's shape-shifting raven familiar who recently defected to our side) flew ahead to prepare the palace and its unguarded inhabitants for battle – leaving just me and the elves to make it all the way through the mountains, which is at least a full-day's hike.

Yeah, I know. I'm not happy about our separation either.

Speaking of which, let's hurry up and get this show on the road, because I've got poisonous claims to eradicate and gorgeous incubus boyfriends to tackle. And fae kingdoms to save, of course.

(If you're not feeling particularly confident in my abilities, don't worry, that makes two of us!)

XOXO,

Talia

And now, without further ado…

Part 3

ALL'S FAIR IN LOVE AND WAR

"How wonderful it is that nobody need wait a single moment before starting to improve the world."

— Anne Frank

I.
Radioactive Spiders

Tired, hungry, and harboring sand in the most unfortunate of places, the elves and I wandered through the desert like biblical pariahs. And while it didn't take us forty years to reach the mountains on the eastern side of the Wastes, the hours certainly seemed to pass like seasons. But after five solid ~~months~~ – er, *hours* – of traipsing, we finally managed to find the elusive entrance to the tommyknocker mines: a small, unmarked tunnel hiding beneath the shadow of the towering mountain ridge that separated the Western Wastes from the rest of the continent.

As we approached the wood-framed mouth of the cave, it wasn't relief I felt, but a wave of cold dread – one that reminded me how utterly ill-prepared I was for whatever might be lurking deep within the bowels of these mountains. Despite Zayn's assurances that the mines would be safe, I'd seen a solid two-thirds of the Hobbit trilogy, and therefore considered myself well-versed on the topic of hollow fantasy mountains. Orcs, dwarves, goblins, gold-hoarding dragons – whatever might be waiting for us down there, I wasn't about to be caught off-guard this time around. During our nighttime hike through the desert,

I'd not only memorized every single existing rune on my body, I'd hand-drawn a few more from memory – slightly less effective than their needle-etched counterparts, but hey, lightning is lightning.

Although… I frowned at the sky. *How does that work if I'm* inside *a mountain?*

While I considered that question, Biscuit's tattoo flared with heat.

Talia, a soft, husky voice filled my ears, making my heart leap into my throat. *Are you there?*

Zayn, I sighed, pressing my hand to my fluttering chest. *How are you? How's Mavros? Is she doing any better with the separation sickness?*

She's determined to help, so she's hanging in there. His soft laugh brushed against the inside of my ears. *I can only think of one other creature that's more head-strong and obstinate than she is.*

I grinned. *You're talking about Biscuit, right?*

Yeah, he snorted. *Sure.* His tone shifted. *Hey, we're approaching the palace now. Be safe, okay? Don't forget to freshen up your Revitalization Runes every so often, and make sure you don't touch anyone – no handshakes, high-fives, nothing. I'll be here, impatiently waiting for you on the other side.*

I nodded – not that he could see it. *Give my mom a hug, okay? Especially since…* I swallowed, blinking back tears. *Well…you know.*

Talia, Zayn's voice was as hard as steel, *we're going to figure this out. So help me God, I* will *get that mark off your shoulder. You have my word.*

"Talia?"

"What?" I started, whirling around to find Korinne's lantern-illuminated face.

"You've been standing there for a long time. Do you want us to send a scout ahead?"

"No." I shook my head, silently bidding Zayn goodbye for the moment. "Just make sure everyone is on high-alert. And maybe tell those with working shields to activate them ahead of time, in case there are any, like, dragons inside."

"Dragons nest inside volcanoes, not in underground mines," she replied matter-of-factly. Then, pitching her voice lower, she added, "Some of the soldiers aren't doing great. They're injured, tired, grieving… Even the Revitalization Runes don't seem to be taking as much of the edge off as they should."

I shifted the two daggers slung around my waist: the curved, gold-encrusted dagger the elves had gifted me and the cold-forged iron dagger from my mother. "What can I do to help?"

A grateful smile feathered at the corners of her lips. "Well, there are a few ingredients down in the caves that can be used for healing tonics. If you see any bioluminescent snails, for example, let me know. Or any illuminated crystals. Or, now that I think about it, there's a type of spider that glows pink in the dark—"

"In other words, if it glows, I should mention it?"

"Essentially, yes." Korinne tapped her chin thoughtfully. "Although if you see any floating glowing lights, definitely don't follow those because they'll most likely be will-o'-wisps." Upon seeing my confused expression, she added, "Small sprites that steal the light from your lantern and then cheerfully lead you off a cliff."

"Lovely," I muttered. Then, after casting the elves a glance that was meant to be reassuring, I rolled up my sleeves and ducked beneath the low wooden overhang, holding my lantern out at arm's length.

A long, carved-out passageway stretched before me, seemingly with no end. Tapping on Biscuit's tattoo, I gently woke him up from his nap. He appeared with a wide yawn, ruffling and unruffling his head feathers as he stretched first his left leg behind him, and then his right. Even at night, the faint decorative lines of tribal scrollwork accenting his plumage stood out like fine golden thread, and his long, glittering tail feathers gleamed with every color of the fae rainbow, as brilliant and lustrous as finely-cut gems.

"Good morning," I smiled, booping the tip of his beak. He nibbled on my glowing finger playfully.

"Touching him doesn't hurt you?" Korinne asked, referencing Sol's claim on my shoulder.

I shook my head. "I think, because we share a soul, that the Requisition Rune can't tell the difference between us. He's essentially an extension of me… Aren't you, little buddy?" Biscuit's feathers ruffled in contentment as I kissed the top of his head. "At least I can still touch *someone.* I'd never realized how important physical touch was until I found out I'd never be able to hug anyone ever again."

"El'thanek lo máreth íbna," Korinne muttered, which I now understood meant something along the lines of "that son of a bitch," but far less polite. *"Sevyán'the sivích'en váşi!"*

I stumbled over my own foot. "You hope *whose* lover has venereal pustules?"

"Oops," she said, her pointed ears turning several shades of pink. "I keep forgetting you can understand Elvish[1] now… Uh, well"—she rubbed the back of her neck self-consciously—"in our culture, we don't just say 'Fuck you' or 'Fuck him.' Our curses tend to be a little more…"

"Elaborate?" Safir offered, ducking beneath the low overhang of the cave entrance to join us.

---

[1] Elvish Glossary found on page 384

"To say the least," Korinne grinned. "The Elvish equivalent of 'Fuck you,' for example, is 'May your lover have genital pustules' – the implication, of course, is that the lover gets them from someone else and then gives them to you."

"Of course," I nodded solemnly.

As we cautiously made our way inside, Biscuit flew ahead, igniting the unlit torches on the tunnel walls one at a time. The dazzling rainbow fire made the stones of the corridor dance with every color of the fae light spectrum – all two dozen of them. I smiled at him as I swapped a lantern for one of his colorful burning torches, favoring him with a quick head scratch that elicited a blissful birdy sigh.

"And we don't simply call someone a 'son of a bitch,' like you do in English," Safir continued. "It's misogynistic, for one, not to mention boring. Elves say…" Her eyes quickly darted to the others, who were falling into step behind us. "Well, I won't say it in Elvish, but the translation is something like, 'I will have intercourse with your childhood milkmaid, in your current marital bed, where you have not once succeeded in bringing your romantic partner to…'" She frowned, tapping her chin.

"Climax," Korinne supplied.

"Hmm." Safir's frown deepened. "It sounds much better in Elvish. I will teach you when we don't have so many listening ears."

"I look forward to it," I grinned.

Impromptu expletive lessons momentarily set aside, we made our way farther into the narrow, downward-sloping tunnel, leading the rest of the group, who had fallen into step behind us. The stony walls of said tunnel now looked like an underground hippie den, thanks to Biscuit and his growing line of tie-dyed torches. But instead of smelling like marijuana and patchouli oil, the air smelled like pine needles and damp stone, growing mustier and warmer the deeper we traveled.

As we walked, Safir kept darting glances in my direction.

"What?" I finally asked. "Do I have something on my face?"

"It's just…you are glowing so much brighter than you were yesterday."

"I was wondering about that too," Korinne admitted. "Is your Concealment Rune fading?" She cocked her head to peer down at my ankle, where the light from my delphinium ink tattoo could be seen even through the heavy purple fabric of my *kœrta* – a long-sleeved, high-collared jumpsuit with a sweeping overskirt that was as functional as it was elegant. (And it had pockets!)

"No, I…" My hand fluttered to the hollow of my throat, where my gold locket used to rest. "My, uh…" I swallowed painfully. "My pendant broke. When Sol stole the vial of blood that hung from my neck."

Korinne's expression darkened. "You mean the fae talisman your father gave you? The one that masked your magical signature?"

I nodded. "Zayn promised me he'd fix it as soon as possible, but…" I tried to laugh, the sound catching in my throat. "I just feel so naked without it."

"If Zæynek is able to repair it, then it will be even better than before." She flashed me a smile that I'm sure was meant to make me feel better, but the sadness and pity etched around her eyes only made my stomach knot. Worst of all was the flicker of fear she'd failed to conceal; it immediately roused my own frightened thoughts, which I'd been trying – and failing – to suppress all day.

He has my blood.

Sol, the most powerful and terrifying creature in two realms, had finally gotten his hands on gold blood. Paired with Zayn's stolen grimoire, who knew what fresh kind of hell that monster would be able to unleash. *At least his last Runemaster is dead.* A shiver snaked down my back as I remembered the sickening crunch Calus's neck made when Sol snapped it.

No one touches my claim but me... No one.

We walked in silence for several minutes before Korinne cleared her throat, snapping me from the barrage of traumatic memories and worsening what-ifs that had been pummeling my amygdala into an anxious slurry.

"Keep an eye out for geometric spider webs," she said cheerfully, drawing perplexed looks from Safir and me. "*Işík-arényen* are known for the intricate spiral designs they weave into their webs to attract—*aha!*" she exclaimed, darting into a dark corner where, indeed, the threads of a weirdly beautiful spiderweb were catching in the rainbow light.

While Korinne ducked in and out of the shadows to snatch up whatever bioluminescent creepy-crawlies she could find for her forthcoming healing tonics, Safir and I hung behind, walking in thoughtful silence. Once or twice, I caught her watching Korinne's back with a fond smile.

"So..." I cleared my throat. "Did you know her from, uh...before?"

She started at my question, the tips of her pointed ears turning pink. "Wh-Who? Kor'ínthe?"

I nodded.

"Yes," she answered, absentmindedly running her fingers through her long, dark hair. "I know her from many years ago. I was working at the palace as a royal cartographer, which you wouldn't think would be a dangerous job"—she bit her lip, clearly working to suppress a smile—"and yet I always found some way to end up in the medical quarters, where she was working as a palace healer."

"Ah, I see." I nodded. "Does she know you love her?"

She jerked her head at me, white showing all around her brilliant topaz irises – mostly likely due to my "total lack of personal boundaries," as Zayn had recently put it. But if I'd learned anything this past week, it was that life is too short and unpredictable to keep your feelings bottled up.

I cocked my head. "Well?"

"I…" Safir grimaced, her ears darkening to scarlet. "Is it so obvious?"

"What's obvious to me is that Korinne's amazing, and you clearly have great taste," I answered honestly. "So…why not tell her how you feel?"

"I…I do not know if she feels the same way," she answered, pitching her voice even lower as Korinne knelt to examine a brightly-glowing orange snail nearby. "Besides, she returned to the settlement just days ago, only to discover that her entire family had perished in the aftermath of the war."

"Oh." Sadness knotted in my chest, followed by a sharp stab of guilt. "I…I didn't know." My shoulders stooped heavily. "I didn't even ask."

"Your arrival brought her much joy, Tálya al'Dídra," Safir said, unconsciously slipping back into Elvish. "And it was you who freed her from her forced servitude. There simply has not been time to properly catch up. Do not blame yourself for that." The warmth of her smile immediately made me feel better. "As for Kor'ínthe's family, it is possible they survived and fled to the Northern Demesne, where there are rumors of a hidden elven settlement… But as there is no evidence of such a place, what else can she assume but the worst?" She shook her head sadly. "No, Tálya… I cannot put more on her shoulders by making selfish declarations. I can only offer her my friendship and hope it is enough."

I wanted to say more, but Korinne returned at that moment, gently dropping a handful of live, squirming, glowing pink spiders into a leather pouch.

"I won't be able to milk the venom from these until I have the proper type of cloth," she said casually, oblivious to my wince of revulsion, "but once I do, they'll make for a powerful *Vidgæ'dren* potion."

"Don't forget all the sand serpent saliva I selflessly donated to the cause," Safir added drily. "What did you say that was good for?"

Korinne tried to hide a wry smile. "The enzymes found in sand serpents' salivary excretions can be used for all sorts of healing and fortifying potions. It's a highly coveted Extractant. So, your 'donation' is much appreciated."

"Wonderful," Safir said, once more combing her fingers through her long, still-partially-matted ponytail.

Behind us, Éyrel was quietly snickering. Safir shot him a dirty look over her shoulder while his father, Tanak, swatted him over the head.

"Do not be so quick to laugh," he told his son, "when there are blood-thirsty, elf-eating demons that roam these mines." He flashed me a quick wink. "Éyrel has spent his entire life in the settlement, so he's never laid eyes on a tommyknocker before."

His son's eyes grew wide. "Tommyknockers are demons?"

"The scariest kind of demon you can think of," I replied, doing my best to keep a straight face. "They have these scruffy, blood-soaked beards, and coal-black eyes that see straight into your soul. And noses that are so big, they can smell your flesh from a mile away."

"Tell Éyrel about their claws," Safir grinned. "How they're long and jagged…"

"Oh, yes." I shivered. "The perfect shape for pulling out the brains of their prey through their ear canals—"

"Brains?" Éyrel scoffed. "What for?"

"For eating. They like to smear them over crackers, I hear."

"Crackies?" Up ahead, Biscuit made a dramatic mid-air U-turn. "Where crackie?" His beady, greedy little eyes honing in on the leather pouch Korinne was holding, he hopped on her wrist and snatched it out of her hand.

"Hey!" she cried, grasping for it.

Ignoring her, he violently shook out the pouch until it exploded in a shower of bright pink spiders, resulting in twin shrieks of terror from him and me.

"*Raaaawk!*" he screeched, hurling the pouch to the ground. "Spi-yer!"

"This is why you ASK FIRST, you walnut-brained numbskull!" I shouted, simultaneously swatting an errant arachnid from my bangs.

Poor Korinne let out a long-suffering sigh as she knelt to the ground to re-collect her precious radioactive spiders. With a pinch-faced grimace, Safir chivalrously crouched beside her, plucking the spiders from the ground with her thumb and forefinger and then hastily dropping them in the pouch with a visible shudder.

Meanwhile, Éyrel was still looking around nervously, as though a monster might leap from the shadows at any moment. "You were just making jokes before, right?"

"Jokes?" I asked innocently. "About the brain-eating tommyknocker demons?"

"Yes."

"Not at all," a menacing voice uttered from right behind us.

"Auuugh!" Éyrel yelped, jumping two feet in the air.

"In fact," the stealthy tommyknocker grinned, displaying a full set of green-tinted teeth, "the best way to serve elven brains is with larkberry jam and crumpets!"

II.
Hard Knock Life

Éyrel's hand shot toward his dagger.

"Take it easy," I said, reflexively clasping his wrist, which I quickly dropped with a wince. "We were just pulling your leg."

"No one was pulling me!" he sputtered, reminding me that Translation Runes don't handle idioms very well.

"Please forgive our rudeness!" Korinne swiftly interjected, inclining her head at the rogue tommyknocker. "We truly meant no disrespect."

The three-foot creature stepped out of the shadows, and as he did, twenty more tommyknockers appeared in the shadowy corridor just ahead of us. "On the contrary, what you said about our noses was quite flattering," he beamed, one gnarled finger tapping the side of the prodigious, wart-riddled bulb protruding from his face. "In fact"—his bushy eyebrows wiggled up and down—"large noses are often seen as a sign of sexual prowess among male tommyknockers."

Korinne pressed her mouth into a tight line – a far more polite response than my ungainly snort.

"I am Boris." The tommyknocker removed his pointed hat to make a sweeping bow. "How may we be of service to you this fine evening?" Without giving anyone the chance to answer, he quickly barreled on, "We did just recently discover a brand-new vein of *nivadium* ore that's highly conductive, as well as a pocket of *denzanite* crystals so transparent, you'd almost mistake them for glass – though they most certainly aren't made of glass," he added a little too quickly. "We're also pleased to offer a wheel of *tommindale* cheese, crafted from the finest mountain sheep's milk and fermented until the molded rind turns a delicious fuzzy green—"

"We're not here to barter, Boris," Korinne interjected while I stifled a gag. "We came to seek safe passage through your mines—"

"Not here to barter?" Boris's fox ears drooped. A synchronized groan erupted from the gaggle of tommyknockers up ahead.

"Now, hang on a minute," I said, casually smoothing out my layered skirts. "I mean, there's always room to barter, right? As we were telling Morris just the other day—"

"Morris?" Boris's ears perked right back up. "That's my cousin!"

"Oh?" I asked, feigning surprise. "Well, as Korinne and I had just mentioned to our dear, close tommyknocker friend, Morris—"

He let out a star-struck gasp. "*The* Korinne, who has stolen the heart of our cousins in the Obsidian Cliffs? Why, you are even more lovely than Morris claimed!" Boris whirled on me as I coughed out a laugh. "And you must be Korinne's lusty assistant, Zaffre!"

My laughter cut off abruptly. "Lusty?!"

"Zaffre?" Safir muttered to Korinne.

"Why, yes! My cousin told us how enthusiastic you were in offering up your sweet kisses in exchange for *durajellan* truffles!" His coal-like black eyes lit up with excitement. "It just so happens that we have many varieties of fine truffles here! Not to mention dried *oshaoli* lichen grounds, which, as you no doubt know, is an extremely powerful aphrodisiac—"

"Raawk!" Biscuit clucked impatiently.

"*Boris*," I stressed, gritting my teeth in what probably looked like a maniacal smile, "listen to me. As we stand here discussing fungus and sexual performance enhancers, an army of demons is headed to the Summer Palace to slaughter a hundred unarmed elven refugees." A knot appeared in my throat at the thought of Zayn, Lam, and my mother being among them. "So, we're trying to get there as fast as possible to stop Sol from—"

"Sol?" Boris interjected sharply, a low growl slipping between his pointed teeth. "You speak of the ruthless, greedy demon who rules from his obsidian fortress on the High Plateau?"

"Yes, him. Why—*hey!*"

I jumped out of the way as Boris shoved past me to join the growing cluster of now at least fifty tommyknockers, who had erupted into an angry tizzy upon hearing Sol's name. Their voices grew low and frantic as they pressed their pointy hats together in a tight huddle. Every so often, one of them would pop up like a gopher to glare suspiciously at us, then drop back down to join the muffled buzz of whatever heated discussion they were having amongst themselves. At some point, one of them broke off and ran down the dark corridor, returning a few minutes later with several dozen more tommyknockers.

As their numbers grew and their debate became more and more spirited, the rest of us began to shift uncomfortably.

Finally, Boris turned around, locking his black, beady eyes on mine. "Do you intend to dissuade Sol from his present course of action by means of political dialogue or swift assault?"

My hands balled into fists. "Our intention is to annihilate him completely."

His eyes narrowed into contemplative slits before he spun on his heels to rejoin the huddle. The knockers' whispers grew louder and more fervent over the next minute or so, until the meeting abruptly adjourned – at which point, one hundred stony-faced tommyknockers turned around to glare at us, forming a tight barricade that blocked the entire corridor.

Korinne and I exchanged nervous glances.

"Madam Zaffre," Boris said, the edges of his voice hard. "Our business – the entire mining industry, in fact – is controlled, overseen, and regulated by Sol. It is because of him that our workload and output has tripled in recent years."

Shit. My shoulders slumped. There was no way we could convince them to help us now. Hell, if these little guys were that far into Sol's pocket, they might not even let us through the mountain.

My fingers absentmindedly crept toward my Fulmen Rune.

"It is because of him that we starve, unable to profit from the fruits of our toils," Boris continued, bolstered by a chorus of affirming grunts. "It is because of him that we have been relegated to these mountains, that we work from sun-up to sundown every day, just so he and his associates can pocket seventy percent of the minerals we unearth. It is because of him that we fear for our very lives as this mine edges closer and closer to exhaustion. *He* controls the realm-wide price of fine gems and metals, forcibly inflating their values to further line his pockets with gold," he snarled, wringing his cap in his hands, "all the while digging a proverbial muddy boot into our backs!"

Stunned, I let my hand drop to my side.

He yanked his hat back over his ears with two hands, spitting in the dirt. "If it is war you seek with the red-eyed devil, then it is war you shall have! And as you ride into battle, hastened by gnawing rage and the unquenchable thirst for justice, the tommyknockers shall ride alongside you, lifting our sharpened axes to victory!"

His small army of compatriots, who had been fervently nodding alongside Boris's impassioned speech, raised their pickaxes to the air, echoing his cry.

Chewing on my lip in consternation, I exchanged perplexed looks with Korinne and Safir, then glanced over my shoulder at the rest of the elves, who looked equally bewildered at the knockers' vociferous – and wholly unprompted – pledge of support. When I met Tanak's eye, he and the other officers could only offer me baffled shrugs.

"Um," I said, turning back around to Boris, "when you say you'll help us 'ride into battle,' does that include leading us through this mountain as quickly as possible?"

Once more removing his hat, Boris swept into a dramatic flourish, displaying his shiny bald head and fox-like ears. "Milady Zaffre, you shall see the other side of the mountain before moonrise tomorrow!"

I turned to Biscuit, who, like the elves, merely gave me a half-hearted shrug.

Sighing, I rubbed my temples. *I mean...what's the worst that could happen?*

A swift and bloody massacre, that's what, I immediately answered myself.

"Umm..." While opening my mouth to politely-yet-firmly turn down his offer, I couldn't help but meet the fervent, hopeful stares of each of these overworked little men. They gazed up at me with shiny black puppy dog eyes, wringing their pointed hats in earnest.

Fuck me, I sighed, knuckling my forehead.

"Well?" Boris asked.

"Well," I replied, weakly swinging my fist in front of my chest, "looks like we're all riding into battle!"

The tommyknockers burst into raucous cries, throwing their hats and mining tools in the air.

"Come!" Boris called over his shoulder as he and the others turned on their heels to scamper down the passageway. "Our glorious battle awaits!"

Flashing one last mystified glance over my shoulder, I pushed my heels off the ground and half-heartedly jogged after them, with the rest of the elves following suit a few paces behind me.

"We did say we needed all the help we could get," Korinne huffed, lifting her skirts around her knees as Biscuit flew ahead, illuminating the passageway with a rolling wave of rainbow fire.

"Oh, yeah," I agreed. "And now that we've gathered ourselves a small army of three-foot-tall men, we'll win this battle for sure."

"What is it you say in English?" Safir asked. "When something is twisted helically around an adjacent plane but also means all hope is lost?"

I frowned. "Uh… Screwed?"

"Yes," she nodded solemnly. "I would definitely say we are all very screwed."

We made our way deep into the mountains like the first elementary school field trip of the year, with the tommyknockers excitedly running ahead and hollering for us to keep up. The elves and I, of course, were the sleep-deprived parents and teachers, trailing behind in a heavy-lidded, caffeine-deficient cluster. By then, we were all completely exhausted and nursing varying degrees of injury and loss. And even though the knockers had offered to let us sleep in their network of caves for the night, we didn't have time to stop and rest. We just had to push through, offering encouragement and support to one another as our energy continued to wane. Despite being exhausted ourselves, Korinne and I continually weaved back and forth through the group, placing Revitalizing and Stamina Runes on the elves who needed them most. She'd managed to escape the elven settlement with a handful of tattoo machines, but only a few vials of standard ink, so I donated blood whenever I could to make sure the runes worked to their full extent. But even gold blood has its limits, particularly when its living vessel is steadily fading from food and sleep deprivation.

"You are as white as an umbra," Korinne gently chided me, snatching the empty glass vial from my hand before I had a chance to refill it via the self-inflicted cut on my palm. "Here," she poured a stream of cool, milky liquid over the gash, which bubbled and foamed like hydrogen peroxide, leaving a pale scar in its wake.

"But—"

"No buts, little sister. I promised Zæynek I would look after you, and I do not relish being made into a liar."

"But I feel fine," I protested.

"You are not *fine*." She frowned, looking me over from my tattered head to my toes. "Just because you have the power to help, doesn't mean you should further injure yourself to provide it. You have done all you can," she said firmly, cutting off whatever argument had been forming in my mouth. "Do not give more until you have more to give."

"Kor'ínthe is correct, of course," Safir agreed as she fell into step beside us. "You are forging a life debt too great to repay, Tályа al'Dídra. It would dishonor us if you harmed yourself any further in your desire to help."

My shoulders slumped at the thought of their homes – their sanctuary – being reduced to nothing but smoldering ash and sand. "I just feel so horrible about everything that's happened to all of you. You've lost so much."

"We have survived far worse than this," Safir smiled. "And because of your help and generosity, we will make it through this dark time to see the dawn."

"The dawn of Zæynek *Pádeşah* and our new elven Summer Court," Tanak agreed from behind us.

"Pádeşah," I repeated softly. "You already call him 'king,' even though we haven't won yet?"

"One does not have to bear the crown to earn the title," Safir remarked blithely. "Zæynek al'Bâramahd's selfless actions have made him a savior to our people. Furthermore, he is of royal blood, and the only surviving heir to the queen. With his return, the elves have a legitimate claim to the throne, allowing our people to once again rule this domain as the Creator intended."

I arched an eyebrow.

"And it is because of you, *Paşahdî'mtha*, that he – and we – have found our true purpose once more as the stewards of this land."

"I'm not your queen," I blurted out, wincing. "I mean, it's not that I don't…" The sensation of several dozen sets of elven eyes burning into the back of my neck made me stumble. "Look, I'm just a tattoo artist from Miami, okay? And I only got that job because Zayn took pity on me when no one else would. Before that, I was an unemployed art school drop-out. Hell, I didn't even know this realm existed until last week!" My cheeks flushed with chagrin as I forced myself to add, "I am, quite literally, the least qualified person in this cave to be called queen."

When I finally mustered up the courage to meet their gazes, the elves appeared utterly nonplussed.

Confused, I tapped my Translation Rune. "Did you guys not understand me, or…?"

The officer standing beside Tanak – *Laleh,* I recalled from our prior interactions – cleared her throat. "King Saedis, may he rest in peace, was a cobbler before Queen Jaína presented him with a seed from the Great Phoenix Tree—"

"The traditional elven way of requesting someone's hand in marriage," Korinne supplied helpfully.

"Yes." Laleh nodded. "So, as you can see, Tálya *Paşahdî,* it was not Saedis's vocation or education that earned him the crown, but the eminence of his blood. Only those with the purest souls and bloodlines can be blessed with gilded blood. It is an Endowment by the Creator herself."

Walking backwards, I arched an incredulous eyebrow, waiting for someone to jump in with the obvious rebuttal to that: that blood is a matter of genetics, not religion or creed.

But no rebuttal came.

I let out a frustrated sigh. "But Saedis had a bunch of other qualifications as well, right? Like political experience or maybe, like, a master's degree from an accredited university?" My voice was getting shriller with every question. "A basic understanding of fae world history, at the very least?"

Laleh and the other elves stared at me blankly.

I stared back at them in disbelief. "What about intelligence? Honesty? Morals? Does none of that matter when it comes to wearing the crown?"

She gave me a patient smile. "As I said, blood determines all of that. Yours is gilded. And after witnessing the miracles you conjured during the attack of our settlement, we now recognize that you are the wisest, strongest, and most honorable person among us. In this entire realm, even. We are privileged to march beside you." She bowed her head deeply, as did at least a dozen other elves who had been listening to our conversation.

I froze in place, at a loss for words. There had to be some way to convince these people that I wasn't pre-ordained or divinely-endowed; I was just a mutt – a veritable freak of nature.

"Come along, Zaf–erm, Talia!" Boris called from up ahead. "We are nearly at the Great Crystal Cavern!"

"How far is that from the other side of the mountain?" I hollered back, forcing my heavy, aching feet to keep moving forward.

"Oh, we are getting very close now! Only about ten more candles to go!"

"What's a candle?" I asked Korinne.

She paused, as though mentally calculating numbers in her head, then answered, "About an hour and twenty minutes in Terran time. So, ten candles would be, ohh…a little over thirteen hours?"

"Kill me," I whimpered.

She went to pat my back, stopping herself at the last second with an apologetic grimace.

Biscuit swooped down to land on my shoulder, chattering excitedly. "Crissies!" he squawked. "Biiig crissies!"

"The Chrises are back?" I gasped, remembering Sol's dim-witted incubi henchmen, whom I'd not-so-lovingly nicknamed Pine, Hemsworth, and Evans. "Where are th—"

My question broke off in a choked gasp as a blast of hot, muggy air hit me in the face. The narrow tunnel we'd been walking through abruptly ended, dumping us into an enormous cavern that was as wide as it was tall, at least three football fields on all sides. Colossal, water-clear crystals, some nearly scraping the thousand-foot-high ceiling, towered above us like redwood trees. They sprouted from the ground, the walls, and the ceiling at every angle, crisscrossing over one another and throwing prismatic rainbow reflections all over the cave. I stepped aside as more and more elves entered the cavern, their expressions as awe-struck as mine. Even among the many splendors of the Fae Realm, I had never seen anything this magnificent. I had to remind myself to breathe as I spun in a small circle to take it all in, sucking down a mouthful of uncomfortably warm, humid air.

"This is the one part of our mines Sol has not yet been able to purloin," Boris said, appearing at my side while the rest of the tommyknockers clustered just ahead of us, wringing their hats at the cavern in reverence. "In fact, he does not even know of its existence – not yet, at least. But with every passing day, our minecarts grow lighter and lighter. Soon, they will be empty, and Sol will send his demons deeper into the mountain to verify all of the mineral veins have been tapped. If he were to discover this place, to learn of the secret we've been keeping from him…" He swallowed tightly, twisting his hat between two calloused hands. "Well, let's just say it would be a very dark day, indeed."

"I did not know any of the ancient crystal caverns survived the pillages of the Great Fall," Safir breathed, pressing her hand against the smooth, iridescent side of a "small" crystal scepter that towered some fifty feet above her head. "The only other crystal cavern I have heard of is far north, and its splendor is but a fraction of this."

"It is a secret we have not dared breathe to any outsider." Boris's look was a pointed one. "But time is of the essence, and circumnavigating this cave would add at least five candles to your journey."

"We won't tell a soul," I promised, and the elves nodded their agreement.

"Rawk!" Biscuit agreed from his perch on my shoulder.

"Good." Boris replaced his hat with a business-like flourish. "Then follow me, please, and do be sure to stay close. Will-o'-wisps are drawn to these crystals like moths to a flame."

Gulping, I hastily fell into step behind him and the other knockers. They led us down a winding path that twisted underneath and around the forest of jutting crystals, some of which we had to physically hoist ourselves over in order to stay on the "trail" – a.k.a. a vaguely worn-down footpath that I could barely make out, but the knockers seemed to know by heart. Every so often, I'd spot a dark archway or corridor in the distance, which no doubt led to even more tunnels and caverns that made up this vast underground labyrinth. I couldn't imagine trying to traverse it without the knockers as our guides; we'd probably never find our way back out.

"Ugh," I muttered, wiping my brow with the back of my hand. The thought of getting lost in this place made me perspire more than I already was. The air was so warm and humid, sweat dripped down my back and matted my bangs to my forehead. I unbuttoned the high collar of my dress, wishing I could peel the entire thing off. But I'd already been called "lusty" once that night, and somehow, I didn't think walking around butt-naked would help my reputational precedent.

"Here," Korinne said, her own brow dotted with sweat. "You must be starving." She handed me a canteen and a small chunk of what looked like a slice of pound cake.

I practically wept at the sight.

After breaking off a small morsel for Biscuit, I greedily scarfed down the rest. The cake was dense and buttery and sweet, with a slight hint of lemon. The familiar, comforting flavor brought me back to my first night in the Fae Realm; this was the same bread Zayn had given me inside the tent where we were forced to share a sleeping bag to keep warm. That was the evening I realized that my feelings for Zayn might not actually be one-sided – that he was, perhaps, fighting his repressed feelings for me just as fiercely as I was fighting mine for him.

Hunger satiated, I winced as another kind of pang unfurled in my core; I could vividly remember his hot, quickening breath brushing against the back of my neck. His fingers clutching my waist like he couldn't bear to let me go. The entire length of his hard arousal, pressing against the small of my back…

"Talia," he'd whispered, his voice ragged with the last, unraveling vestiges of his self-control. *"Tell me no. Tell me no and—"*

Biscuit let out a startled squawk as my left foot collided with the back of my right heel, pitching us both forward. Instinctively, Korinne grabbed my arm to keep me from falling, eliciting a sharp yelp of pain from me.

"I'm so sorry!" she cried, immediately letting go.

"It's okay," I gasped. Clutching my shoulder, I took a deep breath to collect myself. "It was my fault – just please don't try to catch me if I fall again," I added with a pained chuckle.

She said nothing in response, though her eyes were pooling with sympathy as I forced her a tight smile, then quickly turned away.

So long as this stain stays on my body, I thought, blinking back tears, *I'll never be able to share a sleeping bag – or any other kind of bed – with Zayn ever again.*

III.
WISP REPELLANT

We walked for hours, sustained by runes, small pieces of elven bread, and the ardent desire to return to our loved ones. The crystals jutting from the ceiling and walls grew smaller and smaller the longer we walked, until they were no bigger than the size of my fist – but still dazzlingly beautiful.

At one point, the ground on either side of the path fell away, revealing a chasm of inky blackness that we had no choice but to traverse across. A narrow wooden bridge stretched into the darkness, of which there seemed to be no end; the ground was so far below, I couldn't tell where the shadows ended and the earth began. Worst of all, the only thing separating us from the endless abyss was a fraying, knee-high rope railing. My stomach lurched into my throat as I minced across the bridge – no wider than a city sidewalk – sandwiched between a long line of tommyknockers ahead and an even longer line of elves trailing behind me. The dancing, multicolored flames from our torches reflected against the crystal stalactites that hung high above us, creating hundreds of prismatic rainbows that were quickly smothered by blackness.

Hands and knees trembling, I forced my eyes back to the wooden planks beneath my feet, which creaked and rocked as we made our way deeper into the void.

"Um, B-Boris?" I called, trying to keep my teeth from chattering. The air was as hot and muggy as ever, but my courage had abandoned me well over thirty minutes ago.

"Yes?" he glanced at me over his shoulder.

"How long is this bridge?"

"Oh, just another half-candle or so of walking," he beamed, "and then we'll arrive at the end."

An involuntary squeak slipped through my lips. "And y-you're sure it can hold this much w-weight?"

"Oh, certainly! This bridge could easily support up to three hundred tommyknockers!"

"What about elves?" Éyrel called from a few feet behind me, his voice as shaky as my knees. "We're twice your height!"

Boris stopped dead in his tracks, making me and the line of elves behind me lurch to a stop.

"Oh." He frowned. "I hadn't thought of that. In that case, it's probably better to spread out the weight." He raised his voice, adding, "Elven friends, I suggest leaving a span or so in between you and your neighbor to avoid overburdening the bridge! Knockers, carry on!"

I waited until I could just barely make out the glint of Boris's axe, then gingerly made my way forward, shooting one last petrified glance at Korinne.

"I'll be right behind you," she called. "Well, a few spans behind you, anyway."

I squeaked out an affirmative whimper, then glanced at Biscuit, who was casually preening himself on my shoulder. "Think you could help link me with Zayn? It might be nice to say goodbye before the two of us plunge to our deaths."

Shaking out his feathers, he chirped, "Bisskiss not die. Bisskiss fly!"

"Wow," I remarked dryly. "How do you fit so much love and compassion into such a tiny body?"

"Luvyu!"

"Do you?!" I balked, shaking my head. "Just call Zayn already!"

"Zayn!" he squawked, his shrill echo reverberating throughout the cavernous expanse.

I was just about to wring his scrawny neck when a familiar voice murmured in my ears, *Talia, where are you? Are you okay?*

At the sound of Zayn's voice, relief flooded my body. *Yeah, we're okay – just enjoying a nice walk through an underground cavern.* I grimaced, doing my best not to look down. *How are you?*

I'm—

IS THAT TALIA? My mother's voice flooded the link, as though she'd just burst into Zayn's not-so-personal space. *IS SHE OKAY? DID YOU REMIND HER TO DRINK PLENTY OF WATER SO SHE DOESN'T GET DEHYDRATED? WHEN ARE THEY GETTING HERE?*

Yes, it's Talia, Zayn answered her. *She was just about to tell me where they are.*

DID YOU TELL HER ABOUT WHAT HAPPENED AFTER DINNER? AND THAT YOU FINISHED THE 'CALRISSIAN' INK?

No, I haven't had the chance—

Zayn, I interrupted, *would you kindly tell my mom to shove a sock in it for a second?!*

What? I can't tell her that!

Zœynek! Lamswyth's voice echoed through the link. *Are you in there? I believe I've found the source of the trow infestation!*

OH MY GOD! DID YOU TELL HER ABOUT THE TROWS? Mom interjected. *TALIA, DID HE TELL YOU? WE FOUND A WHOLE NEST OF TROWS IN THE NORTH WING!*

Dee Dee, please. I haven't been able to tell her anything yet—

Zœynek! Lam's voice was steadily growing in both volume and distress. *I think you'd better come see this!*

You should go, I sighed.

I am so sorry, Tal – but, quickly, you're okay? Absolutely nothing is wrong?

I stole one last glance at the bowels of oblivion on either side of me, feeling the cavern spin as I did, and replied, *Nope! Everything's great!*

I cannot wait to see you, he said, a warm pang of longing heating our link. *In fact, I—*

A sheep-like bleat sounded from somewhere close to Zayn, cutting him off.

Go, I urged. *We'll be there soon...another eight or nine candles, I'd guess.*

Candles? His laugh warmed me from the inside out. *You sound positively fae-like, Sevyánim. Okay, I'd better—*

Zayn, wait – before you go... I hesitated, working to get the pronunciation exactly right. *Kalb'ímtha azá'ye dáşti.*

Ve kalb'ímtha azá'ye dáşti, jiyâné kalb'ímtha, he replied, the heat of his words wrapping me in warmth. *I love you too, life of my heart.*

My own heart thrummed like a hummingbird, sending a fresh bounce to my step.

Biscuit made a disgusted grunt, abruptly severing the link.

I stuck my tongue out at him. "Oh yeah? Well maybe if you took a page out of Zayn's book, you and Mavros might actually…uh…"

My voice trailed off as a little ball of pulsating blue light floated before my vision, lovely and curious and mesmerizing. Crossing my eyes over my nose, I stared at the flickering orb – neither a firefly nor a trick of the light – utterly entranced.

"Hello there," I breathed. "Where did you come from?"

Its response sounded like delicate, tinkling bells.

"You're so pretty…" I reached a tentative finger toward it. "Biscuit, isn't it pretty?"

He nodded, gazing at our new friend in rapt wonder.

Darting just out of reach, the little ball of light hovered in the darkness, imploring the two of us to catch it. I took a step closer. Biscuit leaned forward on my shoulder, his head bobbing from side to side as he trailed its movements, similar to a cat stalking a laser beam.

As if playing with him, the orb landed right between his eyes, only to gracefully flutter away when he tried to catch it with his beak.

"Don't worry, buddy, I'll get it," I murmured, reaching forward. As I stretched out my fingers, I vaguely registered the sensation of taut, scratchy rope pressing against my knees. The torch tumbled from my slack hand, a plummeting pinprick of color that was quickly extinguished by the darkness.

With another soft tinkle, like distant sleigh bells, the pulsing orb entreated me forward, floating mere inches from my grasp.

"Almost…got you…" I grunted, straining to reach it.

"*Talia!*" someone shouted, momentarily snapping me from my trance.

I jerked my head just in time to see Korinne and Safir rushing toward me, yellow light erupting from their palms.

The sound of tinkling bells abruptly turned to a high-pitched, gleeful shriek of laughter as the rope digging into my knees buckled and I plunged forward, belly-flopping straight into the black expanse.

"AAAAAA—*AUGH!*"

My bloodcurdling scream turned into a strangulated grunt as a glowing lasso ensnared me by the waist, forcing the air from my lungs. After yo-yo-ing up and down for several innard-jolting seconds, I hung there, dazed and suspended, like a stuffed animal ensnared by an arcade claw machine. Meanwhile, Biscuit was dangling by his own hog-tied claws a few feet away, squawking and flailing in indignation.

Several yards above, a staggered line of heads popped over the edge of the bridge, the light from their rainbow fire torches painting their faces in varying shades of shock and relief.

"Are you two okay?" Korinne called down.

"Yeah," I wheezed, just as Biscuit bawked, "*No!*"

"We'll pull you up – just hang on!"

I bit my tongue, suppressing a snarky retort.

A dozen elves and knockers worked together to hoist us up, with every lurch and tug bringing my stomach closer and closer to the bilious brink. The moment my disheveled head and Biscuit's entwined feet appeared above the bridge, Safir hurriedly chicken-snatched him by the ankles while Korinne regarded my outstretched hand warily.

"Don't worry, I got it," I huffed, kicking up an ungainly leg to hoist myself up and over the ledge.

Zaffre.

I froze mid-heave, my head snapping behind me; there was only darkness. And yet, I had the distinct, unsettling feeling that someone was watching me.

I shook my head roughly. It was an idiotic thought, of course – what else did I expect, given the several hundred sets of eyes that were presently gawking at me?

The elves backed away as I flipped over on my back, panting heavily as I regarded a shimmering cloud of multi-colored orbs that hovered near the ceiling.

"Will-o'-wisps," Boris said with a shrug, as though this were a perfectly normal occurrence. "It seems they are particularly attracted to your lovely golden skin."

"How flattering," I grunted, hoisting myself on my elbows. "Did anyone remember to bring wisp repellant? Heh heh." I couldn't help chortling. "Get it? *Wisp* repellant?"

Laleh cleared her throat. "If you are referring to aerosol rebarbarbatives, no, we did not bring any."

"There's no need for chemical repellant!" one of the nearby knockers *tsked.*

"Norris is right!" Boris said. "We've devised a superb anti-wisp method that works far better than any spray or enchantment!"

"Yeah?" I pulled myself into a sitting position. "And what's that?"

"Singing, of course!" He beamed. "Will-o'-wisps despise the sound of it! Curiously, we've found that they especially hate songs sung in the key of E-flat!"

"Naturally," I grumbled.

"No, flat E," Boris frowned.

Once my lungs had been properly refilled with hot, muggy air, I staggered to my feet, muttering, "Just when I thought this trip couldn't get any more hellish."

"What was that?" Boris asked.

"I said, 'Oh yay, I'm so excited for this.'"

"Indeed!" he clapped. "Norris, if you wouldn't mind?"

Norris reached into his hat, from which he retrieved a small silver object. After giving it a good shine with the soiled hem of his shirt, he blew into it to produce a harmonica-like note – E flat, I had to assume. The other knockers hummed the same note, then cheerfully spun on their heels to continue our perilous, mid-air march through the will-o'-wisp-infested cavern. While the elves and I fell back into a well-staggered line behind them, the tommyknockers broke into a perfectly-harmonized ditty, as though they'd spent lots and lots of time practicing in the mines.

O, we traipse and trek and tromp and trudge,
Chipping away at rocks and sludge
To make Sol's pockets swell and bulge,
We'll mine these mountains 'til morning!

O, we thwack and crack and strike and split,
Upon sore rumps we cannot sit
Until we've dulled our diamond bits
We'll mine these mountains 'til morning!

Before the tommyknockers had even reached the end of the first stanza, the cloud of murderous Tinker Bells had scattered in every direction, letting out agonized, tormented screeches as they fled.

Unfortunately, five minutes and eighteen stanzas later, *I* was on the brink of doing the same thing. Biscuit, who was perched on my shoulder, wings folded over his ears to block out the noise, looked up at me with pleading puppy dog eyes. An image of Mavros appeared in my head – an entreaty for me to let him go check on her.

Sighing, I glanced at the empty space on my arm, where his tattoo would have otherwise been if he were napping in his two-dimensional form. "You're gonna teleport there through the link?" I asked, having to shout over the din of bellowing tommyknockers.

He nodded eagerly.

"Are you sure you're not just using this as an excuse to raid the castle larder?" I arched my eyebrow.

Biscuit's eyes got even wider, as if to say, "Who, me?"

"Ugh, fine. Go home! But you'd better bring me back some cheddar stat – oh, and some ear plugs too."

"Rawk! Luv yu!"

Before I could even reply, he'd already disappeared in a kaleidoscopic flash of feathers and light – just in time to miss the twentieth stanza of the knockers' interminable song, which they broke into with even more gusto than before:

O, we sift and sieve and sort and strain,
Picking through gems and golden veins,
Our poor backs ache, we can't complain,
We'll mine these mountains 'til morning!

"Traitor," I grumbled, glaring down at Biscuit's tattoo while the knockers restarted their whole damn ditty from the beginning.

At that point, having absolutely nothing else to do, I threw my hands in the air and joined in, shouting, "O, WE TRAIPSE AND TREK AND TROMP AND TRUDGE, CHIPPING AWAY AT ROCKS AND SLUDGE, TO MAKE SOL'S POCKETS SWELL AND BULGE, WE'LL MINE THESE MOUNTAINS 'TIL MOOORNING!"

Whether they'd been waiting on my cue, or, like myself, simply capitulating to the relentless melody, one by one, the elves begrudgingly joined in. Before long, every single one of them was singing at the top of their lungs, giving the tommyknockers a run for their money. Not to be outdone, the knockers started singing even louder, until little bits of stalactite debris rained down on our heads from the vibration.

And anyway, that's how I found myself clomping through an underground faery cavern with an army of elves, belting out tommyknocker shanties at the top of our lungs to ward off a squadron of homicidal fireflies. Would I have preferred to be in Miami, binge-watching Korean soap operas and gorging myself on a family-sized bag of white cheddar popcorn like any other Friday night? Yeah. I most definitely would have preferred that. But as we've already established, I'm an idiot who makes terrible choices.

And yet, as I looked over my shoulder to find two hundred previously grieving, injured elves singing that ridiculous tommyknocker jingle at full volume…I somehow didn't regret any of them.

IV.
FOLLOW THE YELLOW LIT ROAD

Ballads and bonding aside, by the time we emerged from the eastern entrance to the mines nearly thirty Terran hours after we started our journey through the Western Wastes, even the knockers – who proudly and repeatedly proclaimed they could go days without sleeping – looked worse for the wear. As for me, I sank to the ground the moment cool, fresh evening air hit my nostrils, unable to take a single step further. I'd never gone so long without sleep in my entire life, nor walked so far. Every joint in my body hurt; even my blisters had blisters. If it hadn't been for the gloriously comfortable soft-soled boots the elves had given me, I don't know what I would have done.

Died, probably.

"Water, my wilted flower?" Boris asked, passing me his canteen.

"Thank you," I rasped as I gratefully accepted its last dregs. "Where are we?"

Korinne, who was leaning against the mouth of the cave for support, glanced up at the sky, where three small crescent moons were shining high above us. "We are close to the Great Phoenix Tree," she grunted, pushing away from the rock. "I can feel it."

I followed her gaze into the distance, though all I could see were craggy, moonlit mountains surrounding us – including the lone peak that housed the Summer Palace, its glowing windows flickering warmly in the distance.

Zayn. I struggled to my feet, spurred by his proximity. I hadn't been able to reach him in hours, not after our asshole familiar had traveled back through our link and then never returned. Four or five candles ago, I wasn't sure whether to feel anxious or aggravated by that fact. Now, as I surveyed the calm tranquility in this neck of the mountains – with nary an Unseelie army in sight – I was decidedly more aggravated than anxious. The little shit was probably still in the larder, stuffing his beak with cheddar.

My empty stomach rumbled crankily at the thought.

"*Ay'aşéya*," several of the elves murmured, pointing to the sky. *Moon Mother*.

A warm, tingling flush spread through my body as the clouds parted to reveal the realm's fourth and largest moon. Its rose-pink crescent and half-shadowed rings appeared in all their silvery splendor, making my breath catch. It was the first time I'd witnessed all four moons hovering in the fae night sky.

Tilting her head back, Korinne held out her hands to her sides, absorbing the moonlight. As more and more elves filtered outside the caves, they followed suit, lifting their faces to Ay'aşéya while wordlessly locking hands. The Lunar Runes on their bodies pulsed with a growing power that crackled in the space between them as, hand in hand, the elves began to chant.

Ayi'şík emæ yem beşévi,
Aşeki'rûm emæ muhávsi,
Væyéni'k̂aan emæ hafízi,
Aşeyái'preyám'en emæ korsávi.

Their words mingled with the cool breeze of the evening as pink moonlight suffused their bodies; the longer they chanted, the brighter their runes began to glow. Something deep within me stirred, urging me to join them, coaxing my feet forward. Unable as I was to clasp anyone's hand, I forced myself to resist, lingering near the mouth of the cave with Boris and the other knockers. But I couldn't help but tilt my face to the moons, whispering the English words quietly beneath my breath.

May the light of the moon nourish us,
May the grace of the Creator protect us,
May the blood of our veins preserve us,
May the blessings of the Mother sustain us.

As I spoke the words, the Lunar Rune on my left arm flickered to life, starting with the largest crescent moon, then trickling through the smaller satellites. Suffusing my cold, shivering body with warmth, the honey-colored glow continued to spread across the veins and arteries in my arm, illuminating every rune it passed, until my entire body hummed with energy. I closed my eyes and breathed deeply through my nose, swathed by a quiet tranquility I'd never felt before. Gone were the anxious thoughts that constantly flooded my mind, along with the fear, tension, and self-doubt that had plagued me my entire life. In their place was power – raw, simmering, untapped power. It wasn't overwhelming or forceful. It was just there, patiently waiting to be used.

Patiently waiting for *me*.

When my eyes popped open once more, the elves had stopped chanting. They, along with the tommyknockers, had all turned to stare at me, white showing all around their brilliant gem-colored irises.

"Who *is* she?" Éyrel murmured to his father.

"*Ema k̂aan krâliyet vaşía,*" his father replied, making my stomach lurch. *She is of royal blood.*

I shook my head vigorously, as stunned as I was confused. "No." I tried to laugh, but my voice came out in a hoarse whisper. "I'm not."

Korinne stepped forward, and in her wide amethyst eyes, I could see twin reflections of my own glowing face, burning as bright as a candle. Even the hairs fluttering around my head shone like golden threads. Following her gaze to my shoulder, I let out a soft gasp; like all of the other tattoos on my body, the circle of *corissian* ink was blazing so brightly, it was visible even beneath the heavy fabric of my dress.

"What the hell?" I sputtered.

Her reassuring smile didn't quite meet her eyes. "The moonlight appears to have boosted your runes."

"Why did Tanak say I have royal blood?" I demanded, my voice cracking.

"My apologies," he bowed, making my stomach lurch yet again, "I meant no offense, my queen."

"I'm not your queen!"

When an eagle screeched from somewhere above, I somehow *knew* it was mocking me.

I jerked my head in the direction of the sound, letting out a low curse. That same massive, crimson-headed eagle was perched in the highest branch of a nearby tree, head cocked straight at me, its piercing blue eyes catching in the moonlight like two polished aquamarines.

"Stuff a sock in it!" I snarled, chucking a rock in its general direction.

Emitting a noise that sounded dangerously close to a cackle, it flew off the branch, disappearing into the darkening blanket of stars to the east.

"Yeah, you'd better run, you dumb chicken!" I bellowed hoarsely.

"Talia," Korinne warned, her voice firm. "You're tired. We all are. And it's not safe to linger in these woods after sundown. Let's get back to the palace, where we can eat, rest, and *then* talk about whatever it is you want to discuss." She squeezed my hand, and for the first time in days, Sol's mark barely hurt.

"I just want to be able to remember my dad as the funny, kind, *regular* guy he was, okay?" I whimpered, furiously scrubbing the tears from my eyes. "Because if I have to hear about *one more* blood-related bombshell that he kept from me all those years, that I'll *never* have the chance to ask him about, I'll…I'll…" The sob I'd been trying so hard to suppress burst from my throat, and I covered my face in shame.

"Shh, it's okay." Korinne wrapped her arms around me in a tight hug before quickly pulling away. "Talia, the most important thing you need to know about your father is that he loved you more than life itself – that much is clear."

My hand fluttered to the empty hollow of my throat, where a fresh sob had lodged. "But—"

"No buts." She shook her head firmly. "Now, as your honorary big sister, I'm going to tell you the same thing he would if he were here right now—"

"To hurry up and get my *tuchus* inside 'cause it's after curfew?" I sniffed pitifully.

"Exactly," she smiled, guiding me forward. A hundred tommyknockers immediately fell in line behind us while a couple hundred more elves practically jumped aside to let us through – several bowing their heads as we moved past them.

My stomach twisted at the sight.

Taking that opportunity to hide my face, I dropped into a crouch and pressed my fingers against the Greater Concealment Rune on my ankle, the sole purpose of which was meant to hide the magical signature of my blood. When I stood up a few moments later, I was still glowing, but noticeably less than before.

"Good idea." Korinne nodded. "We can't have you gleaming like a lantern in the middle of the Royal Forests. Now, come on. The faster we hike, the sooner we can sit down to a hot meal."

"Assuming Biscuit hasn't cleaned out the entire larder," I muttered to no one in particular as I started down the rocky path. The mines had spit us into a natural crag between two mountain peaks, which formed a stark valley that immediately swept back up to become the western slope of the lush, waterfall-strewn mountain that housed the Summer Palace.

Gazing up at the fortress, which was easily three-thousand feet up – my least favorite hiking direction – I suppressed a moan. *I* might have resolved to quit complaining after seeing everything the elves had silently endured, but my burning, jellified leg muscles had made no such resolution. Furiously protesting all the steps we'd yet to take, they were already threatening to buckle before the last leg of our journey had even started.

Lucky for me, I smiled grimly, *I just happen to know a guy with a flying dragon.* And after my two-day, nonstop schlep through the desert and mountains, I knew Zayn would be more than happy to tap in, thereby allowing me to tap the hell out.

Already yawning at the thought of a warm, soft bed, I touched my fingers to Biscuit's tattoo. *Zayn? Biscuit? Are you guys there?*

No answer.

Guys? I tried again, my fraying anxiety unraveling even further. *Zayn...? Biscuit...?*

A full thirty seconds came and went, with every passing moment making my heart gallop faster.

Finally, Zayn's husky voice rustled like dry leaves between my ears. *Tal – please tell me you're safe.*

I'm fine, I breathed a sigh of relief. *We just exited the mountain.*

After a long pause, he muttered, *Thank the Creator.*

What's going on? I frowned.

Another pause. *Uh...we've got...complications.*

Complications??

Everyone's okay, he quickly reassured me. *Just... Well...you'll see. Here, draw this rune on something you can easily carry.* He showed me a relatively simple design. *Rock, scrap of paper, whatever.*

Okay... I bent down to pick up a rock. On it, I scrawled the rune he was showing me with one of the Sharpies in my purse. The moment I drew the final line, the rock lit up like a glowing neon-yellow sign. A blazing streak of buttery light shot from it, zigzagging up the side of the mountain like Sonic the Hedgehog.

So, I just follow the yellow light? I asked. When he didn't answer right away, I frowned. *Zayn?*

Yes – sorry. It'll lead you straight here, quickest route. A stab of anxiety shot through our link. *Talia, I am so incredibly sorry, but I have to go. I love you so much.* A split second passed before he hastily added, *Don't touch any plants on the way up. Remember, the prettier the flower, the worse its bite.* After that, everything went completely silent.

Stopping in my tracks, I stared at my arm in bewilderment. "What the actual fuck?"

"Was that Zayn?" Korinne asked. "Is everything—"

"We have to go," I interrupted. "Right now."

She nodded, worry creasing between her brows.

Breaking into a sprint, I shouted over my shoulder, "Everyone who isn't too tired or injured, follow me! The rest of you, shields up!"

"What's wrong?" Safir asked, quickly falling in beside me. "Is it Sol? Are they under attack?"

"I don't know," I panted, pushing every drop of waning energy I had into my burning thighs. The only thing I did know was that it took a lot for Zayn to get flustered – and I mean, a *lot*. Whatever was going on up there, it had to be bad.

Sucking down a shallow breath, I picked up the pace, burning through my Stamina Runes like a Hummer guzzling gasoline.

Above, the lights in the castle windows flickered ominously.

V.
A CLEAN SLATE

After a two-mile sprint – and by "sprint," I mean "wheezing slog" – I dragged myself up the very last step of that godforsaken stone staircase, my entire body covered in sweat, dirt, and the stinky green slime of a bulbous, waist-high plant the elves like to call "The Fool's Pustule" – and no, I don't want to talk about it. Panting, I pressed a grimy palm against the hidden Unchaining Rune embedded in the forty-foot doors of the castle, moaning in relief when they swung open on hinges that no longer screamed, but politely mewled.

The moment I staggered into the foyer, a gasp slipped through my lips. At various points throughout our interminable schlep through the mountains, I'd done a spectacular job of ensuring my traveling companions' expectations of the abandoned Summer Palace would be as low as possible, using words such as "dilapidated," "grungy," and – my personal favorite – "post-hurricane chic." Now, as dozens of travel-worn elves crowded inside the entryway, no doubt expecting to find the dingy shell of a ruined castle I'd repeatedly warned them about, they all looked at me as though I were insane.

All of the candles in the glittering crystal chandelier had been lit, casting warm light and splashes of rainbows on the perfectly restored mosaic walls – every colorful, rune-embedded tile of which had been scrubbed until it gleamed like new. The towering stained-glass depictions of Saedis and Jaína – which smelled faintly of ammonia – literally sparkled, utterly pristine in their restored states. And the shining tile floors were so meticulously spotless, you could eat off them without a care or worry.

For a brief, hazy moment, I wondered if I'd accidentally stumbled into the wrong palace…until I saw the shoes: dozens and dozens of them, which had been neatly stacked in a perfectly straight, two-tiered row against the wall.

As though telepathically summoned, a blurry figure appeared behind the stained glass, flinging the doors open to reveal the Hygiene Faerie herself.

"TALLY!" my mother cried, throwing her arms around me.

By now, the corissian ink had faded back to normal, and a pained gasp slipped through my lips.

"Sorry, I keep forgetting!" She winced as she quickly pulled away. Lucy and Ricky – my parents' Chihuahua familiars – skittered between my mother's feet, barking excitedly. "I'm just so glad you're home safe!"

"M-me too," I stammered, instinctively taking two steps backward.

Despite her stained apron and frizzy bottle-blonde hair, my mother looked beautiful – in a decidedly unsettling way. Her skin was as pale as the flour that dusted her clothes, her lips as red as the raw meat she'd developed a sudden affinity for, and her irises… I gulped. Her irises were the lightest shade of blue

I'd ever seen in a human eye, more ice than storm. And while the ladies at her Thursday night Scrabble meet-up might have asked her what new expensive skin regimen she'd embarked on, or which hoity-toity celebrity's makeup products she was using, I knew the truth.

This transformation had nothing to do with Sephora.

"What's the matter with you?" she demanded, closing the gap between us. "You look like you've seen a ghost!" Without giving me the chance to answer, she spun me around by the shoulders.

"Ow!"

"Oy, look at you!" she clucked, ignoring my yelp of pain. "I've been so worried about you! What the hell were you thinking, traipsing through the desert? Who do you think you are, Moses?"

"No, I—"

"For Pete's sake, you're not even wearing a jacket!" My mouth opened with a snarky retort about not having to have time to grab one during the surprise battle, but her attention had already shifted behind me. "Shoes off, please!" she barked, wildly gesticulating at the growing cluster of elves and tommyknockers trudging in from outside. "*Oy gotenyu*, I *just* scrubbed these floors!—Hey!" she whistled. "You boys in the back – leave those filthy boots on the steps before you track more mud in here!"

I dragged a heavy hand across my face. "Mom! They're not boys, they're tommyknockers!"

"Yeah? Well, I'll tommy-knock them out if they track mud all over my spotless palace!"

"Are you out of your mind?" I hissed, drawing my face close to the marble-white pallor of hers. "We have literally been walking for *two days*—"

"Exactly!" She planted her hands on her hips. "Tracking God knows what from God knows where all over the house! Now, everyone, hurry up and come inside before you let all the cold air in," she cajoled, ushering everyone into the foyer. "Shoes off, wash up, then come to the dining hall for dinner. I made brisket for the meat eaters and *kasha varnishkes* for the vegetarians!"

With expressions ranging from fright to bewilderment, our frazzled houseguests quickly slipped off their muddy footwear and skirted inside, offering polite nods and murmurs to my vamshee mother as they passed.

"We're a very packed house so we'll need to fit at least four people to a room," Mom hollered after them, scooping up a yapping dog in each arm to keep them from nipping at everyone's ankles. "Make sure to use Greater Laundering Runes on all your clothes before you sit on the furniture! And use plenty of soap when you wash your hands!—Oh!" she added, almost as an afterthought. "Zayn asked me to tell all of you that the wine cellar is full of banshees, so if you see one, you're probably not dying. They're just here for the family reunion."

The remaining elves froze in their tracks, right in the middle of removing their shoes.

"*What?*" I rounded on her. "What do you mean, *family reunion?*"

"Oy, would you calm down already?" She rolled her eyes. "You wanted help to beat this *meshuggeneh* sex pervert and his army of vampire *schreken*, right? Well, vampires are terrified of banshees, so *you* do the math!—*Ah ah ah!*" she called to a cluster of tommyknockers. "Shoes go in *that* corner! And make sure you wipe the *schmutz* from your hands and beards before dinner!"

"Mom, you are literally killing me," I moaned, rubbing the growing ache in my head with the heel of my palm. "Where's Zayn?"

"Oh, he's somewhere around here…" She gestured into the palace idly. "But before you go rushing off to fornicate, who is this Aunt Ko-Ko Moishe keeps telling me all about? He said she helped the two of you escape some sort of vampire sex club?!"

Korinne, who was at that exact moment trying to shrink past the two of us without getting caught in the verbal crossfire, abruptly straightened at the sound of her name. "Uh, hello," she waved feebly, unleashing another series of yips from the squirming dogs.

I rolled my eyes. "His name isn't Moishe, it's Biscuit!"

"According to Zayn, his *full* name is Hibiscus! If you can name my grandbirdy after a cracker, why can't I call him Moishe?"

Korinne was again slowly inching away from us. "You know, if this isn't a good time, I can just come back la—"

"What are you talking about? This is a perfect time!" Mom said, setting down the dogs – who immediately went barking and scampering into the palace – to scoop the startled elf into a tight hug. "Moishe was right – you *are* beautiful!" she enthused, gripping Korinne's wrists like handcuffs. "Do you think you could share some of your beauty tips with my daughter?" She gave my purple hair a not-so-gentle tug. "I mean, look at this! You know, when Tally was a little girl, she had the most gorgeous chocolate-brown hair just like yours! But ever since she went through puberty and decided to become a 'rebel,'" she said with accompanying air quotes, "she feels the need to turn herself into a new sorbet flavor every other—"

"MOM!" I exploded, once more making everyone unlucky enough to still be in the foyer jerk to a startled stop. A hot tendril of anger unfurled in my chest, as powerful as it was surprising.

I took a long, deep breath and held it, letting my next question come out as a slow release of air. "Where... Is... Zayn?"

"Where *did* I see him last?" Mom scrunched up her brow. "I want to say he's still dealing with the nest of *trows* Lambchop found in the guest quarters... Although," she tapped her chin thoughtfully, "he might have gone down to the basement to have a word with the banshees after that little hiccup they had with the elves."

"Hiccup?"

She rolled her eyes. "Oh, you know, their usual Seelie-Unseelie *mishegas*—Oy, you! Mr. Dwarf! Toss those muddy boots back outside!"

"Dwarf?" Boris huffed indignantly. "Tommyknockers look nothing like dwarves!"

"Oh, I beg your pardon," Mom apologized. "I thought that all mountain men of a certain, uh, *stature*, were dwarves."

Upon hearing the contrition in her voice, Boris relaxed. "It is an all-too-common misconception, sadly. Dwarves are lumbering and stockier – and, if you ask me, quite uncouth – whereas tommyknockers are much more agile and clever." He puffed out his chest. "Similarly, where dwarves have only their crude iron tools as protection, tommyknockers possess a unique form of earthen magic that is tapped directly from the stone we mine. Of course, the classification of stone is quite important, as metamorphic rock, compared to, say, igneous rock, possesses far more terramantic potential for transmutation..."

"You don't say!" she replied, feigning interest.

Using that opportunity to make my escape, I quickly and silently slipped through the doors and out of my mother's sight. Safely on the other side, I found myself standing in the palace's enormous, dazzlingly-clean throne room, where a few hundred elven soldiers and refugees were tearfully reuniting. Among the tight embraces and emotional hellos, fragments of conversations buzzed in the air, tickling my ears.

"...lost the Great Mother, may the leaves of the Great Phoenix Tree shade her..."

"...safe because of the pádeşah and his gilded paşahdî..."

"...of nowhere, completely annihilating our defenses..."

"...not for her, we never would have been able to escape..."

As I made my way through the crowd, I could feel the elves' eyes on the back of my neck, which was flushing with chagrin. I ducked my head and dropped my eyes, searching for Zayn among the many beautiful bronzed faces, until I literally ran smack-dab into Lamswyth.

"Talia!" he blustered, stumbling backward. "I thought I heard your distinctive voice!" His horizontal pupils narrowed at my disheveled state. "Are you in need of medicine or aid? I've set up an ad hoc medical ward in the east wing—"

"I'm fine, Lam," I answered tiredly. "Have you seen Zayn?"

He rubbed the back of his neck. "Ah, yes, well, it's been quite a hullabaloo these past two days, what with the elves arriving, and then the banshees..." He shuddered. "Poor Zæynek has been darting around like a panicked pixie, putting out proverbial fires... Actually," he corrected himself, "one of those fires was, in fact, a literal fire. And a large one at—"

"Lam!" I interrupted. "*Where* is Zayn?"

He stroked a furry hand across his bushy beard. "Let's see...when I last saw him, he was in the kitchen creating several batches of ink, while his familiar was tending to a rather sick raven... Of course, that was after the incident with the dryad—"

"Dryad?!"

"—or perhaps it was before that?" Lam scrubbed his eyes with his palms. "I'm sorry, my pet, it has been a very long and sordid day."

"Tell me about it." I sighed. "What time is it, anyway?"

Lamswyth glanced at the large candle that flickered from a small alcove. "Just after midnight. I—ah." A smile suddenly tugged at the edge of his jowls as he turned back to face me.

"Talia."

I whirled around, letting out a small sob. "Zayn!" I cried, throwing myself into his arms. Pain zinged through my arm, all the way down to my fingertips. But in that moment, I didn't care.

Pressing his face against the top of my head, he held me tightly for one brief second, then, after gently pulling away, he reached forward to tug down the top of my sleeve. The sigh of relief he made upon seeing the intact circle on my shoulder quickly turned into a frown. "The corissian ink looks darker than it did yesterday morning. How did you…?"

"Lunar Runes," I smiled wanly. "All four moons were out tonight, and when I joined the elves' chant, their Moon Mama apparently saw fit to give me a power-up."

Zayn's frown deepened, accentuating the dark circles beneath his eyes. As he opened his mouth to inquire further, a gushing torrent of chattering tommyknockers spilled in from the foyer.

At the sight of them, Zayn's jaw dropped. "What the…"

I shrugged my shoulders, flashing him a sheepish, chattering grin. "Surprise?"

It was at that moment I noticed my breath had condensed in front of my face, hazily swirling against the rapidly-chilling air. A cold shiver spider-walked down my spine as a door on the far wall swung open, sending tendrils of icy white fog creeping into the throne room. The crowd hushed, parting as the fog spread. Ice crystallized beneath the expanding plume, until the marble floor was more frost than tile.

And then they appeared.

Not one, but *six* banshees emerged from the doorway, their flowing white hair and ghostly nightgowns fluttering in an invisible breeze. The low hum of murmurs came to an abrupt halt as the deathly procession made its way into the throne room.

The most chilling part of all: every set of the banshees' wide, milky eyes were locked directly onto me.

VI.
Family Reunion

I clung to Zayn's sleeve like Velcro, my eyes growing wider and wider as the line of banshees floated across the tiles, leaving a trail of fog and ice swirling behind them. On the right side of the chamber, the tommyknockers were clutching their pickaxes between white-knuckled fists, while on the left side, every elven hand was inching toward a gem-encrusted gold dagger. Beside me, Zayn had become as stiff as a plank, but since he made no move to run or attack, I did my best to follow suit – even though my feet were on the verge of carrying me out of there with or without my mind's blessing.

The banshee at the front of the line stopped less than a foot from me, peering down at me with piercing, pale irises, which swirled and glinted like two pools of liquid pearls. My breath caught at the sight of her. Despite her colorless features, she was almost pretty – in a creepy, ghostly sort of way. Younger, too, than I had imagined, though I couldn't tell if she was thirty or sixty. Hell, in this realm, she might have been six-*hundred* and sixty and I'd never know the difference.

"Daughter of cloven heritages, whose gilded blood is like none before her," the banshee whispered, her voice frosty, but not cold. "I am Saoirse – sister of your great-grandmother."

I should have been utterly terrified of the bloodless hand she was extending in my direction, but when she pressed her cold fingertips to my forehead, a strange feeling of comfort and familiarity swept over me.

"H-Hello, Sheer-sha," I stammered, warily eyeing her smooth, ageless features while no doubt butchering her name.

Zayn stepped between us, breaking the contact.

Saoirse's pale, unblinking eyes remained affixed to mine. "We have felt ripples of your presence spreading across the realm – in the seas, in the air. You breathe life into a land where death has long festered." Her eyes then swept to Zayn, narrowing slightly. "And you – lord of Seelies and Unseelies both, whose heart is as sundered as his bloodline – we see you and your efforts to unite this continent. Now that all have gathered here in witness, speak truthfully, wholly and without equivocation: What rights would you bestow upon your lover's kin, were you to ascend Saedis's throne?"

Zayn followed her gaze to the dais, where two thrones, each made of dead, interwoven branches and vines, loomed above us. Judging by the pile of withered leaves and flowers beneath them, it was clear the thrones had once been lush and green – maybe even alive.

The knot in his throat bobbed. "I wish to atone for my stepfather's sins, not revive them. Therefore, your rights would be no different than theirs"—he gestured to the elves—"or hers,"—he nodded at me—"…or my own. We are all equals in the eye of the Creator."

At *that,* the elves suddenly managed to find their voices.

"Blasphemy!"

"These creatures are harbingers of destruction!"

"Death-bringers are not welcome in the Summer Court!"

A shrill, high-pitched whistle sliced through their protests like the screeching brakes of a locomotive. The crowd parted as my fuming mother stormed toward us, holding her mop aloft like a wizard's staff.

"*Again* with this *mishegas*?" she demanded, slamming the wooden handle on the floor for emphasis. "What did I *just* say to all of you the *last* time you had this argument? There are no enemies inside these walls! The bad guys are out *there!*" She jerked a finger toward the front doors, glaring down the startled crowd.

The room had fallen so silent, you could hear the elves awkwardly shuffling their bare feet. My mother took her place between Zayn and me, while everyone else subconsciously crowded around us in a segregated triangle, with the banshees, elves, and knockers each taking up separate sides.

Seeing that, Mom's left eye twitched. "During the Holocaust, did the Jews bicker among themselves, saying, 'You were born in a different ghetto so I don't like you,' or 'Your complexion is darker than mine, so we're enemies'? Of *course* not – the Nazis were doing a good enough job of that all on their own!" She spun around in a slow circle, meeting the gaze of every elf, tommyknocker, and banshee that had the courage to meet her withering glare. "For those of you who aren't familiar with Earth's Second World War, *six million* of our kind were rounded up and slaughtered like cattle, for no reason other than made-up differences between our blood and theirs.

"Now, my mother, a Jewish banshee," she continued, fighting to keep the waver from her voice, "survived unspeakable things – both on this planet and mine – all of which were rooted in fear and hatred." She quickly scrubbed a tear from her cheek. "So enough already with how you are *different*, and start figuring out all the ways you are *alike*. Because there is a big, nasty sex pervert coming this way to take that throne from this wonderful young man," she jerked a thumb in Zayn's direction, "and I don't need a crystal ball to know that the only way we will survive that battle is together!" Flinging her mop in the air like a general rousing her troops, her voice rose into a roaring crescendo. "NOW, GO WASH UP AND GET TO THE DINING HALL, BECAUSE I DIDN'T SLAVE OVER A HOT STOVE FOR *THREE HOURS* SO ALL OF YOU COULD SIT AROUND KVETCHING!!!"

By the time her verbal assault had come to an apoplectic conclusion, the room had fallen so quiet you could have literally heard a pin drop. One second passed, and then another. And then, after three seconds of complete, spine-prickling silence, the *entire fucking room* exploded in triumphant, euphoric cheers.

Mom merely spun on her slippered heel with a stately *harrumph*, then marched straight through the crowd, parting the applauding sea of fae like Moses himself.

Saoirse appeared at the empty place to my left, her expression wholly inscrutable as she watched my mom disappear into the kitchen. When the commotion finally died down, and the crowd began to disperse, she sighed. "*That* is a banshee to make all other banshees weep."

"Is that…good?" I asked, frowning.

She nodded, her lips pursing as though she were trying to suppress a smile. "She – and you, Talia-*grādh* – would have made your grandmother very proud… Now go on," she urged, gesturing me forward. "It is never wise to keep a banshee waiting."

"Come on. Let's get you cleaned up," Zayn murmured against my ear.

Nodding, I took his sleeve in mine.

As we turned to leave, I distinctly heard Saoirse mutter, "I wonder what her *other* grandmother would think about these developments."

I stopped dead in my tracks. "What did you just say?" I demanded, whirling around.

But she and the other banshees were already gone, leaving nothing but ice and fog in their wake.

Zayn led me to the same room we had slept in a few nights before – a lilac-themed guest bedroom with a large canopy bed, three pieces of matching white furniture, and heavy drapes that had been tied back to expose a beautiful stained-glass window overlooking a glittering lake and pink forest below.

He quietly shut the door behind us, paused, then slowly turned around to face me, his shoulders rising and falling in what looked like a deep, steeling breath. Taking a cautious step toward me, and then another, he stopped himself when our toes were less than an inch apart.

I had to clench my hands at my sides to keep myself from reaching for him.

Neither of us said anything for several breaths. When Zayn finally opened his mouth to speak, his voice was as rough as sandpaper. "There is nothing in this world I wouldn't do to be able to hold you right now." Our eyes simultaneously trailed to my shoulder, his shifting to black as they did.

My nails dug into my palms. During the last two days, there had been at least a dozen instances where the thought of this exact moment was the only thing that had kept my feet going forward. But now that Zayn and I finally were finally granted our long-awaited moment of quiet togetherness, an ominous, invisible wall loomed between us. I hugged my body tightly, trying to smother the tendrils of bitterness and grief that were tightening around my ribcage, making it hard to breathe.

"There are some duraberries and Revitalizing Serum waiting for you beside the sink," he said softly, "as well as a palliative balm for your feet, which I'm sure are aching…" He swallowed hard. "I wish—"

"Where is he?" I interrupted. "And how long until he gets here?"

"We sent out a small team of scouts early yesterday morning. It looks like his army has set up a temporary camp in the Zaffrenpine Woodlands, a two-days' trek from here." A muscle in Zayn's jaw tensed. "Earlier this evening, they sent a pack of strigas flying to the east. We think it's a convoy meant for Fire Island, most likely to further bolster their numbers."

"What kind of fae live on Fire Island?" I asked, my stomach sinking even further.

"Go get cleaned up." He smiled tightly. "We'll discuss everything once we've caught one another up over dinner, and you and the elven soldiers are properly fed. The good news is that our scouts will know once Sol's army starts moving again, giving us a two-day advantage."

I nodded, suddenly feeling very tired. "I just need a few minutes to clean up… Wait for me?"

"Always," he replied, the word soft, yet filled with ardor.

Swallowing tightly, I forced myself to turn away from the smoldering intensity of his gaze, my heart thrumming against my chest like a helicopter propeller. Once the bathroom door had clicked shut behind me, I pressed my back against the cool wood, clutching the collar of my dress. I'd seen that same, tensed expression on Zayn's face so many times in the last two years, believing it to be deep concentration, or even irritation. *But now*... The lump in my throat had grown too painful to swallow. Now I fully understood it for what it actually was: a glimpse of the effort it took to control himself – to control his urges, his incubus nature, and his desire… His desire for *me.*

Just as I'd felt the constant need to do around him, believing my feelings were unreciprocated.

We'd denied ourselves to one another for so long.

And now…

Choking back the sob that was welling in my chest, I turned on the faucet and splashed ice-cold water on my face, then grabbed the brush on the edge of the sink and tore it through my tangles of knotted hair, using the pain to distract myself from the enormity of my grief.

Once my tresses had been tamed, facilities used, hands washed, and medicinal remedies consumed, I gripped the edge of the sink, staring at myself in the mirror. Except it felt more like I was staring at a portrait of a stranger than a reflection of myself. The woman who gazed back at me was someone I'd never seen before. Her jade eyes were illuminated as if by fire, her radiant skin dusted with gold, and her violet hair was longer and thicker than it had been in years, spilling in soft cascades across her squared shoulders. Though her borrowed elven-made dress was fit for royalty, she somehow managed to carry it as though it were her own. But strangest and most striking of all, the woman standing before me looked capable. Powerful. Resilient enough to weather whatever came her way.

She took a deep breath at the same time I did, her chest and shoulders rising alongside her solidifying resolve.

Sol had believed that staking his claim on my body was enough to make me his property, his vessel – a possession to be utilized as he saw fit. But he would learn soon enough.

This body belonged to *me.*

VII.
LA PETITE MORT

When I emerged from the bathroom a few minutes later, Zayn was sitting on the bed, his hands clasped in his lap. He glanced up as the bathroom door clicked shut behind me, that same tight, controlled expression plastering his face.

"Korinne dropped off a dress for you to change into," he said, patting the gold-threaded, scarlet *kœrta* that had been carefully laid out beside him.

I tried to speak, but couldn't find the words. After silently unbuckling the wide belt with my two daggers hanging from it, I let it slide to the floor. Then, slowly, wordlessly, I brought my hands to the row of gold buttons on the front of my dress, starting from the top and working my way down as I unsnapped them one by one. The Adam's apple in Zayn's throat bobbed forcefully as he watched, eyes burning with countless unspoken emotions. But, like me, he said nothing.

After unfastening the final button of the dress, just above my navel, I peeled away one sleeve, and then the other. He didn't move, didn't breathe, as I shimmied out of the split skirts, letting the garment fall to a rumpled pile on the floor.

Leaving only me.

Fire erupted behind Zayn's irises as he took in my naked form from head to toe. His hands gripped the comforter in two clenched fists, as though physically restraining himself. My body blossomed with heat, longing for his touch, but I remained in my spot, meeting his smoldering gaze with my own.

Taking one step forward, and then another, I ran my hands down my breasts, my waist, my hips, imagining Zayn's hands caressing my body. A low rumble vibrated through his chest as he watched, his feet glued to the floor as though he'd grown roots. Slowly, deliberately, he unclenched his fists and brought his fingers to his own shirt buttons, exposing a triangle of taut, bronzed skin underneath. The last button undone, he peeled away his shirt and tossed it to the ground. My eyes raked across his naked torso, taking in every inch of him. In the short time we'd been apart, he'd added more runes to his body. The intricate tattoos began at his wrists, twining around his carved forearms and biceps, curling up and over his rounded deltoids and shoulders, and stretched across his chest like armor. My fingers longed to trace the hard edges and ripples of his body, so I traced the soft curves of mine instead, biting my lip.

His hand inched toward the fly of his pants. When his eyes caught mine, I nodded. But instead of unzipping it, he ran his hand over the growing bulge beneath it, rubbing his palm up and down the prodigious outline of his shaft in one slow, controlled motion.

I followed his lead, sliding my own hand down my navel and toward the apex of my thighs, which throbbed with hot, wet longing. A soft moan escaped my lips as my fingers slipped between that wetness. My other hand gripped the edge of the nightstand beside the bed, steadying my trembling knees.

"Zayn," I moaned in a soft whisper, touching myself.

Watching my fingers slide between my legs, his eyes glinted so brightly, so wickedly, I thought he might actually reach out and pull me on top of him. The muscle in his jaw clenched as he unsnapped his fly, reaching down to expose the part of himself that nearly made *me* lose control. His member was rock hard and glistening at the tip, beckoning me to slide on top of it. My fingers picked up speed as I imagined myself climbing into his lap and straddling him, his hands clutching my ass cheeks while I took every inch of him deep inside of me, our hips grinding against one another with growing intensity as our bodies moved as one…

"Fuck," I gasped, lowering myself on the edge of the nightstand for support.

A growl rumbled deep in Zayn's throat as I spread my legs for him, showing him exactly what my hand was doing. His own hand grasped his arousal, gliding up and down from base to tip. I imagined the entire length of him thrusting in and out of me in much the same way. My fingers were soaked with my desire for him.

With less than a foot separating us, our hands moved up and down together, our motions perfectly synchronized. My core coiled like a spring while my quivering thighs clenched around my hand. But it wasn't enough. I slipped one finger inside myself, and then another, imagining they were his, and let out a deep moan of pleasure. Back arched and head lolling back, my hardened nipples pointed at the ceiling, begging to be sucked. Seeing this, the muscles in Zayn's core began to flex as his hand movement became faster and harder.

Oh God, how I wanted him inside me.

I slid my fingers deeper, using the palm of my hand to massage the hot, tingling bundle of nerves just above my opening. As I did, I imagined Zayn fucking me on that bed without restraint, hard and raw and relentlessly. The spring deep in my core wound tighter and tighter, tense and quivering. My toes curled with exertion as I pleasured myself with mounting fervor, my fingers and thighs dripping with yearning.

Zayn watched me from the edge of the bed with the intensity of a hungry lion, a sheen of sweat covering his chest – whether from exertion or restraint, I couldn't be sure.

"Come for me, Talia," he growled. *"Mæthir ama'yla, Sevyá'mtha."*

I gasped his name as the knot in my core unexpectedly snapped like a rubber band, sending wave after wave of pleasure coursing through my body.

"Oh, fuck," Zayn gasped, clutching himself. "Fuck, Talia!"

I could taste his intoxicating pheromones from there; the lure of Zayn's glamour, which had been inadvertently freed from his self-imposed shackles, called to me like a siren.

And I was his all-too-willing prey.

More reflex than thought, I shoved off the nightstand and mounted him in one fluid motion, my knees tightening around his hips as I slid myself onto his rock-hard arousal. He grabbed my wrists as though to push me off, stiffening as I rocked my hips against his, taking him deep inside me from throbbing tip to thick, quivering hilt. As another spasm shuddered from deep within, I kicked my head back, crying out his name.

"Talia," he groaned against my neck, raking his fingers down my spine as he emptied himself inside of me.

Zaffre.

My cry of pleasure turned into a ragged gasp.

"Tal—!" My name lodged in Zayn's throat as a bestial snarl. As quick as lightning, he lifted me off of him and gently laid me down on the bed.

"It hurts," I choked out, clutching my shoulder.

Is that you, Zaffre?

I shook my head violently, trying to rid myself of the ringing in my ears, which almost sounded like—

"Let me see," Zayn ordered, drawing back the moment I pulled my hand away.

Faint, throbbing black veins splintered from the center of the poisonous spider, while the surrounding skin had become shiny and red-streaked. The blue circle of runes was still intact, but the festering blight it contained pressed against the border of the corissian ink, threatening to seep into the rest of my body.

The poison was overpowering the cure.

The whites of Zayn's eyes had become black as pitch. I winced, expecting him to reprimand me for my recklessness, but he remained deathly quiet.

"D-Do we have enough corissian ink to fix it?" I whimpered, already cringing from the terrible pain I knew was coming.

Zayn shook his head slowly, his face as white as a sheet despite the sexual energy that had permeated the room moments ago.

"We don't?" I could feel the panic rising in my throat. "But I thought… I mean, you said—"

"I prepped the ink, Talia. An entire vat of it. But…it's failing."

"Failing?" I whispered, brushing my fingertips across the swollen, angry lines. I tried to swallow, but the lump in my throat was like molasses, fusing to my vocal cords. "Wh-What do you mean, failing? As in, losing its effectiveness?"

He didn't answer.

"Zayn?" I shakily pushed myself into a sitting position, feeling the room swim in front of my vision. He couldn't bring himself to look at me. And in that moment, I understood why: If the ink truly was failing, then it didn't matter how careful we were, or even if we vowed to never touch one another again.

I was already dying.

This time, I retouched the circle of runes myself, biting back an agonized sob as I did. Zayn could only watch while I worked, murder etched into every deepening line of his glower. Once, he'd mentioned that even Sol could barely handle the pain of touching up this particular tattoo; for me, it took everything I had not to pass out.

When I finished, he wordlessly handed me some healing balm and the very last of his remaining duraberries, got dressed, then strode over to the window. When he threw it open, I stifled a gasp. Suspended in a black, star-studded sky, the two smaller moons hovered above the Great Phoenix Tree, which towered hundreds of feet above the surrounding forest. Ribbons of scintillating magic furled and unfurled around its upturned leaves like living vines. Each individual leaf glowed as though soaking in the light of the moons, while every bud and branch radiated life and power – a beacon of hope against the night. As I took a step toward Zayn, the Lunar Rune on my arm flickered in the column of moonlight that trickled inside.

I wanted to stand beside him, to rest my head on his shoulder, and take his hand in mine.

Instead, I got dressed in silence, careful not to drag the fabric across the raw, inflamed skin surrounding the Requisition

Rune as I pulled my new kœrta over my head. After clasping the buttons to my collar and twisting my loose hair into a high bun – which I skillfully set with a Sharpie – I did a little twirl in front of the wardrobe's oval mirror. Cherry-red and velvet-soft, this "casual" elven dress was by far the finest garment I'd ever worn. It was sewn with shining gold threads that started from its high collar and ran all the way down its bell sleeves and long hem. Unlike the purple dress I was wearing earlier, the bodice of this kœrta was cropped, displaying a narrow strip of bare midriff. Just below that, the layered skirts split down the middle to reveal close-fitting gold leggings when they swished back and forth.

Turning to face Zayn, I cleared my throat softly. "What do you think?"

He glanced over his shoulder, warily taking me in from head to toe.

"You don't like it?" I asked, seeing his pained expression.

"You look…like a queen," he finally answered. Reaching into his pocket, he withdrew the gold locket my father had given me, its chain replaced and the hinge repaired. He dangled it into my hand by the clasp, taking two steps backward the moment I closed my palm around it. "I, uh…" He rubbed the back of his neck. "I fixed the rune. When you put the necklace back on, it should once again diminish the magical signature of your blood, but it won't be able to fully camouflage it. I don't think anything could at this point. Not here, at least."

Heart thrumming, I carefully clasped the chain behind my neck, sighing in relief as the cool, comforting weight of the locket settled against my sternum. Almost immediately, the irradiated hue of my skin returned to a dull golden glow.

"I was able to repair the inside as well," he added softly. "That photo of your father carrying you on his shoulders is beautiful. You can clearly see the love you had for one another."

I clutched the pendant in a trembling hand, overwhelmed by both gratitude and sorrow. "Thank you."

"There's…something else," he said, a crease forming between his eyebrows. "When I removed the photo to repair the glass, I found a hidden rune behind it."

"What kind of rune?" I asked, raising an eyebrow.

"I have no idea." He brandished a small piece of paper from his pocket. "Here, I drew it for you so you wouldn't have to remove the photo… It's a symbol I've never seen before."

I took the parchment from his hand, scrutinizing it.

"Are you sure this is even a rune?" I murmured, squinting at the paper.

"No," Zayn admitted. "It might be as mundane as an initial, or a non-warded symbol. I've seen similar markings in the marshes, not far from the Blighted Forest. Maybe the banshees will know what it is."

As if on cue, my mother's voice thundered from somewhere in the castle, "TALIA! COME DOWN TO EAT, YOUR DINNER IS GETTING ICE COLD!"

"WE'RE COMING!" I shouted back, making Zayn's hands fly to his ears.

A split second later, someone started rapping on the door like a woodpecker.

"What?!" I snarled as I flung the door open.

"Tal-ya!" Biscuit lifted his claw to wave at me from the ground. "Din-din!"

"Yes, I heard." I rolled my eyes, scooping him off the floor. "Where have *you* been, you little traitor?"

He looked up at me with a quivering beak and glittering puppy dog eyes.

"After finding him holed up in the larder, devouring his *second* wheel of cheese"—Zayn shot Biscuit a reproachful look—"I put him to work. He's been helping me round up herbs and put out various fires… Although one of those fires was actually his fault—"

"Raawk!"

Ignoring him, Zayn held the door open for me. "After you," he said, nodding graciously as he gestured me forward, "*paşahdî'mtha*."

"Please don't," I griped as I stepped through the doorway. "I have a hard enough time getting the elves to stop calling me 'queen.'"

I expected him to laugh, but he just quietly fell into step beside me, his hands shoved deeply in his pockets.

Sighing, I turned to Biscuit, who was perched on my shoulder preening a lock of hair that had fallen from my bun. "How's Mavros?"

Wings drooping, he showed me an image of a black cat curled up in a tight ball beside the kitchen fireplace. "Sad."

"Have you tried giving her almonds? She seems to like those."

He nodded.

"What about chocolate? Zayn says it's good for familiars who've been separated from their masters."

Biscuit ruffled his feathers in annoyance. "Biss-kiss give Mavvie almond, choccy, *an'* cheese!"

"All of that?" I let out a low whistle. "Well…try not to worry, okay? If there's a way to help her, we will. I promise."

Zayn cast me a grim look before heading down the grand staircase. The throne room was completely empty and silent, save for the sound of our bare feet softly plodding across the pristine marble floors. As we made our way to the wide double doors in the far back corner of the room, a knot appeared in my stomach. A dusty pile of skeletons had been shoved in this corner just days before. Had any of those bones belonged to Zayn's family members? And if so, where were they now? I glanced at him out of the corner of my eye, but his face was stone-smooth as he pushed the doors open.

Several hundred forks lowered to their plates as we stepped into the dining hall, momentarily halting the polite drone of various dinner conversations. The elves, knockers, and banshees were seated among three sprawling tables, though pointedly separated by race. I had to work to keep my jaw in place as I gaped at the colossal room that stretched before us. An elaborate crystal chandelier hovered above each of the three banquet tables, hung from an arched ceiling that was at least thirty feet high. The walls of the dining hall were covered in the same intricate ceramic tiles as the throne room and foyer, but the ceiling…the ceiling was a masterpiece. An entire two-dimensional world stared down at us, millions upon millions of glittering tiles that, all together, painted a picture of the continent, from the silvery mists of the north to the glittering cobalt-blue forests of the south. Emerald-green seas crashed upon the shores of the Obsidian Cliffs while fires erupted from a southeastern island that seemed to be made entirely of lava. I spun in a slow circle, taking it all in.

It wasn't until I finally pulled my eyes away from the breathtaking mural that I realized everyone else in the room was on their feet and waiting for us to sit down.

My face flushed several shades of gold as I quickly caught up to Zayn, taking the empty seat he pulled out for me at the head of the center table. Once he'd taken his place beside me, everyone else sat as well, casually falling back into hushed conversations. Most of the tommyknockers sat together at the table to our left, with elves taking up most of the center table where we were seated, as well as the one to our right – save for the handful of banshees who sat at the very end of it, closest to us. Ice had formed on that lone section of the table, and neither elf nor knocker dared sit less than four empty seats away from them. Judging by the surly looks the banshees were casting the rest of the room, they didn't seem to mind.

A door on the far end of the dining hall banged open and my mother and Lam stepped through, wearing matching pink aprons and carrying two plates each.

"Oh, Talia, there you are!" Mom called. I made a move to stand but she waved me back down. "Oy, sit, sit! You've been walking for days!"

I let out a grateful sigh as I started to sit back down—

"And anyway, we cooked, so you two can do all the dishes!"

—which turned into a loud groan.

"Just kidding!" She grinned, setting down a big plate of brisket, wilted greens, and a hunk of purple-tinged elven sweet bread that Korinne no doubt had a hand in baking. "Now eat up, or else you won't have any more fat in those adorable cheeks for me to pinch!" She reached forward to do just that, dropping her hand when Zayn hummed a low warning.

"Dee Dee, I cannot emphasize enough how important it is that you do *not*, under any circumstance, touch your daughter right now."

"So you've been telling me!" Her eyes narrowed at him, betraying the slightest glimmer of crimson. "But you still haven't told me why I can't!"

"Because it'll k—"

"Cause me a lot of discomfort," I swiftly interjected, flashing him a hard look. "But only until we kill Sol, and then it won't be a problem anymore…right, Zayn?"

The muscle in his jaw clenched. "Right."

With a hearty throat clear, Lam set one of his two plates in front of Zayn. He then pulled out the empty chair to my left for my mother, which she sullenly accepted, before finally seating himself directly to Zayn's right.

"Sire." He nodded his head formally.

No one else in the dining hall had resumed eating, though their plates were still piled high with food. I could feel the eyes of every person in that room trained on us, so I raised my gilded fork and knife and began to cut into my meat, spurred on by the voracious grumblings of my hollow stomach.

Zayn and the rest of the room followed suit as I shoved a hunk of tender meat in my mouth, doing everything I could not to let out what I knew would be a borderline-sexual moan when that first bite hit the back of my tongue. Beside me, my mother was ravenously attacking her raw piece of meat, using a spoon to slurp the residual juices from her plate like tomato soup.

"Aren't you worried about E. coli?" I asked, stifling a gag.

"There is no E. coli in this realm," she answered primly, "otherwise, vampires would get food poisoning all the time, wouldn't they?"

I gritted my teeth into what I hoped looked like a smile. "You're not a vampire."

"You're right. I'm a vamshee!"

I rolled my eyes, stifling what would have been a biting retort had we been anywhere but here.

Biscuit hopped from the back of my chair and onto Lam's, peering down at the satyr's food like a half-starved seagull. Just as Lam had settled in to take a big bite of steamed weeds, Biscuit flew down and snatched them from his fork.

"Away, foul beast!" Lam snarled, wrapping a hairy arm around his plate like a mother protecting her young.

Biscuit spat the greens back onto Lam's plate in disgust. "Bad goat food!"

"Biscuit, *where* have your manners gone?" Zayn admonished.

"Seriously, stop begging for scraps like a dog!" I said as I tossed him a hunk of buttered bread that he deftly caught in one claw.

Zayn gave me a pointed look.

"What?" I asked, shoving the rest of the roll in my mouth.

Several chairs down the table, Safir rose to her feet, lifting her goblet. The drone of elven conversations hushed as everyone at the table turned to look at her. "On behalf of those who escaped the southern territory with their families and their lives intact"—she smiled, tilting her glass at us—"I would like to extend our deepest gratitude to our gallant saviors."

Chairs grazed across the stone as Korinne and the rest of the elves quickly stood alongside her, raising their glasses toward our end of the table. Seeing this, the tommyknockers scrambled to refill their empty goblets from the few remaining bottles at their table, then pushed out their chairs with loud scrapes. Despite a handful of disdainful glances from the elves, they too raised their glasses high in the sky. Saoirse and the other banshees, meanwhile, remained seated in their icy corner of the room, watching the rest of us with equally icy expressions.

I downed my hunk of bread with an audible gulp as Safir continued, "Had Zæynek *Pádeşah* and Talia *Paşahdî* not risked everything to first give us warning, and then to selflessly fight beside us, none would have escaped the ruthless, unprompted attack upon our settlement. None would have survived to tell the story of what would have been our futile demise. None would sing the songs of the elves' lasting endurance to our ancestors beneath the shade of the Great Phoenix Tree. But because of your noble sacrifice, such songs may yet be written."

“Hear, hear,” Korinne and several of the other elves murmured – about a quarter of them clutching young children against their hips.

“And without the graciousness of our hosts, Lamswyth *Şahéni’musáf* and Dídra *Paş’aşéya*,” Safir shifted her glass toward the two of them, “our bellies would be as light as our traveling bags.”

That elicited several chortles from the elves.

“*L’chaim!*” Mom and Lam – the newly-dubbed “queen’s mother” and “king’s advisor” – simultaneously called out.

The blush in my cheeks deepened.

“And lastly,” Safir continued, “we would still be wandering those mountains, perhaps being led to our deaths by impish will-o’-wisps”—her eyes playfully darted to me—“if not for the masterful guidance and very loud singing of our new friends.” With a solemn nod, she raised her glass to the tommyknockers, many of whom nearly choked on their wine when the rest of the elves followed suit.

Having recovered from his initial shock, Boris lifted his sloshing glass high above his pointed hat, prompting his compatriots to do the same. “To new friends…and vanquished enemies!”

Laughter turned to cheers.

“To new friends and vanquished enemies!” everyone else shouted back, toasting their neighbors.

While Zayn shifted uncomfortably to my right, I stared into the untouched goblet of red wine sitting in front of me, remembering the rivers of blood snaking across the sand just days ago. Elves, I had come to understand, don’t mourn death the way most humans do; according to their beliefs, the Great Phoenix Tree welcomes home all pure elven souls, granting them new life as saplings beneath the shade of her branches.

I, however, was still reeling from the violence and loss of the last few days.

When a cold shiver slithered down my back, it took me a moment to realize that it wasn't from the chilling memory of battle, but rather from the next table over. The air around Saoirse and the other banshees had cooled to fog, turning their breaths into icy puffs of crystallized anger.

"Fools," she hissed, her voice cutting through the reverie like a cold knife. "You sit upon your high hill, drinking to toasts you have not yet earned. Have you learned nothing from the skeletons resting beneath these blood-stained stones?"

Silence fell upon the room as, one by one, the elves and tommyknockers all lowered their goblets.

"The gathering storm promises to be a hard-fought battle you shall bleed for, but not win." The air grew colder as Saoirse's voice steadily grew stronger. "For when the Killer of Kings begins his march upon these lands, the true battle of this age will begin. And mark you our words—"

A visible shiver spread through every person her cold, silvery gaze fell upon.

"—of the five hundred and sixty-two living souls in this room, not one of you will survive the scourge Solomon brings."

Her eyes fell directly on me, stealing the breath from my chest.

"Not one."

VIII.
A Cold Awakening

Silence billowed across the room like winter fog.

I stared at Saoirse in shock, my knuckles aching from clutching the edge of the table so forcefully. "Then what do you propose we do?" I asked, mechanically rising to my feet. "Are you saying we should surrender? Without even trying?"

Her eyes narrowed into silver slits. "I am saying that you will join the skeletons beneath these walls should you decide to remain here, meager in number as you are."

"Is this opinion or prophecy?" Zayn demanded, pushing out his chair.

"As sure as the moons will rise, it is written."

He took a step backward as though he'd been slapped. "Is…Is there truly nothing we can do?"

"Fool boy!" the banshee cackled. "There is always something to be done, but raising your glasses to a war you've not yet won will not save you from the blight that comes for you

– and for *her.*" Her inhuman eyes once more settled on me, making Zayn's fingers twitch.

"Then…we will gather others," he declared. "I've already sent messages—"

"And who has replied?"

The Adam's apple in Zayn's throat dipped. When the rest of Saoirse's sisters rose, his was not the only hand to reach for a dagger.

But the banshees didn't notice – didn't even blink – as their eyes shifted to pure, glowing white. When they opened their mouths, many of the elves' hands instinctively shot to their ears. And yet, what followed wasn't a scream, but a perfectly synchronized chant that swirled in the air like the frigid breath of winter:

Lord of Seelies and Unseelies both,
Whose birth wrenched the realm in twain,
Stake your claim upon the throne,
And blood shall fall as rain.

But if an ally you should find,
Far north, beyond the plains,
The shepherd of this land may rise,
And dawn shall come again.

Then, their ghostly echoes still lingering in the air, the banshees disappeared, their bodies evaporating into fog. As snow swirled around her nightgown, dissolving her lower body into cold mist, Saoirse's frosty gaze settled on me.

"The fate of this world rests on a razor's edge, Talia-*grādh.* Journey to the Blighted Forest with Zæynek alone at your side, and you may find that which you both seek." Her eyes trailed to Zayn. Gentle snow had begun to fall from the ceiling, dusting his hair and lashes. "When the collective scream of the banshees rises above the cries of the battlefield, the war will be over. Pray it comes at dawn, not dusk."

And then she was gone, leaving nothing but ice and silence in her wake.

A long, tense moment passed, followed by another. And then, all at once, the room erupted in shouts; shouts of anger and outrage, of questions and doubt, of fear and distress.

Zayn and I exchanged a long, haunted look amid the heightening chaos.

"Wait a minute! *Wait a minute!"* my mom hollered at us, drawing the attention of several nearby elves who had stopped shouting to listen in. "Let me get this straight… If we try to fight with just the people in this room, we're doomed? But if we find some allies from the north, we'll be okay? But only if the banshees scream in the morning, not at night?"

"That does seem to be their general insinuation, yes," Lam said, stroking his beard thoughtfully.

Mom shook her head in irritation. "Who do they think they are, the Illuminati? Back in Brooklyn, if you've got something to say, you just say it! You don't chant in ominous riddles and then disappear in a puff of smoke! And what's this *mishegas* about some kind of blighted forest?"

"The Blighted Forest is where Saedis banished the Unseelies in the years leading up to the Blood Wars," Lam explained. "It's why it's otherwise known as the Path of the Banished."

"It's also where Sol secretly planned their uprising," Zayn added, tiredness creeping into his voice. "It's not the most hospitable of regions."

"Indeed," Lam nodded fervently. "Seelies have not entered those woods since…well, since before the Great Fall! For the banshees to even suggest that Talia should set foot in there is…well, it's madness!"

I opened my mouth to answer, then snapped it shut upon realizing that the rest of the room had gone completely silent and was listening to our conversation with rapt attention.

Lam's horizontal pupils narrowed as he turned to me. "Surely you aren't considering such a perilous – and frankly nonsensical – notion? Even to find some hypothetical ally, it's decidedly not worth the risk!"

Most of the heads in the dining hall were nodding in agreement as they too swiveled in my direction, no doubt expecting me to concur with Lam's unassailable reasoning.

Zayn looked at me, and I looked at him, while everyone else waited with bated breath.

"The Blighted Forest is one of the last places I would have you venture, if given the choice…" He sighed, dropping his voice to a low murmur. "That said, it was once considered the crossroads of the north. And I can't imagine the banshees would have mentioned it if it were not somehow important that we start there."

A small smile tugged at the corner of my mouth. "I mean…what's the worst thing that could happen?"

My mother groaned into her hands while the rest of the room once more exploded into verbal mayhem.

"But the werewolves!"

"They'd never make it back!"

"It's obviously a trick!"

Lamswyth brought his panpipes to his lips, emitting one extremely shrill, prolonged note that brought the pandemonium to a complete standstill, then turned to Zayn. "How would the two of you even travel there and back?" he asked, hiking his bushy eyebrows halfway up his furrowed forehead. "The Waypoint in that region has been enchanted – one may only portal in, not out. And those who try to leave by hoof face the very real risk of being mauled by werewolves – and that's only if they're lucky enough to die before succumbing to their venom!"

A line appeared between Zayn's brows. He – and every other person in the dining hall – turned back to me, awaiting my response.

I chewed on the inside of my lip. "Tesseract Runes?"

Zayn hesitated, then nodded. "Assuming the proper ingredients are nearby, the ink would take me about two hours to make."

"I can help!" Korinne called. "I found a cluster of *fœchíra* pods outside just this morning."

"But we can't just leave," I said, darting a glance at my mother. "I mean, not unless we evacuate everyone else first."

That sent the tommyknockers into a flurry of incensed titters.

"Evacuate – meaning *surrender?*" Boris shouted. "Never!"

"Yeah, but you heard the banshees!" I protested. "If we stay here, we're doomed—"

"Which is why you and His Highness are going to find us more allies!" Norris chimed in. "Besides, we've already notified our cousins in the Obsidian Cliffs, who are on their way to help!"

"*More* tommyknockers?" Zayn grumbled under his breath.

I rubbed at the growing ache in my temples.

"Your Highnesses, with all due respect," Safir spoke up, "Tanak, Laleh, and I can stay behind to ready a strategic battle plan—"

"To which I can certainly lend my expertise," Lam offered. "After all, I did spend decades as King Saedis's most-trusted advisor!"

"Once the ink is done, I'll take on a group of apprentices and continue warding the castle," Korinne added.

"We can help fortify the palace as well!" Boris chimed in, oblivious to the handful of incredulous stares that statement had earned him.

Wincing, I mustered just enough courage to turn and face my mother, from whom I was expecting a swift and fiery barrage of protests. Indeed, she had a stern look on her face, but, shockingly, it wasn't directed at me. "And I'll help organize everyone else," she volunteered, hand raised. "Plus, my special banshee sixth sense will let me know if Tally and Zayn are in trouble, or worse, if Captain Creepy prematurely decides to pay us a visit! I'll be a human alarm system!"

"WEEE-oooh-WEEE-oooh!" Biscuit shrieked helpfully.

"That's my Moishe!" Mom beamed.

I gaped at her in shock. "Just… Just like that? You'll let me go?"

She made an exasperated shrug. "Would I prefer to keep you from leaving this castle by using my own body as a barricade? Yes, obviously! But, like you keep reminding me, you're a grown woman. And anyway, the longer I watch you here, the more I can see you were born to do this."

An unexpected twinge of emotion knotted in my chest.

"You were always destined to do great things, Tally. Your father and I never doubted that for an instant. I'm just glad you're expanding your talents beyond hanging around a bunch of biker gangs in some schlocky tattoo shop. No offense," Mom added quickly, casting Zayn an apologetic look.

"Uh, none taken," he replied, shifting his attention from her to me. "So…you really want to do this? Even in your…condition?" His eyes darted to my shoulder.

"*Especially* in my condition," I answered fiercely. "Whatever we can do, whoever we can find to help us take this guy down, I'm there. Oh, and before I forget," I added, crossing my arms smugly, "we're heading into *my* family's neck of the forbidden woods. So, you'd better stick close to my side and listen, if you know what's good for you."

Despite his best efforts, the corner of Zayn's mouth quirked up. "You've got it, Boss."

We scarfed down our midnight meal quickly, then left the others to embark on their various duties: Korinne would make the ink Zayn and I needed for the Tess Runes, while Lam, Safir, and the other elven officers hauled dusty maps onto cleared-off banquet tables to start talking battle strategy. The mothers and children who were too young to fight helped my mom organize supplies, and any elves with a knowledge of runes were sent off to continue fortifying the castle walls with strict instructions from Zayn. Meanwhile, the tommyknockers made a beeline for the dungeon, chattering excitedly about "metamorphizing" the igneous rocks of the foundation – whatever that meant. After ensuring everyone else was in proper order, Zayn set about packing our belongings for the journey while I was saddled with the crucial task of "taking a goddamn nap before you collapse from exhaustion."

Despite my vociferous protests, the minute my head hit that pillow, I was dead to the world.

When Zayn gently roused me two hours later, I rubbed my eyes groggily, my jaw cracking with a yawn as I stretched my arms over my head.

"Here, stick out your tongue," he said softly, holding up a dropper of bright pink Revitalizing Serum.

I did as I was told, feeling a familiar invigorating zing shoot through my body when the minty liquid hit the back of my throat.

"Thanks," I muttered, shaking my head to clear away the last vestiges of sleepiness.

"When this is all over, you can sleep undisturbed for a week, if you'd like." He smiled, though it came nowhere close to meeting his eyes.

"When this is all over, I'll be doing nothing *but* disturbing your sleep." I flashed him a half-hearted wink. "Do you know what it's like to hang out with the sexiest creature you've ever laid eyes on and not be able to lay a finger on them?"

"I have some idea," he answered, the edges of his voice coarse as his eyes raked across the thin undershirt and panties I'd slept in.

I swallowed tightly.

Muttering Elvish obscenities under his breath, he withdrew a charged tattoo machine from his bag and sat down next to me on the bed. "The fæchíra ink came out perfectly, and the cartridge is already filled. I'd offer to put the Tess Rune on you myself, but…"

"I know, I know." I sighed. "Is yours done at least?"

"Yes." He held up his palm, where a triangular Tesseract Rune had already been tattooed. "I'm ready to go when you are…so long as you're absolutely sure you still want to do this."

I rolled my eyes. "I'm sure. I'll just need your spellb—" I snapped my mouth shut, remembering that Zayn's priceless family grimoire was now in the hands of his arch nemesis – along with a gleaming vial of my blood. "Oh God… We are so screwed," I moaned into cupped hands.

"It's going to be okay, Tal," he said softly. "And if at any time you want to go home—"

"I *am* home," I interrupted, looking him square in the eye. "Wherever you are is home. Now shut up and give me the tattoo machine."

Mouth quirking into that adorable half-smile that had long ago stolen my heart, he gently placed the machine in my hand, careful not to let his fingers brush against mine. "Here – I'll sketch out the design so it's easier for you to copy."

I took a deep, steeling breath – muttering obscenities beneath it – then flicked on the machine. "No need, I remember." Ignoring his look of surprise, I began free-drawing the rune on the inside of my left hand, pretending the gold liquid seeping through the lines of my palm was metallic ink – not the result of a you-know-what carving into my skin.

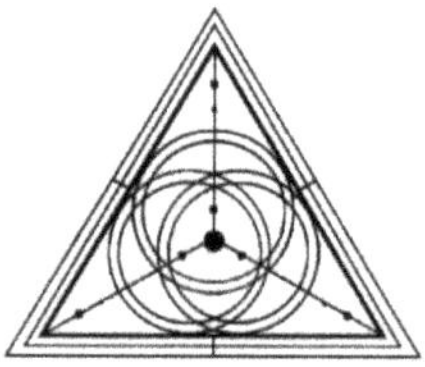

Zayn watched intently as I quickly etched the main triangle into my palm, followed by the surrounding ones. "You're remarkable," he murmured.

"I'm an idiot savant who happens to be good at drawing," I grunted back. "How many uses of this thing are we going to get?"

"Of the rune? Three."

"Even with my blood?"

"Tess Runes are so powerful – and use up so much magic – not even gold blood can prolong them. What gold blood *can* do, however, is allow you to bring extra passengers along with you…hypothetically, of course, since it would require you to physically touch them."

I ground my teeth together as I pulled the third line of the third triangle. "Speaking of passengers, where's Biscuit?"

"In the kitchen, saying goodbye to Mavros. She hasn't moved from her spot by the fireplace since yesterday."

A worried knot formed in my throat. "Will she be okay until we get back?"

He shifted uncomfortably. "I was able to mix up some herbs to help with the separation anxiety. And she allowed me to place a ward on her that will make it that much harder for Sol to Manipulate her, should they cross paths again. But Tal, if we kill Sol…"

My heart sank. "She'll die too…won't she?"

He nodded.

Tears began to blur my vision, forcing me to pause my work. "Does Biscuit know?"

"Raaawk?" Biscuit appeared atop my head in a dazzling blaze of rainbow feathers.

Zayn plucked him off of me like a chicken, setting him between us on the bed. "Talia was asking if you knew about, um…"

"Almond butter," I blurted out. "I was asking if you'd ever heard of it."

Biscuit's eyes grew as wide as saucers. "Almond…*buttie?*"

"Mm-hmm," I nodded swiftly. "You can smear it on toast or dip apples in it. I'll buy some for you, if…er, *when* we get home."

Zayn's eyes met mine.

"Almond buttie!" Biscuit cheered, flapping his wings. "Lessgo!"

"I'm almost done," I said through gritted teeth. "Just a few more circles."

"Start with the outer ones, then work your way clockwise and in," Zayn reminded me. "Incorrectly-drawn Tesseract Runes have been known to teleport inexperienced mages into, well…unfortunate circumstances. Some were never seen again.

They might have ended up in an ocean trench or the center of the earth, for all we know."

"How delightful," I muttered, then quickly changed the subject. "So, this Blighted Forest…is it really as bad as the elves make it sound? Or are they just blowing it out of proportion because it happens to be in prime Unseelie Territory?"

Zayn didn't answer right away.

After finishing my next set of circles, I momentarily flicked off the tattoo machine and looked up at him. "Zayn? Did you hear me?"

"Between runes and nepotism, I'm sure we'll be okay," he finally replied.

I arched an incredulous eyebrow at him. "Are you just trying to make me feel better?"

"Um…"

Setting down the tattoo machine, I pinched the bridge of my nose with my good hand. "Okay, can you at least tell me what we'll be dealing with? Are we talking glaistigs? Werewolves? I mean, we survived a legion of vampires, strigas, and manticores. Nothing in there can be worse than a flying lion with a poisonous scorpion tail…right?"

Zayn didn't answer right away. Instead, his gaze drifted to the belt I'd draped across the footboard of the bed, from which two daggers hung: one gem-encrusted gold and the other cold-forged iron.

After a long moment, he sighed. "We'll need to get you bigger weapons."

IX.
Into the Woods

Dawn came.

With fresh runes tattooed on our bodies, Zayn and I gathered our things and made our farewells. It took some effort to get my mom to release her death grip on the black travel cloak I'd borrowed from Korinne, but after about twenty minutes of reassurances, promises on my father's grave to come back in one piece, and a little help from Lamswyth – who made up some spur-of-the-moment lie about finding mice droppings in Mom's closet – I was finally able to extricate myself from her clutches. But I still had one last thing to do before Zayn, Biscuit, and I could commence our journey.

While Zayn finished up an impromptu strategy session with Safir and the other officers, I made my way to the kitchen, where Korinne was busy grinding a pile of what looked like metallic butterfly wings into a fine iridescent dust. A large cauldron of silver ink was simmering inside the roaring fireplace a few feet behind her, and lying on the stones just in front of it was a curled-up black cat resting her head on her paws.

"Hey sweetie," I murmured, kneeling beside Mavros to scratch between her ears. The Requisition Rune on my shoulder didn't protest, probably because Mavros belonged to Sol, making her an extension of him…

Just like me, I couldn't help thinking.

"Um, listen," I cleared my throat, "I know you're sleepy and probably not in the best of moods, but I'd love it if you would come with us…please?"

She cocked one green eye at me, her faint voice fluttering in my mind. *Tired.*

"I know you're tired, baby girl." I gently scooped her into my lap, kissing the top of her head despite her small mewl of protest. "But I can't bear the thought of leaving you here. And who knows? Maybe we'll find something out there to help you feel better. So, please, would you come? I know Biscuit would be so happy if you did."

With a rather human-like sigh, she stepped off my lap and stretched out her long spine, claws kneading at the stone as her entire body erupted into dull black flames. Upon burning away, a tiny black mouse remained in their place, anxiously clutching her tail between two tiny paws.

"Atta girl," I smiled, scooping her into the warm inside pocket of my cloak.

"I'm glad you're taking her with you," Korinne smiled. "She really seems to have taken to you – just like everyone else in this realm."

"Well, we can't fault all of you for your terrible taste," I joked.

She chuckled. "How's your shoulder?"

"Fine," I lied. In truth, it hadn't stopped hurting all day; I'd just gotten better at ignoring it.

"Do you have everything you need? Food, ink, supplies…weapons?" Her eyes trailed to the revolver strapped to my hip.

I followed her gaze, wincing. "I guess Zayn had stashed this at Lam's place decades ago, then forgot about it. It's got five iron bullets, but…" I laughed dryly. "I've never shot a gun in my life. I mean, look at me. I feel ridiculous – like a teddy bear decorated in artillery."

Her eyes roved over my outfit, taking in its absurdity: black knee-high boots, one of them hiding a four-inch switchblade; siren-hide leggings, tough enough to withstand even a werewolf's claws according to Zayn; a wide belt strung with several Sharpies, two knives, and the aforementioned iron-loaded handgun; a white peasant shirt, its sleeves rolled to my elbows to partially expose the tactical runes I sported from wrist to shoulder; a sturdy siren-hide corset to help protect all of my vulnerable and squishy organs; and the hooded traveling cloak Korinne had lent me, the fabric a beautiful crushed velvet that had been dyed the color of ripe berries.

"You don't look ridiculous," she said in a serious tone. "You look like a force to be reckoned with. I'm frankly grateful to be fighting on the same team as you and would follow you to the ends of the earth…Your Highness," she inclined her head in a bow that was neither ironic nor condescending.

"You can't tell me you believe in this gold blood nonsense too!" I protested. "Jesus, Korinne! More than anyone else, you must realize how utterly unqualified I am—"

"I believe that fate brought you to this realm to help us," she interrupted. "And whether your blood was gold or red, magical or mundane, my faith in you would remain staunch… Now, you must hold your chin up high." She gestured, raising her own in illustration. "After all, half of leading is believing in yourself – or at least giving others the false impression that you do." She flashed me a quick wink.

"Yeah, yeah," I muttered, turning to go. Biting my lip, I stole a glance at her over my shoulder. "Hey, Korinne?"

She looked up from her mortar of crushed butterfly wings. "Yes?"

"You have feelings for Safir…don't you?"

"I…" Her mouth opened, then closed, her cheeks flushing the color of maraschino cherries. "Um…"

"You should tell her how you feel," I smiled. "If this week has taught me anything, it's that life is too short and too fragile to keep things inside…you know?"

She swallowed, then nodded mutely.

"And on that note…" I turned around to face her. "I want you to know that I love *you*, Ko-Ko. You're the big sister I never had but always wanted." My smile wavered slightly. "So don't you dare let anything happen to you while I'm gone, or I'll ring your beautiful neck."

"You too, little sister." Her amethyst eyes grew glassy with emotion. "Promise me you'll be safe out there."

I nodded, touching my hand to my heart. "Anak'tha al'preyámi, Kor'ínthe al'Rahími."

Korinne did the same, bowing her head once more. "Anak'tha al'preyámi, Talia Kestenbaum. May the leaves of the Great Phoenix Tree shade you on your journey."

"Hiiii Ko-Ko!" Biscuit's shrill squawk punctuated our touching moment as he flew through the kitchen doors, landing gracefully on Korinne's shoulder. "Almond?"

"You little scavenger." She chuckled, withdrawing one from her pocket.

He snatched the nut with one claw, balancing on her shoulder with the other as his head swiveled around the room, looking for Mavros.

"Right here," I said, showing him the sleeping mouse in my pocket.

He gazed at her with an inscrutable expression, his gold-flecked pupils dilating with the reflection of her curled up little body. And then, as though suddenly remembering what he was clutching, he attacked the almond, sending a shower of shell fragments onto the countertop where Korinne had been meticulously working.

"Hey, watch it!" she exclaimed, shielding the contents of her mortar with two hands.

"Biscuit, what have I told you about harassing people when they're working?" Zayn asked as he strode into the kitchen, an absolute vision in his high-collared, siren-hide vest and black cloak. He was slinging a heavy messenger bag over his shoulder, the tattoos twining up his chiseled bronze arms rippling with every subtle flex and movement of his muscles. When his eyes fell on me, his expression softened. "Are you ready to go, Tal?"

"As ready as I'll ever be," I answered, feeling a flush creeping into my cheeks.

"That's all any of us can hope for." He smiled tightly. "Well, no sense stalling your Tesseract lessons any longer. Biscuit?"

With an affirmative "Raawk!" Biscuit disappeared in a flash of color, reappearing on the inside of our forearms in two-dimensional form.

"How will Talia Tesseract to the Blighted Forest if she's never been there before?" Korinne asked, setting down her pestle. "She has to be able to visualize where she's going."

"I'm going to show her," Zayn replied, touching the tattoo of Biscuit on his arm. "Tal, close your eyes."

I did as I was told.

"Now, can you see the image of the Waypoint I'm showing you?"

Our link flared with warmth. A gray and peeling Waypoint fluttered in front of my vision, its lamp glowing a sickly puce green.

"I see it," I answered.

"Good. Now clear your mind of all other thoughts and images, keeping that Waypoint firmly in your vision. When you activate your Tess Rune, I want you to say 'The Blighted Forest Waypoint,' loudly and clearly, concentrating on the image of it in your mind. Okay? Any questions?"

I shook my head, swallowing tightly. "No…that seems straightforward enough."

"Okay." His husky voice was centimeters from my ear as he positioned himself behind me. I felt him clasping my cloak in his hand, the closest he'd let himself come to touching me. "We'll leave on your signal."

Trying to ignore all other distractions – like the delicious, intoxicating scent of Zayn's body, so unbearably close to mine – I focused on the green glow of the Waypoint he was showing me, burning the lamppost into my memory. Then, with a deep breath, I held my open palm out in front of me, my hand erupting with heat as the Tesseract Rune triggered to life.

I took a deep breath, making sure to speak my next words clearly and concisely. "The Blighted Forest W—"

"Talia!" My mother's shrill voice punctured straight through my concentration. "What are you still doing here?"

"Dee Dee, no!" Zayn shouted, but it was too late.

My "clear and concise" command dissolved into a series of hacking coughs as thick, red smoke enveloped my entire body. Squeezing my eyes shut, I concentrated as best as I could, mentally groping at the flickering image of the Waypoint.

"Th-The B-Blighted Forest Waypoint," I tried to sputter out once more, but my tongue evaporated into smoke halfway through, relegating the words to nothing more than a jumbled string of syllables in my head.

A smothering column of smoke swirled around me, searing my throat with its acrid stench. My eyes watered, but before I could even sneeze, the entire kitchen dissolved into a roiling sea of crimson, reducing my mother's shrill voice, Zayn's sharp rebuke, and Korinne's panicked cry to nothing but diminishing echoes from a distant land.

I fell into a violent fit of sneezes as the smoke bled away, revealing a dark, lifeless forest devoid of all leaves and sunlight. The earth pitched beneath my feet; I instinctively reached for Zayn, but my hands groped at nothing but cold air.

Something shrieked nearby, making me whirl on my heels. Gnarled, dead trees surrounded me on all sides, their bony, mangled branches reminding me of broken limbs and twisted claws. Panting, I spun in a full circle, trying to catch both my balance and my breath. My eyes darted from tree to tree, searching for the sickly green glow of the Waypoint in the distance. But there was no light to be found.

Zayn! I called out silently.

Nothing.

Biscuit! Are you there? I glanced down at my arm. Biscuit's frame was empty, meaning he was with Zayn – wherever that was.

Zayn? I tried again. *Zayn!*

My heart was crashing against my ribcage, sending a torrent of blood rushing straight to my eardrums that momentarily drowned out all other thoughts. Shivering, I wrapped my cloak tightly around my body, startled by the series of shrill squeaks coming from the inside pocket.

"Mavros!" I whispered, scooping her out. "Oh, thank God, you're here!"

She looked around frantically, wringing her paws.

"I don't know where they are." I chewed on my lip, half-expecting a one-legged fachan to pop out from between the trees at any moment. "Are you feeling well enough to do a quick survey of the area?"

She nodded. After appearing to struggle for a few moments, black flames enveloped her furry little mouse body. When they cleared, she was still a mouse, but with long black wings – a flutter-mouse.

"Oh, so *that's* why the Germans call bats *Fledermausen*," I joked weakly, fighting the urge to fling her to the ground. For whatever reason, Rabies-prone flying rodents have never been my thing.

Seeing me recoil, she cocked her head at me. I had to admit – despite her elongated finger bones and creepy, membranous bat wings – her furry little bat-face was actually kind of cute.

"Don't go far, okay?" I whispered. "If you can't find them in five minutes, come right back!"

She let out an affirmative chitter, then launched off my hand and fluttered away. I listened as her tiny squeaks of echolocation faded into the darkness of the surrounding forest, sucking down a deep, shuddering breath when I could no longer hear them. The cold ground crunched beneath my feet as I took one tentative step forward, and then another. Lifeless and grim, the forest looked like something straight out of a Halloween slasher movie

– save for the tiny red orbs that hovered in the air, all around, like fireflies.

Please, God, don't let those be will-o'-wisps, I grimaced.

My hand moved to my iron dagger, the hilt of which had been wrapped in crisscrossing ropes of leather to protect my skin from the poisonous metal. I'd touched plenty of iron-containing materials back on earth, but as a creature with mixed fae blood, this cold-forged meteorite iron had sloughed the skin right off my hand the last time I'd been forced to use it. I gulped at the terrible memory of Sol plunging it into Zayn's back, nervously taking in my surroundings.

So, what do I do? Go back to the castle? My eyes darted to the faded Tess Rune on the inside of my palm. It only had two uses left, and we didn't have another drop of that particular type of ink to spare – it was a miracle that Korinne had managed to brew anything functional from the paltry handful of brittle fœchíra pods she had collected.

No, I chewed my lip. I couldn't waste the trip – not yet, at least. I just had to pray that Zayn and I would find each other before something much bigger and scarier did.

"Zayn?" I whisper-called into the darkness, taking a ginger step forward.

When I was a kid, my parents had always drilled in my head to stay put if I ever got lost, that someone would eventually find me and take me home. But something told me these woods were not the ideal place to be found by a stranger. My feet took three more cautious steps forward, every snap and pop of dried twigs beneath my boots making me wince. I risked a skyward glance, trying to locate the sun. It had been dawn when we left the castle, and this place was farther east, which meant it was later in the day. So, where the hell had all the daylight gone?

I hugged my body even tighter as I willed my feet forward. A twisted cluster of trees lay just ahead of me; faintly-glowing, putrid-green fruit dangled from their otherwise-bare branches like shrunken heads. Something small and black darted between the trees' rotted boughs – a squirrel, perhaps? I shuddered to think what rodents in these woods might look like. Would they have three sets of venomous fangs? Glowing red eyes? Claws sharp enough to tear your face to shreds?

"Zayn?" I tried again, raising my voice slightly. "Are you there?"

A twig snapped behind me, making me whirl around.

"Who's there?" I gasped, clenching my iron dagger in a trembling hand.

There was no answer.

"Z-Zayn?" I gulped. "Biscuit? Is that you?"

I took a timid step in the direction of the snapping twig, mentally running through my body's inventory of new runes. *Fulmen for lightning. Ligature for binding. Smoke Screen for…uh…smoking?* My eyes trailed to the complex set of squares embedded on the inside of my wrist. What was that one for again – killing or blocking?

Something howled in the distance, sending an icy shiver trickling down my spine.

Hello, Zaffre, a sumptuous voice whispered in my head, stopping me dead in my tracks. Sharp, icy shards sliced through the Requisition Rune on my shoulder as Sol's voice slithered between my ears. *What sort of trouble have you gotten yourself into this time?*

"Get out of my head," I rasped, pressing my palms against my ears.

Strange that I can hear you so clearly… Heightened emotions, perhaps? Or is my claim on you strengthening? His laugh scraped against my eardrums, bringing tears to my eyes.

I could practically feel his knee shoved against my groin, his hot breath on my face as he leaned in to crush his bloody lips against mine.

So much fear…so much terror. If I only knew where you were, little jay, I'd come rescue you.

The memory of his crimson eyes – glinting with savagery as he slammed my head against the rocks – flashed in my mind, filling my throat with bile.

I sank to my knees, gnashing my teeth together. "Get out of my head!"

A pair of inhumanly yellow eyes appeared between the trees to my right. I could hear the wet snorts of whatever lurked there, could see twin plumes of steam that huffed through its flared nostrils.

Show me what you see, little one.

More and more amber eyes blinked into existence – two sets to my left, two more to my right, three more just ahead. I could feel their hungry stares roving across the soft, vulnerable parts of my body, burning into my flesh.

Werewolves, Sol hissed, fear and fury abrading the edges of his voice.

I cried out in pain as the Requisition Rune burned as cold as dry ice, then quickly clamped a hand over my mouth. Spurred forward by the sound, the monsters appeared from the shadows: massive black wolves, their mangy fur blood-soaked and heavily scarred, as though their coats had been torn open again and again. Their eyes burned like yellow flames in the darkness, while their bared muzzles revealed several jagged, crowded rows of fangs – as sharp and serrated as a shark's.

My eyes darted to the Tesseract Rune on my palm. "The Summer Palace!" I gasped, bringing an image of the foyer to my mind. The rune didn't even flicker. "Take me to the Summer

Palace!" I shouted again, concentrating my full attention on the front doors of the palace.

Nothing happened.

Meanwhile, more and more yellow eyes had appeared in the darkness, as one by one the wolves drew closer.

Terror made me forget how to breathe. I was clutching the dagger so tightly, my knuckles throbbed with pain.

Calm yourself, little jay. We can't have werewolf venom tainting that precious blood of yours. Iron won't do the trick. But fire will.

Fire? I started as though I'd been slapped, then shoved my sleeve past my bicep, exposing the Ignis Rune just above my elbow. Replacing my dagger in its sheath, I staggered to my feet. The werewolves – all eight of them – were closing in, eyes glinting and jowls frothing.

Burn them, Zaffre. Fury filled my heart, as ferocious as it was foreign. *Burn them all.*

The werewolf directly in front of me lunged, its three jagged rows of fangs bared. My hands instinctively flew in front of me to block his attack, and as they did, hell unleashed. Like a dying star violently ejecting its outermost layers, a white-hot halo of fire exploded from my body, careening outward with the force of Sol's rage… *My* rage. The closest werewolf immediately exploded into flames, his entire body disintegrating within seconds. Howls of surprise turned into brays of agony as the blaze engulfed three more werewolves, utterly wasting them. Four managed to flee the hellish inferno and stumble back into the forest, licking their wounds and yelping in terror.

I remained rooted in the eye of the firestorm as the wall of flames raged on, ravaging everything within a twenty-foot radius. Only when there was nothing left to burn, and the flames had nothing but themselves to consume, did the fire eventually die out. I stood inside my scorched circle of ash, fists clenched and breath ragged, adrenaline and fury coursing through my veins.

A low growl sounded from somewhere behind me. I spun on my heel just as a lone, uninjured werewolf launched himself from the ground, his serrated fangs primed for flesh-tearing.

Time slowed to a trickle, with my crashing heartbeats counting the fleeting moments till death. My eyes darted to the place where my Ignis Rune used to be, now completely empty, then back to the wolf, whose monstrous body was arced, midair, and poised to kill. He unhinged his powerful, bloody jaws, his amber eyes flaring with vengeance and hunger as they honed in on my exposed jugular.

As I squeezed my eyes shut, preparing to die, I vaguely registered the high-pitched, haunting scream of a distant banshee.

X.
Scorched Earth

A shrill yelp punctuated the air, followed by a heavy thud.

My eyes shot open to find the crumpled body of a werewolf splayed out at my feet, a silver arrow protruding from its bleeding eye socket. A second arrow – this one blazing with rainbow fire – hit it in the chest; within moments, its entire body had burst into flames. The acrid scent of burning fur and scorched flesh permeated my nostrils, making my stomach churn.

“Talia!” a familiar voice shouted, breaking through my mental daze.

With difficulty, I managed to tear my eyes away from the grim scene. Zayn was bounding into the scorched clearing, gripping his gleaming silver bow. Biscuit soared just behind him, his plumage alight with dazzling rainbow flames and a little black bat fluttering in tow.

“Talia!” Zayn called again, picking up his pace. But when his eyes settled on mine, he staggered to a stop. “Tal…?”

As my adrenaline subsided and my galloping heart rate began to slow, a whisper scraped between my ears – so soft and distant, I wasn't even sure it was real.

See you soon, little jay.

"Tal?" Zayn repeated, taking a cautious step forward. "Are you…hurt?"

I shook my head, partially in answer to his question, but mostly to clear the haze that had settled there. "No," I managed to reply. "I'm okay."

Biscuit landed on Zayn's shoulder, his feathers returning to normal. The two of them silently took in the scorched circle of carnage surrounding us, which included the smoking remains of five werewolf carcasses.

"Did… Did you do this?"

"Yeah." A fresh wave of nausea rose in my stomach as I took in the death and devastation. "I guess I did."

His hand tightly clenched his bow as he took three more steps in my direction, closing the distance between us. Biscuit actually recoiled as they approached, attempting to hide himself behind Zayn's ear. Even Mavros chose to land on Zayn's other shoulder, forsaking mine.

"What?" I demanded, glancing behind me. Finding nothing there, I whirled back around. Zayn, Biscuit, and Mavros were all looking at me with wary expressions, as though I'd suddenly sprouted devil horns. "Why are you guys staring at me like that?"

"I've never seen such a powerful Ignis attack," Zayn finally replied, pointedly ignoring my question. "Biscuit and I were half a mile away looking for you when we saw the flames." In spite of his obvious relief, his eyes narrowed. "How did you know to use fire against werewolves?"

"I…" I opened my mouth to answer, then closed it again, shame and guilt heating my cheeks. Zayn and I hadn't touched each other again since last night. And yet, the Requisition Rune on my shoulder was throbbing painfully, a constant reminder of its strengthening presence.

"Tal…" He took a step closer, his hand reaching for my cheek, only to freeze mid-air. "What is it?"

Head bowed, I rubbed at my arms, as though I could somehow expunge the invisible stain from my skin. As though I could somehow abrase the filth *he* had left on my body. But I couldn't. Because unlike the link Zayn and I shared – born from our love and the intermingling of our souls via Biscuit's rebirth – Sol's mark had been forcibly imprinted on me, corrupting me. Defiling me.

It was a stain I'd never be able to rub off, no matter how hard I scoured.

"How long, Tal?" Zayn asked softly. I stiffened. He was standing so close to me, I could feel the heat and pheromones radiating from his body. "How long has he been in your head?"

I couldn't bear to look at Zayn as a tear trickled down my cheek. "I first heard him back at the elven settlement, just before he attacked. At the time, I thought I was imagining it – like a trauma response. But I heard him again, just now. He…He *saw* them – the werewolves – through my eyes. And then he…he told me how to kill them. Not because he cares, but to keep my precious blood from being tainted by their venom." Digging my fingernails into my palms to keep from crying, I kept my gaze glued to the blackened earth. "What if he can see you, or where we are right now? What if…What if he's been using me to spy on you this whole time?"

I averted my gaze as Zayn knelt to the ground in front of me, his stunning, glassy emerald pools probing every inch of my face. "Tal, look at me."

I shook my head roughly, clenching my jaw.

"Tal," he tried again, his voice soft and undeservedly gentle. "You would know if he were in your head. Hell, after seeing your eyes a few minutes ago, *I* would know too. From what you've said, it sounds like he can only sense you when your emotions are at their peak… And I suspect that goes both ways."

I started, remembering the anger – the hunger – I'd felt right before Sol arrived at the settlement. The fury that flowed through me as the werewolves attacked – the fury that wasn't my own, and yet spurred me to… I gulped.

To kill.

"I don't want him inside of me, Zayn," I wept, hugging my body tightly. "It's bad enough his blood is under my skin! But this?" I shook my head so violently, the forest spun. "I can't stand it! You have to help me get him out of my head – *please!*"

Zayn's irises were darkening as I spoke, until they were two smoldering coals of fury. "If I have to tear him apart with my own two hands, Talia, I will. On my mother's grave, I swear I will destroy him."

My fingers dug into my arms as I nodded, choking back a fresh sob.

He slowly rose to his feet, his hands clenched into shaking, white-knuckled fists. But when he spoke, his voice was as gentle as I'd ever heard it. "Come, *Sevyá'mtha.* The sooner we find this ally, the closer I will be to killing Sol."

I withdrew my inhaler from the pocket in my cloak, took a deep, shuddering breath of aerosolized steroids, and exhaled shakily. "You're right," I agreed, gulping down another deep breath. With my windpipe properly open, the oxygen I inhaled actually managed to reach my deprived brain, blunting the worst of my anxiety. "Now that we're here, where do you think we should start look—" My words cut off in a gasp.

Just past Zayn's shoulder, sitting at the top of a nearby tree, was a large crimson-headed eagle, its piercing blue eyes locked directly onto mine.

Frowning, Zayn followed my gaze. When he saw the eagle, he immediately stiffened into a protective stance, positioning his body in front of me.

"Raaawk!" Biscuit screeched angrily, his feathers flat against his body.

Mavros fluttered to the ground, where – with what appeared to take a tremendous effort – she transformed into a sleek black fox, her teeth bared and hackles raised.

Unperturbed, the eagle hopped onto a lower branch, where it cocked its head in my direction.

"What—" I swallowed, then tried again. "What do you want with me?"

It gazed at me for a long, tense moment, its eyes probing me so deeply, I felt like they were boring into my soul. Then, apparently satisfied with what it saw, it flew off the branch, its powerful wings catching in the breeze, and soared into the sky.

Zayn's fists clenched and unclenched as he regarded the eagle's shrinking form. "What – or rather *who* – the hell is that? And why has it been tracking you all this time?"

"I don't know." My next words tumbled out of my mouth before I'd even registered the subsequent thought. "But I think she wants me to follow her."

"What?" He whirled around to face me. "Follow her where?"

I nodded in the direction the eagle had flown. "That way, if I had to guess."

"East…to the marshes?" A hard line appeared between his brows as he considered my words. "But there's nothing there except—"

"Harpies," I finished, both dread and resolve pitting in my stomach.

Zayn raked his hands through his hair, tilting his face toward the shrouded sky as he cupped the back of his neck. "The one region on this continent that's even more dangerous than the Blighted Forest…" He turned around to look at me, worry creasing his face. "Are you absolutely sure you want to do this? We have no idea what that…creature…wants with you. And I can't imagine the ally we're looking for is in the marshes."

"No," I agreed. "Probably not. But…" I chewed my lip anxiously, then sighed. "Something in my gut is telling me to follow her."

Zayn rubbed the bridge of his nose with one hand while the other reached into his vest pocket, retrieving what appeared to be a smooth river stone. "Lam, are you there?" he spoke into it.

The stone glowed, and a moment later, Lam's voice vibrated through it. *"Are you alright, Your Highness? Diedre recently came down with a terrible stomachache and has been fervently insisting that something is wrong. I was just about to call you—"*

"Talia and I are both okay," Zayn interjected. "What are the scouts saying, Lam? Has there been any movement at the enemy camp?"

"No, sire, they appear to be waiting for something, though we cannot say what."

"IS THAT TALIA?" My mother's voice blasted through the stone. Zayn tried to smother her booming roar between his sandwiched hands, but it didn't do much. *"WHAT IN GOD'S NAME IS GOING ON OUT THERE? MY HEARTBURN HASN'T BEEN THIS BAD SINCE I WAS PREGNANT!"*

"Mom, *shhhh!*" I hissed, searching for stray werewolves over my shoulder. "Everything's fine! I'll call you back as soon as—"

"You'd better!" she shouted, only slightly less volubly. *"If I don't hear from you in the next hour, I'm sending out a tommyknocker SWAT team to bring you right back here!"*

"I. Will. Call. You. As. Soon. As. I. Can." I repeated through gritted teeth.

"In the meantime," Zayn added, "keep us apprised of any and all new developments, Lamswyth."

"Of course, sire."

Zayn prudently switched off the rocky-talkie before my mother's shrill voice could come blaring through again, then turned to me. "Just to be clear, is this the same 'gut feeling' that spurred you to go swimming with sirens and befriend giant sand serpents?"

I nodded solemnly. "The very same."

"Fantastic," he muttered as he gestured me forward with an expression that can only be described as bone-weary resignation. "In that case, by all means – lead the way."

"Can't we just Tesseract to the marshes?" I asked, my eyes darting to the seemingly-defective rune on my hand.

"Tess Runes are so powerful, they require a six-hour recharge period."

My panic spiked at the thought of being trapped in the Blighted Forest for five and a half more hours. "But Lam said there's no other way out of here!"

"Lam is a biased old goat who doesn't know his ass from his hoof." Zayn rolled his eyes. "These woods aren't literally 'cursed' – not anymore, at least. The enchantments that Saedis's soldiers placed to keep the Unseelies trapped inside were destroyed long ago. Apart from the one-way Waypoint, the only obstacles to getting in or out are fear and old superstitions. And while it is true that some of the most dangerous Unseelies linger on the outskirts of the Blighted Forest, after seeing you utterly waste that pack of werewolves, I'm not terribly worried."

"Why is that?"

The corner of his mouth quirked into a wan smile. "Because you, *Sevyá'mtha*, are by far the most dangerous thing lurking in these woods."

By the grace of God – and possibly my distant banshee relatives, since a cold, frosty breeze seemed to be at our backs regardless of which direction we walked – we made it to the edge of the Blighted Forest with nary a disaster or murderous fae in sight. It took about four hours of walking before the gnarled trees had begun to thin and patches of teal afternoon sky could be seen through the veil of darkness that shrouded the entire forest. After that, the ground became squishier with every step we took, until our boots were covered in thick, gloopy mud.

When we saw the sickly green glow of the Waypoint we were supposed to arrive at together, Zayn breathed a sigh of relief. "We're almost out of the forest. All we have to do is cross the river, which is just up ahead."

"Hang on one sec," I panted, wiping the perspiration from my brow as I leaned against a dead, fallen bough. "My feet feel like they weigh fifty pounds each."

"Let's take a break," Zayn agreed. Before sitting down beside me, however, he retrieved a glass canister of salt from his enchanted messenger bag, flipped open the top, and made a large white circle around us and our temporary bench.

"So it's true, then, that fae hate salt?" I asked as he sat beside me, careful not to brush against my leg. It was just the two of us by that point, as Biscuit and Mavros had both settled in for naps: he in his ink form, she in her pocket-sized mouse form.

"Not all fae." He removed his pack, rubbing the back of his neck. "Saltwater mermaids, for example, have no problem with it. But pure halite crystals possess anti-magic properties that can temporarily strip certain fae of their powers. Unseelies, in particular, can have unpleasant reactions to it."

"But not you?"

"You'll notice I don't handle the salt crystals directly." He winked. "But in all seriousness, not really. I'm lucky that my elven heritage takes precedence in that area."

"What was it like?" I asked, gnawing on a hangnail. "Being a half-incubus in a family of elves, I mean. I know your stepdad was a dick, but what about your siblings? Were they…kind to you?"

Zayn was quiet for a long moment, his eyes roving across the thinning trees and clumps of moss that dotted the otherwise barren, muddy landscape.

"I'm sorry," I said softly. "You don't have to answer that if you don't want to."

"It's fine," he smiled, his shoulders rising and falling in a deep breath. "Painful or not, I'm happy to finally be able to share my past with you."

Warmth flared in my chest, making it all the more difficult not to take his hand in mine.

He cleared his throat. "My siblings and I didn't interact much, which I'm sure is no surprise to you. My sisters were much older than me, and as different from one another as night and day. Maránthe, the oldest, was very kind and soft-spoken, like my mother. She would sometimes bring me gifts, like books and maps, but wouldn't linger. She was nearing adulthood when I was born, which meant there was a growing line of suitors constantly vying for her time and attention. Yenna was much wilder and self-centered. Because it didn't benefit her in any way to have a relationship with me, she treated me as most others did – with quiet disdain. But that was only when she remembered I existed, since I lived and worked among the palace staff."

A lump appeared in my throat, which I forced back down. At that moment, the last thing I wanted was my emotions taking over – Zayn, was the one who needed comforting, not me…not to mention the fact that heightened emotions might allow Sol to slither his way back in.

I shuddered. "A-And your brother, Mikhæl? What was he like?"

"Mikhæl." Zayn sighed the name. "Mikhæl was…complex. He was very much like Saedis, in that he had strong convictions and always believed he was right. He was also arrogant and entitled, even though he resented being Saedis's first successor."

"Why wasn't Maránthe the successor? Wasn't she the oldest?"

Zayn glanced at me from the corner of his eye. "It all comes back to blood, and his was stronger than hers."

"But not as strong as yours?" I hedged.

"No." Zayn's expression was grim. "Saedis liked to boast that all three of his offspring were silver-blooded, since each could harness three of the four types of magic. But Maránthe and Yenna's skills were Limited, and the only Universal ability Mikhæl had was Extracting. I was the only one of my mother's offspring with true silver blood, since I am a Universal Benefactor who can also Extract and Endow in equal capacities."

All the more reason for his father and siblings to resent him, I thought wistfully. "So why was Mikhæl unhappy about the fact that he was first in line to the throne? As entitled as you say he was, you'd think it'd be the other way around."

Zayn's gaze was far away. "Because it took hard work, particularly on the scholarly side of things. He wasn't interested in reading much, which is how my mother's grimoire came to me, not him." When his expression tightened, I knew he was thinking about her spell book currently being in Sol's possession.

But not her blood, I thought with grim satisfaction. Because, as it turned out, the powerful bloodstone that Sol had long worn on his finger, the one Mavros had asked me to destroy when she helped me free Zayn from Sol's vault, had been forged from Jaína's blood. Why Sol had chosen hers, when he could have used any other Benefactor's blood, was a mystery – unless his choice had been purely sentimental. After all, for all we knew – or rather, were beginning to strongly suspect – *he* had been the incubus who had crept into her bed all those years ago, impregnating her with a "demonspawn," and subsequently plunging the realm into the darkest days of the Blood Wars.

"Anyway," Zayn continued, "my relationship with Mikhæl was…erratic, to say the least. He was older than me by some years, but immature. So, in that respect, we were near-equals. And even though Saedis had forbidden him from interacting with me, there happened to be a war raging, so he was distracted more often than not. On those days, my brother and I would sneak off and play in the forest together, sometimes for hours. Miki was simultaneously the funniest, most playful person I knew, while also being the quickest to lash out and the slowest to forgive – much like his father."

I reached down and plucked a twig from the ground and started peeling away the bark layer by layer with my thumbnail. Anything to keep my hands busy, when all they wanted to do was reach forward and pull Zayn into a hug.

His smile was grim as he stared out into the distance. "There were days when Miki acted like we were best friends.

Brothers, even. He'd confide all of his secrets and regrets to me, claiming that I was the only one who understood him. But the next day – usually after some argument with his father, or another disparaging comment from one of his tutors – he'd lash out at me, in ways I couldn't understand. One minute we'd be playing, and the next, he'd shove me in a ditch or drop a venomous snake down my shirt." My jaw dropped in indignation, but Zayn just shrugged. "Whenever he became angry with me, I saw it as some sort of failing on my part, so I'd try to earn his love again – offering gifts, favors, writing school papers for him. I even earned myself several nasty lashings in my attempts to draw my stepfather's foul moods away from Miki."

"Oh, Zayn," I said softly. "That's awful."

"He was the closest thing I had to a sibling," Zayn said simply. "I'd have done anything for him – anything to make him love me again. But the more I tried, and the older we got, the more he seemed to resent me. And then one day…he just stopped talking to me altogether. He died several years later."

Tears were pooling in my eyes, which I quickly scrubbed away. "Were you there when he…I mean, when they…" I trailed off, unable to say it.

He gave me a sidelong glance. "When they were killed?"

I nodded.

"Yes."

I waited for him to say more, but his mouth just pressed in a tight line. Eventually, I went back to my twig, which I had whittled down to the width of a toothpick, and rolled it between my fingers. When Zayn finally spoke again, his voice was so quiet and fragile, I had to strain to make out the words.

"They were all gathered in the throne room, where an altar had been erected with the unsigned Peace Accord. Seelie factions from all over the realm had gathered there for the first time in decades, their surviving leaders standing beside Saedis with quills in hand. I watched from the balcony with the rest of the servants. My brother and sisters stood behind their father, while my mother watched from her throne. She looked so pale and fragile that day…even more than usual." Staring straight ahead, Zayn leaned against the fallen bough, as still as a statue – save for the small circles he was making with his thumb and forefinger. "They came from underground, through a secret escape tunnel that only a top-ranking palace official would have known about, outnumbering us by threefold. There was no warning. Before the screaming had even started, bodies just started…dropping."

Zayn's voice was hollow and flat as he recounted these events, though his hands shook with all the emotions he'd long been repressing.

"There was so much blood," he continued, "you couldn't see the stone underneath. A pack of vampires attacked my sisters, ravaging their bodies beyond recognition. Calus – who had been freed from his cell in the dungeons – slit Mikhæl's throat, while Sol himself plunged an iron dagger into my stepfather's back. And…my mother…" He closed his eyes before the tears that had been gathering there could fall. "My mother was dragged away by three of Sol's sons, kicking and screaming for her children. I'd made it down the stairs by then, stumbling over bodies to try to save her, but…"

"They ambushed you," I whispered, unable to look at him for fear of bursting into tears.

He nodded. "I don't know exactly what they did to her. All Sol ever told me was that she suffered…greatly."

As he leaned forward on his thighs, head bowed, my mouth fluttered open, desperately trying to find the words – *any* word – to comfort him. But what he had endured was beyond anything I could even begin to imagine. Losing my father to his long, ugly battle with cancer was the hardest, most devastating thing I'd ever had to go through. It literally shattered me – at least until Zayn came into my life and quietly helped me glue the pieces back together.

"Zayn, I…"

He glanced up at me, his eyes glassy with the unspeakable memories he'd just relived on my behalf.

I took a deep breath, working to keep my voice steady. "I know that I can never take away the pain in your heart. And I would never diminish that pain by claiming to understand it…" A rogue tear trickled down my cheek, which I quickly wiped away. "But what I *can* do is love you – unconditionally, and with every fiber of my being – for the rest of my life." My cheeks were burning from the daunting intimacy of my own words as I forced my tear-filled eyes to meet his. "And who knows? Maybe, with time, some of the pain you carry might be displaced by love…or, at the very least, hurt just a little bit less."

Courage spent, I quickly dropped my eyes to my lap.

To my chagrin, Zayn said nothing in response, but I could feel his silent stare boring into me, deepening the flush in my cheeks. I took that opportunity to put my full attention into picking apart my already-ravaged toothpick, mentally kicking myself. Throughout my many failed relationships, I'd staunchly avoided any and all forms of emotional intimacy, and for damn good reason: love hurts. My father's death had only reaffirmed that. Why I thought that exact moment had been a good time to—

"Talia," Zayn cleared his throat, "I…" Hesitating, his voice dropped to a whisper. "Thank you."

My head snapped up. "What?"

"Thank you," he repeated. His voice was strained, as though he were working as hard as I was to keep his own emotions in check. "For everything you've done for me. For loving me. For making me believe that I could even be worthy of your love."

"Oh, Zayn," I whispered. "Of *course* you're—"

"Yes, yes, we get it!" an aggrieved voice called from behind us. "The two of you are frantically and hopelessly besotted with one another!"

Zayn and I whirled around, a silver dagger materializing in his hand, and a gold one appearing in mine.

Less than ten feet away, a barefoot old woman with startlingly-blue eyes, wild red hair, and exposed, dangling breasts stood with her hands on her hips. Except her hips weren't human hips – they were covered in brown feathers, along the entire lower half of her body. And her bare "feet" weren't feet at all, but mud-covered talons.

As though enjoying our shock, a smirk tugged at her lips. "What's the matter? Have you swallowed your tongues?"

Zayn was the first to regain his wits. "Who are you?" he demanded. "What do you—"

"Silence, beguiler!" She cocked her head sharply as her owl-round eyes darted from him to me. "Save your sweet nothings for later, for I have words to exchange with my granddaughter that are long overdue."

With that, she transformed back into an eagle and launched into the eastern skies.

XI.
A Rare Bird

I froze, unable to move, unable to speak, unable to breathe.

I wonder what her other *grandmother would think about these developments,* Saoirse's voice echoed in my ears before dissolving into a shrill ring that smothered all other thoughts. In the back of my mind, I vaguely registered Zayn trying to talk to me, but I couldn't make out his words over the muffled ringing. When my legs took one step forward, and then another, it was reflex, not thought.

Before I knew it, I was sprinting at full speed, my boots sinking into the spongy ground and kicking up clumps of mud and moss as they propelled me forward. My heartbeat thumped heavily against my chest, in my rushing ears, and in my shoulder, which was throbbing in tandem.

I pushed the pain from my mind, burying it.

Biscuit appeared in a dazzling flash, launching from my arm to survey the path ahead, while Zayn appeared at my left, wordlessly keeping pace with me. He didn't try to warn me, or stop me, or implore me to think before acting. He was just right there beside me.

A river appeared after several minutes of running, and I stumbled to a hard stop. Less than fifteen feet across, its waters were still, murky, and red-tinged from the blood-colored moss that grew along its muddy bank. I stopped a few feet from the edge of the water, my hands clutching my thighs as I worked to catch my breath.

Biscuit remained in the sky, flying in wide, glittering circles above us as he kept watch.

"Are you okay?" Zayn asked softly, his hand hovering above my shoulder.

"No." I shook my head, panting. "How do we cross?"

He looked around, his shoulders tensing as he searched for signs of danger. "This river marks the western edge of the marshes. We can certainly cross it, but before we do, I need you to understand what will be waiting for us on the other side."

Still breathing heavily, I straightened to look him in the eye. "I'm listening."

Relief softened the crease between his brows. "The fae that lurk in these marshes are among the most dangerous creatures on the continent: kelpies, glaistigs, ballybogs – and, of course, harpies."

I tried to swallow the growing lump in my throat, but it didn't budge.

"Ballybogs are shy and won't generally attack unless you step directly on them. Glaistigs, you know, of course. They're extremely rare and only target lone males…usually." He rubbed his forehead, almost certainly remembering the unprompted she-goat attack from the other week. "Kelpies, I don't have to explain, except to remind you that they shoot poisonous barbs similar to manticores." He licked his lips. "But harpies—"

"—won't kill me," I interjected, my words sounding far more confident than my actual feelings on the matter. "Not if my gr—" I winced, unable to bring myself to say the word. "Er, not if that red-headed harpy has any say in it."

Zayn looked like he might argue, then decided against it. "Your Fulmen Rune"—he pointed at my fancy lightning-conjuring tattoo—"should be enough to scare off all but the most nefarious water fae. But, please, do me a favor, and don't try to make friends with anything we meet in there. Apart from selkies, who are usually polite, almost everything in these swamps will happily try to eat or maim you."

I nodded, impatience making me bounce on the balls of my feet.

"Lastly," he finished, giving me a pointed look, "it is absolutely crucial that you do not let any part of your body touch these waters."

"Uhh…" I regarded the opposite side of the riverbank, no less than five looming yards away.

"You see those tendrils down at the bottom of the river?" He pointed.

I took a careful step forward, leaning my face over the surface of the water to get a closer look. A forest of what appeared to be bright red kelp swayed back and forth from the murky depths. "You mean the seaweed?"

"Yes – except that 'seaweed' is sentient. If you dip even one toe in this river, those tendrils will immediately snatch you by the ankle and drag you beneath the surface, where they'll bind your every limb in venomous fronds, instantaneously paralyzing you. Death, on the other hand, comes much more slowly." He pointed to a kelp-swathed skeleton I hadn't noticed before, which swayed alongside the ghostly fronds at the very bottom of the river.

I gulped. "So…how do we cross without turning into, uh…that guy?"

Zayn's eyes darted up the bank as he rubbed his jaw thoughtfully. "There's a bridge about a mile south, where the river forks, but a family of trolls lives underneath it. Since time is of the essence, I think a Smokescreen will suffice. Luckily, you still have the one you stole from Salen." He pointed at a small, faded yellow rune on my left arm – the last of the tattoos I had accidentally Extracted from Sol's daughter.

I tiredly raked my hands across my face. Had that truly only been a week and a half ago?

Zayn crouched to the ground, balancing on the balls of his feet. "I don't have one, so I'll need to make mine from scratch."

I knelt beside him as he started to draw the same rune in the mud with his finger.

"A Smokescreen Rune is sort of like a low-powered Tess Rune, except it's typically used for defense, and you can only teleport up to…" He paused, most likely converting fae measurements into American units. "Uh, just under twenty feet, give or take a few inches. It'll be tight but manageable, I think."

"You *think*?" I demanded, regarding the other side of the river – which suddenly looked much, much farther away than it had a few seconds ago.

"I'm talking about mine," he chuckled. "Your tattoo, however, could probably take you twice as far."

I rolled my eyes skyward. "Oh, well, gee, I feel much better if *you're* the one to drown."

Once he'd finished sketching the rune, I held my hands over it, Endowing it with magic. A warm glow swept up my arms, disappearing beneath my rolled-up sleeves. A moment later, the muddy, crisscrossing lines ignited, illuminating the entire symbol with pulsing power.

"I will never not be in awe of the power of your blood." Zayn exhaled sharply, pressing his hands against the glowing lines. "Okay, before triggering your Smokescreen, I want you to focus all your concentration on the other side of the bank, exactly where you want to land. I recommend right there, where the river narrows."

My eyes followed his index finger directly across the red-tinged water. Unlike the flat, barren ground where we were standing, the other side of the bank was covered in gnarled willow trees with long, sweeping branches that nearly brushed the ground. But unlike their Earthly counterparts, these willow trees had brick-red bark and yellow fronds, reminding me of something from a Dr. Seuss book.

"Are you ready?" Zayn asked.

I nodded wordlessly.

"*Nathværé*," he said, enunciating every syllable as he gestured for me to do the same.

"Nath-vow-ray," I repeated.

Thick, navy-blue smoke swirled first around his legs, and then mine. But instead of the world turning to smoke, as it appeared to do when summoning a Tesseract, the Smokescreen Rune dissolved my actual body into smoke from the feet up – a wholly disconcerting sensation, I might add. At least *this* magical smoke didn't trigger a sneezing fit, since, you know, sneezing requires the presence of lungs.

When my eyeballs resolidified from smoke to matter a few disorienting seconds later, I shook my head roughly, trying to clear the literal fog from my brain. For some reason, the sky, river, and distant trees had all been replaced by curtains of bright yellow fronds, while my legs lay splayed out in front of me, resting on a large pile of hay, feathers, and sticks. Feeling something hard and lumpy digging into my back, I twisted my arm uncomfortably behind me – gasping when my hand brushed across something as smooth and round as a melon.

"What the…?" I held the mystery object – a spotted blue egg – in front of my face, waiting for my brain to catch up with my vision.

"Talia!" Zayn called from somewhere far below.

I craned my neck, trying to spot him through the drapes of leaves that were surrounding me on all sides.

"Talia!" he yelled again, fear creeping into his voice.

"I'm up here!" I shouted down to him. "I think I Smokescreened into some sort of…nest?"

Zayn let out a sharp curse. "Tal, get down from there! Now!"

I scooted over to the edge of the nest, which was spacious enough to hold at least three more of me, trying to spot him. "I'm working on it!" I yelled, still clutching the egg against my chest. "I just need to—"

A massive gray eagle – at least twice the size of an American bald eagle – landed on the opposite edge of the nest. Orange eyes rounding in surprise, it dropped the zebra-striped, ferret-sized lizard that had been dangling from its beak – which prudently took that opportunity to scurry away for dear life – and let out an enraged squawk.

"H-Hold on!" I stammered frantically, my eyes darting from the egg I was clutching to the raptor's rapidly-narrowing glare. "I-I know this looks bad, but—"

The eagle lunged at me at the same time Zayn shouted, "Talia! What's happening up there?"

"*Aah!*" I flinched, dropping the egg to shield my face from its sharp, entrail-shredding talons. But instead of clawing out my eyeballs, the eagle snatched me by the shoulder straps of my corset, yanking me upward. "Ow!" I yelped as branches and fronds violently whipped at my face. "Hey—wait!"

We burst through the topmost branches of the tree, letting out simultaneous shrieks – mine of terror, hers of annoyance.

"Stop – put me down!" I cried, my stomach plummeting to my toes as the eagle lifted me up, up, and away. Eyes tearing from the wind, my head rolled back, and I found myself face-to-underfloof with a bird so enormous, its wings must have been fifteen feet wide.

A silver arrow whistled by, but the eagle casually veered out of its path.

"Talia!" Zayn's frantic voice sounded unnervingly far away. "TALIA!"

As the eagle and I rose higher and higher, soaring farther and farther away from Zayn, I fought against my own corset straps, furiously trying to wrestle out of them – until I happened to glance down and realize that the tree I'd been snatched from was at least a hundred feet below my dangling boots. At that point, I abruptly ceased struggling and grabbed onto the eagle's scaly yellow ankles for dear life.

"Hey!" I yelled again, spitting wild locks of windblown hair from my mouth. "Would you please put me back down? I didn't mean—"

"Silence, human," the eagle replied, making my jaw tumble open. "You will face the flock's judgment soon enough."

"You can talk?!"

"My brain is nearly thrice the size of yours, and *you* are surprised? It is a wonder your kind is able to produce any sort of intelligible speech at all."

"I… That's…"

"Hiiii!" another voice cheerfully interjected.

I jerked my head to the right, where – to my immense relief – Biscuit had appeared at my side, soaring lazily beneath the shade of the eagle's massive wing. "Hi, Tal-ya bird!"

"Biscuit!" I cried. "Help me!"

The eagle tilted her head in our direction, but otherwise didn't seem bothered by his presence.

"Tal-ya bird *FLYYYY!*" Biscuit screeched happily, utterly oblivious to my plight as he tumbled into a glittering barrel roll.

"That is not helpful!" I shouted at him, kicking my feet.

The eagle tightened her massive talons around my shirt straps before cranking her wings and diving from the sky beak-first.

"No wait!" I shrieked, plummeting toward the ground like a screaming missile. "I changed my—*AAHHHHH*!"

My stomach lurched into my throat, cutting off my bloodcurdling scream. The ground rose up faster and faster, a green and brown blur that would soon be splattered with gold blood. I gritted my teeth, bracing for impact. Just as the eye-watering stench of dead fish and decaying plant slop hit my nose, the eagle released me.

"Come back!" My hands blindly groped at the sky, catching nothing but air.

A split second later, my feet smashed into the ground – not with the leg-shattering impact I'd been expecting, but with a sticky, slurping squelch. My eyes shot open in shock, only to find the lower half of my body completely submerged in muck.

"What the—" I stammered, my head swiveling around frantically. Smack-dab in the middle of a sprawling marsh, a wide ring of towering red and yellow willow trees surrounded me on all sides, like an amphitheater. Almost every branch was occupied by one of hundreds of huge eagles that ranged in color from bone-white to ebony-black. And yet, as varied as their plumages were, every single one of them was gazing down at me with matching scowls.

Thankfully, when Biscuit gracefully landed on the exposed root of a nearby Cypress tree a few seconds later, the eagles didn't spare *him* but a cavalier glance. Likewise, he seemed utterly unperturbed by them, casually preening his feathers as though I weren't half-submerged in a pool of muck, surrounded by massive winged scavengers that were eyeing me as though I were a dying antelope.

With immense effort, I wrenched one arm from the squelching sludge, and then the other, trying to pull myself out. I may as well have been trying to hoist myself out of quicksand.

"Biscuit!" I hissed. "Go find Zayn!"

He took his sweet time preening a particularly bright green feather, then leisurely moving on to a watermelon-red one, before casually ruffling and unruffling his wing feathers… And then the little shit started on his tail feathers.

A low, inhuman snarl rumbled from deep in my chest.

Mavros took that opportunity to stick her tiny mouse head out of my shirt pocket. Upon seeing a marsh full of eagles, she let out a panicked squeak and dove back inside.

"Biscuit!" I let out a savage growl. "If you don't go get Zayn *right this minute*, I swear to God you will never get another almond as long as I live! Which, at this rate, won't be much longer unless you *get out of here and find him!*"

Rolling his eyes – as though *I* were somehow being the birdbrained nincompoop – he took off into the marshes, cheerfully whistling the tune to *I Love Lucy.* I gaped at his shrinking tail feathers in disbelief, wondering where exactly Zayn and I had gone wrong as parents.

Moments after Biscuit's departure, one of the eagles swooped down from the trees, landing on the bough of a rotted log a few feet in front of me. Its enormous brown body and crimson head marked it as the same bird that had been following me around the continent for the last few days.

"You!" I sputtered. "What the hell do you want from me?"

Emitting a noise that sounded like a muffled cackle, the eagle shook out its crimson head and tail feathers before its upper torso morphed into that of a middle-aged, blue-eyed woman with feathery red hair that stuck out in all directions.

I gaped up at her in wordless shock. Her feet were still talons and her arms were still wings, but her head, neck, and torso were featherless, and even now, she didn't seem even the slightest bit perturbed that her bare bosom was exposed for all the world to behold.

"Hello, Granddaughter," she grinned down at me, her breasts swinging from her chest like two unsettlingly-hypnotic pendulums.

"I..." I started, my jaw dangling wordlessly. "You..."

"Oh, come now," the harpy cocked her head in a notably avian manner, "I'd expected you to be far more talkative than this, given the unrivaled garrulousness of your banshee mother!" The other birds let out whistling titters in what I could only assume were peals of laughter.

"I... You know my mom?"

The harpy rolled her shockingly-blue eyes. "Yes, yes, I know your ghastly mother, Diedre, and your dearly departed father, Hæren, whom the humans refer to as *Howard*," she practically spat out the name. "*Fenaaa,* such an ugly language."

My mouth remained fluttering open in stunned silence, as though the part of my brain responsible for speech had shorted out completely.

"Anyway," she continued breezily, "I am Xianis, matriarch of the harpies and guardian of these marshes. And you, my little plum, are on trial for trespassing upon restricted nesting territory."

"But I—"

"Cease your squawking!" she interrupted, waving the tip of her wing in my face like a condemning finger. "Now where was I…? Oh, yes, trespassing! To save precious time, the flock and I have already concluded your trial, and we have determined that you are unquestionably guilty of infringing upon our cossetted sanctuary—"

The other harpies erupted in a series of jeering whistles.

"—the penalty for which," Xianis continued, her owl-round eyes glinting with wickedness and glee, "shall be your swift and immediate death."

XII.
JEWISH AMERICAN PRINCESS

"My *what?!*" I screeched.

"Ah, so the little lark *does* have spirit," Xianis grinned. "Do not fret, child. I was merely tugging your talon. Now, come along. There is much to discuss." As she extended her wing to me, the feathers melted away, morphing into a bare human arm with outstretched fingers.

My jaw dropped even further, until a nearby buzzing fly – and the long, sticky tongue that shot out of the mud to swallow it – made it snap shut with a painful clack.

"Come now," the harpy's penetrating blue eyes glinted as wickedly as her grin, "I won't bite."

After hesitating for a long moment – during which a series of bubbles less than an arm's-length away reminded me of Zayn's dire warning about all the *other* dangerous fae that lurked in these swamps – I tentatively extended my hand toward hers. She clasped my wrist with surprising force, hoisting me out of the mud and onto the log. The second my feet hit solid ground,

I immediately yanked my hand away. Shoulder zinging, I teetered atop the unsteady log, trying to catch my balance. As I did, I noticed all the narrow wooden walkways that had been built above the marsh – boardwalks, of a sort. One of them jutted all the way out to the log, close enough to hop onto – which I clumsily did.

With two breezy flaps of her wings, Xianis landed beside me. "Come, my plum. Walk with me."

Not knowing what else to do, I fell into step beside her, my muddy boots squelching beside her long, clacking talons. She folded her wings behind her back and let out a sharp whistle. Two of the eagles flew down from their branches – one brown and one white – morphing into their half-human forms as they landed behind us. Like Xianis, these harpies were wide-eyed females with short, feathery hair that stuck out in all directions. Though one can never really tell with fae, the tall, brunette harpy didn't appear much older than me, while the one with shock-white hair and hunched shoulders looked at least a century old.

"What, uh…" I started, stealing another quick glance at them over my shoulder. "What were you wanting to discuss, exactly?"

"Oh, just the usual small talk between a caring grandmother and her beloved, long-lost granddaughter," Xianis replied as she reached down to pluck a small lizard from the ground and swallow it whole.

"Oh?" I squeaked, stifling a gag. "Usual things, such as…?"

"You know," she clucked. "School, work, boys – though it appears you've already scooped up quite the catch." She waggled her eyebrows impishly. "The uncrowned king of the Fae Realm, eh? It would seem my granddaughter's tastes are nearly as refined as my own."

"Oh y-yeah?" I gulped, doing my best to match her casual tone. "D-Does that mean you, uh, have a boyfriend? Or um, *did* you? At one point or another…?"

One of the harpies snorted, reminding me of their looming presence. I hugged my body tightly, glancing around for Zayn. But there was still no sign of him or our rainbow familiar; just muck, a bunch of strangely-colored willow and Cypress trees that jutted out of the muck, and this boardwalk, which forked and multiplied in at least a dozen directions just above the muck.

"Ha!" Xianis squawked, slapping her feathery thigh as we walked. "I have entertained more suitors than there are knots in a *goolygroot* tree!"

"Oh." My shoulders slumped.

She stole a glance at me out of the corner of her eye. "We do not prevaricate among these parts, child. Ask the question you intend to ask. Our time together is short."

"Fine, you want blunt?" I abruptly stopped walking, causing the white-haired harpy to stumble into my back with an annoyed squawk. "Then tell me, who was my grandfather? And why – no, *how* the two of you could just abandon my dad like that?" I demanded, my voice cracking. "You left him all alone, on a strange planet – and for what? To let him die? How *could* you?"

My grandmother cocked her head, taking me in from tousled head to muddy toe. "Yes," she nodded slowly, musing to herself, "there indeed is that spirit I was hoping for…as well as your banshee mother's uncouth tongue!" She swatted the back of my head with her wing. "You will show your grandmother the respect she is owed!"

"Respect?!" I blustered, rubbing the growing ache in my shoulder. "Look, lady, you might be my grandmother, but I've never seen you before in my life! So, if you want even an iota of respect, answer the question – who was my grandfather, and why did the two of you dump my dad like yesterday's trash? And another thing!" My hands balled into fists. "Where's the human child you kidnapped in his place?"

Without bothering to see if I was still following her, Xianis resumed her brisk, clacking walk, wings primly folded behind her back. "Your grandfather," she tossed over her shoulder, "most likely would have killed your father had he learned of his existence…and the human child I 'kidnapped,' as you so crudely accuse me of, is dead."

I gaped at her, momentarily stunned into silence before anger once more took hold of my tongue. "*Dead?* You kidnapped a perfectly healthy baby, and then…" My mouth had run dry, making it impossible to swallow the dread and fury building in my throat. "Y-You just killed him? A helpless *infant?*"

Xianis abruptly froze in her tracks, swiveling her head a full 180 degrees to scowl at me. The rest of her body followed, eventually catching up with her craned neck. "Has that banshee truly spoken so poorly of me – to make you believe such dung and venom?"

"She's said *nothing* about you, except that you abandoned my father to die as a baby, then came running back to Earth thirty years later once you realized his 'progeny' had gold blood! Oh, no, sorry – she also said that you then tried to kidnap me every chance you got, to the point that she and Dad were forced to travel to the Fae Realm to spend all their savings on some necklace that would hide me from you and every other dangerous fae just like you." I crossed my arms coldly. "I guess that's your M.O., huh? Kidnapping and murdering helpless babies?"

Click…click…click… Her razor-sharp talons clacked against the wood as she slowly approached me, the shaggy feathers on the back of her neck raised like hackles. "First of all," she squawked, thrusting the tip of her wing in my face, "the child I swapped out for your father had a fatal heart defect that neither science nor magic could cure." Sadness flickered across her features, making my eyes widen in surprise. "That boy's parents would have mourned their child's death for the rest of their lives. Instead, they were bequeathed a beautiful, healthy infant—"

"*Healthy?!* My father was sick for most of his life!" I snarled. "Maybe if you'd actually kept him – like any mother with even *half* a heart would have done – he would have thrived here and not…not…" My eyes filled with hot tears, which I furiously blinked away. "Did you know he spent the last year of his life in agony, stuck with needles and poisons that leeched the life from him. Did you know that? Did you even *care?*"

She took a step backward.

I took a step forward. "Had he been allowed to stay here, among his own kind, soaking up your planet's magical blue sunlight, he might still be alive! Do you ever think about that?"

Xianis's wings and tail feathers drooped. "Perhaps that is true. Perhaps I should have done more to keep him here, to find another way to shield him from his father's wrath… But remember this, granddaughter: you would not exist had he not met your mother on Earth. You would not have been blessed with those coveted gilded veins, making you the most powerful fae in two realms, perfectly poised to retake your grandfather's forsaken throne!"

This time, I was the one who took a step backward. "My grandfather's *what?*"

Her eyes darted to the large bubble that erupted from the mud just a few feet away. "It is not safe for you to linger in these parts, child – your blood rouses too much attention. Come. Your courageous paramour has breached the boundary of our nesting grounds. My kin have made a generous exception for you, Granddaughter, but they will not grant him the same favor."

With that, she spun on her talon, sharply gesturing for the accompanying harpies to follow.

I sank to the boardwalk, my legs too numb to carry me.

Upon seeing this, Xianis stopped, sighed, then muttered something to her feathered sentries. Nodding, they assumed their eagle forms and abruptly took to the west…leaving just the two of us.

She crouched beside me. "Talia," she said, referring to me by name for the first time, "what I am about to tell you cannot be heeded by any other ear in this realm – not even Zæynek. Especially not Zæynek," she amended. "My attendants will see to it that he makes it to you safely, but you must promise me that you will not utter a word of what I am about to tell you to anyone – least of all him."

I said nothing. A few feet away, another gloopy brown bubble surfaced, then popped with a squelch.

Eyeing that, my grandmother's voice dropped to a whisper. "A ballybog lurks nearby. We must keep our voices down, lest we wake it," she said, settling in beside me. "Now, I will talk, and you will listen."

I nodded mutely.

"By now, you must know of the queen's infidelity?" When I didn't answer, she took my silence as an affirmative. "Zæynek's mother was not"—her wide eyes darted around the swamp as she lowered her voice even further—"the only royal to have an affair."

"No," I whispered hoarsely. "Please…don't…"

"You will listen to what I have to say, child," she clucked gently. "Now, you may see the deep furrows in my brow, the lines etched around my eyes"—she patted her chest—"and my bosom, which is but a sagging vestige of its former glory—"

Groaning, I pressed the palms of my hands to my eyes.

"—but I was once as young and radiant as you. And when I took my featherless form, there was not a fae in this realm who did not lust for me. Our affinity for charming and attracting is how we harpies have kept our numbers so high, despite those many decades of bloodshed," she added with a note of pride. "Now, you may believe me or not, child, but I once lay with the highest fae in the realm, at the very height of his rage over his wife's affair – not once, but thrice."

"Xianis, please," I croaked. "I don't want to hear this. I can't—"

"Ah, but you must – and so you will, child. I lay with him – willingly and for my own personal gain. But when the product of our amorous tryst was born exactly one maternal cycle later, lo and behold – the child was not a she, but a *he*."

I crossed my arms over my knees, burying my face in them as I rocked back and forth.

"Newly-hatched harpy males quickly perish, and so I cradled my child against my breast, knowing he would not last through the night… But against all odds, he persisted. Not through one sunrise, but seven. The youngling was not hardy, not with his mixed-elven blood – a sanguineous combination that had not occurred in centuries. But he had the determination of a king."

She was quiet for a long moment – long enough for me to sneak a blurry glance at her. Her lined, weathered face had grown contorted as she gazed out into the distance, reminiscing; when she caught me looking at her, she quickly recomposed her expression into a tight smile.

"I did not want to abandon him, you must understand. But if his father were to discover his existence, he would have been killed – not only to keep the line of succession secure and untarnished, but to hide his infidelity. For, you see, Saedis did not love me as he loved Jaína," she said softly – almost wistfully.

"I would not have been able to protect my son as she had doggedly protected her own. And so, child, I did what no mother should ever have to do – I took my son far, far away, where he could never be found…and I left him there."

Sniffing, she turned her head away from me. "Shortly after your grandfather's premature death, I came back for my son. But by then he was a fully-formed child, happy and thriving. His human parents had done more for his sickly disposition than I ever could have. And so, I continued to watch in secret, sharing in his joy and accomplishments from afar. I even attended your parents' betrothal ceremony, from the hidden branches of a nearby tree… Of course, when you were conceived sometime later, I had my share of selfish whims – this realm had been plunged into terror, after all. Who better than my granddaughter – a gilded one with a royal heritage, no less – to put the pieces back together? But your parents heartlessly denied me my own son's progeny, going so far – as you said – to secure an ancient fae talisman that hid you from my sight…until the fateful day you arrived in your ancestral plane, and your true magic was unlocked."

By then, I was trembling so badly, her expression morphed into a look of pity. When she reached out to pull me into a hug, I recoiled from her touch, shakily rising to my feet. "If what you're saying is true…that is, if you're not completely full of shit," I amended, doing everything I had in my power to keep my voice steady, "then that means my father…"

"Is the *true*, long-lost prince of this realm," she answered solemnly, drawing an envelope from a small frond-woven pouch hanging at her side. The letter was weathered but unopened, and bore a blood-red wax seal.

I took the envelope in two shaking hands, choking back a sob. The seal bore the same mystery symbol as the one Zayn had recently discovered on my locket.

"This is a copy of the letter I gave to your father, shortly after you were born, explaining everything – though I am all but certain he did not share its contents with your mother."

"W-What does this symbol mean?" I forced myself to ask, afraid of the answer.

"It is the harpy pictogram for 'crown,' marking you for what you are," she inclined her head solemnly. "As the gilded, *rightful* successor to Saedis's throne, you will have the full support of my entire flock, granting your assured triumph in the coming war...provided you do one thing first."

The knot in my stomach felt as heavy as a lead brick. "And what is that?"

Her eyes flashed darkly. "You must kill Jaína's bastard prince and take the summer crown as your own."

XIII.
WITH FRIENDS LIKE THESE

I stared at her for a long, protracted moment. "Are you out of your mind?"

"Yes," she replied wryly. "But that does not mean I am wrong."

A chill snaked down my spine as I remembered the banshees' prophecy – the one that came right after Saoirse looked me dead in the eye and said that every single one of us would perish in the coming war:

But if an ally you should find,
Far north, beyond the plains,
The shepherd of this land shall rise;
And dawn shall come again.

I took a step backward. *The shepherd of this land... Were they talking about* me?

"No," I whispered, pushing the haunting whisper from my mind.

"No?" Xianis's unkempt eyebrows were steadily creeping up her forehead. "You would turn down our offer of alliance, one that is as munificent as it is unprecedented?" Her eyes narrowed, reminding me of a falcon's. "You would risk your life, simultaneously condemning this realm to further death and tragedy. And for what? To protect your current bedmate?"

"My current *bedmate?*" A rueful laugh slipped from my mouth as anger slowly began to displace shock. "I'm not even going to dignify that comment with a response. But as far as everything else – the answer is no. No, I will not kill the man I love, for reasons that go without saying. And no, I will not steal the crown from the Summer Court's rightful heir. Not only do I have *zero* interest in being queen, but that would be an incredibly douchey thing to do."

The harpy's eyes narrowed even further, until the whites of her eyes were completely shrouded in shadow. "Think very carefully about your choice, child – it may be the greatest mistake you ever make."

"If these are your terms, *Grandmother,*" I squared my shoulders, ignoring the dread pitting in my stomach, "I have no interest in striking a deal with you."

Xianis scowled at me for a long, terrible minute, but I managed to keep my chin high, staring her down.

Finally, she shrugged. "Then you will not have our support. We do not need another elven king to subjugate us."

I scoffed. "You're so quick to judge Zæynek based on the actions of his stepfather"—I gritted my teeth together, doggedly refusing to consider my own familial link with the late Summer King—"and yet, you don't know the first thing about him. Well, let me clue you in: he was raised as a servant, treated with contempt every day of his life, and then enslaved by the demon who killed his mother. He is the *last* person in this realm who would ever—"

My sentence ended in a yelp as Zayn's feet slammed onto the boardwalk, triggering a veritable clusterfuck that unfolded in slow motion before my very eyes: A swamp creature from my literal nightmares erupted from the previously-bubbling muck, letting out a vicious roar that turned my insides to applesauce; the two harpies that had been carrying Zayn landed on either side of my grandmother, poising for attack; and a rainbow-colored comet streaked from the sky, wings flared and claws outstretched as he let out an eagle-like shriek.

"TAALLLL-YAAAAAA!"

At the sound of Biscuit's battle cry, Mavros somehow managed to wriggle her way out of my pocket, then leap like a flying squirrel from my chest, black fire engulfing her tiny mouse body as she soared through the air – but when the flames dissolved, she was still a tiny mouse. The poor thing let out a petrified squeak as she tumbled to the ground, rolling to a woozy stop at the sharp talons of three keen-eyed raptors.

At that moment, time jolted back to life like a defibrillator greeting a flatlining heart, and everything happened all at once: silver arrows flew, rainbow fireballs launched, bog monsters screamed, incubus boyfriends snarled, eagle sentries lunged, and terrified mice shrieked for dear life. In the split-second window I had to make my decision, I dove forward, scooping Mavros into my cupped hands just as the brown eagle's beak snapped at empty air. Then, after shoving her back into my pocket, I planted my feet on the dock, fists clenched at my sides.

"EVERYBODY STOP!" I screamed, bordering on banshee-mode.

Pandemonium skittered to a halt.

The bog monster, from which one of Zayn's quivering arrows protruded, popped back into the mud with a *squelch.*

Zayn's next arrow, which was currently nocked and aimed directly at my grandmother, froze in place. Biscuit paused his colorful missile assault mid-air, doing a corrective barrel roll to land on my shoulder, momentarily teetering for balance. The two eagle sentries positioned themselves in front of Xianis, wings flared for battle. And my grandmother…

My grandmother burst into laughter, clutching her feathered stomach from the wheezing force of her inexplicable mirth.

Zayn, whose eyes were smoldering with feral intensity, hazarded me a glance out of the corner of his eye. "Are you okay? Did they touch you?"

I quickly shook my head no.

"Are you sure? Because if they did—"

"I'm okay," I assured him, gently pushing his arrow away from my grandmother's exposed bosom. "And no one touched me."

"And if we had?" Xianis taunted Zayn. "Would the deranged incubus have killed us all in a fit of jealous rage?"

"Touch her and find out," he snarled.

"Hey," I swiftly interjected, directing my words at him. "They didn't touch me. I'm okay."

His coal-black eyes darted to my shoulder – which was admittedly hurting, but not because of anything my grandmother had done.

"Well?" she chided, tapping her talon. "Aren't you going to introduce us?"

"Uh…yeah." I sighed, gesturing between the two of them half-heartedly. "Zayn, I'd like you to meet my grandmother, Xianis."

At that, he promptly lowered his bow. Green flickered back into his eyes, though the crease between his brows didn't soften. "This…is your father's…?"

"Mom – yeah."

"Indeed!" Xianis's eyes rounded with the intensity of her own smoldering gaze. But even then, she motioned for her sentries to step aside as she circled Zayn like a hawk, taking him in from head to toe with the occasional poke or prod. "And I suppose *this* is the incubus who has stolen my granddaughter's heart…not to mention her better judgment!"

His expression tightened with anger.

"Zayn, don't – it's not worth it." I shook my head wearily. "And anyway, I was just telling my *grandmother* goodbye."

"Already?" Her head swiveled around like an owl's. "You won't take more time to consider my proposal?"

"No," I replied, pointedly avoiding Zayn's probing look. "You've made your position clear, as have I. I was raised with a Jewish mother – I know better than to argue with someone who can't be reasoned with."

I turned to go, but Zayn remained, his bow lowered and his eyebrows raised. "Are you sure, Tal? Did you get all the answers you needed?" He cast a suspicious glare in my grandmother's direction.

"I heard all I needed to hear," I replied coldly, directing my tone at Xianis.

As I turned to go, Mavros let out a soft squeak as she once more tried – and failed – to transform. This time, tiny black sparks ignited in my pocket, fizzling out before they could even turn to flames. Seeing this, Biscuit let out a mournful cluck.

"Your blood incarnate," Xianis blurted out, her voice tinged with desperation. "It is unwell?"

Zayn shot her a dark look. "He's fine."

"Not that one." She waved a dismissive wing at Biscuit. "The one in my granddaughter's pocket."

"Yes, she's sick," I replied. "But she's not an incarnate – she's a familiar who's been separated from her master. He was…mistreating her."

Xianis peered into my pocket to get a closer look. "Pah! It is not separation sickness that ails this one, but Manipulation sickness."

I regarded the tiny, curled-up mouse in my pocket, whose breaths were coming quick and shallow, even for a rodent. "What do you mean?"

"This familiar is not bonded to her master by soul, but by blood and hostile control. The ailment that has befallen her comes from the constant fatigue of doing what she believes is right, while simultaneously resisting the urge of her master's compulsion from afar."

Biscuit and I exchanged wide-eyed glances. "So, what do we do?"

"You have gold blood." She shrugged, feigning nonchalance. "And you are clearly already bonded. You need only Manipulate her into being well again."

Zayn rolled his eyes.

"Do not balk!" she snapped at him, then turned back to me. "If you use your blood to free her from her master's hold, he will not be able to ensnare her again, for gold blood trumps all! I should know, since harpies, of course, are master Manipulators… And speaking of Manipulation," she added, not bothering to mask the disdain in her tone, "it would seem this little mouse is not the only creature in this marsh who has been ensnared and Manipulated by a demon." She cast Zayn a salty look.

"Not that it's any of your business," he snapped, "but I love Talia, deeply. There is nothing in this realm or the next that I wouldn't do for her."

My stomach did a little flip at the fervor of his words.

"But I suppose the concept of love would be foreign to you, wouldn't it?" He glared at her. "You are, after all, a mother who left her own child to perish."

Pointedly ignoring Zayn's last remark, Xianis approached me, wing outstretched as though she might take me by the hand. "Come, my plum, let us go somewhere more private to finish up our chat from earlier, hmm?"

Zayn swooped between us. "Don't touch her."

"Stand aside, boy," she squawked, shoving past him.

"I said," Zayn growled, his irises turning to molten fury as he again positioned himself between us, "*don't touch her*."

The two eagle sentries, who had been casually surveying our interaction until that moment, snapped to attention.

"Shame on you for debasing yourself in such a way!" Xianis shot an accusatory feather in my direction. "Allowing yourself – a powerful and proud descendant of harpies – to be claimed by a demon such as this! To be defiled and reduced to mere property—"

Zayn took a menacing step toward her, a snarl far more beast than human slipping between his bared teeth.

"It's okay," I told him softly, repositioning myself between them.

He stepped aside, making room for me, but his white-knuckled grip on his bow didn't loosen.

I turned to Xianis. "I am not his property, and I am not his claim." I took a deep breath, then pulled down the collar of my shirt to expose the Requisition Rune on my shoulder.

My grandmother's eyes doubled in size as she took in the festering affliction eating away at the shiny, red-streaked skin that surrounded it – the mark that was slowly killing me.

"Every time someone touches me – Zayn included – the poison leeches farther into my veins."

It appeared to take great effort for Xianis to pull her horrified gaze away from the affliction. And though I expected an onslaught of questions, indignation, and even anger, for the first time since meeting her, she'd fallen speechless.

“Sol did this to me,” I explained, though she deserved no explanation. “We don’t have a cure, short of killing him before his claim kills me. It’s part of the reason I came to you for help.” Digging my nails into my palms to curb my mounting emotions – fear, anger, and crippling disappointment, to name a few – I squared my shoulders. “You say we’re family, Xianis, but based on the demands you’ve made of me today, I can see this relationship boils down to nothing more than shared blood. Now, since it would seem we have no allies in this swamp, Zayn and I would like to use what dwindling time we have to find someone who *is* willing to help. Will you let us leave in peace, or is this going to get ugly?”

I rolled up my sleeves, casually displaying the wide assortment of deadly runes embedded underneath.

After a long moment of silence, she abruptly shook her head as if to clear it from a daze. “No,” she whispered, then cleared her throat. “No. You may, of course, leave in peace. That path”—she pointed to a walkway forking sharply to our right—“will take you back to the western edge of the marshes. I…I will personally ensure you are not harried by any among my flock.”

“Thank you,” I answered curtly, before motioning for Zayn and Biscuit to lead the way.

Zayn gave me a reassuring nod as he passed, though his steely gaze quickly darted back to my grandmother and her stony sentinels. Hopping onto his broad shoulder, Biscuit’s head swiveled 180 degrees to shoot her an equally-wrathful glare.

Without another word, I turned to follow them.

“There is one,” Xianis blurted out.

Pausing halfway between her and Zayn, I sighed. “One what?”

“One who may serve as your ally. One who is perhaps powerful enough to defeat the scourge that comes for you.”

Turning around, I surveyed her expression, searching for any trace of deception. "A…harpy?"

"No. It is someone *he* knows." Her eyes darted to Zayn, who had frozen in place. "One from his distant past who dwells deep inside the northernmost peaks, ensconced in stone and self-pity."

But if an ally you should find, far north, beyond the plains…

"What are you talking about?" Zayn demanded. "Which person from my past?"

Ignoring him, my grandmother's eyes once more settled on me, her expression tight and wary. "May the Almighty Eagle protect you, child. I pray that your ally in the Winter Court can be of more service to you than I."

Zayn's face blanched of all color. "The Winter Court?"

The shepherd of this land shall rise, and dawn shall come again.

Xianis didn't spare him a glance. Her eyes lingered on mine for a long, loaded moment. And then, without another word, she transformed back into an eagle and soared away with her sentries.

Zayn and I regarded their shrinking forms in stunned silence, then turned to one another with matching expressions of shock and confusion.

"Do…we go?" I asked, chewing my lip.

"I don't know." Zayn ran his hands through his hair, cupping the back of his neck. "Xianis could be full of shit. Harpies are notorious liars, after all."

I shook my head. "I don't think she was lying."

A muscle in his jaw clenched as he glanced at his watch. "We're running out of time, and I worry this might be a wild goose chase. But…I trust your judgment." Zayn sighed. "By now, our Tess Runes should be fully charged again. If you think it's the right move to go—"

“It’s the only other lead we have.” I chewed on my lip. “So yes, I say we go.”

“Okay.” Zayn nodded, resolution hardening his features. “But fair warning, I’ve never been to the Winter Palace – no one from the Summer Court has. The closest we’ll be able to safely Tesseract is to the base of the mountain. And it’s going to be a cold and miserable hike up to the peak.”

“Aw, shoot,” I forced a weak smile. “And here I thought this trip was going to be warm and pleasant.”

The corner of his mouth quirked up. “Okay. Then it’s settled. Are you ready?”

I hesitated as my hand fluttered to my back pocket, where the letter my grandmother had given me felt like it was burning a hole through the fabric.

No secrets, I reminded myself.

Taking a deep breath, I turned to Zayn. “Before we go…we need to talk.”

Part 4

One Is Silver and the Other…

XIV.
Blood for Blood

Endless white stretched before us.

White ground. White trees. White sky. White mountains.

I hugged my traveling cloak tighter around my arms as another gust of frigid wind lashed at my face. The cloak's hem was flapping in the breeze like a banner – a welcoming splash of crimson that broke through the otherwise bleached, silent landscape. I rubbed Biscuit's colorful tattoo on my goosepricked arm, half-wishing he'd appear – but he'd already made it abundantly clear that he'd rather do just about anything else than spend even one minute in this arctic tundra. Mavros – who hadn't poked her nose out of my pocket since we'd Tessed here two hours ago – apparently wanted nothing to do with it either.

Squinting against the blowing snow, I stole a glance over my shoulder at Zayn, who was trudging behind me with his bare arms crossed and his head down. Far more torturous than the biting cold and endless blizzard was the silence that stretched between us.

I'd told him everything before we left the marshes, offering to let him read Xianis's letter over my shoulder – an exact copy of the message she'd sent my father twenty-five years ago, according to her. Bearing the harpy symbol of the crown, the tear-stained parchment explained everything in painstaking detail: my father's "salacious" conception, and why it had been necessary to hide him on Earth; the true identity of his biological father (a.k.a. my grandfather); and Xianis's hopes that my parents would return me, her gold-blooded, royal progeny, to the Fae Realm so that I, Saedis's "rightful" heir, could take back his vacant throne.

The letter went on, outlining Xianis's vision of a world where harpies were finally acknowledged as the superior race and treated with such favor from the highest seat in the land. She saw my eventual ascendance as a way to rekindle her "stolen" relationship with her abandoned son and begin anew. I could only imagine my father angrily crumpling up the original letter before hurrying my mother to the Fae Realm, bolstered by this newfound reason to hide me.

After that, I told Zayn about Xianis's outrageous proposal, i.e., the harpies' absolute support in the coming war, so long as I killed him and absconded with the Summer Crown. And even though – in *my* mind, at least – it went without saying, I did emphasize the fact that I had zero interest in taking her up on her offer. I'm not sure what I was expecting Zayn's response to be, though I assumed it would fall somewhere between rage, shock, and uncontrollable laughter – after all, the notion was as preposterous as it was shocking. But he was none of those things.

He was just…quiet.

And he remained quiet, his brooding silence continuing long after we arrived at the base of a towering mountain so high, its snow-capped peak was completely obscured by clouds. After showing me a basic rune for keeping (mostly) warm and gesturing in the general direction we'd be trekking, the only two sentences Zayn had uttered to me were "Are you warm enough?" and "Do you need to stop and rest?" Otherwise, the two of us spent the afternoon trudging through the knee-deep snow in complete silence.

An hour passed.

And then two.

After several hours of strenuous hiking, where the only sound I could hear was my own labored wheezing, I couldn't take the silence anymore. Pivoting in the snow, I marched right up to him, jabbing a frost-nipped finger in his face.

"*What* is your *deal?*"

He started as though I'd roused him from deep thought. "Huh?"

"I mean, I get it, okay? This whole thing is absolutely insane, not to mention borderline-creepy, since we're technically step…somethings…" I scratched the top of my head, where a layer of snow had accumulated, trying to work out the genealogical implications of the bombshell my grandmother had dropped.

"Your father would have been my stepbrother," Zayn said softly, not quite meeting my eyes.

"I—Oh. Well…I'm not gonna lie, that is *kind* of weird." I removed my hood and shook my head, sending a cascade of snow to the ground. "But whatever! Seeing as we're not in any way blood-related and I wasn't even born until well *after* Saedis died, I don't think we'll need to spend too much money on family therapy sessions—"

"Talia—"

"—and just to be *crystal* clear," I barreled on without pausing for breath, "there's no way you could *possibly* be thinking that I'd ever take Xianis up on her offer, right? Because, apart from the fact that I'm madly in love with you and would sooner kill myself than hurt you—"

Zayn's face contorted into a grimace.

"—the *last* thing I want is that stupid crown. Well, not stupid – not for you, at least. And, I mean, I'm all about uniting this realm and helping you overthrow Sol, but…" My throat tightened.

"But?" he prompted, wariness etched into his face. We were standing in the middle of a small clearing, with snow-covered, cobalt-blue pines surrounding us on all sides. Snowflakes were lightly falling from low-hanging, green-tinged storm clouds, accumulating in large clumps that immediately melted when they met Zayn's red nose and flushed cheeks.

"But the thought of being a queen makes me feel sick to my stomach," I confessed, blinking away the tears and snowflakes that had accumulated on my lashes. "And that terrifies me, because I know your entire plan predicates on *you* becoming king… But I was sort of hoping I could avoid a royal title altogether, you know? I could be, like, Official Girlfriend to the King. Or, um, Associate Runemaster to the King – with benefits, of course. Er, of the romantic variety, that is – not political favors or anything like that…" I ran my hands through my damp hair, groaning in frustration. "What I'm trying to say is, *you'd* make an absolutely brilliant king, Zayn – truly. But me, a *queen?*" I dropped my voice to a barely-coherent mumble, my cheeks burning with embarrassment. "Why are we even kidding ourselves?"

Silence once more fell between us. When I looked up a few moments later, Zayn was watching me with an inscrutable expression.

"What?" I asked, crinkling my nose.

He exhaled softly, shaking his head. "And here I've been thinking how much better *you* would be at leading this realm. That maybe you should have taken Xianis up on her offer—"

My jaw literally dropped.

"Not the part where you kill me," he clarified, waving a casual hand as though we were discussing the unseasonably cold weather, "but ruling in my place."

He abruptly resumed walking, and I had to practically jog to keep up with him – and by "jog," I mean winch my knees up like a can-can dancer to make it through the deepening snow.

"How can you even *think* that?" I panted.

"How can you *not?*" he countered. "I mean, you've got the blood, the claim, the charm… But me? I'm just Sol's ex-henchman. And, short of Calus, I've spilled more blood in this realm than any other Runemaster. Indirectly, yes, and against my will… But blood is blood."

I opened my mouth, readying a razor-sharp retort, but Zayn's hand flew to the breast pocket of his vest, where the illuminated rocky-talkie had started vibrating.

"Lam?" he spoke into it, urgency creeping into his voice. "What's happening?"

"IT'S ME!" Mom's voice blared through the rock. *"AND I CAN ONLY ASSUME MY DAUGHTER MUST BE DEAD, SINCE SHE HASN'T BOTHERED TO CALL ME IN HOURS!"*

"Oy, Mom! I'm right here!" I groaned, taking the stone from Zayn, who was holding it an arm's length from his ear. "Can you please stop yelling? You're gonna set off an avalanche."

At that, Zayn and I both darted anxious glances up the towering mountainside, which, indeed, was covered in a heavy layer of hard-packed snow that looked unnervingly susceptible to a banshee-induced landslide.

"An avalanche?!" she demanded, lowering her voice a decibel or two. *"Where* are *you two? What's going on? And have you found this 'ally' of ours or what?"*

"We're in the mountains, a few days' north of you. Everything's fine. And, um…no," I answered, purposefully omitting certain Dad-related bombshells. From what I'd gathered, my mom absolutely despised her harpy mother-in-law – and, after speaking to Xianis, the feeling appeared to be extremely mutual. There was no reason to rile Mom up further, at least for the moment. "But we did learn about, um, someone in the Winter Court who might be able to help us."

"The Winter Court?!" Lam's voice blustered through the stone. *"Is this true, boy?"*

"Yes," was all Zayn said, likely for the same drama-eschewing reasons as me.

"But no one has heard a peep from the Winter Court in decades! They all perished when Sol—"

"We know," Zayn interrupted. "It's probably a lost cause, but since it's our only lead, Talia and I have decided to go check it out. What's the latest development on Sol's army?"

After a moment's hesitation – during which he was probably trying to decide whether to keep arguing or not – Lam let out a relenting huff. *"We suspect Sol may be waiting out the lunar cycle, knowing the elves will be weaker during the moons' waning phase."*

"When's the full moon?" I asked, glancing at the lunar tattoo on my arm.

"In two nights' time. Of course, if he manages to enlist the dragons to his cause, the lunar phase won't make a difference to him. The scouts also reported what appears to be a legion of blood incarnates, which are steadily growing in number."

Zayn snarled a curse beneath his breath.

"That, we believe, is the real reason for the delay. Sol knows we're gathering an army of our own and is therefore taking the opportunity to bolster his numbers. And since he is in possession of Talia's blood, as well as your grimoire, he and his Runemaster are—"

"Sol doesn't have any more Runemasters," I cut in. "Korinne is back with us, and I watched him break Calus's neck with my own eyes."

"I am sure you did. However, after our sentries reported that they'd spotted a mage in the enemy camp resembling Calus in stature and appearance, Kor'inthe speculates that he may have had a Resurrection Rune somewhere on his body—"

Zayn stopped dead in his tracks.

"—which is, of course, one of the most rancorous forms of Death Magic in existence. His face has been altered, most likely a symptom of the necromantic process... Then again, he does have a predilection for stealing his victim's faces."

I stifled a gag.

"Regardless of the cause or manner, Calus appears to be alive and...functioning." Lam cleared his throat. *"For now, that is all we know, sire. In the meantime, we are doing everything we can to fortify the castle and ourselves, but without additional aid..."* He trailed off, leaving the sobering implication to hang in the frigid air.

I glanced at Zayn to see if he had anything else to add, taking a half step backward upon seeing the black veins pulsing beneath his eyes.

"Uh, th-thanks, Lam," I interjected. "Please let us know if there are any other developments in the meantime. We'll... We'll be back as soon as we can," I finished, a pang of guilt twisting through my stomach. I'd wasted precious hours chasing Xianis into that marsh – only to wind up empty-handed – while

Sol and his zombie Runemaster were busy creating an army of soulless monsters.

"You two be safe out there!" Mom hollered. *"And make sure you're eating enough – oh, and using protection too!"*

I gaped at the glowing rock in my palm. "Using *what?*"

"Protection! I want another grandbaby, but only after *the war is over! In the meantime, say hi to my precious grandbirdy and his new girlfriend for me!"*

At the sound of my mother's voice, Biscuit's tattoo glowed with warmth. I could almost hear his muffled little voice asking, "Mar-zee-pan?"

"Diedre, my pet, if you'll recall, the children aren't even able to shake hands at the moment, let alone procreate. We'll have to find a way to remove the partial claim from Talia's arm before she'll be able to welcome a litter of lambs into the world."

"Do you mean to tell me," Mom seethed, her voice growing angrier and shriller by the nanosecond, *"THAT HORRIBLE SCHMUCK MIGHT ACTUALLY ROB ME OF GRANDCH—"*

After hastily switching off the rocky-talkie before she could trigger either a proverbial or literal avalanche, I lobbed it at Zayn as though it were a hot potato.

His hand shot out to his side and caught it easily. "*Emæ ni ældurúş, Aşek'ye lénim edím!*" he growled, gripping the rock like a hand grenade.

I cringed as my Translation Rune glowed to life. "I know…I want to kill Sol and Calus too. And we will," I added, forcing a tight smile to my face. "The ally we're looking for is at the top of this mountain – I can feel it."

Zayn didn't reply, though the glower on his face darkened and his string of curses got even more colorful as we resumed our interminable, upward slog.

Biscuit appeared on my arm with a matching glower, though his was less "schmuck"-related and more of the snow-hating variety. Without so much as a "Hello," he stuck his head in my travel cloak and unzipped the pocket containing Mavros.

My heart stopped when I saw her curled up inside, eyes closed, barely moving.

"Mavvie?" Biscuit clucked, nudging her with his beak. "You okay-kay?"

She didn't stir.

"Mavvie!" he squawked.

She opened one eye, made a tiny little squeak, then closed it again.

Biscuit hopped onto my shoulder, where he furiously began tugging my ear. "*Rawk!* Tal-ya help Mavvie!"

"Ow!" My hand shot up to my earlobe, where Biscuit had accidentally drawn blood.

He recoiled as soon as he realized what he'd done, but didn't waste time apologizing. "Pease?" he asked, giving me the roundest, glassiest puppy dog eyes I'd ever seen. "Mavvie sick! Tal-ya help?"

"I…" I chewed on my lip, feeling utterly helpless. "I-I don't…"

"Hibiscus," Zayn said, running an exasperated hand through his snow-dusted hair, "there's nothing we can—"

"No!" Biscuit stamped his foot. "Eagle-lady say!" To help prove his point, he dredged up Xianis's words, replaying them in our heads like a taped recording: *It is not familiar sickness, but Manipulation sickness! If you use your blood to free her from her master's hold, he will not be able to ensnare her again, for gold blood trumps all!"*

"Hibiscus," Zayn growled again, "familiar sickness cannot be healed by blood – gold or otherwise!" His eyes darted up the mountain, where the Winter Palace was still far out of sight, and the snow was lashing at the uppermost peak in violent, blowing gusts. "I know you're worried about your friend, but we're running out of time – *all* of us, not just her!"

Biscuit turned away from him, imploring me. "Gold blood?"

Zayn shot me a stern "we need to go" look – which was more than reasonable, given the growing direness of our situation. Sighing, I peeked into my pocket, where Mavros was curled up in the fetal position, scarcely breathing.

My heart couldn't take the sight of it.

"Okay," I relented, eliciting a shrill tea-kettle-like whistle from Biscuit. "I'll…I'll try."

Carefully plucking Mavros from my pocket, I crouched in the rapidly-accumulating snow. Biscuit balanced on my shoulder, anxiously watching. "I know we're in a hurry, but will you help me?" I asked, casting Zayn an imploring look. "Please?"

Muttering more Elvish curses beneath his breath, Zayn knelt beside me – so close, I could feel the heat radiating from his bare arm. "Xianis might be a so-called 'Master Manipulator,' but this *is* familiar sickness. To cure it, you would have to break the bond between Mavros and Sol – which, as I've said, will kill her."

Biscuit made a panicked squawk.

"*Hypothetically,*" I stressed, shooting Biscuit my best attempt at a reassuring smile, "how would we go about breaking that bond?"

"You would smash the bloodstone around her neck. But again – and I cannot emphasize this enough – that will kill her."

Still cradling Mavros's trembling body in one hand, I knuckled the growing ache between my eyes with the other. "Then…I'll need some sort of transference rune – to swap out Sol's blood with mine. Does something like that even exist?"

Zayn started to shake his head, then stopped, his brows furrowing. "Actually…"

"Actually?" I prompted.

"I mean…I can't even begin to imagine how it would work inside a bloodstone, but there *is* a rune that can modify certain types of liquids – a Conversion Rune, which can turn water to wine and the like. If we had a vial of your blood for the transfer, perhaps…" His frown deepened. "But even then, I don't think it—"

"It can't do any harm to try," I whispered, meeting his eyes. "She's already dying."

Zayn's expression softened as he took in mine, though the dubious crease remained between his brows. Without another word of protest, he reached into his bag and retrieved a small, empty vial, as well as a pocket-sized switchblade. "Only if you're completely sure," he said softly, placing them both in my palm.

"I'm sure," I swallowed, carefully passing him both Mavros and Biscuit. "I'll prep the vial. You draw the rune on the back of her pendant in the meantime, okay?"

He did as I asked, while I pressed the tip of the blade into the center of my palm, drawing a small pool of blood. Grimacing, I clenched my hand into a fist, letting the blood drip into the vial, then turned to Biscuit. His eyes were glued to Mavros, as though he were afraid to pull them away.

"Biscuit?" I asked softly. "Do you want…?"

He looked between the vial and the bloody knife I held, then nodded fervently. He hopped onto my wrist, extending one little trembling claw, then turned away, eyes squeezed shut. Sucking down a deep, steeling breath, I took the very tip of the blade and lightly pressed it against the pad of one of his claws, withdrawing a single drop of blood that I squeezed into the vial. Biscuit swayed as though he might pass out, but Zayn placed a hand on his back to steady him.

"I've got you, little buddy." He smiled tightly, then turned to me. "Okay. I drew a Conversion Rune on her pendant. Now we just have to add the corresponding rune to the vial of blood."

I handed it to him, forcing a shaky smile to my face as he gently transferred Mavros back into my good hand. "Thank you."

"Always," he murmured, catching my gaze over the top of the vial as he worked.

The snow continued to fall silently, dusting our bodies and belongings as Biscuit and I sat, waiting with bated breath while Zayn drew the final rune. Mavros's chest was barely moving by this point, and her body was so cool, the snow had begun to accumulate atop her fur rather than melt. Biscuit stood stock-still, watching her waning breaths with wide, unblinking eyes that were becoming glassier by the moment.

Once Zayn had finished drawing the accompanying Conversion Rune, he handed me the vial of blood. "I added a few drops of my own blood to it. Every little bit, right?"

Gratitude welled in my chest as I took the vial from him. "Yes. Every little bit." I swallowed. "So…what do I do now?"

"Trust your heart," he answered, flashing me a wan smile. "It always seems to know what to do."

Great. I grimaced.

Taking a deep breath, I did my best to ignore the chorus of doubts in my mind, and simply allowed my fingers to move without thought. After smearing a drop of blood across the rune on the back of her pendant, I gently laid Mavros's body atop the snow, then placed the gleaming vial right beside her. Edging as close to Zayn as I could without touching him, I took Biscuit's claw in my right hand, motioning for Zayn to take the other. The result was the two of us crouching side by side, with Biscuit balancing atop both of our hands. Finally, I reached forward and clasped Mavros's paw between my thumb and forefinger, while Zayn gently pressed his fingertips against her stilling body.

"She doesn't have long," he whispered softly.

Biscuit's entire body began to quiver.

Nodding, I took one more deep, shaky breath, focusing my attention solely on the task at hand. The Conversion Runes on her necklace and the vial of blood flickered to life. Not knowing what else to do, I did as Xianis had told me, gently prodding Mavros's mind until I could just scarcely hear the final, fading whispers of her innermost thoughts.

Mavros, can you hear me? If you can, I need you to try to let go of your bond with Sol. I know it's hard. And I know it's scary... But I need you to trust me, okay?

Her tiny voice brushed against my ears, softer than a whisper. *Let...go?*

Yes, Mavros, I said, pushing my power into her name. *You have to find the strength in your heart to go on without him. And after this moment, you can't ever let yourself be compelled again. You are your own master now. Your soul belongs to you, and only you.* I swallowed tightly. *It's time to let go.*

I could feel Biscuit's claw tightening around my hand, and I knew he was doing the same to Zayn's.

"Tal," Zayn murmured gently, "it's now or never."

Stay with me, Mavros.

Shifting my attention to the runes, I focused first on the scarlet bloodstone, and then the gold vial, Endowing them with magic.

At first, nothing happened.

I ground my teeth together, pushing my magic deeper into the runes. Golden light began to spread through my fingers and hands, washing up my arms, past my elbows, and all the way to my shoulders. I could feel its warmth creeping into my neck and cheeks.

Beside me, Zayn let out a soft gasp. A tiny drop of red liquid had appeared in the vial, swirling like a delicate, crimson cloud against a golden sky. At the same time, a sparkle of gold appeared in Mavros's pendant, steadily infusing the bloodstone with metallic flecks. My breath caught in my throat, but I kept my concentration firmly on the runes, mentally guiding the conversion. Within moments, the vial's liquid had turned completely red, while Mavros's bloodstone swirled with liquid gold.

Her tiny chest rose in a long, deep breath…

And then it didn't move again.

Biscuit's claw was gripping my hand so tightly, I could feel his talons digging into my skin.

Mavros, I whispered, once more prodding her mind. *Wake up, little friend, and be free.*

She didn't stir.

A sob caught in my throat, but I choked it back for Biscuit's sake. *You're not alone anymore, Mavros. Biscuit, Zayn, and me – we'll be your new family. My mom and Aunt Ko-Ko too. You just have to push through and come back to us.*

I watched her unmoving body with bated breath, afraid to speak or breathe. Seconds passed, up to the better part of a minute.

Still, she didn't budge.

Zayn's shoulders slumped forward. "Damnit," he whispered, pressing the heel of his palm against his forehead.

Biscuit jumped from our hands and into the snow, nuzzling her body with his beak. "Mavvie?" he cooed softly. "Wake up, Mavvie!" When she didn't budge, he tried again. "Mavvie? Mavvie want almond?"

"Biscuit," I whispered, my eyes welling with hot tears. "I don't think—"

"No!" he squawked angrily, then whimpered, "Mavvie? Mavvie!" He nudged her harder. *"Mavvie!"*

I pressed my hands against my mouth, stifling a sob, while Zayn's head sank to his knees.

Biscuit let out a long, mournful cry, one that wrenched my heart in two. Sinking beside him in the snow, I pulled him into a tight hug.

"I'm so sorry, Biscuit," I whispered against his feathers. "I tried my best, but it…it just wasn't enough."

He nuzzled his face against my chest, whimpering.

Zayn made a strangled noise. "What the—"

My head snapped up just in time to see Mavros's motionless form erupt in black fire. Within seconds, her tiny body had been entirely consumed – and yet the flames continued to burn, seething like boiling ink against a backdrop of pure white snow.

Snatching Biscuit away from the strengthening blaze, I staggered to my feet alongside Zayn. The three of us backed away as the obsidian fire exploded into dazzling gold flames that were so hot and bright, we had to shield our faces from the intensity. The flames grew higher and higher, towering above our heads like a coruscating tractor beam that melted every last drop of snow within a twenty-foot radius. A bowel-shaking roar erupted from behind the curtain of golden fire, ricocheting through the snowy trees and sending a tremor through the earth itself. My hand reached out instinctively, clutching Zayn's cloak.

And then, all at once, the flames disappeared.

In their place, a colossal gold dragon loomed above us, with shimmering waves of heat radiating off its metallic body. Ribbons of fire and smoke curled from its glittering jowls, while its gilded scales gleamed like polished bullion.

As I gazed up at the magnificent creature, another deafening roar splintered through the air like a thousand shattering tree trunks, sending a jolt through my body that reverberated all the way down to the bone. Only this time, the roar hadn't come from the dragon.

It came from the avalanche the dragon had triggered.

Flayed from the entirety of the eastern peak, snow stampeded down the mountain like a thunderous herd of wild horses, devouring everything in its path.

Zayn and I turned to one another, our eyes rounding in horror.

But before we could do so much as scream, the avalanche was upon us, a crashing deluge of slush and fury that stole the very scream from my lungs.

XV.
Uninvited Guests

Snow detonated all around me with the force of a dozen grenades, dousing the entire world in white. But somehow, instead of being buried beneath it, I found myself being propelled upward and *through* the explosion. As a blast of cold wind lashed at my face, my eyes shot open and a scream formed – and then immediately caught – in my throat. I hadn't been entombed beneath masses of snow and broken boughs, as I should have been; instead, my body was soaring *above* the avalanche.

"Are we dead?" I whimpered, still clutching Biscuit against my chest.

As I considered the distinct possibility that this was an out-of-body experience, we burst through a heavy layer of clouds, where curtains of shimmering snow flurries sparkled against the blinding light of the cerulean blue sun.

"Oh fuck," I moaned. "We really *are* dead."

Rather than sticking around and waiting for the Jewish version of the Pearly Gates to appear – which I assumed would include a lunchtime spread of lox and bagels, at the very least – Biscuit wriggled free and away from my grasp, letting out a jubilant shriek as he launched even higher into the sky.

"Hey, wait—!" I started, choking on my own words when I noticed the massive gold dragon grinning down at me. A few feet away, safely encased in the dragon's opposite claws, was Zayn, who was gazing up at the creature in wide-eyed astonishment.

Whether seconds or minutes had passed since we'd been rescued from what should have been our snowy tombs, I wasn't sure. But before I knew it, Zayn and I were once more being gently lowered to solid ground. Lightheaded, I yanked my inhaler from the pocket of my siren-hide leggings and took a good, long huff. There were no trees at this elevation, just a small island of sunlit snow jutting up from an endless ocean of clouds. In the center of the snowy peak, which stood less than a hundred feet above us, a mighty black fortress rose up from the mountain, encased in a glimmering layer of ice.

The Winter Palace, I gasped, my bulging eyes darting between it and the stunning creature that had brought us here.

Loosing one final roar, the gilded dragon towering before us dissolved into golden flames, revealing an "ordinary" black raven that was sitting in the center of a perfect, dragon-sized circle of melted snow. She gazed up at me, her bright green eyes sparkling with life and vigor, and her gold-tipped feathers glinting in the sunlight.

"MAVVIE!" Biscuit screamed, dive-tackling her into the snow.

"BISSKISS!" she screeched, tumbling alongside him in a heap of powder and feathers.

"Mavros?" I whispered, emotion welling in my chest. "Is it really—*augh!*" I cried out as a cold stab of pain ripped through my shoulder. Pushing my cloak away, I clutched my arm, searching for a wound that didn't exist.

"Talia!" Zayn gasped, running to my side. "What is it? What's wrong?"

The overwhelming joy that had filled me at the sight of Mavros, alive and well, promptly evaporated. In its place, seething fury exploded inside my chest, cutting off my air supply and turning the edges of my vision blood-red. I fell to one knee in the snow, clutching my body in genuine fear that my ribcage might split apart. Zayn fell beside me, seizing me by the front of my cloak, but I couldn't hear the words he was shouting.

So…you've stolen my familiar from me.

My mind flailed and sputtered, but I couldn't find the words to speak.

First you take my Runemasters, and then my glamour, and now you rob me of my favorite familiar. A fresh stab of pain shot through the Requisition Rune. Rage poured from the throbbing ink and into my veins, seizing my limbs like a strung-up marionette.

Gasping, I pressed one numb hand against the frozen ground, trying to steady myself, and the other against my chest to smother the roaring flames that blazed there.

Paired with your flagrant disregard for my claim, and I'm beginning to think you have a death wish, Zaffre… Perhaps I should just put an end to your misery right now.

"No!" I tried to cry out, only to be gagged by a wave of nausea. Choking, I fell into a fit of coughs that were so violent, gold flecked the palm of my hand just before I pitched forward and vomited into the snow.

"Talia!" Zayn's animalistic snarl punctuated the storm raging in my head.

My eyes rolled up to meet his. He was there, so close…and yet he couldn't touch me. Couldn't do anything to shield or protect me.

Inches from the man I loved, I was utterly alone.

I will *take back what is mine, Zaffre – all of it. And then, I will take everything that was once yours – your familiar, your lover, your crown, your body… Soon, all will belong to me.*

Curled up in the fetal position, I clutched my ribs tighter, gasping for breath. I couldn't tell where Sol's fury ended and mine began.

"Get *out!*" I screamed, cupping my ears. As another fit of coughs gripped my body, the snow became spotted in gold.

"Talia!" Still clutching me by the cloak, Zayn brought his face close to mine. "Tal, I'm right here!"

Get away from my claim, Sol hissed, his hatred for Jaína's son filling me from the inside out…except, I realized, it wasn't just hate. Shame, guilt, jealousy – even grief – fueled the seething maelstrom of Sol's wrath, sucking me into the growing abyss where he lurked, waiting for me.

"Tal, you can fight this," Zayn whispered fiercely, the edges of his voice as sharp and serrated as a knife. "You have to push him out, close the link—"

I'll kill every last one of them, you know, Sol's voice once more pervaded my mind, drowning out Zayn's fervent pleas. *Every elf – female and child alike.* His anger twisted through my chest as though he'd plunged a serrated dagger through it. *I'll drain the life from your mother's eyes, until they're as dead and unseeing as your father's were… I can see him so clearly – his frail, withered body as he lay dying, the IVs draped around his hospital bed like garlands…* Surprise flickered through our link. *Wait—what's this?*

"No," I whispered against the snow, doing everything I could to force the contents of the harpy's letter from my mind. But it was no use. There was no corner of my mind Sol couldn't see.

Of course… Sol marveled, his mix of relief and glee dampening the pain of his rage. *That's the real reason Zæynek keeps you close, isn't it? Far more than a vessel of blood, you're his literal key to the kingdom, aren't you?*

"That's not true," I gasped, panting for breath. "He loves me!"

Oh, Talia, can't you see how he's used you? Aren't you ashamed of your feelings for him, knowing they'll forever be unrequited?

"Talia," Zayn whispered, his nose just millimeters from mine, his beautiful green eyes red-rimmed and glassy. "I *do* love you, with my entire being!"

Lies, Sol sneered. *Zæynek, like everyone else who pretends to care about you, is just using you for your blood and your lineage – even your mother merely sees you as a pig to be auctioned.* I could feel his power pressing against my skull, and as it did, his words began to make more and more sense. *They all want a piece of your soul, don't they, little one? But you belong to* me, *Talia. And together, we'll make them pay…won't we?*

Sol's ruby-red eyes flickered in front of my vision, replacing the lush emerald green of Zayn's. The anger that pulsed in my core was like nothing I'd ever felt before – hot and venomous and all-consuming. But somehow, like cooling balm to a burn, Sol's words made them better.

He's right, I realized, the edges of my lips curling into a smile. *When the crown is mine, and all the rest of them are dead, there'll be no one else to use me. There will just be me and Sol and our boundless kingdom—*

Gold and rainbow flames exploded inside my head, making both of us cry out in surprise. For the briefest moment, I found myself in the middle of a thick forest of glowing, cobalt-blue pine trees. Truck-sized insects and black-clad Unseelies were spreading like poison through a nearby grove, razing it to the ground. Every time a tree fell, its glowing pine needles flickered weakly, then faded to black. Sol's oldest son, Soren, stood several yards away, resting his hand on the muzzle of a massive black wolf whose powerful shoulders nearly came to his own. When he and the wolf turned to look at me, their eyes were glowing twin shades of crimson.

Except they weren't looking at me – they were looking at Sol.

Fury once more snatched me by the windpipe as he worked to wrest control from me, but the rainbow-and-gold flames blazed warm and bright, forming a barrier between our two minds. The blue forest burned away, and in its place, fire-laced images of almonds, chocolate, butterflies, sunflowers, fireflies, cheddar cheese, and warm summer rain danced in front of my vision. I squeezed my eyes shut, focusing on those images and nothing else, until my heart rate had slowed and the anger coursing through my veins had all but dissipated.

"Talia?" Zayn whispered, his voice swathing me like a warm fleece blanket.

I sat bolt upright with a wheezing gasp. Biscuit and Mavros landed at my feet, fire once more returning to feathers as they gazed up at me with round, worried eyes.

"Tal?" Zayn knelt beside me, his face contorted with fear and pain and fury. "Are you…"

"I'm okay," I choked out, wrapping my snow-covered cloak around my trembling body. If it weren't for the warming runes, I'd have long ago succumbed to hypothermia. "H-He's gone."

"For now." Crouched in the snow, shoulders hunched, Zayn raked his fingers through his hair and squeezed his eyes shut. Tears glittered in his dark lashes. He was clenching his hair so tightly, his knuckles were white and his fists were shaking. "This has gone too far," he rasped. "I have to get you away from here. From him. From this realm."

"It won't work," I whimpered. Biscuit and Mavvie hopped on each of my shoulders, nuzzling my tear-stained cheeks. "He's inside me. No matter where I go."

Zayn's eyes popped open, dark and dangerous as I'd ever seen them.

I let out an audible gulp.

He quickly looked away from me as though ashamed, and took a deep breath. With visible effort, he fought to keep his voice steady – even then, he bit out his words one by one, through gritted teeth. "No more side trips. No more stalling. I'm taking you back to Miami, far away from here, and hunting down Sol alone."

"Zayn," I whispered.

He couldn't bring himself to look at me.

"It's not your choice whether I stay or go," I said softly. "It's mine. And I'm *choosing* to stay because this fight is just as much mine as it is yours." I reached up to stroke the top of Mavros's head, doing the same for Biscuit when he made a low grunt. "Mavvie was able to free herself from Sol—with help, I know," I interjected, stealing the words from his mouth. "The point is, she survived. And she's free now…not to mention stronger and more beautiful than ever." I kissed the top of her ruffled, gold-dusted head, eliciting a grateful coo. "Thank you, by the way, for helping Biscuit snap me out of…well, whatever the hell that was." I shuddered.

"Welcome!" Mavros chirped.

"Luvyu!" Biscuit chimed in.

Forcing what I hoped was a reassuring smile to my face, I turned back to Zayn. The vein in his temple was still bulging, but I knew that *he* knew better than to argue with me.

"Tal," he finally said, the quiver in his voice catching me off guard, "if anything were to happen to you—"

"I know." I swallowed, trying and failing to clear the painful lump from my throat. "But worrying alone isn't going to fix this."

He nodded mutely, his eyes betraying the emotions he was so clearly trying to keep in check. It made my own eyes prick with tears as I struggled to my feet, dusting the snow from my damp clothes. Zayn did the same, hovering millimeters from my arm.

"Now"—I forced a tight smile after hastily scrubbing my eyes—"we've come all this way. So, I say we just march right up to the front door of the Winter Palace and—"

"Vemme är dul?" a voice called from behind us.

Zayn and I whirled around so fast, both birds nearly toppled off my shoulders.

A group of two dozen men and women were standing several yards away, each aiming a silver crossbow directly at us. Their pointed ears marked them as elves, but that was where any resemblance to the elves from the southern territory ended. Where Zayn's cousins were bronze-skinned and dark-haired, these elves were so pale, their skin glittered like freshly-fallen snow. Their hair – which both the males and females had gathered into matching braided buns – was platinum-blonde, almost silver. And unlike the gem-colored dresses and tunics of their southern brethren, the elves of the north were swathed in pale leather pants and white furs.

"I thought you said the elves in the south were the last surviving settlement," I muttered to Zayn out of the corner of my mouth.

He didn't reply; he just gaped.

One of the elves, who had woven a set of small antlers into his hair with leather twine, stepped forward. *"Vemme är dul?"* he asked again, triggering my Translation Rune. *Who are you?*

"Varre är besköre från sködra holvret," I answered, spurred by Zayn's blank expression – he didn't have a Translation Rune on his body. "We are visitors from the Summer Court…and we come in peace," I added quickly. "Um…who might *you* be?"

"We are part of the Royal Guard," he answered, lowering his crossbow only slightly. "And *you* are trespassing on the king's land."

"What did he say?" Zayn demanded.

I rubbed the bridge of my nose. "He says they're from the Royal Guard, and we're trespassing on the king's land."

"The *king*?" Zayn repeated, his face blanching of all color. "Who the…I mean, *how*—" He shook his head forcefully, regathering his wits. "Ask if we can meet their king. Tell him that we've come with urgent news, as well as an offer of alliance."

I nodded, quickly translating his words.

The elf with white antlers cocked his head at me, his pale, almond-shaped eyes roving across my face as though trying to decide whether my glowing skin was real or a trick of the light, then falling on Zayn, where they narrowed even further. Finally, he replied, "We will take you to our king. But beware, he does not take kindly to visitors – especially those that appear unexpectedly, and without invitation. By which appellation shall we announce you to him?"

Darting a glance at Zayn, I muttered, "He wants to know our names. Should I tell him?"

He hesitated briefly, then nodded. "Yes."

I cleared my throat. "Um, you can announce us as Talia Kestenbaum and Zæynek al'Bâramahd, stepson of the late King Saedis."

Upon hearing that, every member of the elven guard visibly stiffened.

I opened my mouth, briefly considering whether I should mention the part about me being Saedis's granddaughter, then closed it again. I had no proof of that – only the word of a capricious, mentally-unstable harpy. Furthermore, something in my gut told me it wasn't the best idea to go around announcing myself as the former Summer King's illicit grandbaby.

The members of the Royal Guard exchanged long looks with one another, and for a moment, I thought they were going to tell us to buzz off – or worse, set up a meet-cute between us and the pointy ends of their crossbows.

Finally, tightening his grip on his crossbow, the leader replied, "Come, Zæynek al'Bâramahd and Talia al'Kestenbaum. We will take you to the Winter King."

The palace now loomed just fifty iced-over steps above us, the highest point on the highest peak in the entire realm. Biscuit had gone back home to rest, while Mavros, in her golden dragon form, was soaring in wide, glittering circles high above us. The elves routinely glanced up at her as we climbed, as though they'd never seen anything like her before…

Which, to be fair, they probably hadn't.

How are you doing, Mavvie? I silently called up to her. *Are you feeling okay?*

With a mix of reassuring feelings and images, she let me know she was okay – albeit worried about me.

I'll be alright, I reassured her.

Her disbelieving sigh was quickly replaced by a detailed image of her removing Sol's charred head from his body, followed by a rasping laugh that tickled my eardrums.

I couldn't help but smile, even as the enormous, uninviting outline of the Winter Palace loomed ever higher.

"It's nice to see you smiling," Zayn said softly, his expression mirroring my own.

Seeing his, my own smile deepened. "You too."

He cleared his throat roughly. "Are you sure you don't want to Tess back to Korinne and the others?" he asked – again. "I mean, you don't…" He swallowed visibly. "You don't look well, Tal. I'm worried about you." His eyes darted up to Mavros, whom he could apparently hear in his head as well. "We're all worried about you."

"I'm not abandoning you here – and I don't feel sick." *Well, no sicker than usual,* I silently amended. My shoulder was throbbing like crazy, even though the corissian ink appeared to be holding, and my earlier spell of nausea still hadn't dissipated. But *where* I was didn't make a difference in how I felt. The Requisition Rune was slowly poisoning me, and for the moment, nothing could be done about it.

Nothing except destroying Sol, I thought, even as the knot in my stomach tightened. After all, we had no guarantee that killing him would actually release me from his claim.

"Is he still…there?" Zayn asked, as though reading my thoughts.

I shook my head. "So long as I keep my emotions in check, I can't hear him at all… And speaking of emotions"—I regarded the towering steel doors of the Winter Palace, now a mere ten steps away—"I'm doing my absolute best not to freak out right now. But dude – the Winter *King?*" I squeaked. "I thought you and Lam said he and his court were wiped out in the Blood Wars!"

"They were," Zayn answered stonily. "I have no idea who's currently sitting on the throne, or why he hasn't made a peep in the fifty years since his predecessor died."

I let out a low *harrumph.*

As we approached the towering, iced-over, ornately-carved front doors, the elf with antlers – Kløssen, as he'd eventually introduced himself – ungloved a pale hand to reach forward and trigger an Unchaining Rune embedded in the wood. With a keening creak, the doors swung open, revealing inky darkness inside. He politely gestured for us to enter while he and the other elves fell into synchronized step behind us.

Zayn and I exchanged one last wary last glance before stepping inside.

Unlike the bright, colorful splendor of the Summer Palace, the Winter Palace was dark, cold, and smelled of isolation. There was no grand entryway, nor a well-intentioned "Hygiene Fairy" hocking everybody to take their shoes off. It felt like any other old, neglected manor.

Once everyone had entered, Kløssen dismissed all but four of the other elves; the two pairs that stayed behind stiffly took their positions on either side of the front doors, which swung shut with an echoing bang.

"Are these all of your weapons?" he asked, gesturing to my belt, which held two knives and a gun loaded with iron bullets.

"I also have a switchblade in my boot." *And half a dozen lethal runes on my body,* I added silently. "Do you want me to leave them outside?"

"No need. However, if you withdraw them, you'll be killed instantly."

"Fair enough," I muttered, then passed along his warning to Zayn, who seemed to find the comment amusing.

With a casual wave of Kløssen's hand, two lines of torches ignited on both sides of us, throwing the chamber in dim, flickering shadows. This was apparently the Winter King's throne room, where an unadorned stone dais rose several feet above our heads. A single empty throne stood in the center, comprised of dozens of antlers and a pelt of spotted white fur that had been draped over them. To my dismay, a large and varied assortment of animal heads had been plastered on all four walls of the throne room. Some looked just like the deer and elk back on Earth – others…not so much. There was a large cat head that resembled a saber-toothed tiger, but with powerful, moose-like antlers. Another creature, which looked like a cross between a raccoon and a badger – but at least twice as big – snarled at us in frozen fury, its bright green, forked tongue permanently dangling between two sharpened tusks. I shuddered, pulling my eyes away from the trophies with a mix of pity and fear. Had we just been hiking in the same region where these nightmarish creatures freely roamed?

I didn't really want to think about that.

Apart from the assortment of mounted animal heads, there weren't any other decorations in the room – no banners or sigils or art of any kind. It was just a modestly-sized chamber, with a tall pointed ceiling that probably ended as one of the castle turrets, and two darkened, doorless archways that ostensibly led to other parts of the castle.

I rubbed my arms briskly, trying to warm them. Seeing this, Kløssen casually pointed a finger at an unlit fireplace. Glowing runes on a neatly-stacked pile of cobweb-adorned logs erupted into flames, casting the room in warmth, but not comfort. That's when I noticed the black markings embedded in Kløssen's pale hand – runes. Many of them.

"Niya chamak Padeşáh'tho ta?" Zayn asked, slipping into the southern Elvish dialect.

Kløssen just stared at him blankly.

Sighing, I grabbed a marker from the pocket of my cloak and scrawled a symbol on the back of this hand – which turned out to be a rather difficult feat since I couldn't grab his hand to steady it. Nevertheless, the fresh Translation Rune flickered to life a moment later.

"Where is your king?" Zayn asked again, this time in the proper language of the north.

His stern features somewhat relaxing, Kløssen replied, "He will be here presently. In the meantime, please make yourselves comfortable." At that, two chairs – smaller antler-and-fur versions of the throne – appeared before the fireplace.

Zayn eyed his tattoos warily. "You're a Runemaster?"

"I am," the elf replied, regarding Zayn's tattoos with a matching look of cool appraisal.

"Under whom did you train?"

"I am self-taught," Kløssen answered in a clipped tone. "None of *our* Runemasters were fortunate enough to survive your stepfather's war," he added, keeping his expression carefully schooled. "Why? Do you consider my knowledge of Runes inferior to yours?"

Zayn stiffened. "I meant no offense – I was merely curious."

Kløssen turned to look at me, his eyes once more roving across my face and crossed forearms. "Is that some sort of cosmetic trick you employ, or is your blood actually…?"

"Gold?" I supplied. "Yeah…it's about as gold as it gets, or so I'm told."

His left eyebrow raised imperceptibly. "Are you a Runemaster as well?"

"Yes," Zayn cut in. "She is."

I darted a questioning look at him, but he was too busy staring down Kløssen to notice – most likely trying to determine just how dangerous of a threat he would be, should discussion turn to dispute. He crossed his arms in front of him, one finger absentmindedly tapping one of the more lethal runes on his bulging bicep.

Kløssen stiffened as a shadow fell across the floor, his pale gray eyes darting just past Zayn's shoulder.

The two of us whirled around to find a broad figure emerging from the nearest darkened archway, his large antlers and billowing cloak swathed in shadows.

Taking Zayn's cue, I abruptly fell to a single, trembling knee as the man strode into the room, his cape of quilted animal pelts swishing across the stone floor. Though Zayn's gaze was respectfully glued to the floor, I darted a quick glance up at the man, taken aback by his bronze complexion. Apart from the furs and antlers he sported, he looked nothing like Kløssen or the other northern elves. In fact, he sort of looked like—

"Zæynek al'Bâramahd," Kløssen said, straightening from his own deep bow, "stepson of the late King Saedis, and his gilded companion, Talia al'Kestenbaum, I humbly present to you Metkäyel, Flame of the Mountain, Guardian of the Keep, and Sovereign of the North."

Following the Runemaster's lead, Zayn and I slowly returned to our feet, exchanging anxious glances.

Who is *this guy?* I wondered, chewing on an already-ragged nail. *Oh, God – what if he's in cahoots with Sol? What if this whole thing is a trap?* My hand slowly crept to the leather-wrapped hilt of my iron dagger, pulse fluttering and fingers trembling.

As torchlight fully illuminated the stark edges and deep grooves of the Winter King's tightening expression, Zayn let out a ragged gasp.

"*Mikhæl?*"

XVI.
A Chilly Disposition

I stumbled backward with a gasp, looking between the two men who were staring each other up and down like two wolves meeting in a forest. Indeed, the man Zayn had called Mikhæl bore a slight, albeit hardened, resemblance to Zayn. But that wasn't the reason for my shock.

No, what stole the very breath from my lungs was how much this man looked like the thirty-year-old version of my father, from his deep-set gray eyes, slightly too wide for his face, to his dark, cropped beard, to the small divot on the tip of his aquiline nose…

I took another step backward, pressing my hand to my mouth.

"After all this time," Mikhæl growled, switching to Zayn's mother tongue. "Has Sol finally sent you to kill me, *brother?*" He all but spat the word.

"Miki," Zayn whispered, his face as white as I'd ever seen it.

The king swept his cape back as he made a slow circle around Zayn, who stood frozen to his spot. "I'd heard rumors of your survival, that you'd sold yourself out to your baser kind moments after those accursed demonspawn raped and ravaged our family." The king's eyebrows narrowed into predatory slits as he stopped pacing directly in front of Zayn. "Despite overwhelming evidence to the contrary, I could not let myself believe them, convincing myself you'd sooner *die* than sell your soul…until now."

Zayn said nothing in his own defense; he just stared at his brother as though he were seeing a ghost, his wide eyes roving from the gold-dipped antlers resting upon the king's head, to the gem-encrusted sword he wore at his waist, finally settling on the mink-like stole he'd wrapped around his neck. "But I…I saw Calus slit your throat, Miki. I saw you fall to the ground, bleeding—"

"That ignorant roach didn't press his blade deep enough," Mikhæl sneered, unwrapping his fur scarf to expose the ugly scar that stretched from one side of his throat to the other. "I was forced to lie in a puddle of my own blood, watching the life drain from my father's eyes, before darkness eventually took pity on me. When I awoke, I found myself lying atop our sisters' broken bodies, in a mass grave that had yet to be covered."

Zayn looked as though he might faint.

As for me, I still couldn't pull my eyes away from the king's face; it bore so much resemblance to my father's, I could hardly register anything that was being said.

"And so, I ask you again, *Zæynek*," Mikhæl sneered, taking a step closer. "Have you come to finish your master's work?"

At Kløssen's sharp gesture, the four guards stepped forward, their hands reaching for their crossbows.

"N-No," Zayn blurted out, finally snapping from his trance. "No, I-I've freed myself from Sol's enslavement – or rather, Talia freed me."

Only when Mikhæl's familiar gray eyes darted to mine did it finally hit me – if my father truly was Saedis's illicit son, then that meant…

Oh, God.

My knees buckled, and I crumpled to the floor.

"Talia!" Zayn hissed, shoving past his brother to fall to his knees beside me. When Kløssen made a move to do the same, Zayn let out a vicious snarl, and the Runemaster took a startled step backward.

The king's eyes darkened, making my shallow breaths come even quicker. "Explain yourself."

If my Dad and Mikhæl share the same father…

"She's been cursed by Sol, just as I was." Zayn closed his eyes, as though he were steeling himself against his own words. "But unlike my mark of slavery, the mark Sol left on Talia's body is slowly killing her."

Then that makes him…

Mikhæl turned his hawklike-gaze back to me, while realization sank to the pit of my stomach like a stone.

My uncle.

I forced myself into a sitting position, groaning against the accompanying wave of nausea. Still, the pain emanating from my stomach was nothing compared to the growing agony of my shoulder, from which there appeared to be no relief in sight.

"What can be done for her?" Kløssen asked. His flat tone made it hard to tell whether the question was coming from a place of curiosity or sympathy. "Which herbs does she require?"

"Nothing can be done," Zayn said through gritted teeth. "Heightened emotions – particularly negative ones – open the channel between her and Sol, allowing him to poison her from the inside out."

"I'll be okay," I wheezed, doing my best to take a deep breath. "Just n-need…to calm…down."

Mikhæl looked between the two of us, the wheels in his head spinning. "So, this girl is your…claim?"

"She belongs to me, and I to her," Zayn snapped, sending another wave of emotion straight to my throat.

The king's expression softened, but only slightly. "Then you truly have not come to kill me, brother?"

Tell him, I mouthed to Zayn, urging him to stand.

After hesitating for the briefest moment, Zayn rose to his feet to face his half-brother. "On our mother's memory, Miki, I swear I haven't. I didn't even know you lived until you set foot in this room."

At the king's subtle nod, the four elven guards returned to their posts beside the entrance, the tips of their crossbows once more aimed at the floor.

"Come," Kløssen said, beckoning me to my feet. He led me over to the fireplace, where I slumped into one of the two chairs with an exhausted sigh.

Zayn watched the two of us like a hawk, turning back to face Mikhæl only when I shot him a *stop-worrying-about-me-and-go-talk-to-him* glare.

"So," Mikhæl's shoulders finally seemed to relax, "if not for me, then why have you come?"

"Sol is raising an army, hell-bent on killing every last Seelie on the continent," Zayn answered, the fatigue in his voice evident. "After evacuating the southern elven territory, Talia and I have been building an army of our own to stop him. We are several-hundred strong and mostly comprised of elves, though our numbers and strength are meager in comparison to his. That's why we've traveled north – to try to find allies for our cause." Zayn lowered his head in a show of deference, making my lips purse into a frown. "I claimed the crown believing I was the last survivor of the Bâramahd bloodline. However, I'll gladly cede the throne to you, brother, in exchange for your help. I don't care which of us leads, so long as Sol and his disciples are defeated in the process."

Mikhæl stared at him for a good, long moment…and then burst out laughing. Before Zayn could even react, the Winter King scooped him into a massive bear hug, crushing him against his chest. "Brother, you *live* – not as a traitor, but as a warrior! And for that, I cannot tell you how happy I am!"

"You are?" Zayn wheezed.

The king slapped a hearty hand on Zayn's shoulder, making him flinch. Apart from his prodigious gold-dipped antlers, Mikhæl was at least an inch shorter than his brother, and stockier in build, though far less muscular – that much was clear even beneath his pompous, oversized fur cloak. And yet, Zayn shrunk beneath his older brother's piercing gaze, stooping his shoulders in a way that made him seem small in comparison.

My frown deepened.

Biscuit appeared on my arm in a subdued flash, his feathers raising like hackles as he watched the exchange between Zayn and Mikhæl. At the same time, a tiny sparrow sailed through one of narrow arrow slits in the upper turret, landing on my other shoulder with a chirp. Mavros ruffled and unruffled her lustrous black and gold feathers, which gleamed against the dancing light of the fireplace.

Kløssen regarded my familiars with a raised eyebrow. "Blood incarnates?"

"More like emotional support animals," I muttered.

Mikhæl glanced at a large candle burning beneath a mounted kelpie head in one of the shallow alcoves. "It's nearly time for the midday meal, brother. Let us dine, drink, and fill one another in on the events of the last fifty seasons!"

"And...what of the coming war?" Zayn asked warily. "As much as I too want to reminisce and catch up, Miki, our window of opportunity is quickly closing—"

For some reason, that elicited another peal of laughter from the king. He wiped a tear from his eye as he roughly clapped another hand on Zayn's shoulder. "Oh, Zæynek. You always were prone to theatrics. This 'war' you speak of is a problem for the Southern Demesne. And if none of our kin remain in the Southern Demesne, then it is really not a problem at all, is it? It simply becomes a matter of increased border control to ensure those spineless, licentious demons stay in their own demesne – no offense intended, of course," he quickly added.

The flicker of pain that darted across Zayn's face made me want to rip the antlers off his brother's over-inflated head and shove them up his ass.

"And anyway," Mikhæl continued, as jovial as he was oblivious, "Sol knows better than to brave the perils of the north. You'll simply have to bring your 'army' to the Winter Palace, where we can spend our days ensconced in warmth and safety. After all, life is short enough, brother – there is no reason to kick down death's door, as you're so zealously attempting to do. Now, let's set aside this talk of war, and move to drinking and dining! Kløssen!" He snapped his fingers at the Runemaster. "Notify the kitchen staff that we have guests, and then fetch me our finest wine!"

A look of surprise crossed the Runemaster's face. "You wish to uncork the last bottle of your father's vineyard, sire?"

Mikhæl ushered Zayn toward the darkened archway. "My only brother, the last remaining flesh and blood of my kin, has returned!" He bellowed over his shoulder, not bothering to spare me or anyone else a second glance. "What better cause for celebration could there be?"

A low growl slipped from my throat, while Biscuit and Mavros both ground their beaks in irritation. When Zayn darted an apologetic look at me over his shoulder, I quickly composed my face into a tight smile, motioning that I was right behind him. But the moment he turned back around, my expression reverted to a simmering glower that Biscuit was mirroring and then some.

"So," I muttered to him under my breath, keeping pace several feet behind Zayn and his brother, "I take it you're not a fan of this 'Miki' either?"

Biscuit shook his head in a fervent "No!"

"Did you ever like him?"

His hardened, gold-flecked eyes met mine. A split-second later, a memory flashed in front of my vision, momentarily replacing the darkness of the hallway. I – or rather, Biscuit – was perched in a tall oak tree, watching two teenage boys splashing in the river. One was the lanky, boyish version of Zayn, who had just dived beneath the surface. The other was his scowling older brother, who immediately plunged his arm beneath the water, trapping Zayn's head underneath. My breath caught and held as five seconds passed, and then ten, and then twenty.

Bubbles erupted at the surface.

Biscuit let out an angry squawk, diving from his tall branch. Mikhæl's head jerked toward the sound, his arms instinctively covering his head as Biscuit snatched him by the hair, narrowly dodging Mikhæl's flailing fist. Zayn popped up from the water with a series of sputtering, doubled-over coughs, while his brother's furious glower immediately morphed into one of feigned innocence.

"What? You said you dropped your crystal – I was just helping you look for it!"

My fingernails dug into my palm as the memory faded back to shadows. "Coming here was a big mistake…wasn't it?"

Biscuit didn't answer; he was too busy glaring at the back of Mikhæl's neck.

The three of us ate alone in a surprisingly small dining room, which housed a fifteen-foot-long wooden table, four stark chairs, and a single, unlit fireplace. Some sort of meat and potato stew was set in front of us by a stout, frosty female elf, while another elf that could have been Kløssen's brother – sans the decorative antlers – poured and served us three pewter goblets of hearty red wine. Remembering my last experience with fae wine, I limited myself to tiny sips, silently watching Zayn, who sat at my right, and his brother, who sat on the opposite end of the table, over the top of my goblet. Meanwhile, Biscuit and Mavros were camped beside my elbow, annihilating their third chunk of buttered bread.

Despite Zayn's obvious discomfort, Mikhæl spent a good thirty minutes regaling himself with fond memories of their childhood – even though many of those memories had nothing to do with Zayn. When he brought up some story about Yenna rooting through their mother's bag of potions to find a suitable *expungeant* – which turned out to be a powerful dye that stained her hands pink for the better part of the summer – Mikhæl finally grew silent.

"Do you…" Zayn started, then tried again. "Do you know…what became of her? Our mother, that is."

His brother was silent for a long moment. Then, after picking up his wooden spoon and shoving a massive hunk of potato in his mouth, he answered, "No."

Zayn dropped his eyes to his own untouched bowl of stew. After several moments of heavy silence, he took a deep breath, then said, "Aunt Elínya is dead."

"She and everyone else in the family," Mikhæl grunted.

"No." Zayn shook his head. "I mean she died recently – just days ago. She survived the war and had taken up the helm of Great Mother in the southern elven sanctuary – as their High Priestess," he added, most likely for my benefit. "She and nearly thirty other elves died in the unprompted attack that Sol launched against them."

My stomach knotted at the memory. Minutes after learning that her nephew hadn't, in fact, been a complete traitor to his kind, the Great Mother took a venomous manticore barb to the neck and collapsed, never to open her eyes again.

Mikhæl stuffed another hunk of meat in his mouth, which he downed with a large swig of wine that dribbled out of the sides of the goblet and onto his beard. Frowning, he dabbed at his face with the cloth napkin from his lap. The clumsy motion was so human-like, my chest constricted. Though he and my father appeared to have nothing in common personality-wise, whatever genes Saedis had passed down to his two sons must have been strong, because the outward traits Mikhæl and my father shared were unnervingly similar.

"Did anyone else we know survive?" he asked, keeping his tone carefully blasé.

"Korinne, one of the palace healers, and Safír, the cartographer – she's become the ad hoc captain of the elven guard. Lamswyth is alive, as well. He's currently helping the soldiers with battle logist—"

"That old goat survived the war?" Mikhæl interrupted. "How?"

"By fleeing with so many of the others, I suppose," Zayn answered, ice creeping into his voice. "Why? Are you dismayed to hear that?"

His older brother scoffed. "I have nothing against the satyr personally. I just can't begin to understand the Creator's reasoning – allowing the greatest king of all time to die, while sparing the life of a lecherous sheep."

A muscle in Zayn's jaw clenched. "And you, brother? You say you woke up in a mass grave after Calus failed in his attempt to kill you. But that does not explain how you arrived here, in the Winter Court's abandoned palace, and managed to crown yourself King of the North."

I glanced at Zayn out of the corner of my eye, surprised – and heartened – by the brazenness of his tone. He was staring pointedly at his brother, who also appeared caught off-guard.

"When I realized there was no point in fighting, save to hasten my return to the shade of the Great Phoenix Tree," Mikhæl answered, his chin raised defensively, "I joined a caravan of elven survivors from the north. Their numbers had been decimated through decades of war, reduced to several hundred from tens of thousands. When they learned of my argent blood and royal lineage, they beseeched me to be their king. After much thought, I humbly accepted."

I exchanged an incredulous look with Biscuit, whose belly was slightly rounded from an overabundance of bread. Even Mavros, once more in her preferred, raven form, rolled her eyes.

"I see." Judging by the incline of Zayn's brow, he wasn't exactly sold on Mikhæl's version of events, either. "And, of those several hundred survivors, how many remain?"

"Including the elven town of Northstead, which I personally helped conceal along the western slope, we now sit at well over one-thousand strong," Mikhæl answered, squaring his shoulders with an air of pride.

Zayn nodded, clearly impressed. And yet, instead of lavishing his brother with praise, as Mikhæl no doubt expected, he rested his chin on steepled fingers, cocked his head, and said, "You have more elves in the Northern Demesne than anywhere else on the continent, and yet you refuse to come to the aid of your southern brethren?"

That wiped the blithe smile from the Winter King's face. "As I already told you, *little* brother, the travails of the south are no concern of mine – particularly when such travails come with no hope of triumph."

"No concern of yours?" Zayn repeated. "You are of southern blood – you are a prince born and raised in the Summer Kingdom. It is one thing to seek asylum when you believe there are no other survivors to be found. But we have come here, telling you of your surviving kin who are in dire need of help. Hundreds of innocent elves, tommyknockers, and banshees stand to be massacred if you don't—"

"Did you say *banshees?*" When Zayn didn't correct him, his brother let out a howl of laughter, slapping the table. "Why in the Creator's name should I concern myself with the plight of banshees? Let those witches of pestilence rot, for all I care!"

It was only when a sharp pain zinged through my jaw that I realized I'd been gnashing my teeth together. Biscuit angrily hopped up on my shoulder, calling to mind a haloed image of his beloved *bubbe* and her valiant Chihuahua hellhounds.

"And tommyknockers!" Mikhæl wiped a glistening eye. "You expect me to put my life on the line for 'men' whose noses barely reach my belt loop?"

Zayn's scowl darkened.

"Brother, I am sorry for any offense you have chosen to take from my words." Mikhæl waved his hand in a flippant gesture.

"But your brief dalliance with power has clearly softened your head! Damn the banshees, as I've already said, and send the knockers back to their mines, where they belong. At that point, you and the others are welcome in the Winter Kingdom, where no foreign invader would dare set foot. Even Sol, belligerent as he is, has no doubt picked up a history book in the last century or two – or at the very least, his advisors have. There is not a general on this continent who would stroll into the unforgiving tundra of the north and expect to survive the bitter chill of Winter's wrath." He shoved another hunk of meat in his mouth. "Bring the surviving elves here," he repeated, guzzling another prodigious swig of his father's wine, "and we shall make a home for them all in Northstead."

"Mikhæl—"

"And I'll tell you this, brother," he continued on as though Zayn hadn't spoken, "while you'll never bear the crown in this demesne or any other, we'll find you a suitable honorary title, one that befits the son of a queen. Well," he amended, chuckling to himself, "a title that befits a halfling prince born to a queen out of wedlock, at the very least."

"Are you fucking kidding me?" I exploded, the first words I'd uttered since having the misfortune of sitting across from this narcissistic doorknob.

Mikhæl started, as though he'd forgotten I was there, then grinned. "Ah, so the waif speaks."

I shot him a glare so withering, my "witch" of a mother would have been proud. "Yes, the 'waif' speaks. And the 'waif' would like His Royal Highness to know that she finds him to be a pompous, insufferable prick."

The king's spoon clattered to the table.

Zayn leaned back in his chair, pressing his lips into a tight line – whether to suppress a grin or a grimace, I wasn't sure.

Frankly, by that point, I didn't care.

Flinging my napkin to the ground, I rose from my seat, gripping the edges of the table. "I came here expecting to find a king – instead, all I see is a frightened little man drinking his daddy's wine while hiding from the world in this moldy excuse for a castle!"

The Winter King slowly rose from his own seat, pressing his palms to the table as he glared me down. "Watch your tongue, child, or the next words you speak may be your last."

Zayn pushed out his chair, rising to his feet.

"You're an idiot if you think Sol will stop at the southern border," I replied, ignoring Mikhæl's threat. "He's power-hungry and out of his mind, not to mention the fact that he's using your mother's grimoire and your family's blood to create an army of soulless monsters. And yeah, I'm pretty sure those monsters would *gladly* take a refreshing hike through the mountains to rob the hermit king of his stolen castle, or literally anything else he asks them to do, *because that's the whole freaking point of blood incarnates!"*

"How dare you speak to me this way!" Mikhæl snarled. "*You*, who are nothing more than decorative chattel!"

"At least I'm not a walking ass with teeth!" I shot back.

His jaw literally dropped.

Goddamn, I thought, stealing a satisfied glance at my Translation Rune. *Elvish insults really* are *savage.*

"And you!" The king's furs swirled at his heels as he furiously rounded on Zayn. "For you to just stand there like a troll, allowing this *child* to speak to me in such a way! Control your female's tongue!"

Zayn's shoulder rose and fell in an indifferent shrug as he came to stand beside me. "Who am I to control her? I'm her lover, not her keeper… Besides"—he cast me a lightning-quick wink—"I can't say I disapprove of a single thing she does with her tongue."

In the single beat of silence that followed, the deepening flush abruptly drained from Mikhæl's cheeks. "Wait…what do you mean, 'my family's blood'?" His eyes darted to Zayn. "Is she talking about you?"

"I realize you may have been distracted when Kløssen announced us, since you haven't seen your brother in fifty years," I said, casually bending down to deactivate the Concealment Rune on my ankle, then unclasping my father's locket from my neck. My faintly-shimmering skin ignited like a lantern, casting Mikhæl's stunned expression in warm golden light. "So it's possible you missed the part about me having gilded blood."

Biscuit and Mavros took that gloriously-timed opportunity to launch themselves onto my shoulders, erupting into dazzling flames as they did. Our three illuminated silhouettes reflected in the king's widening eyes, which were darting between Zayn and me as though he were seeing us for the first time.

"Sol's got a vial of *my* blood," I said softly, "which means he's got a vial of our family's blood."

Mikhæl's chair scraped against the floor as he took a step backward. "And just who in the three realms are *you?*"

"So nice of you to finally ask." I inclined my head in a polite bow. "I'm Talia, daughter of your half-brother, Howard…the younger, lesser-known son of King Saedis."

XVII.
Blood is Thicker Than Water

"What kind of trickery is this?" Mikhæl demanded hoarsely, his wide eyes darting between me and Zayn. "My father loved my mother with every fiber of his being! He…" The knot in his throat bobbed forcefully. "He would never betray her."

After re-clasping my locket around my neck, I casually tossed Xianis's letter in his direction. It slid to a stop a few inches in front of his emptied goblet. "I haven't gone on daytime TV to take an official DNA test yet, but based on how similar you and my father look, I'm gonna assume the contents of this message are accurate."

Mikhæl hastily withdrew the letter from its torn-open envelope, then sank into his chair to read it with shaking hands. Anger crossed his face, followed by confusion, shock, disgust, and, finally, horror. When he set the letter back down a few minutes later, his cheeks had lost all their color. "First, my brother returns from the dead, and now you desecrate my father's memory with this…this"—he reached forward and crumpled the letter in a shaking fist—"this *nonsense?* My father, the most powerful and revered king in elven history, would lay with a *harpy*, of all things?"

I crossed my arms, saying nothing.

He leapt to his feet, slapping the letter on the table. "Not only that, but you expect me to believe that loathsome creature then birthed a living son who *only now* claims to be my half-brother at the *exact same moment* Zæynek 'accidentally' appears at my doorstep?" He shot an accusatory glare at Zayn before jerking his head back to me. "Since this abomination has not the courage nor honor to face me with these allegations, I demand you bring me the conniving bastard so that I may interrogate him myself!"

Zayn took a step forward, his hands balling into fists. I tugged him backward by the hem of his shirt, shaking my head. A muscle in his jaw flexed as he regarded me, though he did manage a small, begrudging nod.

I turned back to Mikhæl. "My father is dead," I replied coldly. "He died on Earth, several decades after being abandoned there as a changeling."

"Abandoned as a *changeling?*" Mikhæl recoiled as though I'd blurted out a racial slur, then shook his head roughly. "My father would never do something so contemptible!"

"First of all, your father never knew my grandmother gave birth to his child. Xianis claims she left my dad on Earth for his own protection. And secondly," I continued, doing everything I could to keep my temper corked, "I'm pretty sure your father *would* do something like that, since he tried to do the exact same thing when Zæynek was born!"

"That was different!" Mikhæl snarled. "*That* creature wasn't his blood. It was merely the accidental by-product of a demonic parasite!"

Zayn stiffened, yet said nothing – as though he were used to this kind of dehumanization.

Molten-hot fury flared in my chest and shoulder – so hot, I literally saw red; so powerful, my fraying defenses were knocked aside in one single, violent blow. For the first time in my life, I actually felt as though I had the capacity—no, not just the capacity – the acute, overwhelming *desire* to kill someone.

My lips curled into a gleeful smile as I took a menacing step toward the king. *And what better life to take than that of this vile, horrible, self-important narcissist?*

Zayn let out a sharp hiss. "Talia!" His arm jerked forward as if to grab me, freezing when he remembered he couldn't. "What are you doing?"

Kill him, a voice whispered in my head, pulsing in time with the throb in my shoulder. I nodded, my palm glowing with power.

Mikhæl merely stood frozen in place, staring at me as though I'd lost my mind.

"RAAAWK!" Biscuit screeched, flapping his wings from my shoulder, while Mavros gave my ear a sharp tug. Gold and rainbow flames once more appeared in front of my vision, searing away the crimson filter.

I stopped in my tracks, blinking furiously. "Oh, God," I whispered, staring at my glowing palms.

Deftly positioning himself between Mikhæl and me, Zayn probed my eyes for a long moment. Apparently placated by what he saw – or maybe what he *didn't* see – he softly asked, "Are you alright?"

"I…" I tried to swallow, but my mouth had gone completely dry. "I-I think it's time we leave. Right now."

"Agreed." He nodded.

"What?" Mikhæl demanded, striding toward us. I ducked behind Zayn, keeping my distance more for his brother's sake than for mine. "You just got here!"

"We came looking for help," Zayn answered frostily. "Seeing as there is no help to be found, we'll be on our way."

He started to turn away, but Mikhæl reached out and roughly grabbed him by the shoulder. "You can't leave," he rasped, the desperation in his voice catching both of us off guard. "I thought my entire family had been slaughtered. And now I find my brother and m-my—" His eyes darted to me, then settled firmly back on Zayn. "Well…it seems our family line has persevered beyond what I thought possible. Bring the other elves here, I implore you. You'll all be safe within the walls of my dominion, far beyond the reach of the demon that took everything from us." His voice cracked, and he cleared his throat roughly. "Please, brother…don't let him take you from me again."

Zayn started at the unexpected show of emotion. "I…"

Biscuit hopped from my shoulder to his, nuzzling his face against Zayn's cheek. "Luvyu," he chirped softly.

Zayn reached up and scratched our familiar on the head, mustering a weak nod. After a protracted moment, he turned back to his brother. "If I survive the coming war, I pray you and I will have the opportunity to start over…" He clasped Mikhæl's wrist, forcing a tight smile. "If not, perhaps I'll see you in the next realm."

Mikhæl froze, a look of panic crossing his face. He opened his mouth as though to continue pleading with his brother – but his eyes quickly tightened, and he roughly pushed Zayn away instead. "Let the others know what I have offered, lest they show a little more care for their lives than you do."

Zayn pursed his lips in what I'd hoped would be a sharp retort…then exhaled softly through his nose, shaking his head. "Come on, Tal. It's time to go."

Nodding, I gladly fell into step behind him.

"Zæynek!"

At the sound of Mikhæl's sharp appeal, Zayn slowly turned around, wariness etched into every line of his face. "Yes?"

The king motioned him over. "One more word, brother. Please."

With an exasperated sigh, Zayn turned around to approach him, while Mavros and I remained by the door.

Mikhæl ushered him into the far corner of the room, darting a furtive glance in my direction as he dropped his voice to a low whisper.

I rolled my eyes and crossed my arms, unable to hear a word he was saying – fortunately, however, Biscuit could. Casting me a mischievous wink, he transmitted Mikhæl's words directly to my ears via our telepathic bond:

"Brother, listen to me. I'm not exactly sure how these incubus 'relationships' work, but I can assure you, you don't have to plunge the entire realm into war to free this girl from the demon's claim. Return with the other elves. Once you've settled in, Kløss will help you find a cure so you can once more feed on her – or whatever it is you do – since you're obviously so pent up you're not thinking straight."

Zayn's back stiffened.

"And if that doesn't work, there are plenty of other eligible females to choose from. Why, in Northstead alone, we have several hundred *lonely females of mating age—"*

Shame and humiliation heated my cheeks, while anger knotted through my chest.

"—some of whom, I'm sure, would gladly give you the chance to prove what all the overblown incubus fuss is about, so long as you can assure them of your sterility—"

Mikhæl's words cut off in a sharp *whoosh* as Zayn's hand shot out and gripped him by the throat, slamming his back into the wall.

"Oh, shit!" My hands flew to my mouth.

"Now that you've said your piece, allow me say something to you, *brother,*" Zayn growled, his voice as coarse as gravel. "For years, you forced me to *earn* your companionship – and even then, it was only because you were 'munificent' enough to grant it to a creature as unworthy as me. You taunted me endlessly, making me think I was no better than the mud that tarnished your boots – and for years, I believed you. I tolerated your insults and abuse as charity, blaming myself for my own pitiful existence."

The wooden door to the kitchen swung open to reveal the wide-eyed female elf who had brought us our dinner – only for her to immediately dart back inside and return two seconds later with a half dozen royal guards and at least twice that many wide-eyed kitchen staff. While the latter stood in the corner whispering salaciously among themselves, the former poured into the room, their crossbows trained directly onto Zayn – who was still clutching the Winter King by his windpipe.

I reached for the Ligature Rune on my arm, but Zayn held up a hand to stop me, releasing his iron grip on his brother in the same motion.

Mikhæl let out a wheezing gasp as his own hands flew to his mottled, scarred throat.

"This woman"—Zayn pointed at me—"is the single greatest thing to have ever happened to me. And while I'm certainly not 'plunging the realm into war' to save her alone, believe me when I say there is nothing I wouldn't do to protect her." He took a menacing step toward his brother, ignoring the half dozen arrows that were aimed at every exposed point on his body, until their noses were millimeters apart. "*Nothing.*"

Mikhæl's face contorted into a dark glare…only to miraculously transform into something vaguely resembling contrition. "I am…sorry, Zæynek."

I couldn't be sure who was more shocked by the apology – Zayn or the kitchen staff.

His brother stole a quick glance at me, then dropped his gaze to the floor. "I…did not realize you cared for the girl in such a way."

"More than I could ever say," Zayn replied, his shoulders finally relaxing. "For the first time in my life, Miki, she makes me feel deserving – worthy, even – of love."

Tears unexpectedly filled my eyes.

"I don't know what kind of demons you are harboring about your own past," he continued, "but I suggest you deal with them – quickly. Because I promise you, Miki, Sol *will* come for the Winter Court – and when he does, I doubt he'll be considerate enough to leave survivors this time."

At that, the guards and kitchen staff dissolved into quiet, uneasy mutters.

"I am well aware my previous misdeeds will bar my soul from the shade of the Great Phoenix Tree when I die"—Zayn's face softened into a rueful smile—"but *you* still have a chance to do some good in this world."

Mikhæl's head bowed.

Zayn reached forward and gripped the back of his neck, pressing his forehead against his brother's. "The Creator saw fit to spare your life, Miki," he said softly. "Don't squander it."

Turning his back to the Winter King – who neither moved nor spoke after that – Zayn strode back over to me.

"Come on," he murmured, risking the most feather-light of kisses against the top of my head. "It's time to go home."

The massive doors of the Winter Palace slammed shut behind us, once more sealing its reclusive king and his cloistered keepers away from the rest of the world. While Zayn and I trudged down the icy stone staircase, Biscuit and Mavros soared in ascending spirals above us, leaving overlapping contrails of glitter as they crossed paths in the darkening green sky.

Dread and hopelessness weighed on my shoulders like twin fifty-pound bags.

"How many more hours until our last Tesseract replenishes?" I asked Zayn, casting him a worried side eye. He looked exhausted – both mentally and physically.

He regarded me with equal, if not greater, concern. "A couple of hours. I was thinking we could ask Mavros to transform into a dragon and carry us back to the Summer Palace, but the trip would probably take the better part of the night. And then there's always the chance of me sliding into you if we hit a rough patch of air."

"Yeah," I sighed, remembering the last time we rode on Mavros's back. I had been clinging to her scaly neck like Velcro, while Zayn – who, I learned at the same time, is *not* a fan of heights – had his arms wrapped around my waist like an iron vice.

"I could ask her to change into a horse so you don't have to walk while we wait," Zayn offered, surveying me like a Fabergé egg with a hairline crack running down the seam.

"I'm fine," I replied, tightening my cloak around my shoulders as a bitter gust of wind lashed at our faces. "Frankly, I could use the exercise. Helps keep my mind off...well, you know. Everything else."

He nodded, hovering as close to me as he safely could as we carefully minced the rest of the way down the icy steps.

Of course, nothing could keep my thoughts from returning to the Winter King – the uncle I never knew I had. Mikhæl looked so much like my father, it had been like seeing a ghost. And yet, personality-wise, the two of them couldn't have been more different. Where my dad had been warm, loving, and endlessly patient, his half-brother was erratic, self-absorbed, and bitter at the entire world. Still, I couldn't help but wonder if their differences came down to personality alone, or if, in the end, my father truly was the lucky one. After all, Dad's human parents had showered him with love when he was a child, which he then showered me with.

The thought made me miss him so badly my heart physically ached. But for the first time since his death, I didn't try to push the pain away. I gave it space, allowing it to fill the hollow void his absence had left.

And somehow, I felt better for it.

When we reached the bottom several minutes later, an untouched field of white loomed ahead of us; I could hardly tell where the snow ended and clouds began.

"Let's head that way." Zayn pointed. I squinted, following his finger to a lone cluster of pine trees located several hundred yards down the southern slope of the mountain. "I'll make us a fire while we wait for our Tess Runes to recharge. No point tiring ourselves out in the meantime."

Nodding wordlessly, I fell into step behind him, awkwardly attempting to re-trace his footprints in the deep, powdery snow. The sun had disappeared below the skirt of clouds that encircled the upper peak of the mountain, letting me know it was sometime in the late afternoon. My warming runes were still active, taking the worst of the bite out of the cold, but they didn't stop the wind from whipping at my face or the ice crystals from stinging my nostrils. It was impractical and stupid, no doubt, choosing the bitter cold of the high tundra over the relative warmth of Mikhæl's palace. But for Zayn and me, it hadn't even been a conversation. Both of us, for our own reasons, needed to get the hell out of that castle.

As we trudged through the wind and snow, neither of us cast a single look back.

We arrived at the tight cluster of trees about twenty minutes later. Zayn cleared away a circle of snow from the ground, then arranged a cone of broken branches and dead pine needles that I ignited with an impromptu Ignis Rune. We then dusted off a fallen bough and settled in beside the fire to warm our hands. Not long after, Biscuit and Mavros landed on a low branch of a nearby evergreen. With a soft coo, Mavros lowered her head, and Biscuit started dutifully preening her head feathers while she nuzzled against him.

Emotion welled in my chest as I watched them, though I hadn't even realized I was crying until Zayn knelt in front of me.

"What is it, Tal?"

Sniffing, I used my cloak to quickly scrub away my tears. "I just, um…I was thinking about what your brother was saying to you – about you being so pent up you're not thinking straight."

Zayn's expression darkened. "Tal, don't you dare give his idiotic, half-formed assumptions a second's thought. I lo—"

"I know you love me," I interrupted. "I do. And I love you, more than anything in this realm – or any other realm for that matter. But…"

Zayn's eyebrow arched. "But?"

"But…you're exhausted," I whispered. "I know love is so much more than physical touch. But I'm looking at you and…" My voice caught, so I cleared my throat and tried again. "You need energy, Zayn. If we have any hope at all of pulling through this alive, you can't traipse into battle half-fed – you need to be at full strength." Zayn opened his mouth to argue, but I hurriedly barreled on, "I – *all* of us – need you to be at full strength. And if there are elves in Northstead who would be willing to"—I winced, unable to bring myself to say it—"you know, to give you energy…then you have to go. Whatever you need to do, you have to do it, because I…"

I swallowed, desperately trying to choke down the sob that was threatening to burst from my throat. "I can't give you what you need. I can love you – unconditionally and with all my heart – but I can't…I can't *nourish* you. I can't strengthen you. In fact…" I took a deep, steadying breath, doing everything I could to keep my emotions in check. "All I am to you at this moment is a liability."

"Tal—"

"No, you have to listen to me! What almost happened back there…" I squeezed my eyes shut, clenching my cloak in two trembling fists. "Zayn, I…I wanted to kill him. Your brother – I truly, literally wanted to kill him. Whatever this poison in my shoulder is, it's fucking with my head. When I get angry, or scared, or sad…I hear him. If I were to lose myself…if I were to h-hurt you—" My sentence broke off abruptly in a sob. I hugged my body as tightly as I could, imagining Zayn's arms embracing me, and sucked down several deep mouthfuls of air to wrench my emotions back into submission.

When I was sure I'd regained control of myself, I forced my eyes open, meeting the smoldering intensity of Zayn's gaze.

"Tal…you are the life of my heart. Your love sustains me in a way nothing else ever has, or ever could. In fact, I…" He reached into his pocket, where he tightened his hand around something but didn't withdraw it. "I…" Zayn shook his head as though he were fighting an internal battle.

When he withdrew his hand again, it was still empty, but clenched and trembling. "Talia, if the banshees are right, and my time in this realm is coming to a close…then I can't bear the thought of spending one single moment without you."

A soft cry escaped my lips.

Zayn gripped both sides of my cloak, drawing his face close to mine. "I love you. I am nurtured by you. And I want nothing more than to share every moment of the rest of my life with you – be it the next five hours or five centuries."

"But I don't have five centuries to offer you," I sniffled pitifully. "Maybe a full-blooded elf would, but not me."

"Between your fae blood and the light of this sun, I truly think you and I could spend eternity together."

"Oh, Zayn…" I sighed, shaking my head.

His expression tightened. "Too long?"

"No," I whispered softly. "Not nearly long enough."

XVIII.
Scream Queens

The sun was setting behind the mountains when we finally arrived at the Summer Palace, weary, downtrodden, and, in my case, on the verge of throwing up – whether from Tessing, the poison slowly building up in my veins, or the sheer, unbridled dread of what was to come, I couldn't be sure. Whatever the cause, acid roiled in my stomach and my head throbbed so fiercely, the edges of my vision had become blurred. I gritted my teeth and kept my discomfort to myself – not because I was trying to keep secrets from Zayn, but because he already knew I was in pain, and there was no sense in further torturing a tortured man.

"I've got this," I told him, pressing my hand against the Unchaining Rune embedded in the cool wood.

As it glowed to life, Zayn shook his head ruefully. "I should have realized you had royal blood the first time you unlocked these doors."

I cast him a weak smile as they creaked open. "For what it's worth, I wouldn't have believed you, anyway."

With our feathered familiars in tow, the two of us stepped into the dimly-illuminated foyer, which was surprisingly devoid of any sort of welcome party. After taking off our shoes and setting them beside the long line of neatly stacked footwear against the wall, we pushed the doors open and entered the throne room. That too, was uncharacteristically empty – no shrieking Jewish mothers, yapping Chihuahua familiars, or lusty, blustering satyrs.

"Where is everyone?" Zayn muttered to himself.

While Biscuit and Mavros flew off to find my mother – or, more specifically, the bar of marzipan she was guarding in her purse – I approached the pair of thrones sitting atop the dais, frowning to myself. When I'd last seen them, they'd been made of nothing but dead, interwoven branches, and a collection of withered leaves and flowers decomposing underneath them. But now…

With a trembling hand, I reached forward to brush my fingers against one of the many green buds that had sprouted among the withered vines. The moment my fingertips touched it, petals unfurled from the bud, blossoming into a beautiful sunset-colored rose.

"Z-Zayn?" I stammered. "Have you seen th—"

An earsplitting scream sliced through the air, loud enough to make me clap my hands against my ears and shrill enough to cause a long, splintering crack to appear in the nearest stained-glass window panel.

"I DON'T CARE HOW MANY KINGS' TABLES YOU'VE SAT AT – KIBBITZ ME *ONE MORE TIME* ABOUT MY BRISKET BEING TOO SALTY AND I'LL *SHOW* YOU WHAT SALTY LOOKS LIKE!"

"DON'T YOU TAKE THAT INSOLENT TONE OF VOICE WITH ME!" another, equally-strident voice pierced the air, echoing against the castle walls and bringing me to my knees. "I'M FOUR TIMES YOUR AGE, WHICH MAKES ME AT LEAST FOUR TIMES SMARTER THAN YOU!"

Another crack formed in the stained glass – this one traveling all the way up and through the stone that encased it. Zayn was at the top of the dais in three strides, dropping beside me with his own hands clamped over his ears. "They're going to bring down the castle!"

"SMART?! MORE LIKE SENILE! I THINK YOU'VE FINALLY GONE SOFT IN THAT BIRD-BRAINED HEAD OF YOURS!"

"I'LL HAVE YOU KNOW MY 'BIRD-BRAIN' IS THRICE THE SIZE OF YOURS!"

The doors to the dining hall swung open, crashing into the stone walls behind them, and two women stormed out – one aggressively stirring the contents of the bowl she was clutching against her chest, while the other one hovered several feet in the air, her wings beating as briskly as the spoon my mom was wielding.

"OH YEAH? THEN EXPLAIN TO ME WHY—Oh, hi Tally!" My mother waved her ladle at me, sending a glob of purple Hollandaise sauce sailing at the other creature's cheek.

After flinging the goop off her face, the harpy swiveled her head 180 degrees, her talons landing beside my mother's slippered feet with a soft click. "Hello again, little plum! We didn't expect you back so soon!"

"*Xianis?*" I gasped. "What the hell are you doing here?"

"So, you *have* met!" Mom rolled her eyes. "Why didn't you tell me you ran into this *chalerya* out there? If you'd've called me like you promised, I might have been spared *four hours* of nonstop heartburn!"

Xianis shot her an aggrieved scowl. "What have I told you about taking that tone with me, devil woman? I carried your beloved husband in my womb for months, suckling him with this very teat!" She jiggled a bare, dangling breast in my mother's direction. "And *this* is how you talk to me?"

"Stop waving that wrinkly old boob in my face and go do something useful!"

"*Do something useful?* With you hovering over me like a storm cloud? What 'useful' thing could I possibly do that wouldn't result in your incessant carping? Honestly, Diedre! WHO RE-SCOURS A POT MOMENTS AFTER IT'S ALREADY BEEN WASHED?!"

Zayn let out a pained gasp as another crack appeared in the glass.

"WHO WASHES A POT IN COLD, DIRTY WATER THAT'S BEEN SITTING IN THE SINK FOR HOURS?" My mother shot back. "MAYBE IF YOU HADN'T BEEN RAISED IN A FILTHY *SWAMP,* YOU MIGHT'VE LEARNED A THING OR TWO ABOUT BASIC HYGIENE!"

"Hey!" I shouted at the two of them, still clutching my ears.

The cellar door banged open and Boris and about twenty other tommyknockers burst through. "Oh dear," he lamented, seeing the cracking stone. "It looks like this wall will need more fortifications. Tally ho, knockers!" He gestured for the others to follow him to the wall, where they immediately set about banging mallets and jamming pickaxes into the crumbling rock. "Put your backs into it now, or the entire structure might collapse!"

"FOR YOUR INFORMATION, SWAMPS – *LIKE SINKS* – CONTAIN A VERITABLE HOST OF SALUBRIOUS BACTERIA THAT ARE VITAL FOR PROMOTING HEALTHY GIZZARDS!"

"Hey!" I tried again, my voice completely drowned out by Lucy and Ricky, who burst through the kitchen doors at that very moment, barking at the top of their lungs. Biscuit and Mavros waddled in just behind them, kicking their beaks back and howling like hellhounds as they stalwartly defended their maltreated *bubbe*. Meanwhile, a line of a dozen bare-breasted harpies had appeared on the upper balcony as the ad hoc peanut gallery, contributing to the cacophony with a series of offensive squawks directed at my mother.

"WELL IN THAT CASE, LET'S ALL JUST GO OUT AND BATHE OURSELVES IN MUCK!"

"MAYBE IF YOU'D EXPOSE YOURSELF TO A LITTLE 'MUCK' INSTEAD OF WORSHIPING THOSE FOUL-SMELLING CHEMICALS, YOU WOULDN'T BE SO PINCH-FACED AND CONSTIPATED ALL THE TIME!"

My mom's face abruptly turned the color of an *asgera* mushroom as she whirled on her mother-in-law, clutching her ladle like a sharpened dagger. "WHAT DID YOU SAY TO ME?"

"I SAID—"

"WOULD BOTH OF YOU SHUT UP!" I screeched at the top of my lungs.

The cracking pane of stained glass abruptly exploded into a thousand pieces, sending the tommyknockers into a fit of aggrieved titters.

Zayn's head snapped in my direction, his entire body tensing.

Though the scream fest in front of me had come to a swift and immediate halt, behind me, the tommyknockers had redoubled their castle-fortifying efforts, with the resulting stream of *bangs*, *clanks,* and *whacks* steadily gnawing on my last nerve. Doing my best to ignore them, I stomped straight up to my mother and grandmother, backpaddling a half step when

Mom shifted her glowing, red-eyed vamshee glare from Xianis to me.

"Talia!" she snapped, planting a hand on her aproned hip. "Don't you *dare* cop an attitude with me, not after—" Upon seeing my face up close, whatever diatribe had been forming on her tongue abruptly evaporated. She hurriedly closed the gap between us, frowning at me with what appeared to be genuine concern. "*Bubaleh,* you look…terrible." When I didn't immediately offer up some snarky retort, she bit her lip, giving me a glimpse of her new, unnervingly-sharp canines. "You know what, I'm not actually mad at you for not calling, Tally… I-I'm sure you were just really busy out there."

At that, I took *two* steps backward; either my mom was on drugs, or I looked *way* worse than I'd imagined.

Xianis ruffled her feathers in impatience.

I gaped at her. "Seriously, what the hell are you doing here?"

She waved a condescending wing in the air, as though I should have already figured it out. "I may disapprove of your bedmate, your general life choices, and the vulgar, hysterical banshee that fledged you—"

My mom let out a threatening growl.

"—but a harpy does not abandon her progeny in her greatest time of need!"

"HA!" Mom snorted. "*A harpy does not abandon*—DO YOU EVEN HEAR YOURSELF TALK?"

"WHEN YOU ARE AROUND, *NOBODY* CAN HEAR THEMSELVES TALK!" Xianis shot back, once more setting off a jeering audience of birds and Chihuahuas.

My hands again flew to my ears. Between their nails-on-chalkboard screeching and the five-alarm accompaniment of squawks, barks, and the stone-smashing racket the knockers were making – not to mention the throbbing migraine I had developed as of five minutes ago – I literally wanted to claw my eardrums out.

Grinding my teeth, I squeezed my eyes shut to try to drown out the pandemonium. But I could feel my last thread of self-control fraying, the edges of my vision darkening to crimson, and the brittle shards of fury that were scraping against the inside of my ribs, threatening to—

"ENOUGH!" Zayn roared, snapping me from my trance.

In the beat of heavenly silence that ensued, I sucked down a deep breath, working to loosen my chest and clear my vision.

Meanwhile, every banshee, harpy, and braying familiar had jerked their head in his direction, though the tommyknockers continued with their incessant hammering, oblivious to the danger – i.e., me – that had been brewing just a few yards away from them. The door to the kitchen creaked open as Korinne and Lamswyth timidly peeked their heads out. She offered me a weak wave when our eyes met, while more and more elves appeared at the balcony and atop the twin staircases to peer down at us. Judging by their traumatized expressions, the horrific scream-fest had been going on for some time.

Zayn came and stood beside me, his hands clenched into white-knuckled fists.

"Why are you yelling?" my mother demanded.

Xianis rolled her eyes. "Incubi can be so melodramatic."

"Talia. Is. Dying," Zayn spat through gritted teeth, eliciting a series of gasps around the room. Even the tommyknockers stopped what they were doing to stare at him.

My mom's ladle clattered to her bowl. "Dying?"

"What do you mean, *dying?*" Xianis demanded.

I stumbled backward as they zeroed in on me like two lionesses stalking the same rabbit. Zayn positioned himself between us – an action that made both women's nostrils flare and their eyes narrow into predatory slits.

"Talia, get out of here," he muttered to me over his shoulder. "I'll fill them in on everything – Mikhæl included."

"But you shouldn't have to do that alone—"

"*Talia,*" he growled, turning around to face me head-on. To my surprise, the veins beneath his eyes were pulsing with fury – as well as genuine fear.

Swallowing tightly, I regarded my own face in the glassy reflection of his pitch-black irises. Gone was the golden luster from my skin; instead, a drawn, colorless face stared back at me, nearly as pale as a banshee's. I raised my fingers to the dark circles stamped beneath my eyes, my breath catching in my throat when the strange reflection did the very same.

"You won't be able to maintain control around these two – not while they're acting like this," Zayn continued, working to keep his voice steady. "Go get some fresh air. I'll take care of this mess, then have Biscuit find you when the time comes to discuss our next steps…okay?"

Guilt cleaved through me at the thought of leaving him to share the bad news – namely, that we'd failed in our mission, and would most likely die fighting an unwinnable fight before the end of the week.

But in that moment, all I could do was nod. "Y-You're right. I'll…I'll go try to calm down."

"Just don't wander too far, okay?" he murmured softly.

I nodded again, turning to go.

"Tal?"

I slowly turned back around to find Zayn looking at me with glassy eyes.

"I love you."

A lump the size of a tennis ball appeared in my throat. "I love you too."

Stealing one last glance at Xianis and my mother, who were both gawking at me with wide-eyed, barely-contained hysteria,

I quickly strode to the foyer, snatched my shoes without putting them on, and shoved the front doors open.

The second they swung shut behind me, chaos erupted inside the castle – loud enough for me to clearly hear my mother and Xianis through the heavy stones and enchantments that separated me from them. As I jogged down the many stone steps, putting as much space between me and my loved ones as I could, I had to wonder if it was enough to protect them from myself.

As if in answer, the rune embedded in my shoulder throbbed tauntingly.

I ambled downhill for a long time, lost to the turmoil of my own thoughts.

After some hazy, indeterminate amount of time, my knees began to shake and my thighs were burning from the exertion, but I didn't slow down. It was a welcome pain, one that distracted me from the throb in my head, the nausea in my stomach, and the ever-growing ache in my shoulder. When my chest started to burn sometime later, panic jolted through me like an electrical shock; I let out a wheezing sigh of relief when I realized it was just the beginnings of an asthma attack, not Sol.

Sucking down two deep breaths from my inhaler, I glanced above me, surprised to find the Summer Palace looming hundreds of feet above my head. By then, the sun had all but disappeared beneath the jagged black line of mountains stretching out behind the castle, casting the sky in bands of teal, gold, and green. In its place, the smallest of the four moons had just appeared above the horizon, making the Lunar Rune on my arm flicker faintly.

And yet this side of the mountain was as bright as day.

Less than a mile to the east, the Great Phoenix Tree towered hundreds of feet above the surrounding forest, a beacon of hope and life that seemed to touch the sky itself. Ribbons of glittering light swirled around its glowing leaves and branches, illuminating the entire mountainside – including the sprawling evergreen forest to the east and the groves of cotton-candy-pink trees to the south. I found myself being drawn to the breathtaking sight like a moth to a flame; ignoring the protests of my rapidly-weakening body, I followed the sound of rushing water to a nearby waterfall, which cascaded into a large lake several dozen stories below. A narrow footpath zigzagged alongside the waterfall, eventually depositing me at the bottom of the mountainside, where the forest of pink trees came right up to the edge of a glass-smooth, shimmering blue lake.

No, not a lake, I realized. Though it swelled into a wide pool here, beneath the waterfall, the waters continued on, narrowing into a river that disappeared into the pink forest.

I glanced up at the Summer Palace – now the size of a toy castle – tugging my cloak around my goosepricked arms. Part of me knew it was time to go back – that Zayn had asked me to stay close, and I'd already wandered well past the confines of "close." But the magnificence of the Great Phoenix Tree was calling to me, suffusing me with an overwhelming sense of longing that made my feet move of their own accord. As I ventured into the forest, the trees' magenta leaves blotted out the evening sky, while their snow-white bark faintly glowed from the inside out. In fact, pretty much everything in this part of the forest glowed. Bright blue and purple fireflies hovered in the air, and bioluminescent moss cushioned my feet as they made their way forward, spurred by a mounting, gnawing feeling that I couldn't place or name.

A soft rustle sounded behind me, and I whirled around with a gasp. Fifty feet away, a dozen silver unicorns quietly appeared from between the trees, approaching the shimmering lake to dip their muzzles for a drink. My breath caught at the sight, and for one brief moment, the weight that had long been crushing my chest was lifted, leaving hope and tranquility in its place.

I watched them, rooted to my spot, memorizing every last detail of the magical scene: the way their coats gleamed like liquid silver against the light of the Great Phoenix Tree; how their spiraling horns were somehow both translucent and iridescent, reminding me of polished diamonds; the graceful way they shook out their platinum manes, which sparkled in the moonlight… Once they'd finished drinking, several in the herd turned their heads in my direction, inclining their muzzles in such a way that I had to wonder if it was in greeting. Not wanting to be rude, I nodded back, hand pressed to my heart as they made their way back into the forest.

When the last pearlescent tail once more disappeared between the trees, my shoulder throbbed painfully, reminding me of the time – and the Unseelie army marching this way. But whatever was pulling me forward had only paused long enough to let me catch my breath, redoubling in strength once the unicorns had come and gone.

I continued onward.

Peeking through the interlacing branches of the canopy, the Great Phoenix Tree rose higher and higher, until I couldn't see the top of it no matter how far back I craned my neck. The pain in my shoulder was steadily getting worse, while exhaustion seemed to creep deeper and deeper, leaching all the way into my bones. But my feet kept going, spurred by more and more invisible vines that both ensnared and tugged me forward with increasing persistence.

Eventually, I stumbled all the way to the edge of the pink forest, my breath catching at the magnificent sight before me. The Great Phoenix Tree stood alone in the middle of a large clearing, the surrounding trees forming a wide, almost reverent ring around it. Its swirling ribbons of magic illuminated the entire area as though it were midday, and the air itself twinkled with millions of tiny white orbs that gently swayed with the breeze.

I kept walking until I was directly beneath the tree's "lowest" branches, which extended a hundred feet above my head. But even from this distance, I could see the magic that swirled inside every individual, umbrella-sized leaf. The tree's roots, too, which spread a hundred feet in every direction, suffused the ground itself with pulsing light – as though the tree were nourishing the earth, and not the other way around. Multicolored mushrooms and toadstools sprouted all along the expansive root system, burning as bright as bulbs. As I made my way forward, I carefully stepped around them – both for their sake, and mine. Before I knew it, the base of the tree trunk was less than ten steps away. The pull of its magic was so strong now, I couldn't have turned back even if I tried.

And so, I surrendered to it – wholly and without restraint.

Five steps…

I stretched my hand out in front of me, surprised to find it was glowing as brightly as the tree itself.

Two steps…

My gold fingertips buzzed like a live wire as they stretched out to meet the trunk, where veins of magic trickled through the cracks and ridges of the bark like sand flowing down a stream. The moment my fingers pressed against it, the runes embedded in my skin erupted like neon signs, stealing the breath from my lungs.

Talia.

I glanced over my shoulder, searching for the source of the voice…and found no one.

When I turned back around, the bark of the tree was glowing so brightly, I had to squint against the blinding light. It spread up my hand, coursing through my arm and completely enveloping the runes on my skin. Within seconds, the light had become so intense, the rest of the forest was completely bleached away. Just when I thought it couldn't get any brighter, the bark beneath my palm fell away, revealing the purest, whitest light I'd ever seen. Coruscating and infinite, it called to the magic of my veins, inviting me in.

Without thought, my body responded in kind, and I stepped through the portal.

XIX.
THE THIRD REALM

Dazzling, endless white light stretched as far my eyes could see, in every direction, engulfing the entire world. It was so powerful, so infinite, I couldn't tell where my body ended and the light began. I was adrift in an endless sea, except it didn't feel like I was being carried away. It was as if I were part of the ocean itself – a current, rather than a piece of driftwood. I floated in those tranquil depths for what may have been seconds or hours, my troubles and pain completely forgotten.

And then, slowly, details began to emerge.

The light didn't dim, not even a little, but the trunk of the Great Phoenix Tree gradually rematerialized, magic blazing through every ridge and divot of its bark. The forest floor reappeared as well, its upturned roots, multicolored moss, and clusters of mushrooms glowing even brighter and more vividly than before. My feet once more pressed against solid earth – though "solid" might be a bit of a misnomer. I stared at my boots for a long minute, waiting for my brain to catch up with my vision. I could almost see the ground beneath my feet – both of which appeared to be more light than matter. In fact, my entire body was shaped from warm, golden light, through which I was fairly certain a solid object would be able to pass without hindrance. I held my hands in front of my face, slowly turning them over; they, too, were vaguely transparent.

Curious, I knelt to the ground to see if I could pick up a small twig, which shone just as brightly as everything else in this place. Not only could I pick it up, but I could almost *feel* it – not just the sensation of it resting between my fingers, but the gentle pulse of energy it exuded. No more or less than me, this twig…*lived.* Gently setting it back down to its spot, I stood up to inspect the rest of me. My cloak, shirt, and pants still looked the same, albeit transparent and shimmery.

But when my eyes fell on my left shoulder, my throat tightened.

There was no light there, only blackness – so dark, it stole the light from the surrounding skin. Ink-black veins splintered from Sol's claim, running halfway down my arm and across the left side of my chest. Pulling the collar of my shirt away from my neck, I peered beneath the thin fabric. There, visible as a faint crimson pulse beneath my translucent skin, was the weak flutter of my own heart, half-shrouded in shadow.

For the first time since entering the portal, fear knotted in my chest.

A soft rustle behind me made me whirl around, hand still pressed to my failing heart. A doe stepped lightly past me, its coat gleaming brightly in the light – or rather, as part of it. The deer, the twig, the ground, myself – we were all beings of light and energy in this otherworldly place, as pure as the magic that hummed beneath the bark of the Great Phoenix Tree.

The deer turned to glance over her shoulder, where the trees burned as brightly as a line of torches. Though I was fairly certain the forest had been bereft of movement moments before, white-robed figures now moved silently and gracefully among the trees. I cautiously moved toward them, my hand resting on the hilt of my gold dagger. As I drew closer, more and more figures appeared, though none of them seemed to notice me. It wasn't until I was less than ten paces from the edge of the forest that I recognized what they were.

Elves.

Dozens and dozens of them, they sat beneath the trees, quietly reading, or walking in pairs, their heads pressed close as they spoke softly to one another. Some of the younger elves were sitting up in the trees, reaching for the glowing red fruit that grew from them, while a group of children who looked no older than seven or eight spun in a circle, laughing. I edged closer, my hand dropping from my dagger and back to my side. The auras that surrounded each of the elves blazed like fire: violet, crimson, cerulean, tangerine, and a dozen more I couldn't name. They all represented every color of the fae rainbow, with one exception.

Even here, I was the only one who glowed with gold light.

It wasn't until I had walked right up to them that any of the elves appeared to notice me – and even then, their gaze seemed to slip right past me, as though trying to decide if I were real or not.

What is this place?

The pain and exhaustion that had been plaguing me all but gone, I made my way farther and farther into the forest, passing elves of every age, size, and color as I walked. The children, in particular, nodded and grinned at me, and one even tossed me a ruby-red fruit from the branch he was dangling his legs from. I bit into it, my eyes widening in surprise; it was the sweetest, most delicious thing I'd ever tasted.

After some time – minutes or hours, I still couldn't be sure – I eventually found my way back to the lake. The herd of unicorns had returned, their coats glowing so radiantly, I had to shield my eyes from the light. This time, they weren't alone. A small cluster of mermaids was treading water near the edge of the lake, their scaled hands reaching up from the shimmering water to stroke their silver manes. My entire body stiffened when they began to sing to them in soft, low voices, but the unicorns just nickered contentedly, enjoying the heavenly lullaby.

My swelling heart lodged itself in my chest. This place was one of love and serenity – a far cry from the feral, dangerous wilds of the rest of the Fae Realm. Which reminded me… I glanced up the side of the mountain, a cry rising and sticking in my throat.

The Summer Palace was gone.

Not out of sight or obscured, but *gone*. What's more, the evening sky had turned to day – not the typical daytime green of the Fae Realm, but a multicolored, iridescent sky, which swirled and shifted like the surface of a bubble. The sun, a dazzling silver sphere, rose high above fluffy white clouds, striping the sky in bands of prismatic color.

My throat tightened at the sight. I was so awestruck, I almost failed to notice the pair of white-robed figures that had appeared several yards to my right. They weren't looking at me, but at their surroundings, their expressions as awestruck as mine. I frowned. Unlike the other elves I'd seen, these elves looked familiar. As I watched them head into the forest, the back of my neck began to prickle as though a spider were crawling down my spine.

Slowly, I turned around, where the air behind me was shimmering. I squinted my eyes to peer through it, but it was like trying to see through a thick wall of ice. Flames rose up from somewhere far away, while small, faintly-glowing silhouettes moved sluggishly, as though trudging through molasses. Every so often, one of the figures would ignite, briefly burning as bright as a torch, then vanish; every time they did, another white-shrouded elf appeared beside the lake. But while some figures blazed like fire right before disappearing, others burned as black as the mark on my shoulder. When those faded from existence, they didn't reappear again – on either side of the veil.

As two more silhouettes flared out of existence, a pair of elves simultaneously appeared a few yards away from me: a middle-aged woman and a young man. They looked around, confusion, and then relief, quickly washing over their faces.

Gasping, I cried out, "Laleh! Éyrel!"

Neither of them appeared to notice me.

"Laleh!" I shouted again. "Éyrel!"

Wincing at the sound of my own voice, so harsh and forceful in such a tranquil place, I jogged over to them. Like the other elves, they were wearing simple white tunics, and their glowing feet were bare. A honey-colored aura surrounded Laleh's entire body, feathering against the seafoam-green halo that belonged to Éyrel.

"Do either of you know what this place is?" I asked, breathless.

The two of them stopped, their eyes rounding with recognition and surprise.

"My queen!" Laleh gasped, rushing forward to scoop me in a tight hug that didn't hurt. Her body felt wispy, almost insubstantial – more light than matter. "I'm both overjoyed and saddened to see you here."

"Here?" I repeated feebly, tears filling my eyes – as though my heart had understood what my mind had yet to grasp. "Where is here?"

She opened her mouth to answer, then stopped, her wide eyes roving over my body – my boots, my leggings, my weapons – and finally resting on the dark blight that was spreading from my shoulder, stealing the light from the rest of my body. "You..." she started, then swallowed. "You're..."

"Not supposed to be here," Éyrel chimed in, cocking his head. "But then, how is she here?"

"I know that gold blood unlocks all magic," Laleh frowned, "but I had no idea it could do *this*." When her eyes once more fell to the blackness of my shoulder, her frown deepened. "Perhaps it is because you were already straddling both realms, due to your growing sickness."

Straddling both...?

"Oh my God." I took a step backward, my hands floating to my mouth. Tears spilled from my eyes and down my cheeks as I regarded the two of them with eyes that finally saw. "You're... You're both...dead?"

Laleh nodded. "It would appear so."

"But don't worry," Éyrel grinned. "It didn't even hurt!"

A rising wave of panic was squeezing the last of the air from my lungs. "How..." I tried to wet my lips, but my mouth had gone completely dry. "H-How long have I been gone?"

"We searched for you for two days before Sol's army arrived," Laleh answered sadly.

Her words were like a sucker punch to the gut. "Zayn?" My hands were shaking so badly I had to fold my arms across my chest to steady them. "My mom? Korinne?"

"Still alive...but perhaps not for long."

Terror and guilt seized me by the heart. "Laleh, I—"

"Do not waste a single moment worrying about us," she smiled. "We are at peace."

"But I—"

"Go," she urged gently.

"Yeah, go kick some demon ass, Your Highness!" Éyrel's smile was a wide one. "And tell my dad I said hi, okay? And that I'm going to be just fine."

I nodded wordlessly, tears still pouring down my cheeks.

"Anak'tha al'preyámi, Paşahdî'mtha," Laleh said, inclining her head.

"May your harvest be bountiful as well," I managed to whisper.

After casting me one last reassuring smile, they joined the other elves that had passed through the veil, their hands outstretched and auras glowing brightly as they made their way toward the Great Phoenix Tree.

Without pausing for breath, I spun on my heels and ran as fast as I could, willing my feet to fly. I ran as though I were in a dream, effortlessly and untethered. My surroundings passed as a shimmering blur; I blew past unicorns and pink trees and elves, barely giving any of them a second glance as I seamlessly wove my way through the trees.

What felt like eons later, I burst into the clearing where the Great Phoenix Tree towered hundreds of feet into the silver sky, every leaf bathed in radiant light. Breathless and choking back tears, I approached the base of the tree, my trembling hands outstretched. The ache in my shoulder had returned, throbbing in time with my thrumming heart.

Whispering a silent prayer, I pressed my palms against the bark. Warmth immediately filled my chest, wrapping me in comfort, and a gentle voice filled my ears.

"Daughter of gold blood, who walks betwixt the three realms as the ancients once did...what is it you beseech of me?"

"I have to go back to the Fae Realm!" I choked out. "My friends need me, and I have no idea how to get back to them!"

"You've not long for that realm, my child. It is why your soul was called to this divine place, which has been made brighter by your beautiful golden light. Should you return to the realm of the living, you will find only suffering and pain waiting for you."

"Please, I'm begging you to let me go back! I-I'll do anything you ask of me – anything!"

"You misunderstand, dear one. The tether that binds your soul to your body is frayed beyond repair... And there is something else you must know, though I fear it will bring you great pain to heed."

"Tell me…please."

A sigh whispered against my ears like a gentle wind. *"The magic that flows through your veins is as pure and potent as that which infuses my own sap. But the blight you bear, were it to spread farther, would tarnish the purity of your soul – perhaps irreparably so."*

My eyes traveled to the darkness unfurling through my body, partially eclipsing the faint glow of my weakly-beating heart.

"This is what you must understand, dear one – if you were to return to the living realm, I fear your soul would be too dim to find its way back to the light."

"Where would I go?" I whispered. "If I couldn't find my way back here?"

The voice was quiet for a long moment. *"A place of infinite darkness, where there is neither light nor hope."*

Blinking away the tears that had flooded my vision, I stole a glance over my shoulder at the beauty and tranquility behind me. A group of elves had gathered at the edge of the clearing, beckoning me toward them.

"Do you understand what I have told you, my child?"

Turning back to the Great Phoenix Tree, I pressed my forehead against her bark, nodding. "I understand. And I ask you once more…please help me return to the people I love."

The voice was quiet for a long moment, considering my request. When it spoke again, it was tinged in sadness. *"Though it pains me to consign further suffering unto you...you have my blessing, Talia, child of golden light. You may once more pass between the veil."*

"Thank you," I whispered fervently, squeezing my eyes against the blinding light that erupted in front of my vision, once more bleaching the world into infinite white.

"Blessings be upon you, my child... Light willing, I shall see you again soon."

XX.
Suppressive Fire

Darkness and coldness and pain exploded all at once.

Agony, the likes of which I'd never experienced before, burned a hole deep in my shoulder, ricocheting all the way down to my fingertips. Gasping, I staggered to my feet, using the nearest upturned root for support. Multiple fires were blazing somewhere in the distance, casting the surrounding forest in ominous crimson stripes. Heavy black smoke billowed from the tops of the trees, blotting out the light of the moons. Shrill, haunting screams shattered from every direction, drowning out all other sound. My heart thudded to a stop. These were not cries of war, but cries of death.

Banshees.

Saoirse's last words slithered between my ears, turning my insides to slush: *When the collective scream of the banshees rises above the cries of the battlefield, the war will soon be over. Pray it comes at dawn, not dusk.*

"No," I whispered, my eyes darting to the pitch-black sky, which was nowhere close to dawn. "No, it's not the end – it can't be the end yet!"

Snatching a Sharpie from my belt, I hastily drew a Resurgence Rune on the back of my hand, which flickered to life before being absorbed into my skin. Then, swallowing back the residual pain, I launched into a full-blown run, the balls of my feet propelling me faster than I'd ever run before. The farther I moved from the Great Phoenix Tree, the weaker I felt, but the Resurgence Rune lent me just enough strength to keep me going. I burst through the trees ten minutes later, my lungs burning almost as fiercely as my shoulder.

What I saw in that clearing would be engraved into my mind for the rest of my life – the end of which, I knew in my heart, was drawing near.

All of the trees on the north side of the lake had been razed to the ground, their gorgeous pink foliage reduced to nothing but smoldering ash. The remaining trees were either burning or at risk of being caught in nearby flames, which lashed from the scorched earth like forked tongues. A dozen bodies were strewn about the fires, so charred and mangled I couldn't tell who – or what – they were.

Nothing else in the clearing moved or stirred.

A screech sounded from above. My head jerked up to find dozens of huge eagles tangled in a midair skirmish with nearly twice as many winged demons. The shrill cry had come from a snow-white eagle, whose talons were entwined with the scythe-like claws of a screaming striga. Trapped in a fierce death spiral, the two of them corkscrewed wildly to the earth, only for the harpy to shove away from the demon seconds before impact.

The striga slammed into the ground with an anguished scream that was abruptly cut short.

Fiery meteors rained down from the night sky, cast by the inky silhouettes of what appeared to be ten-foot reptiles with spiny tails. The white harpy let out another shriek as one of their fireballs hit her square in the back. She landed in a burning heap less than ten feet away from the edge of the lake – the waters of which were no longer glass-smooth and glowing, but red-tinged and murky. I charged toward her, mentally readying a Resurgence Rune in my mind as she melted back into her half-human form. Kneeling beside her, I recognized the woman immediately – the stooped, white-haired sentry that had wordlessly accompanied Xianis during our walk in the marsh. Her eyes were closed, and her chest was still.

I was too late.

I spun around on one knee as a splintering *crack* came from my right, where a twelve-foot-tall fachan was careening through the burning trees, swinging his spiked club high above his head as he chased down a pair of elves. My hand instinctively shot out and glowing yellow ropes exploded from my palm. Ensnared by its one massive foot, the fachan came crashing to the ground like a fallen tree, screeching bloody murder – until its face landed in a smoldering pile of coals that burst to life upon impact. Within seconds, the fachan's body had ignited into a roaring bonfire, one of many that illuminated the makeshift graveyard.

I pressed a fist to my mouth, holding back the wave of nausea that rose in my throat.

"Talia Paşahdî?" one of the elves – a middle-aged woman with graying hair – gasped upon seeing me. "You're alive?"

"The jury's still out on that," I muttered before clearing my throat. "Where are Zayn and the others?"

The second elf, a young man who reminded me so much of Éyrel, my stomach knotted, pointed through the trees. "We are holding our ground, *Talia Paşahdî*, but their Runemaster is readying another wave of incarnates."

He cast me a grateful – albeit worried – look as I pulled out my Sharpie and quickly drew a Shield Rune on his arm, brushed it with a drop of blood from my thumb, and then did the same for his companion. My shoulder screamed with pain, but I ignored it.

"Go help the others, if you have the strength," I grunted, kneeling to the ground to draw an Extinguishing Rune in the smoking dirt with my finger that quickly snuffed out the nearest fires. "But don't tell anyone you saw me," I added.

Puzzled, but far too disciplined to argue, the elves nodded their assent before spinning around and running back the way they and the fachan had come. Casting one more glance at the fallen monster – now nothing more than a smoking carcass – I zigzagged through the burning trees, skidding to a stop when the actual battlefield came into view a few hundred yards later. After ducking behind one of the few trees that wasn't burning, I carefully peered around its wide trunk to get a look. The two elves I'd helped had already sprung back into battle, slashing and burning any demon they came across with a skillful mix of daggers and burning arrows. Dozens of vampires lay scattered across the blackened ground, while several hundred more were hungrily attacking the unshakable army of elves, whose Shield Runes glimmered weakly against the darkness. At a quick glance, there seemed to be at least two vampires for every elf – plus a legion of monstrous, insect-like creatures that scurried around the battlefield searching for prey.

Blood incarnates, I realized with a bone-deep shudder. *Which means Sol must be close.*

Indeed, perched atop a steep hill, far away and above the bloodshed, a black-clad figure stood above the battle, clutching a book to his chest. His face was bone-white, a sharp contrast to his dark beard, which faded into silver sideburns and a wind-swept crop of disheveled platinum hair. The vial of gold blood he wore around his neck glinted against the light of the fires burning below. Even from this distance, his wild eyes and wide grin were evident as he took in the carnage he'd wrought. A cloaked figure stood to his left – his resurrected Death Mage, Calus, I assumed – while Sol's last surviving son, Soren, stood at his right. Hundreds of unnaturally beautiful incubi and succubi stood behind them, their arms crossed and expressions vaguely bored as they regarded the gory scene unfolding below with eyes that glowed the color of blood. The faint, telltale trace of a forcefield surrounded them all, marking them for the cowards they were. That they couldn't be bothered to get their own perfectly-manicured hands dirty, but were more than happy to send in a legion of half-starved vampires, Manipulated demons, and soulless blood incarnates to fight – and die – in their place made the edges of my vision turn red.

But, oh God, that wasn't even the worst of it.

As I crept closer along the line of trees, squinting to make out the details, I suddenly realized that the ring of figures encircling the top of the hill weren't incubi or succubi, but *humans* – glamoured humans, likely kidnapped from one of Sol's many nightclubs, that were being used not only as snacks, but as a literal human shield.

Fury rose in my chest – tamped only by the heat that flared against my back as another barrage of fireballs exploded near the lake. Fists clenched and shaking, I muttered a prayer beneath my breath, praying the unicorns had somehow escaped the carnage. The thought of anything happening to those pure, beautiful creatures made the shards of rage forming in my chest rub together like brittle glass.

Breathe, I reminded myself. *Focus on something soothing – like the other realm.*

But even that brought a lump of panic to my throat.

I cast an anxious glance over my shoulder. If the Great Phoenix Tree burned with the rest of the forest, what would happen to all of the souls dwelling inside of it? Would they be lost as well?

"Not if I can help it," I whispered. Kneeling to the ground, I used my index finger to draw another Extinguishing Rune in the warm dirt, Endowing it with magic while I considered my next move; all the fires blazing within a hundred-foot radius abruptly vanished, though several of the trees on the far side of the lake still burned.

Think, Talia... I sighed, knuckling my aching forehead.

Every spell I cast felt as though it were robbing me of more energy – which, in this case, was surprisingly beneficial. Exhaustion chipped away at anger and my heart rate had slowed significantly, even as I glared at Sol, his army of spineless prisses, and the hundred or so humans they had taken as hostages. As far as I could tell, Sol didn't know I was here – no one did. But if my mounting emotions tipped him off, he'd use his claim to lure me straight to him. Underscoring that fear, a recent conversation with Zayn echoed in my mind.

"Your magic was awakened a week ago – meaning you've barely scratched the surface of your skills," he'd remarked. *"If you could somehow let go of your doubts and your fears, you would be a true force to be reckoned with. That's why Sol hasn't killed you yet, despite his threats."*

"Yeah, well...he's got my blood now, so—"

"It's one thing to use your blood to amplify magic; but if he could find a way to harness your raw strength, he would be unstoppable...just like you."

"Zayn," I whispered, my eyes raking across the battlefield. With all that was happening, it took a long moment before I was able to spot him.

But there – less than fifty feet away – a throng of vampires had converged on a single figure whose coal-black eyes burned as darkly as theirs. Loosing a primal roar that chilled me to my marrow, Zayn's fiery scimitar sliced through three demon throats in one savage motion. The vampires crumpled to the ground, where they remained in a burning, unmoving heap. Black liquid dripped from the end of the curved blade, joining the pool of blood that had accumulated at Zayn's feet.

Guilt was cleaving my chest in two. *We searched for you for two days before Sol's army arrived.*

A vampire appeared behind him, lunging at his back.

I opened my mouth to scream a warning at the same moment Biscuit soared over the battlefield like a true phoenix, blasting a technicolor ball of fire at the vampire, utterly wasting it. Without exchanging a single word, the two of them seamlessly moved into a tandem formation: bare arms covered in sweat and blood, Zayn once again slashed his blade through the neck of the nearest vampire, this time sending its severed head rolling across the ground, while Biscuit set the vampire's body aflame, reducing the rest of it to smoldering ash.

Slice, burn, kill; the two of them repeated the same moves again and again, fighting to reach the top of the hill, where Sol was lazily controlling his bloodthirsty slaves with Zayn's stolen grimoire.

But every time Zayn took a step forward, one of Sol's demons pulled him two steps back.

I have to help him...but how?

"WHY EVERYONE KEEP SCREAMING AND SCREAMING?!"

I jerked my head up just in time to see a massive creature lumbering out of the burning forest, his hands pressed to his ears. At least three times my height, the troll's tattered loincloth, stringy, moss-colored hair, and oatmeal-like complexion identified him as the castle squatter Zayn had made me chase away with an Amplified bell last week.

"Grog?!" I hissed, rubbing my eyes in disbelief.

"BE QUIET!" he bellowed at the crowd as he charged into the clearing, swinging his tree-trunk-sized arms at any creature – in this case, a screeching cluster of strigas – unlucky enough to be in his path. "GROG TRYING SLEEP!"

I jumped as something pressed against the small of my back. Whirling around, I discovered a lone wolf standing behind me, her lustrous black coat glinting as though dusted with gold.

"Mavros!" I whisper-cried, falling to one knee to wrap my arms around her. When I pulled away from her a moment later, her green eyes were brimming with emotion.

You live! She made a little hop on her front legs, her tail wagging. *We have to tell—*

"No!" I shook my head fiercely. "You can't tell anyone – not even Biscuit."

But—

I cupped her furry face in two hands. "Listen to me, Mav…I'm dying." My voice cracked on the last word, but I forced the emotion back down, squeezing my eyes shut to steady myself. "I'm dying…okay? And if Zayn finds out I'm here, he'll try to protect me, probably getting himself killed in the process. But *he's* this realm's last and only chance at peace – not me. If I can get Zayn to the top of that hill without letting him or Sol know I'm here, we might actually have a chance at winning this—*augh!*" I clutched my elbow, biting back a cry as a fresh stab of pain jolted through my arm.

Mavros bared her teeth and let out a low growl.

Uncapping my Sharpie, I hastily scrawled yet another Resurgence Rune on my body, which provided nothing more than a revitalizing tingle. "Besides," I continued, working to keep my expression smooth, "if Zayn can kill Sol, this claim might not be the end of me after all." Judging by Mavros's ensuing whimper, the reassuring smile I'd forced onto my face probably looked more like an agonized grimace. "What do you say, girl…will you help me?"

She glanced between me and Zayn, then let out a resigned huff. A rune popped into my mind, tinged in disapproval and doubt.

"You're brilliant," I marveled, scrawling the symbol on the inside of my wrist. "This will prevent Biscuit from sensing me?"

She nodded sullenly.

"Thank you," I whispered, drawing her in for one last hug. "Now, we just have to break through that forcefield…and take down a few demons along the way."

After quickly taking stock of my non-magical weapons – a switchblade in my boots, two daggers on my belt, and a gun with five iron bullets – I surveyed the battlefield, looking for a clear path that would get us to the hill unseen. When my eyes landed on the small figure clad head-to-toe in purple siren-hide armor, I let out a ragged gasp, then quickly clamped a hand over my mouth.

Safe, Mavros quickly interjected. *Watch.*

Still borderline hyperventilating, I clutched the trunk of the tree we were hiding behind, trying to steady myself. My mother and Lam had just appeared in the middle of the clearing, where they hoisted themselves atop a small mound of unburned grass and pressed their backs together. Without stopping to pause,

Lamswyth started to play a haunting, discordant tune from his panpipes, which instantly brought the five closest vampires to their knees, clutching their ears and screaming. But my mother's shrill soprano screams easily drowned out theirs – as well as every other noise on that battlefield.

"GET OUT OF HERE, YOU BLOODSUCKING CREEPS! GO ON, GET!"

Her scream detonated across the clearing like a percussive bomb, sending the nearest elves to their knees and every vampire within a fifty-foot radius scattering like roaches. Even the strigas, who were locked in an airborne battle against the harpies, zoomed out of there like hell-fleeing, demonic bats. Between their two sets of pipes, she and Lamswyth had arranged a perfect duet; when she screamed, he would catch his breath, and when he played, she would catch hers.

But they weren't always perfectly in sync, and anytime one of them skipped a beat, more vampires would fill the space, like water seeping into a freshly-dug hole.

Every nerve in my body screamed at me to go help her, but I dug my fingernails into my palms, resisting the urge.

Vampires are terrified of banshees, Zayn had told me the last time my mother single-handedly chased away a teeming mass of them. *Their scream is one of the only things in this realm that can send an entire coven scattering. And Lam's pipes are an ancient relic, one of the strongest and most coveted talismans in the realm.*

I sucked down another deep breath, filling my lungs to capacity. As I did, an idea occurred to me. Retrieving my trusted Sharpie, I scrawled a few modified runes on the inside of my palms, Endowing them with blood magic. A moment later, a ring of fire erupted around my mother and Lam, incinerating half the vampires that had gathered there and sending the others running for their half-lives.

"Thank you, *tateleh*!" Mom yelled over to Zayn, who was looking around in confusion. He, too, had suddenly found himself standing in the middle of a ring of burning vampires, thanks to the wall of bright orange flames that had just engulfed them.

"Did you do that?" he shouted up at Biscuit, who shook his head in bewilderment.

Several yards away, a chorus of cheers erupted as the roach-like monstrosity that had been closing in on a group of elves also spontaneously burst into flames.

"I thought your Ignis Rune was out!" a familiar voice called to Zayn.

Relief flooded my body as Korinne and Safir appeared in the middle of the cheering crowd.

"It *is*!" he shouted back, still sporting a consternated look on his face. When his ink-black eyes settled directly on the tree I was hiding behind, my heart skipped a beat. But another, non-burning vampire lunged at him a split second later, pulling his attention away.

Turning to Mavros, I whispered, "C'mon, girl. We've got a forcefield to shatter."

XXI.
Running Up That Hill

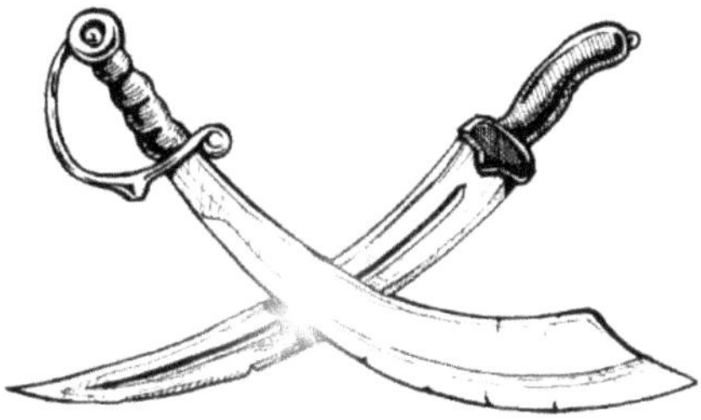

ZAYN

Fires ignited all around my periphery. I spun around, my trance momentarily broken. Dozens of bodies lay all around me, slain by the monster I had finally ceded control to.

"I thought your Ignis Rune was out!" Kor'ínthe yelled. I'd never seen her don anything but fine robes, even as a slave. Now, after a single week of freedom, she'd been thrust into battle, her siren-hide armor splattered in blood and her long hair in tangles.

"It is!" I shouted, my snarl as guttural as a vampire's. My eyes darted to the meager line of trees still standing, searching for the impossible.

"It's her!" Dee Dee cried, echoing my own errant thought. "It *has* to be her!" Using Lam for support, she stood on tip-toes, craning her neck to search among the clusters of fire that illuminated the battlefield.

I flinched at the sight.

After two days, Dee Dee was the only one who hadn't given up hope of finding her daughter. "She's not dead," she'd repeated to me over and over, like a mantra. "She *can't* be dead. I'd know if my only daughter were dead." But the tears in her eyes had betrayed the delusion she'd cast upon herself.

I whirled around as yet another bonfire erupted beneath a nearby blood incarnate – a twenty-foot-long millipede with six-inch venomous fangs. As I watched the ink leach from the monster's burning carcass, that same malicious voice in the back of my mind stirred to life, taunting me.

Maybe it is *her.*

Maybe she's okay after all...

Except we'd searched for her for two days, eventually enacting a Greater Homing Rune – just as I'd done after losing her at the Waypoint two weeks ago. But unlike then, when the beacon led me straight to Lamswyth's bed—my fists reflexively clenched at the memory—the Homing Rune barely flickered to life…then died. It was around that time that Biscuit reappeared, inconsolable. He'd been trying for hours to find her through our link. But every time he attempted to travel through the tattoos that connected the three of us, a proverbial door slammed in his face, preventing him from getting to her.

"Zæynek!"

Kor'ínthe's shrill warning coincided with the blur of movement to my right. My arm moved without thought, silencing the vampire's scream with my fiery blade. Its headless body crumpled to the ground, burning. I relished in the sight of it, in the smell of its charred flesh.

Let them come. I would leave a trail of corpses leading directly to Sol's ravaged carcass.

Activating my Projectile Rune as I whirled in his direction, I shot another glowing barb at that revolting smirk, willing it to hit. But, just as I knew it would, it bounced off Sol's Greater Shield Rune, which his Runemaster had stolen from *my* grimoire, using Talia's blood.

My stomach twisted so violently at her name, I nearly doubled over from the force of it.

Another vampire launched at me, his protracted fangs grazing across my arm as he did. Roaring, I plunged my knife into his eye socket, yanked it out, and wiped away the gore. I then pressed the side of the blade into my skin, cauterizing the wound before the venom could spread. The smell of my own burning flesh filled my nose, and I breathed it in hungrily, relishing in the pain.

I deserved this pain and so much more.

I sent her away, thinking I was protecting her. I sent her out those doors, believing that the runes I'd placed on her body were enough to keep her safe. I lost her…

No.

I *killed* her.

And soon, as sure as the banshees' twilight screams, the rest of us would follow.

I regarded the hundreds of elves I had condemned to death, as well as the dozens of innocent humans who had been dragged into our fractured realm as incubus shields and vampire rations, guilt hewing through my chest. My eyes raked across their blank faces, forcing myself to burn each one of them into my memory. Some of the faces were young, barely a year out of high school. And thanks to me, their short lives would soon be stolen from them.

Just like hers.

Blood sprayed across my face as my blade ripped through another vampire, splitting its trunk open from navel to chin. After setting fire to its body, Biscuit landed on my shoulder, panting.

"Go home," I growled. "Rest – even if it's just for a moment."

He shook his head stubbornly.

Aşek'ye lénim edím, he never used to be this obstinate. Strong-willed, yes – but nothing like this. But she stole his heart the same way she had stolen mine. And now, part of her soul lived in him…the only part of her soul left in this realm.

Blackness feathered my vision as I gasped for breath.

"Enough," I choked out.

Biscuit tugged on my ear, alerting me to the new fires that had appeared – though from what source, I still had no idea. Clusters of vampires spontaneously erupted in flames. Several of the incarnates, too, had been caught inside a wall of fire so fierce, ink poured from their immolated bodies. But for those flames to burn that hot, the Ignis Runes would have had to be augmented by—

"Enough!" I snarled, smothering the flicker of hope that had ignited alongside the mysterious bonfires.

Talia was gone. And yet, even in death, she'd lent me her strength. Façade abandoned and demon unleashed, I had never felt stronger nor more determined. Nothing would take me down, not until Sol's head had been sundered from his body. At which point, I would open my arms wide and embrace death, praying the Creator would allow me even a glimpse of her soul before casting me to the Other – the forsaken realm of infinite darkness.

My eyes roved up the hill, where a clear path to Sol had emerged for the first time. Without even willing them to, my feet moved, carrying me toward him. I launched another projectile at Sol, grinding my teeth when it again ricocheted off the forcefield. He smirked at me, flashing his stolen vial of blood. Taunting me. But something about this smirk was different than before – shaky. Uncertain, even.

I kept climbing, my arm mechanically cutting down anything that moved in my periphery.

Cut off the head of the snake.

I repeated the phrase to myself over and over, focusing on nothing else.

Cut off the head of the snake…

He shouted a muffled command to those behind him. Soren and several of his cousins pressed their hands to glowing runes, unleashing a fresh wave of beasts upon the battlefield – blood incarnates in the form of werewolves, their eyes glowing in a scarlet trance. But even soulless incarnates share certain properties with their flesh-and-blood counterparts, with pyrophobia being chief among them. By some miracle, the mysterious fires kept the werewolves at bay, allowing the elves to stand their ground.

Cut off the head of the snake…

Sol's acolytes would surely kill me within seconds of his death. But the serpent would be dead, along with his incarnates. Plus, Talia had already wounded Calus badly enough that Kor'ínthe and the others would be able to take him out without me. And this time, there would be no Resurgence Rune to revive him.

My attention shifted to the sky, where Xianis had launched her air offensive, despite her grief from losing the granddaughter she had barely gotten to know. She and the other harpies had kept the strigas at bay, even managing to take down some of the beasts Sol had summoned from Fire Island. Once I was dead, she would almost certainly try to take the Summer Throne for herself.

Cut off the head of the snake, I repeated, pushing the troubling thought from my mind.

Halfway up the hill.

I cast one final glance over my shoulder at the Summer Palace, which rose up like a gravestone against the night sky – darkness against darkness. How the tommyknockers had managed to keep those old stones from crumbling against the ongoing assaults, I had no idea. That palace would be nothing but a smoking pile of rubble – and the rest of us buried beneath it – had it not been for Talia and her uncanny ability to make friends—

Fuck.

The stab of pain that sliced through my chest was enough to make me glance down to ensure my armor hadn't been pierced. It hadn't, of course; this pain came from inside me, worse than anything I'd ever experienced.

I hadn't realized I'd stopped moving until Biscuit gave my ear another sharp tug.

"Go protect Kor'ínthe and the others," I gasped, panting for breath. "Please. They need you."

He ignored me, craning his neck as he looked not just for Talia, but for Mavros – our newborn familiar, whom Talia had liberated with her unparalleled selflessness.

The pain in my chest deepened.

If Talia is…dead… My throat tightened as I approached the top of the hill. *Then that means, when I die…*

The realization robbed me of breath.

Hibiscus.

Gently taking him off my shoulder, I knelt to the ground. He perched on my arm, quivering as he looked up at me.

As I gazed into his wide, soulful eyes, I could feel the demon inside me momentarily slipping away. "I don't think I've ever thanked you," I murmured. "For standing by me all these years. For being my only companion when I had no one else. You…" I swallowed, choked by my own immeasurable grief. "You mean more to me than I could ever say. When I'm gone, you have to find a way to persist. Dee Dee will help you fill the void that Ta—" I cleared my throat. "The void that we left. And when this is all over, your *bubbe* will need you – maybe even more than you need her."

Biscuit let out a mournful cluck.

As I regarded Talia's mother, so strong, and yet so fragile, emotion welled up deep inside my chest. I barely knew the woman. And yet, in so many ways, she already treated me with more love and compassion than my own mother ever had…ever *could.*

"Promise me you'll keep going – that you'll look after each other." I gently stroked the colorful crown of feathers atop his head, which Talia herself had created from our own ink and blood.

A choked noise caught in my chest.

Biscuit nuzzled against my cheek, where a lone tear had escaped. Then he hopped on my shoulder. "Go," he clucked, giving my ear a hard tug.

So much like her.

Calus's attacks were raining down on us now, harmlessly bouncing off my shield. The devil knew nothing of real Runemastery – only death and torment.

Ignoring him, I rose on weakened legs, meeting Sol's steely gaze as I did. Thirty feet were all that separated him from me. Thirty feet, a line of innocent humans, and a seemingly impenetrable forcefield. Except… I rubbed the sweat from my eyes, blinking furiously.

"Are… Are you seeing what I'm seeing?" I whispered.

Like me, Biscuit was shaking his head in disbelief.

The forcefield was flickering – as though it were failing. *But from what?*

The line between Sol's brows deepened. He whirled around, shouting something at Calus. And then, all at once, the protective dome shattered, its glowing green fragments dissolving into the smoky air.

When Sol turned back around, his crimson eyes once more caught mine. And in that moment, I saw something there I'd never seen before.

As I approached the crest of the hill, my lips curled into a vicious smile.

TALIA

I sank to the ground halfway up the eastern side of the hill, gasping for breath. A cry had risen up from the battlefield once the elves realized what had happened. Atop the hill, where their forcefield had been obliterated by me, the self-dubbed Ninja of Annihilation, Sol's legion of incubi and succubi – or "in-succubi," as I'd mentally dubbed them – were cowering behind the only shield they had left: their collection of glamoured humans.

Perched on my shoulder in her raven form, Mavros nuzzled against my face, where a sheen of sweat had formed. And yet, in spite of the balmy night air, the heat of the fires I'd cast, and the physical toll of breaking through Calus's shield, I couldn't stop shivering. I carefully peered around the cluster of neon-blue bushes I was hiding behind, doing my best to keep my teeth from chattering. Down on the battlefield, the elves were forcing their way through the thinning partition of vampires, werewolves, and blood incarnates, their sights set on the newly-unprotected hilltop. Those who still had functioning runes sent the occasional magic missile careening up the side of the hill, sending dozens of in-succubi scattering, lest their fancy designer jeans get scuffed.

Which meant it was time for me to do some serious scuffing.

Pressing my fingers to the Fulmen Rune embedded in my left arm, I closed my eyes. The ensuing fork of bright green lightning smashed into the center of the hilltop with such force, my teeth buzzed from the electricity crackling in the air even from this distance. Smoothing out the static halo of hair floating around my head, I peeked over the top of the shrub just in time to see Sol's army of sex demons running not for, but *from* the hills. At the same time, the werewolves down on the battlefield staggered to a halt, their fleeing masters' concentration broken.

A grin spread across my cheeks.

"It's now or never," I whispered to Mavros, pulling my hood over my head. I'd changed all of my clothes to black, using the handy Transformation Rune Korinne had taught me, then ripped off part of the hem of my cloak and draped it across my face to keep it hidden. "You fly out of sight, and keep an eye on my mom, okay? I'll give you the signal when I need you. But listen…"

She cocked her head at me.

"If…" I swallowed tightly. "If I don't make it – or worse, it looks like I'm not in control of myself – I need you to promise to stay away from me, okay? Biscuit, too. I can't risk either of you being Manipulated by me, especially given our blood bond. Okay? Please… Just promise me that."

Mavros looked at me for a long moment, then begrudgingly clicked her beak in agreement. *I promise.*

"Thank you." I kissed the top of her head. "Now be safe."

Nodding, Mavros swooped down and around the hill, keeping low to the ground and out of sight.

Sucking down a deep breath that did nothing to help the throb in my skull or the deepening ache in my arm, I rose to my feet. None of the humans or in-succubi rushing past paid me a second thought as they ran for their lives. I did my best to weave between them, but with every brush and jostle, the agony in my arm spread. By now, I knew another Resurgence Rune wouldn't help the pain, but I scrawled one on my hand for the distraction alone as I trudged up the slope.

What felt like hours later – but was probably only a few minutes – I crested the top of the hill, clutching my thighs to catch my breath. A hundred feet below, the Seelies and

Unseelies were facing off, with the latter far outweighing the former. Worse, a long line of hypnotized humans had been strategically assembled between them, preventing the elves from getting to the in-succubi without harming innocent bystanders in the process. My vision grew increasingly blurry as my eyes roved across the chaos, searching for my mom – but neither she, Lamswyth, nor Mavros were anywhere to be found.

In her absence, the vampires had returned in full force.

As much as my heart screamed for me to help the embattled elves, a much more pressing matter loomed twenty feet in front of me. Zayn had just crested the top of the hill, where Sol, Calus, and Soren were waiting for him. Before he or anyone else could spot me, I quickly ducked behind a leafy purple shrub, my heart soaring at the sight of him.

I clenched my hands into two trembling fists, digging my fingernails into my palms to distract myself. The link I shared with Zayn was fueled by our mutual love and affection, while Sol's claim was triggered by fear and pain. As much as I needed to keep my negative emotions in check, I had to control the positive ones as well, lest I inadvertently tip off Zayn to my presence.

His eyes smoldered like hot coals as they landed on Sol, who'd managed to glamour himself once more – using my stolen blood, no doubt. Once again, he was almost unbearably handsome, designed by nature to lure his unsuspecting prey straight into his arms. Gone were the black veins that had marred his previously bone-white complexion, now smooth and unblemished. The black whiskers on his chiseled jaw faded into a thick coif of platinum hair that was uncharacteristically tousled, and his dark brows were perfectly sculpted. But beneath them, his irises glowed red-hot, betraying the demon that lurked just beneath his flimsy mask.

I tensed, expecting an attack as Zayn approached him. But to my surprise, Sol actually turned his back to his former Runemaster, centering his full attention on the battlefield. As the tattoos on his exposed forearms glowed to life, blood-red columns of light appeared on the ground, from which dozens of terrifying, truck-sized insectoids emerged, pinchers snapping and jaws thrashing.

And still, more demons came.

My stomach sank as I peered out in the distance, where a black cloud of spike-tailed dragons was spreading across the starlit sky. Down on the ground, the elves persisted, despite their increasingly impossible odds, while up on the mountaintop, the flock of resting harpies sat perched on the castle turrets like gargoyles, steadily regarding the coming blight. After a hard-fought battle against the strigas, did they have another fight in them? And what about the elves, who were vastly outnumbered, or the dozens of innocent humans that had been dragged into this mess against their will?

"Hello, *Zæynek,*" Soren called, making my head snap to attention. He and Calus had split off from Sol, circling Zayn like two lions approaching a cobra.

"Hello, *Soren*," Zayn growled, the sound of his voice filling me with longing. He was dressed in head-to-toe black siren-hide armor, though his arms were exposed, revealing the many lethal tattoos running from his broad shoulders to his muscular forearms.

In a brazen display of pretentiousness, Soren had opted to wear a fancy black suit into battle, and was peeling off his jacket with a smug flourish. He rolled up the cuffs of his white dress shirt, exposing a tattooed dagger emblazoned above his left wrist. A moment later, a matching eight-inch serrated blade appeared in his hand – Zayn's work, no doubt.

Calus, on the other hand, had evidently woken up that morning and decided to go with the very practical "mad cultist" look: black robes, black gloves, and a black hood, which cast a black shadow over his repulsive face. He, too, withdrew a savage-looking weapon from his sleeve – a long-handled scythe that made him look like Death himself.

I went to pull my Sharpie from my pocket, intending to light a fresh Ignis Rune under his feet, then hesitated. Anything I did would immediately draw their attention straight to me. Zayn would be distracted, snapped out of the lethal, full-on demon mode that had carried him this far, and I was too sick to be anything but a liability.

My eyes darted to Sol, whose concentration remained firmly glued to the horrors he was orchestrating below.

"Cut off the head of the snake," I whispered to myself, remembering Zayn's words from days before. My hand hovered above the smattering of runes embedded on my arms, trying to decide which, if any, would be strong enough to blast through the powerful shield that surrounded him. Most of my offensive spells were spent, and while I did have my trusty Sharpie, Sol had gold blood at his disposal. Hastily-drawn doodles would never hold up against Calus's perfectly precise tattoo lines, catalyzing ink, and my own blood – all expertly embedded beneath Sol's skin for maximum magical potency.

With a grimace, I dropped my hand to the gun at my waist, hesitating as my fingers brushed against cold steel. A bullet wouldn't penetrate Sol's shield. The noise from it, however, would draw his attention straight to me, the one person he needed most. With so much at stake, now was most definitely *not* the time for my usual strategy of relying on half-formed ideas and sheer, dumb luck.

Think, Talia! I ground my teeth together, trying to keep my mounting emotions at bay.

"You're looking well, Zæynek," Calus sneered, his voice unusually hoarse. "It's a shame your time in the vault was cut so tragically short."

"I unfortunately can't say the same for you, *Niklaus*," Zayn replied. "I didn't think it would be possible for your new face to be even uglier than the last."

"Oh, it's the same face as before – just slightly worse for the wear, thanks to a certain shrew, who, incidentally, seems to be missing all the fun. Where *did* your little whore go, Zæynek?" He clicked his tongue with false pity. "Did your unappeasable lust finally kill her?"

Zayn lunged for his throat.

Calus lazily disappeared in a pillar of noxious smoke, reappearing beside Soren. "Pitiful," he sneered. "You're nothing but a slave to your baser urges, a predator consumed by bloodlust. It's a shame you didn't take my suggestion to become a eunuch years ago."

"I think the real shame, Niklaus, is that I won't be able to castrate something that's already been amputated from your body." Zayn cracked his neck, withdrew a second dagger from his body, then scraped the silver blades across one another to create a shower of sparks. "Luckily, you still have plenty of other body parts I can chop off."

"Enough talk," Soren growled, stepping forward.

"Indeed." As Calus pulled back his hood, my stomach nearly emptied itself. Only a few tufts of hair clung to his otherwise smooth skull, his papery skin hung from his cheekbones, and his eyes were bloodshot and sunken. He looked like the walking dead – a literal zombie with rotting flesh.

I doubled over in the darkness, clutching my stomach. It wasn't just the sight of Calus's resurrected, decaying body; in my entire life, I'd never felt so sick – not even the time I polished off an entire handle of tequila, on my own, in one night. My body was shutting down. And whether I had minutes or hours left, I knew I couldn't waste another second. Rubbing my forehead with the heels of my hands to rid it of the steadily creeping fog, I prayed for an idea to strike.

As if on cue, a clap of pink lightning cleaved the sky in half. It slammed straight down into the lower part of the massive lake, sending up a five-story plume of electrified water. Every hair on the back of my neck standing on end, I crouched on all fours, trying to get a better look…then stifled a gasp.

The waters of the lake were churning and simmering, as though they were being whisked by a giant, invisible egg-beater. I looked around, perplexed, trying to find the source of the disturbance. To my surprise, no one else atop or below the hill seemed to be paying the lake any mind; they'd all fallen right back into fighting.

"It can't be," I muttered, trying to suppress the tiny flicker of hope that had sparked in my chest. *Can it…?*

Another fork of magenta lightning splintered across the sky. As it lit up the battlefield, momentarily bleaching away the fires and ruin, my eyes darted back to the edge of the lake, where a lone, naked woman had appeared. Her damp, black hair cascaded well past her hips, and her jade-tinted, alabaster skin was as smooth as cream – save for the splashes of iridescent fish scales that hugged the various dips and curves of her body. As she gazed up at me, lightning reflected in her fathomless silver gaze.

Hello again, Gilded One.

"Lanmè?!" I rubbed my eyes furiously. "But how…?"

My cousins in the west sent word of your appeal for help against the Siren Slayer.

"Oralay?" I whispered, remembering the school of mermaids I'd spoken to on the way to the Western Wastes. Their interaction with the elves hadn't been particularly amiable, and

I'd frankly considered it a win in and of itself that they hadn't drowned us after my pathetic attempts at diplomacy. "Sh-She told you about me?"

Yes. She thinks highly of you – not highly enough to send reinforcements, I'm afraid. But she has asked me to pass along her wishes that your death be quick and honorable, should it come to that.

"Oh, gee, that's so nice of her."

It was difficult to convince my sisters to ally with pixies and shrieking marsh gulls—I could almost feel Lanmè's wry smile unfurling in my mind—*however, twelve of us have come to offer you our aid.* She gestured behind her, where I just could barely make out the glint of fishtails treading beneath the surface of the lake.

"Oh, Lanmè…" Tears mingled with the light drizzle of rain that had begun to fall on my cheeks. "How can I ever thank you enough?"

Do not thank me yet, as there are many foes, and our numbers are scant. Against this many magical beings, there is not much we can offer you, I'm afraid.

My attention shifted back to Zayn. He, Soren, and Calus were circling one another, their various offensive runes alight as their barbs turned from verbal to physical. They, like Sol, appeared completely oblivious to the mermaids' presence.

"So, what you're saying is, you can't pull another *deus ex machina* and drown all the bad guys in one fell swoop?"

Sadly, no, she mused, almost to herself. *The humans, however, are weak-minded and gullible. We could rouse them from their glamoured trance and drown* them, *if it would help—*

"Absolutely not!" I snapped. "Unless—oh!" I stifled a gasp, struck by a brilliant idea. "Could you draw the humans away from the battle *without* drowning them? As in, lure them to safety?"

She was quiet for a long moment, deliberating my question. Finally, she answered, *For you, Gilded One, it shall be done.*

"Thank you," I whispered, chewing on a ragged nail as I regarded the multitude of scattered fires edging closer and closer to the Great Phoenix Tree. Ominous coils of black smoke twisted into the air, blocking the light of the moons, which the elves desperately needed. "Hey Lanmè – before you do that, could you do one more thing for me?"

Yes, Talia?

"I need you to make it rain."

Another fork of pink lightning lit up the sky, illuminating her answering smile. A moment later, the storm clouds burst open, loosing a veritable deluge upon the burning land. After sloshing back into her watery form, Lanmè's body flowed back into the lake, where she rematerialized beside her sisters. A soft hum rose from the surface, making the back of my neck tingle. Mellifluous and faint, it began first as one low note, but was soon joined by a dozen others, creating a rich, smooth harmony that could just be heard above the sound of crashing rain and clanging steel.

Though no one else seemed affected, one by one, the humans swiveled their heads toward the lake. And then, one by one, they turned and began walking toward it, utterly entranced. Cries of alarm erupted from the in-succubi, who no longer had a partition of human bodies to separate them from the elves. They screamed for their dispersing snacks to come back, but the lure of the sirens' call overpowered theirs. Meanwhile, the pouring rain helped diffuse the billowing smoke and fizzling fires, allowing a glimpse of the four moons. A cheer rose up from the elves as *Ay'aşéya's* faint pink halo shimmered into view. The moment the line of innocents had dispersed, they advanced.

As the battlefield exploded, so did the skies above as the coming maelstrom of winged demons met the answering cries of the harpies. Lightning lit up the roiling sky with an accompanying crash of thunder, illuminating the crimson head and tail feathers of my grandmother, who loosed a shrill battle cry as she and the harpies launched their attack.

A pained grunt jerked my attention back to the fight occurring several yards in front of me. Zayn had crumpled to one knee, clutching his arm as bright red blood dripped between his fingers.

"Poor little drowned rat, have your Shield Runes finally been tapped?" Calus called gleefully.

Vines erupted from his palms, sickly-green and steeped in snaking tendrils of black smoke. They ensnared Zayn by the wrists and throat, draining the color from his cheeks.

Biscuit dove out of the sky like a blazing comet.

"Biscuit, *don't!*" I screamed, my words lost to a simultaneous clap of thunder.

Calus's vines ensnared Biscuit midair, yanking him to the ground. The flames on his feathers went out with a hiss, doused by the puddle in which he'd crash-landed.

I shot to my feet – only to stumble right back to the ground as another wave of sickness overtook me. Crouching in the mud on all fours, I desperately tried to come up with a plan. But my brain was so sluggish, latching onto a coherent thought was like grasping at smoke.

A choked cry lodged behind my tongue as Soren kicked Biscuit aside, then grabbed Zayn by a fistful of dark hair. Wrenching Zayn's own dagger from his hand, Soren pressed its tip against Zayn's jugular, drawing blood.

Fear and bile rose in my throat as I frantically searched for a rune I could use. Most of my offensive tattoos were spent, and the ink from the Sharpie had smeared off in the downpour. All I had left was my faded Fulmen Rune, and with all the rainwater that was pooling on the ground, Zayn would be electrocuted in the process.

Black eyes seething with rage, he fought against Soren with all his might, but the vines held tight, leeching the life from his body.

"Father…?" Soren called.

Sol casually glanced over his shoulder, then nodded. "Kill him."

Terror, the likes of which I'd never felt before, twisted my windpipe into a knot, choking me.

Sol's shoulders stiffened. Concentration broken, he slowly turned around, while the blood incarnates on the battlefield halted mid-step.

"It can't be…" he whispered.

"Father?" Soren asked again confusion tinging his voice. "What's—"

"Silence!" Sol snarled. His gleaming eyes roved across the hilltop while his sumptuous voice slithered between my ears. *Zaffre? Is that you?*

Gulping down mouthful after mouthful of air, I squeezed my eyes shut, doing everything I could to tamp my emotions. But it wasn't enough.

"She's here," Sol breathed.

Zayn jerked his head in Sol's direction, only for Soren to violently yank it back.

"Kill him already!" Calus snarled.

As Soren raised his dagger above his head, time slowed to a trickle. Biscuit squirmed helplessly on the muddy ground, letting out a muffled squawk. Zayn's eyes widened, momentarily shifting from black to green as he fought to crane his neck, looking for me. Calus watched his struggle with visible glee, his yellowed grin splitting his haggard face in two as Soren's dagger arced downward.

Zaffre? Sol called again, worming his way through our link. *Where are you, little one? I've been waiting for you... Come out and say hello.*

Cracks were forming inside of me, like a dam crumbling beneath a deluge. And once that channel opened, I knew there would be nothing left to keep him out.

Time was running out.

My eyes darted to the sky, where the rain had washed away enough smoke to allow the hazy outlines of four moons to shimmer into view.

May the light of the moon nourish us, I whispered silently, the prayer manifesting more from instinct than thought. *May the grace of the Creator protect us.* Moonlight washed over my body, kissing my veins with power. I took a deep breath, turning my face and palms to the sky. *May the blood of our veins preserve us.* The invisible Lunar Rune embedded in my arm all at once flared to life, shimmering with magic; as a golden flush traveled from my fingers to my toes, I could feel my strength growing alongside it. "May the blessings of the Mother sustain us," I finished, tightly clasping my hands in front of me.

Please, Ay'aşéya – lend me the strength to protect them.

Then, with one hand pulling the veil from my face, and the other reaching for the gun on my hip, I shakily rose to my feet.

"Talia!" Zayn rasped.

A sad smile tugged at the corners of my mouth. In all the realms, there would never be a more beautiful sound than that of my name on Zayn's lips. If I died right there and then – and I fully expected I would – at least I'd die with his voice in my ears.

Taking a deep breath, I gripped the gun in two trembling hands, then pulled the trigger three times.

The first iron bullet bounced off Sol's gold-blood-infused Shield Rune, ricocheting wildly into the air.

The second bullet sailed through the side of Soren's neck, eliciting a gurgling scream.

And the third bullet missed Calus altogether as he disappeared in another plume of black smoke, only to reappear right beside me. Before I could move or even scream, he tore the sleeve from my shirt, pressed the tip of his tattoo gun into the ravaged skin of my shoulder, and etched the final leg of the spider in one vicious motion.

I stared at Sol's now-complete claim in wordless horror while it began to pulse with crimson power.

"There." Calus smirked, tossing the cartridge to the ground. "All done." But his sneer quickly dissolved into a grimace as his bleeding leg buckled beneath him and he collapsed into the mud.

Turns out I hadn't missed after all.

With a roar that turned my insides to warm slush, Zayn jerked his wrists to his sides, ripping the vines from Calus's control. In one swift move, he snatched the dagger from Soren's hand and plunged it into his chest.

Soren was dead before he'd even crumpled to the ground.

Zayn whirled in my direction, eyes burning with feral intensity.

"Would you *die* already?!" Calus screamed. He shot his hand in the air, where tendrils of black smoke solidified into a vicious, saw-toothed spear that was aimed at the very center of Zayn's chest.

Biscuit, freed from his binds, launched up from the ground, raking his claws across Calus's eyes.

The Runemaster cried out in anguish, groping blindly at the air.

Meanwhile, Sol – whose son had just been killed before his eyes – didn't even bother feigning a look of remorse. He was too busy staring at me, his mouth curling into a greedy smile.

With Biscuit safely off the ground, I dove at Zayn, wrapping my arms around him as I triggered a Shield Rune that surrounded us both.

The green lightning bolt that tore from the sky slammed into Sol's forcefield with so much fury, the surrounding grass incinerated before it even had the chance to catch fire. Blinding light exploded in my vision, bright enough to sear the inside of my eyelids even as I squeezed them shut.

When my vision had finally adjusted a few moments later, I was still clutching Zayn for dear life. Agony seethed not just in my arm, but throughout my entire body. And yet I couldn't bring myself to let go of him.

His irises erupting in molten fire, he grabbed me by the collar of my cloak and crushed his lips against mine. "We thought he took you," he rasped, quickly pulling away. "We thought you were—"

A pained gasp burst through my lips, sending him stumbling backward. It wasn't the pain of his touch that made me cry out, but the fury that coursed through my blood like liquid fire. Frozen, I could only watch in mute horror as Sol stalked toward us – shieldless, due to the sheer power of my attack annihilating the remainder of his defensive runes, but with nary a scratch on his body.

His mouth contorted into a vicious sneer. "Don't. Touch. My. *Claim*," he hissed at Zayn, his eyes glowing with savagery. My blood swung from the leather cord around his neck as he raised his hand above his head, preparing a killing blow.

"Talia!" Zayn gasped, clutching my shoulders – one of which felt as though a hot knife had been plunged into it and dragged all the way down my arm, flaying my scorched flesh.

Red feathered the edges of my vision. Using the last of my strength to shove Zayn aside, I groped once more for the Fulmen Rune on my arm – but it was gone. Just a few inches above the empty space, the eight-legged spider on my shoulder seethed like a red-hot coal, pulsing in time with my heart. Shards of razor-sharp fury in my chest ground together, the force of it knocking me to my knees.

Zayn sank to the ground beside me.

"TAL-YAAAAAAAAAA!" Biscuit screamed, tearing out of the sky.

A glowing net exploded from Sol's outstretched hand, ensnaring him. Biscuit fell to the ground in a heap, shrieking in anguish as he desperately fought to free himself.

"Talia!" Zayn shouted. "Talia, you have to get out of here!"

With the last vestiges of self-control I possessed, I flung off my weapons belt. "Take them," I wheezed, shoving the knives and gun into Zayn's arms. "Do whatever you have to, just don't let me hurt you!"

"Talia—"

I turned away from him, clutching my stomach. The hate rising in my chest was so visceral, so potent, it took everything I had not to lunge at his throat.

As Sol's muddy boots appeared directly behind him, Zayn staggered to his feet, positioning himself between the two of us. But Sol wasn't looking at him. His scarlet eyes were burning directly into mine, every ounce of his channeled rage gripping me by the throat.

And no matter how hard I tried, I couldn't turn away.

Come to me, Zaffre.

I brought my trembling hands to my ears, trying to force him out. "Stop it!" I screamed, triggering a violent coughing fit that left my palm spotted with gold.

Oh, my poor Talia, Sol crooned, enunciating every syllable of my name as though reciting a spell. *My poor, sweet Talia...Judith...Kestenbaum.*

I let out a pained cry as his power jolted through my body like an electric shock.

You're dying, little one. But if you offer your body to me completely, you'll not only live a long and full life, you'll never feel pain again. You have my word.

I could feel my resolve dwindling alongside my strength. As I gazed up at him, the fire raging in my arm and chest abruptly turned to ice. I let out a sob of relief as icy numbness spread across my body, stripping me of pain, fear, and every other sensation.

And as it did, the rest of the world began to bleed away.

From somewhere far away, Zayn was shouting my name and shaking me by the shoulders, his bright emerald eyes burning into mine.

And then green faded to red…

Red faded to black…

And black dissolved into nothingness.

XXII.
Brother in Arms

ZAYN

Talia stared at me – through me – with vacant eyes that had been cast in shadow by her drawn hood. Gone were the irises of jade and honey I had come to love; in their place were two blazing rubies. I took a step backward, unable to speak. The sleeve had been torn off the shirt she wore beneath her armored corset, exposing the festering black stain that marred her entire arm. She didn't budge. Didn't speak. She just stood there, shrouded in black from head to toe, unmoving and unblinking, like a widow at a funeral.

Sol stood beside her, arms crossed, his mouth curved into a smirk. "Her incessant nattering was so unappealing before. She's nearly perfect now – all that's left is to strip her hair of this hideous color." He pinched a violet lock of hair between his finger and thumb, crinkling his nose.

"There are so few beautiful things in this world…" I whispered, delirious. "And you robbed it of the most beautiful thing of all."

Sol clicked his tongue in derision. "Robbed? Nonsense. It is but our nature to scour the realms for beautiful things, and then claim them for our own." His eyes drifted to Talia, gazing at her body as though she were a fine vase in a museum. "I just happened to claim her first."

"You haven't claimed her. You've ruined her."

"On the contrary – I've just saved her life." He pulled Talia's back against his chest, wrapping a possessive arm across her shoulders. "You should be pleased to know that my claim is no longer suffering, now that she's back in my care – where she belongs."

Rage clawed at my chest, darkening the edges of my vision.

"I can feel her pain, you know," he said, dropping his lips to the side of her neck. Her expression didn't change as he grazed his teeth across her skin, his eyes glinting wickedly as they rose to meet mine. "It's almost completely gone now – unlike the agony she experienced in your so-called care."

The demon inside me was pacing back and forth like a caged lion, commanding me to tear Sol's body apart, one severed, bleeding limb at a time. But in order to do that, I'd have to go through her; I knew it, and so did he.

"Did she tell you we share a blood link?" Sol murmured, kissing her bare shoulder. "Gold blood truly is remarkable. Even incomplete, the modified *Dominans* and *Inferus* Runes I placed on our bodies were extraordinarily attuned to one another. And now…" He chuckled softly. "Well, now, my claim is absolute."

My control, tenuous as it already was, was quickly unraveling. Inky blackness swam in front of my vision as my mind once more threatened to disassociate from my body, unleashing the beast inside. The beast who had witnessed the massacre of his own family, only to be chained like a dog by the very demon who slaughtered them. The beast who, for two days, had believed the only woman he'd ever loved had died by his own hand – only to watch her fall into the arms of the devil himself.

"Can you imagine what it will be like when I take her to bed with me?" Sol continued. "The firmness and vigor of her youthful body, the richness of the blood that flows through her veins…paired with the physical bond we share, the experience will be exquisite." He pressed his nose to the top of her head, breathing deeply. "I'm salivating at the mere thought of it."

I dug my fingernails into my palms, imagining they were gouging out his eyeballs. But even as the beast paced hungrily, desperate to feed, I knew in the deep recesses of my logical mind that I'd only be giving Sol exactly what he wanted. After decades of abuse, I knew his weaknesses better than anyone else; far more than sex, the one thing that truly got him off was torment.

Well, I wouldn't give him the satisfaction.

I would give him hell.

My eyes darted to the ground. Biscuit was still thrashing against the netting he'd been trapped inside, his once-lustrous feathers soaked with rainwater and mud. Talia's abandoned weapons rested a few feet away from him.

That net was designed to nullify magic, I silently whispered to him. *That's why you're unable to portal back home. Conserve your strength for the moment. I'm coming.*

He made a sullen croak, but otherwise did as he was told.

"Once we've finished here and you're lying dead with the others"—Sol gestured blithely to the battlefield, where his army of demons was pushing my surviving soldiers to their limits—"you can rest assured the girl will be kept quite comfortable as my primary consort and Runemaster. Speaking of which…" He glanced over at Calus, who was still gasping and writhing in the mud, the iron wound in his hip leaching the life from the rest of his body. Sol's mouth twisted with contempt. "Get up, you worthless excuse for a mage."

Calus just glared up at him, the skin on his face festering with the blight of cheated death.

Revulsion pitted in my stomach. Resurgence Runes require constant upkeep – a steady stream of victims to maintain the integrity of the ink. How many people had he killed over the years for the ability to bring his own corpse back from the dead?

Sol turned to Talia. "Zaffre, my beloved?"

She looked up at him, her expression blank.

"Here." He handed her my grimoire, pointing to one of the many runes he'd dog-eared. "Be a good girl and dispose of our former associate, would you? The mere sight of his face offends me."

Calus made a strangled noise as Talia took the book from Sol.

"Niklaus tells me you don't even have to draw them," he told her. "Just Endow the printed rune on the page and channel that magic into your intended victim – in this case, him."

"Wait—" Calus started, prostrating himself on his hands and knees. "We can discuss this, Solomon. Please – I'll do anything you ask of me!" At Sol's dispassionate expression, Calus crawled over to Talia, the desperation in his voice growing louder and shriller as he clawed at the mud-stained hem of her cloak. "Rabbit, I swear to you – I'll devote myself to you completely, using every minute of my time to help you become the most powerful Runemaster this realm has ever seen… Please!" he cried out. "You don't have to do this!"

When it was clear there was no sympathy to be found among either of them, his visage shifted from contrition to loathing as he lunged for Talia's weapons belt.

Sol stepped on his wrist, snapping it. Ignoring Calus's ensuing scream, he knelt down to retrieve the gun between his index finger and thumb, then kicked the belt and knives down the hill. "How crude," he muttered, dropping the gun in his pocket as though it were a dead rat.

"Solomon," Calus choked out, clutching his broken wrist against his chest. "Please, I beg y—"

His words broke off in a choked gurgle as a fountain of blood sprayed from his mouth.

Talia and Sol took a collective step backward, while I used that opportunity to snatch Biscuit from the ground. Clutching him against my chest, I turned away, unable to bring myself to watch as the Detonation Rune Talia had cast upon Calus's body – a rune that was never intended for living objects – exploded.

Red misted the earth.

I swallowed the surge of bile that appeared in my throat. "Go," I told Biscuit, yanking the net from his body. "Find Mavros. Together, maybe the two of you can get through to Talia."

He looked over at her, trembling, then immediately launched into the sky.

When I turned back around, Sol had taken out a handkerchief and was wiping a smudge of Calus's remains from Talia's cheek.

"I have to get back to my incarnates," he murmured to her softly. "Now that you're under my complete control, I trust you to take care of the boy. By the time you've killed him, the battle will be over and we can finally return home."

She nodded, the uncharacteristically obedient motion turning my stomach.

"But nothing vulgar," he instructed. "Our lowly bastard prince deserves an honorable death, at the very least. By no means painless – but honorable."

"Painful but honorable," she parroted.

"Good girl." He kissed the top of her head, then cast me a wan smile. "I am sorry it has to end this way, Zæynek – truly. I've lost so many children over the years, just as you've lost most of your family. In another life, I would have liked to have forged a relationship with my last surviving son – my favorite son, if I'm being honest with myself. Perhaps if you'd be willing to don another Dominion Rune…?" Sol shook his head, recognizing the absurdity of his own question. "No, I suppose not… Oh, well. More sons can always be made." He patted Talia's backside, flashing me a wink. "Goodbye, Zæynek. Perhaps we'll meet again someday, in the Other."

His casual admission hit me like a punch to the gut, making the edges of my vision feather. "What's the matter?" I shouted after him, my vision blurred by fury and grief. "Too much of a gutless pig to kill me yourself?"

Sol glanced over his shoulder, his eyes not quite meeting mine. "It's far more poetic to die by the hand of the woman you love, don't you think?"

"Liar!" I snarled. "Admit it – after all these years, you just can't bring yourself to kill me!"

He was quiet for a long moment before finally answering, "If it brings you peace to think so."

With that, he turned his attention back to his blood incarnates, bringing forth a fresh wave of screams from the battlefield.

I stared at his back, shaking with rage. With anguish. For the first time in my life, I inwardly railed at the Creator, who had clearly fashioned me for the sole purpose of torment. The weight of the sorrow I had endured throughout my existence was almost crushing – save for the one, singular bright spot in my life.

And now, she too had been taken from me.

"Talia," I choked out, forcing myself to meet the blistering red eyes that gazed at me from beneath the shadow of her hood. "Please. I know you're in there. If you can hear me—"

A ball of fire exploded from my mother's grimoire without warning, singeing the skin of my left arm as I dove out of the way.

"Talia!" I barked, staggering to my feet. "You have to listen to me—"

This time, blazing yellow ropes erupted from the book, wrapping around my legs and yanking me to the ground. Propping myself on my elbows, I spat the mud and ichor from my mouth as I stared up at her.

"Tal—"

"It's Zaffre," she intoned, thumbing through the grimoire. "Painful but honorable," she muttered to herself. "Painful but honorable…"

My eyes dropped to the ground, where one of the markers she always carried around with her had fallen next to her tapping foot. Engrossed in the book as she was, I managed to snatch it without her noticing, uncap it with my teeth, then quickly start to draw a simple-yet-devastating rune on the palm of my hand: an Immolation Rune. Utterly worthless without the proper ink, of course, but if I could somehow get even a drop of Talia's blood on it, it might be just enough to kill Sol, freeing her in the process.

A blur of movement caught my eye as I drew the final stroke. I craned my neck over the edge of the hill, where I found several hundred white-cloaked figures pouring onto the battlefield. *More demons?* I squinted, trying to make out their pale, shrouded faces in the waning moonlight. By then, the rain had slowed to a patter, allowing the fires to reignite, and their smoke once more all but eclipsed the moons.

"Ah. Here we go."

I jerked my head in Talia's direction, even as a fresh wave of screams rose from below. "Which one will you use?"

"An Exsanguination Rune."

"Ah. That's a good one." I smiled wanly. "Very painful – but fitting, given all the blood I've spilled in my lifetime."

She nodded, her magic setting the grimoire alight in a way no one else's could.

"Do you remember the first time we met? Because for me, it feels like it was just yesterday… Do you remember that day, back in the shop?"

Her eyebrows pinched together the same way they always did when she was working on a complex tattoo design. "The…shop?"

"Yes, my tattoo shop where we used to work together – remember? It was a Tuesday morning. You burst through the door with your entire portfolio in hand. Most aspiring tattoo artists have a digital portfolio, with all their work saved on a tablet. And at least some background in, you know, tattoos. But not you. You came in, totally untrained, with this bulging suitcase. Hauled it right on top of the front desk, knocking over my coffee in the process. You remember that?"

She shook her head. "No, I…I don't remember any tattoo shop."

My eyes darted to Sol, whose attention was consumed by his army of blood incarnates, then back to the battlefield. One of the white-cloaked figures stood alone at the base of the hill, gazing up at me. When he removed his hood, the gold tips of his antlers shone in the light of the fires.

Emotion welled in my chest, gut-wrenching and raw. But, somehow, I managed to keep my face smooth as I turned back to Talia.

"There were tears in your eyes as you apologized again and again, trying to mop up your mess. And it was in those tears that

I first caught the faintest glimmer of a golden aura. I brushed it off as a trick of the light. I mean, what else could it have been, especially in the middle of Miami? But when you pulled out your drawings…they were nothing short of magic. That sketch of you holding your father's hand? It was the most beautiful thing I'd ever seen. The shading, the way you captured the faint veins beneath his skin, the IV that draped across his wrist…it brought tears to my eyes, Tal."

She stared down at me in consternation, her knuckles white as she gripped the spell book in two trembling hands. All I needed was a single drop of her blood – if I could just keep her from killing me for a few moments longer.

"You didn't notice, of course," I continued, pushing myself onto one knee as the Ligature binds she had cast began to loosen, "but the emotion you elicited caught me entirely off guard. How many years had it been since I'd last shed a tear? Or felt much of anything, for that matter? But your drawings, Talia, they stirred something deep within me, something I thought had died a long time ago. When I caught a glimpse of the talisman you wore beneath your shirt, and the faintest of golden auras shimmering around your body, I finally recognized you for what you were. That was the moment that I decided to hire you, so I could safeguard your blood – or so I'd convinced myself at the time."

"Stop it," she whispered, her frown deepening. "That's not… This isn't…"

"But in hindsight, it wasn't your blood, or even your art." The binds slid to the ground as I struggled to my feet. "It was love at first sight, and, unbeknownst to me, my love for you continued to grow with every passing day we worked together. You were compassionate, emotional, and forthright – everything I couldn't be. But you were also broken, lonely, and fragile – just like me. From the moment I laid eyes on you, all I wanted to do was wrap you in my arms. But I was a slave to Sol…just as you are now."

"I'm not a slave," she whispered, her chin quivering. "But I think…" She bit her lip, making my stomach twist at the sight. "I think maybe I do remember you."

My hand inched toward the dagger at my side. *Just one drop…*

Talia's gaze dropped to the makeshift rune on my hand, making my heart skip a beat – but she said nothing. Instead, a tear slipped from her eye, landing on the open page of the grimoire.

Sol's incarnates came to a lurching halt as he whirled around. A growl slipped through his bared teeth as he stalked toward us. "Why is he not dead, Zaffre?"

"I don't know." Her eyes were full of tears as she gazed quizzically into mine.

"It's because you love me," I answered. "Just as I love you with every fiber of my being." I looked Sol directly in the eye. "And there is no claim in existence powerful enough to eradicate that."

He closed his eyes, the muscle in his jaw clenching. A moment later, he retrieved the gun from his pocket, pointing the barrel at my chest. "Perhaps not. But I know something that will."

And then, without a moment's hesitation, he pulled the trigger.

TALIA

A deafening bang, followed immediately by another, roused me from my trance. But even then, it felt like I was looking at the world through a long tunnel, and everything on the other side was far away and hazy. I glanced down at my hands, which had become splattered in blood.

My blood?

No, I shook my head slowly. *Not mine…*

My eyes settled on the man sprawled on the ground at my feet, his face achingly familiar. Blood poured from his chest as another man knelt beside him, desperately trying to staunch the hemorrhage. As I watched the blurry scene unfold, something deep within me stirred, as though I, too, should be mourning the death of this dying man. But it was a distant thought. A fleeting thought. I turned to look at Solomon, who had put a comforting arm around my shoulders, drawing me close.

"Did your brother ever tell you that he was the one who killed your family?" he asked, lazily running his fingers through my hair.

The crouching man glared up at him with a hatred so fierce and deep, I instinctively took a step backward.

Solomon tightened his grip around me. "Your brother was such a fickle and jealous boy," he sighed. "Envious of your talents, of your place in the castle hierarchy, and the special love your mother had for you and no one else. On one particularly emotional day, a stranger approached your brother as he played alone by the creek. He claimed to be your long-lost relative, confiding in your brother that he had come to bring you back to your own kind, where you would be safe and loved. All he needed to know was the best way to sneak in and out of the palace, unseen, so the queen wouldn't try to stop him. To the stranger's amusement, it didn't take much convincing before the poor, love-starved little boy tearfully told him everything he needed to know."

The dying man let out an anguished sob.

Solomon clicked his tongue in pity. "I can only imagine the relief the young prince must have felt the next day, when he found his precious brother was still in his bed, safe and sound. For even though he truly did hate you, he loved you just as fiercely. In time, he forgot all about the kind stranger, and the two of you fell right back into fighting and playing as though nothing had ever happened." His fingertips gently grazed my scalp, nearly lulling me to sleep with his tale. "But the damage was already done, I'm afraid, for the stranger was a very patient man. It wasn't until many years later, when his army was fully formed and the time to strike was nigh, that the stranger used that little boy's jealousy and anguish, entering the castle through a secret passageway known only to the royal family – a secret passageway that was meant to keep them safe in the face of insurmountable danger. Instead, that passageway became the eventual dumping ground for the royal family's lifeless corpses – their final resting place." Solomon's grip on me tightened, steadying my legs, which, for some reason, were trembling. "Save for the two that escaped – with one taking the fall for the other."

"Is what he says true?" the kneeling man asked his brother, his voice hoarse with emotion.

"Yes," the dying man answered. He held up a trembling, blood-covered hand, which his brother grasped in both of his. "What he says is true, brother… It was I who sold my soul to the devil, not you."

ZAYN

I clutched Mikhæl's limp, bloody hand in mine, my vision blurring with tears.

"You're not a traitor," I rasped, the ferocity of my own words catching me off-guard. "You were a broken little boy who made a mistake you did not understand. And now…" Sorrow momentarily robbed me of speech. "Now…"

"And now he'll join Mommy and Daddy in the Other, where their souls can fester together," Sol snickered to Talia, who was staring at us with wide, unblinking eyes.

"I saved your life," Mikhæl choked out.

"I know," my voice cracked, "and I can never—"

"Let me finish," he interjected, switching to our mother tongue so Sol couldn't understand. "I saved your life, brother, so that you may finally right my wrongs." Streaks of iron were snaking up his neck, and the front of his cloak was soaked with blood. His grip weakened as his eyelids began to droop. "Go…" Mikhæl grimaced, straining to speak. "Live your life…in the peace and happiness…that I robbed…from us both."

"Miki," I whispered, dropping my forehead to his.

He pressed his other hand to my cheek…and then his eyelids fluttered closed, and his hand tumbled lifelessly to the ground.

I gripped his limp hand in both of mine. "May the Creator guide your soul back to the light, my brother."

"Enough of this."

I rose to my feet, only to find Sol's gun aimed between my eyes.

"That I was able to facilitate such a tender reunion warms my heart, Zæynek. Truly. But your nine lives are up."

When he pulled the trigger, the gun clicked, but didn't discharge.

Snarling, he pistol-whipped me in the temple, knocking me to the ground beside Mikhæl's unmoving body, then snatched the grimoire from Talia's hands. He thumbed through it furiously, casting anxious glances toward the base of the hill in between pages. The tides of battle seemed to be turning as the elves from the north and south combined forces for the first time in millennia.

A smile crossed my face.

"This one," Sol finally snapped, shoving the grimoire back into Talia's hands. "Kill him now, and kill him quickly."

She nodded, her eyes glowing like molten rubies as she turned the full might of his fury onto me.

XXIII.
Fire and Ice

TALIA

I briefly regarded the man – Zæynek, Solomon had called him – over the top of the spell book before quickly dropping my eyes back to the lethal rune that was staring up at me from the weathered page. I didn't feel dread or even pity at the thought of killing him; if Solomon wanted him dead, he deserved to be dead.

"Attention, Seelies!" he called to the thousands of soldiers scattered across the battlefield. His voice was so commanding and powerful, it brought the fighting to an immediate halt. "Surrender now, and I may find it in my heart to spare those of you who pledge yourselves to me!"

"Talia," Zæynek whispered, once more struggling to his feet. I couldn't understand how a man could fall down so many times, only to stand back up again and again.

Ignoring his entreaty, I turned my attention back to Solomon, entranced by his mellifluous voice. For some reason, the elves weren't as enthralled by his rousing speech as I was, though their rising shouts and jeers only seemed to amuse him.

"Look to your mighty phoenix tree!" he cried out, pointing. I followed his finger to the forest, where the base of an enormous, glowing tree had begun to burn from the many fires that had broached its clearing. "Soon, your precious sanctuary will be razed to the ground, and your lives, your travails, and your imminent deaths will have all been in vain. There will be no leaves to rest beneath, nor heavenly reunions on the other side!"

A wide grin spread across his face as his captive audience devolved into horrified cries. "How the mighty doth fall!" he crooned, setting my heart aflame. "For centuries your people have repressed us, denigrated us, and robbed us of our rights! And now you will all die as the Unseelies do, rotting away in the lightless Other."

"DON'T LISTEN TO THIS SCHMUCK!" a high-pitched cry rose from the battlefield, making Sol – and me – flinch from the shrillness.

My head jerked downward, where a line of white-haired women were gliding over the mud, their bare feet treading across fire and leaving a frosted trail of ice behind them. Leading from the center of the line, a blonde woman clad head-to-toe in purple armor stood with her hands on her hips. Two birds sat on her shoulders, a raven wreathed in flames of gold, and a colorful parrot ensconced in dazzling rainbow fire.

"WE ACCEPT *ALL* CREATURES HERE, SEELIE AND UNSEELIE BOTH! AND I DON'T CARE WHAT YOU ARE – VAMPIRE, ELF, OR THE FREAKING ABOMINABLE SNOWMAN! IF YOU DREAM OF A WORLD WHERE YOU CAN EAT A ROAST BEEF SANDWICH IN PEACE ANYWHERE YOU'D LIKE, THEN YOU ARE WELCOME IN THE SUMMER COURT!"

My eyebrows drew together as I took a step closer to the edge of the precipice. The woman's piercing screech made me want to claw out my eardrums…and yet there was also something inexplicably comforting about it.

"THAT MAN UP THERE IS A PSYCHOTIC DINGLEBERRY WHO ONLY CARES ABOUT HIMSELF!" she hollered at Solomon's soldiers, jabbing a finger in our master's direction. "IF YOU COME JOIN US, YOU'LL NEVER HAVE TO LISTEN TO HIS HATEFUL *MISHEGAS* EVER AGAIN! EVEN YOU VAMPIRES!" she shouted to a nearby cluster of them. "SO LONG AS YOU PROMISE NOT TO BITE ANYONE, YOU'RE WELCOME AT ANY DINNER TABLE OF MINE!"

Deftly weaving his way through the line of banshees, a rumpled-looking satyr appeared at the purple warrior's side. "Every word this remarkable woman – or rather, *vamshee* – is saying is true!" he bleated loudly, sending a ripple of murmurs through the crowd. "There is a place for *all* of you in the Summer Court!"

"Vamshee…?" I whispered, then clapped a hand against my mouth.

Mom.

The strange, unexpected word filled me with warmth.

That's my mother.

Sol whirled around to look at me, and I quickly recomposed my face into a blank stare.

"Zaffre?" he asked, arching an eyebrow.

"Yes, my beloved?" I intoned.

His eyes narrowed slightly. "What is the reason for the delay?"

I opened my mouth, hesitating for the span of a single breath. Nothing had changed; I was still bound to Solomon in a way that went beyond words, beyond even comprehension. Our bodies were intertwined through the unbreakable bond of blood, our souls permanently fused. I'd sooner part with a limb than with him…and yet…

"I…I thought you might want to make his death more of a spectacle – for greater impact." The words toppled from my tongue before the thought behind them had fully materialized. "I've just been waiting for your signal…my love."

His features softened into a smile. "That's my darling girl. Indeed, my runes are spent, little one, and I will need you for this next crucial part."

Nodding, I turned my attention back to the grimoire, hurriedly thumbing through the pages to find what I needed. A few moments later, I cast a Paralysis Rune on the man Sol had called Zæynek, followed by a Levitation Rune. His rigid body hovered in the air beside me, his green eyes full of grief and sorrow. At the sight of him, a cry rose up from the elves. I, however, was just a mysterious figure cloaked entirely in black. Not even my mother recognized me.

My mother.

I swallowed as another shock of clarity jolted through me – one that twisted my stomach into terrified knots.

As the first rays of dawn broke over the mountain, casting the forest and hills in pale gray light, Solomon reached down and yanked Zæynek's brother's limp body from the ground by the bloodied collar. Below, the cries of the elves turned into screams.

To my left, Zæynek could only watch in frozen horror.

"Your Winter King is dead!" Solomon cried, hurling the body down the side of the hill. It tumbled down the steep slope, landing in a heap of broken limbs and bloody robes at the very bottom. "And soon, your unfledged Summer King will join him."

Solomon turned to me. "The banshees will scream any moment now," he murmured, cupping the side of my face. "I need you to kill him, quickly, and then cast a muffling spell over the battlefield. Can you do that for me?"

I nodded. "Of course."

He kissed my forehead, then took a step backward. "In that case, all eyes are on you, little one."

Taking a deep breath, I pushed my hood away, exposing my face to the crowd below.

"*TALIA*!" my mother shrieked.

The earsplitting screech cut through the haze in my brain like sunlight burning through early morning fog. Despite the hundred and one questions swirling through my mind at that moment, there was one thing I knew for certain: My mother was the most intuitive judge of character I'd ever known. If she claimed the incubus I worshiped, lived, and breathed for was a "psychotic dingleberry" and a schmuck…

Oh God.

Sol glanced at me, further weakening my tenuous resolve, but I kept my face schooled. The terrible deed I was deliberating – the equivalent of cutting off my own limb – was going to take every last drop of willpower and strength I possessed.

I turned back to Zæynek, my mind screaming at me to kill him so I could return to the safety of Sol's arms, where I belonged. But my mother's words had been in direct opposition to that. And against all other impulse and reason, my heart was pleading with me to listen to her.

"Talia," Zæynek murmured. "No matter what happens now, I want you to know—"

"Be quiet," I snapped, my eyes darting to the rune on the palm of his hand.

Please help me find what I'm looking for, I whispered silently to his grimoire. For the first time since Sol had given it to me, the pages flipped open obediently, immediately landing on the spell I needed. *Thank you,* I breathed.

My hand hovered above the page, Endowing the rune with power.

"Which one will you use?" Zæynek's voice was soft and gentle, catching me off guard.

"A Laceration Rune," I answered coldly, taking a step toward him. My knees were trembling, and my head felt faint at the thought of what I was about to do. Every nerve in my body was screaming at me, telling me that my mother was wrong.

But if that were true, and Zæynek truly *was* the villain, why was there so much kindness in his eyes?

"Another good one – painful, though not particularly honorable." A crooked smile spread across his face, making my wrenching heart skip a beat. "Would you mind aiming it at my chest, at least, so I bleed out quickly?"

I glanced over my shoulder at Sol. He nodded his approval, his own eyes alight with crimson fire.

Closing the gap between Zæynek and myself, I raised my hand, readying my attack. Down below, hundreds of frantic cries were screaming for me to stop, but I tuned them out, focusing on the spell and nothing else, willing my body to do the unthinkable.

"I love you, Tal," Zæynek whispered, his unbearably kind eyes boring into mine. "Now and always."

I avoided his gaze, where my own, strange-looking reflection gazed back at me, then stole one last glance at my mother. Though everyone around her was shouting up at us, her mouth was clamped shut. She clutched her hands in front of her chest, fingers interlaced as though silently pleading with me. The rainbow bird – *Biscuit,* I suddenly remembered – let out a mournful cry.

I swallowed tightly. "An incubus cannot love, only lust," I replied, turning back to Zæynek. "Or have you forgotten?"

He flinched as though I'd slapped him.

The Laceration Rune on the page blazed to life as my hand shot forward, stopping millimeters from his heart. I took a deep breath, steeling myself against the mounting terror in my chest. I knew full well what was coming; it was just a matter of bringing myself to do it.

By the time my eyes had once more risen to meet his, my entire body was trembling. "Lucky for us, you're half elf."

Zayn's eyes doubled in size as I reached forward and grabbed his hand. Gold blood dripped from the deep laceration that had appeared not across his chest, but down the length of my palm. The rune on his hand, now caught between our entwined fingers, glowed to life.

"Together?" I rasped, turning around to stand beside him.

"Together," he managed to choke out.

"No!" Sol roared, lunging forward, arm outstretched.

Our clasped hands erupted in fire, which then arced through the air, slamming into the center of his chest. A primal scream tore from Sol's throat as his entire body burst into roaring flames.

"*NOOO!*"

The Requisition Rune on my shoulder simultaneously burst to life, blazing as hot as the Immolation Rune Zayn and I had conjured. I fell to one knee, gasping.

Sol screamed in outrage as he raised a burning hand, grasped the vial of blood around his neck, and downed it in one gulp. The flames surrounding his body began to dim.

Biscuit! I cried out silently. *Mavros!*

The raven on my mother's shoulder immediately launched into the sky, her mighty roar shaking the earth itself as she transformed into a colossal gold dragon. Biscuit shot ahead of her, lighting up the sky like a shooting star. A prismatic blast of rainbow fire exploded against Sol's chest, knocking him to one knee.

And then Mavros crested the hill, unleashing a ferocious torrent of golden fire from her jaws.

Wreathed in flames, Sol's burning body illuminated the dusky sky like a lighthouse in a storm. His screams of anguish rose higher and higher as his hair and clothing incinerated and his blackened skin turned to ash.

I clutched Zayn's hand as tightly as I could, feeling as though I, too, were burning alive.

When Sol collapsed to the ground, so did I.

"Talia!" Zayn cried out, falling to his knees beside me. He scooped me into his arms, cradling me against his chest. "Talia, what is it? What's—" His question broke off in a strangled gasp as realization contorted his expression into one of horror.

My eyes darted past his shoulder and to the distant hills, where the sun was cresting the mountains. As rays of pale teal light streaked across the awakening sky, the banshees' mournful cries rose up over the battlefield, sending the remaining vampires fleeing into the smoking remains of the forest. Perched on the castle turrets, licking their wounds, the harpies joined in on the lament. Even the mermaids echoed their cry, and from their requiem, a gentle rain once more began to fall, smothering the fires that glowed at the base of the Great Phoenix Tree.

The edges of my vision were quickly fading to black as I turned to look at Zayn one last time.

"I wouldn't have changed a single thing," I whispered, blinking back tears.

"Please, Tal, don't go." A sob lodged in Zayn's chest as he leaned down and brushed his trembling lips against mine. "I can't live without you."

I lifted my hand to his face, brushing a tear from his dark lashes.

There were so many things I'd never gotten to say to him. So many memories we'd never have the chance to make together. So many regrets I'd never be able to make up to him.

But even still, as darkness overtook me, and the distant echo of Zayn's cries grew farther and farther away, I let out a blissful sigh, basking in the beautiful sound of my name spilling from his lips as I slipped peacefully into death.

XXIV.
Darkness and Light

SOLOMON

Every fiber of my being screamed with agony, growing worse with every passing moment. Upon the commencement of each new and never-ending second, I was certain the pain couldn't possibly get any worse. But it could. And it did. For the first time in my existence, I begged the Creator to put an end to my misery and wrench me from my mortal shell. But Death took its time in taking me, savoring in the interminable moment of my demise.

And then, all at once, the creeping darkness overcame me – and I ceased to exist.

Mercy, I breathed, sinking into the void.

But Death wasn't done with me.

My eyes shot open once more, finding nothing but unending blackness, no different than the inside of my eyelids. All that time longing for oblivion, and my thoughts, my awareness still hadn't left me. I still existed, but how?

And – a far more terrifying thought – *where?*

Panic clawed at my chest as the dark outline of my body materialized into "view," and yet was no more than a black silhouette cast upon an endless black canvas.

Nothing and everything pressed against me all at once, smothering me, pulling me apart.

"Sol?" a voice called.

With a choked cry, I whirled around. At the sight of another, relief flooded me from the inside out. "Zaffre," I sobbed, reaching for her.

She took a step backward, half of her shrouded in shadow, the other half faintly illuminated. Dim as it was, her light warmed the entire realm, and I found myself drawn to her like a dying moth to a flame.

"What is this place?" Zaffre asked, hugging herself for warmth. Her voice sounded muffled and subdued, as though she were speaking underwater.

Wordless whispers scratched at the air behind me, making the hairs on the back of my neck stand on end. But when I whirled around to look, there was only blackness.

Endless, shapeless, everlasting blackness.

"The Other," I rasped, my throat as rough and dry as gravel. "The realm of infinite darkness."

I never expected to see this place; in truth, I'd been alive for so long, I'd almost forgotten about death.

Or perhaps I'd merely convinced myself I could outrun it.

Zaffre jumped, then glanced over her shoulder as though she had heard voices behind her as well. But I couldn't hear any trace of a whisper coming from her direction, and she didn't appear to hear the ghostly rasps scraping against my eardrums like fingernails on sandpaper.

"This place…" she murmured. "It feels…familiar."

"Like the void," I muttered, almost to myself – the pocket of empty space I'd built my Miami nightclub upon, where the veils of our two realms slid right past one another.

"Yes." She nodded slowly, rubbing her shoulder. Her entire left arm was made of matter so black, its inky tendrils leeched into the rest of her soul, stealing the very light from it.

"You shouldn't be here," I whispered, the realization, the weight of my very existence crushing against my sternum. "I… I did this to you." I took another step toward her, propelled by shame and grief – both wholly unfamiliar feelings.

She turned her face away from me.

The ensuing silence filled the space where air used to be, making every labored breath of mine sound deafening. The nothingness closed in on me, crushing my lungs, my body, my soul.

"I never meant…" I started, then licked my lips, desperately trying to put moisture back into my mouth. "I didn't mean for this to happen, truly. I just…" *Just what?* My mind churned through every possible explanation – from the premature death of my own father, to the loss of my beloved Jaína – but every excuse rang as hollow as the void in which I'd trapped us.

"The Seelies took everything from me – *everything*," I raged, desperate to make her understand. "My land, my dreams, my dignity. All I ever wanted was to reclaim what was rightfully mine, to be respected and revered—"

"You wanted to be loved," she whispered.

"I—" My breaths became quick and shallow as I looked up at her – the epitome of goodness and compassion, of beauty and youth. Endless opportunity should have lay ahead of her, had I not stolen it.

"Forgive me," I choked out. As I reached for her hand, the faint aura surrounding her body pulsed brighter and brighter. At the same time – like ink being drawn back into its vial – the hideous black stain bled out of her shoulder, becoming one with the surrounding darkness…

And with me.

She took another step backward.

The whispers at my back grew louder. I stole a glance over my shoulder, where the dark outlines of dozens of specters were creeping closer. When I turned back to Zaffre – to *Talia*, I amended – her aura had grown so bright, she warmed the surrounding darkness. I raised my arm to my tear-filled eyes, shielding them from her radiance.

As her light burned away the very edges of the Other, she cast me a sad smile. "Deep down, there's good in you. I'm sure of it."

I tried to take a step in her direction, only to stumble backward. The darkness pressed in on all sides, like a deep, black ocean, its pressure crushing me. Every time I tried to fill my lungs with air, I felt like I was choking on the nothingness.

"Please don't leave me," I whispered hoarsely. "Please."

Talia glanced over my shoulder, a look of pity crossing her lovely face.

I followed her gaze to the army of hazy figures that had assembled at my back, waiting for me in the darkness. My children, and my enemies – here, one and the same. They converged on me, their familiar faces contorted with both accusation and abhorrence, and yet – to my simultaneous dismay and relief – the one face I'd long been yearning to see again wasn't among them.

Perhaps the boy will see his mother again after all.

"*Aşeki'şík aza muhávsi,*" Talia said softly, her voice growing fainter and fainter as the light seized her. "I pray, one day, your soul will find the light."

"Wait!" I cried out, reaching for her. But the farther my fingers stretched, the dimmer she became. "Wait," I rasped, panting. "Please…"

And then she was gone, and my soul was once more plunged into darkness.

TALIA

Blinding white light surrounded me, cradling my soul like a child. Even still, I hugged my knees against my chest, too afraid to open my eyes.

You have nothing to fear, a gentle voice whispered, wrapping me in comfort.

I squinted one eye open, and then the other, using my hand to shield them from the radiance.

Welcome back, daughter.

When the light finally cleared from my vision, I found myself sitting on one of the upraised roots of the Great Phoenix Tree. Far above, its scintillating leaves fluttered in the gentle breeze. Below, a lush, partially charred carpet of bioluminescent moss and mushrooms cushioned my feet, now safe from the fires that had threatened them from the other side of the veil. And in front of me, filling the entire clearing, stood dozens and dozens of elves – hundreds, even. Most of them were strangers, though some of the faces – like Laleh and Éyrel's – were reassuringly familiar. As I looked closer, I realized it wasn't just elves that had congregated in front of me; there were a number of brightly-glowing tommyknockers and banshees that stood among them as well, while several harpies flew lazily overhead, their feathers as lustrous as the silver sun.

But that wasn't what made me gasp in astonishment.

There, standing front and center in the crowd, were three white-clad figures – one I immediately identified, and two others I recognized only because I'd gazed up at their immortalized forms in the Summer Palace's ornate, stained-glass windows.

I rose to my bare feet, my white robes swirling around my ankles, as the crowd broke into welcoming cheers. But I hardly registered them; I was too busy staring at the elven woman who was motioning to me, her slender arms outstretched in welcome. Ensconced in a pale lavender aura, she was one of the most beautiful creatures I'd ever seen, with shimmering bronze skin, wide green eyes, and midnight blue hair.

"Queen Jaína?" I whispered, clapping my hands to my mouth.

Without hesitating, she stepped forward and wrapped me in her arms, pressing her cheek to the top of my head. "Thank you," she whispered fervently. "Thank you for showing my precious boy all the love we could not, blinded as we were by our corporeal vision."

Tears filled my eyes as I gently pulled away to look between her, Mikhæl, and Zayn's stepfather – the infamous King Saedis himself.

Panicking, I dropped into a curtsy, prompting a low chuckle from the others. He cupped my chin and gently pulled me to my feet.

"My dear granddaughter"—he smiled, his aquamarine eyes twinkling—"there are no titles here, nor hierarchy. There is only love and light – and learning," Saedis added, taking Jaína's hand to brush a gentle kiss against her knuckles. "I echo my beloved's sentiments in thanking you for your compassion, as well as your unwavering devotion to our son – something Zæynek knew so little of as a child." His eyes tightened. "I am deeply sorry for the direct hand I had in that – one of the many reasons I only recently ascended from the Other, unlike the rest of my family, who have been waiting for me for some time." Saedis cast a sad smile at the two young women standing behind him – *Maránthe and Yenna*, I remembered – who both reached out and gripped their father's hand. One was a shorter, softer version of her mother, while the other was poised and statuesque, like her father.

"You were able to leave the Other too?" I asked, suppressing a shudder.

Saedis nodded. "It took me many years of self-reflection and ruminating – all while trapped in a bleak, lightless hell of my own making – before my soul once more found its way back to the light."

Zayn's mother rested her head against his shoulder, drawing my eyes to the faint pale-yellow aura that shimmered around his body.

But Saedis has gold blood like me, doesn't he? I inspected the palms of my hands, which radiated with golden light almost as bright as the Great Phoenix Tree itself. *So why—*

"Talia." Mikhæl stepped forward, pulling me from my reverie. "I would not be here if not for you and my little brother bringing me to my senses… Thank you." He pressed his hand to his heart.

"Amen to that!" a voice called out. My eyes widened as they landed on the speaker – Zayn's Aunt Elínya, the Great Mother herself. "Thank you for getting my people to safety, despite my own stubbornness and ego," she said, pressing a hand to her chest. "And thank you for everything you've sacrificed – not just for our family, but for the entire realm."

"A-Anytime," I stammered.

The other souls in the clearing bowed their heads, echoing her sentiments, while I dropped my gaze to the ground, fighting back tears.

"What's wrong, child?" Jaína asked softly.

"I just…I can't bear the thought of abandoning him there," I whispered, scrubbing the tears from my cheeks. "He's all alone now, just like before—" My words broke off in a quiet sob.

With a soft hum of compassion, Jaína wrapped me in another tight embrace. "My heart hurts for you both, child," she murmured. "But time moves differently here. It will feel like no time at all before his soul comes to join us – your mother's, as well."

A much louder sob burst from my throat as I buried my head in her shoulder, my tears dampening the front of her robes.

She held me for a long time, only letting go when I finally managed to pull away from the embrace. When I looked up at her, I was expecting to find a sad expression; instead, as her eyes darted over my shoulder, a wide smile spread across her face.

I slowly turned around, the hairs on the back of my neck standing on end.

A figure stood before me, his ocean-blue aura among the most radiant in the entire crowd. "Tals," he whispered, his tear-stained cheeks full of life and vigor.

A strangled cry burst from my lips, and I flung myself into his arms, sobbing. "Dad!"

"Shh, shh. It's okay," he whispered, stroking my hair. "I'm right here."

"Dad, I'm so sorry," I wept, clutching him with all my might, too terrified to let go. "It's my fault you spent your last few months hooked up to all those needles. I was so selfish and afraid to lose you – and then, in the end, I wasn't even there to say goodbye!"

At that, Dad gently gripped me by the shoulders and looked me square in the eye. "I was there when you said goodbye, Tals. I heard every word."

My chin began to quiver. "You were?"

Dad nodded. "Yes. And every kind, loving word you and your mother have spoken about me since." His face broke into a wide grin. "I haven't even had the chance to miss you, the way you two chatter on and on about me all the time."

I half-laughed, half-sobbed as I reached forward and pulled him into another hug, this one even tighter than the last. When I finally managed to let him go, he walked over to stand Mikhæl and Saedis – the brother and father he'd never known in life.

The uncle and grandfather I never knew I had.

Saedis put an arm around each of his sons, beaming widely. "Once Zæynek and Talia's mother arrive – a long, long time from now," he added hastily, seeing my crumpling expression, "we'll all be one, big, happy family!"

"Father, you can't tell the poor girl you're looking forward to her loved ones dying!" the taller of his two daughters groaned.

"No, no, certainly not!" Saedis stammered, casting me an apologetic grimace. "I'm just excited for them to ascend to a far better place, that's all."

"Once you've had some time to acclimate, there's no pain here, Tals," Dad said, his eyes twinkling. "No heartache or grief, either. We spend our days learning and growing from our past mistakes, all gently laid bare here, with the intention of making our light a little brighter. That way, the next time we're born, we'll start anew as a better version of ourselves."

"The…next time?" I sniffled.

"Yep." Dad nodded. "We all get to choose the moment we're reincarnated – we even have a small say in the who and where." He grinned again, filling my heart with joy so poignant, it almost ached. "But I couldn't leave before seeing you and your mother again. Besides, she'd kill me if I reincarnated without her. Our marriage vows, as she's repeatedly reminded me, extend into the next life as well."

Another laugh burst from my lips. "You might want to rethink that plan – she's so mad at you for dying before her, you'll never hear the end of it when she finally stomps through that portal."

Zayn's family – *our* family – let out a hearty chuckle at that.

Even still, a fresh lump appeared in my throat. *I* knew I was okay. *I* knew I would see my mother again, in what might even feel – to me – like a relatively short time. But no matter how fluidly time moved in this realm, both she and Zayn would have to live the remainder of their Earth-bound lives without me. Worse, Zayn would spend all those years clinging to the false belief that his soul was too tarnished to ever make it here – that he might never see me again.

"Hey, Dad…?" I chewed on my lip, casting a glance over my shoulder at the Great Phoenix Tree, then back to our rather large audience. "Any chance we could speak in private?"

"Oh – sure thing." He put a hand on my shoulder, gently leading me away from the others, then turned to face me. "What is it, Tals?" he asked, even as a knowing smile tugged at the corners of his mouth.

"I, um…" I trailed off, unsure how I could possibly find the words to tell him—

"You want to go back to them." He said the words simply, kindly, without a trace of judgment or disappointment.

Fresh tears welled in my eyes. "You have no idea how happy I am to see you, Dad. I've literally dreamed of this moment every night since…" I swallowed. "Well, since I lost you."

"Well, lucky for us, I'm not actually lost." He tapped the center of my sternum, just beneath the locket he'd given me. "I'm always right here, no matter where you go."

I flung my arms around him, breathing in the familiar, comforting scent I'd long been bereft of.

He kissed the top of my head, then motioned for me to join him as he crouched beside one of the Great Phoenix Tree's upturned, glowing roots. "Unfortunately, it's not possible to return to our bodies once we've died. Believe me, I tried like heck."

"Oh," I answered, crestfallen.

Dad tucked a piece of golden hair behind my ear, a hint of sadness in his smile. "But as your mother always says, there's never any harm in asking, right?"

He pressed his palm against the root, and I timidly placed my hand atop his, momentarily taken aback by the warmth of it. The last time I'd held my father's hand, his skin had been cold, bruised, and draped in IVs.

I squeezed my eyes shut, burning *this* image into my memory instead, then shook my head to clear it. "But how would I even ask for a thing like that?"

"Like this," Dad grinned, closing his eyes and launching into a solemn, deep-throated invocation. "Oh, mighty Phoenix Tree, Guardian of Light, Sacred Demigod of the Realm of Souls, Almighty Shaper of the Bonds of Aether—"

"Seriously?!" I whispered.

He popped open one eye. "Nah, I'm just pulling your leg. You can just ask normally."

"Oh, thank God." My shoulders abruptly relaxed. "Um, okay…" Squeezing my eyes shut, I clenched his hand in mine, then took a deep, steadying breath. "Um, Great Phoenix Tree…?"

"Yes, daughter."

"Oh, wow! That was fast!" I laughed nervously, then cleared my throat. "Um, listen…I know it's probably really presumptuous of me to even ask, but I was wondering if it might be possible to return to my body—and before you say no, let me just quickly explain my reasoning…"

I turned to my dad for help, though all he did was flash me a hearty thumbs-up.

"Um, so first and foremost," I continued, "my mom will literally die if she loses her only daughter. Like, *die* die. And it's so quiet and peaceful here, you know? I just think it would be better for everyone in the realm if we could hold off on that as long as possible. That way you can kind of prepare the other, uh, 'tenants' ahead of her arrival. I mean, don't get me wrong – my mom's amazing, but she's also pretty…um…voluble."

Dad let out a low snort. "Understatement of the century."

"Also," I barreled on, wincing at my own painfully inarticulate efforts, "as you probably know, Zayn has had, like, the worst life imaginable. And he's such a good person despite all of that, so I think we can all agree he deserves at least a tiny smidge of happi—oh, God!" I gasped, interrupting myself. "I completely forgot about Biscuit! And Mavros too!" I clapped my free hand against my mouth, letting out a muffled squeak. "I've orphaned my babies!"

For some reason, Dad puffed out his cheeks as though he were desperately holding back a peal of laughter.

"Daughter!" The Great Phoenix Tree's tone was surprisingly firm, though her leaves were quivering in a way that made me suspect she too was stifling a laugh. *"I have already answered your question."*

I blinked. "You… have?"

"For mending the divisions of the corporeal realms, as well as your noble sacrifice in defending this sacred demesne, the answer – as I had told you before you had even asked – is yes."

My mouth fluttered open wordlessly.

"It is but a small token of my thanks to you, dear child, for the beautiful light you exude. Radiance such as yours gives me hope that we will one day vanquish the darkness."

Dad gave me a gentle nudge.

"I…thank you," I somehow managed to choke out.

My jaw was still dangling open as my dad helped me to my shaking feet, then wrapped me in a quick, tight embrace. "Give your mother the biggest hug from me when you get back," he said, cupping my dazed face between two hands. "And let her know that the thing she's been looking for is inside a box of ties on the top shelf of her closet, okay? Oh, and if you remember any of this, please tell Zayn that I can't wait to meet him. No man was ever going to be good enough for my only daughter, so I'm glad to see you picked a nice fae instead." He grinned.

"The thing she's looking for...?" I shook my head, frowning. "And what do you mean *if* I rem—"

A bright flash exploded in front of my vision, bleaching my father's smile – and everything else – into an endless, swirling blaze of dazzling light.

I love you, Tals, Dad's voice echoed in my ears, wrapping my soul in warmth. *More than anything in the four realms.*

XXV.
AMENDS

I jolted awake with a wheezing gasp.

"*RAWK! ZOMMIEEE!"* Biscuit screeched at the top of his tiny lungs. He tumbled off my chest and onto the ground, while Mavros fell on top of him with an unholy squawk.

"Talia?" Zayn choked out. He was still cradling me in both arms against his chest, staring down at me as though he were seeing a literal ghost. "What…? *How—*"

He was cut off by a deafening scream unlike any I'd ever heard – not even from a full-blooded banshee. Louder than a locomotive whistle, more powerful than even her window-exploding stunt from the week before last, the force of my mother's scream literally knocked Zayn flat on his back.

"TALIA! YOU'RE ALIVE?!"

"Apparently," I grunted as she and Lamswyth crested the hill, both of them sweating and gasping for breath.

Zayn carefully helped me back into a sitting position just in time for Mom to fling her arms around me, knocking me back to the ground.

"Thank the Creator!" Lam dabbed his forehead with a tattered handkerchief. "From down below, it looked… Well, it certainly didn't look good, to say the least."

"She went five full minutes without a heartbeat, Lam," Zayn muttered, his face as white as a sheet.

"Baruch Hashem!" Mom wailed at the sky, strangling me in the process.

"Zommie!" Biscuit squawked again, flapping his wings in agitation.

"I'm not a zombie!" I barked, sending him cowering behind Mavros, who was cowering behind Zayn. "*Oy,* Mom – please! I can't breathe!"

The second my mom clambered off of me, Zayn reached forward and scooped me into his arms, hugging me so fiercely, a choked gasp burst through my lips.

"I thought I'd lost you," he rasped, only to quickly pull away so he could inspect me.

Our breaths simultaneously caught at the sight of my bare shoulder.

The entire area was covered in angry red welts, as though I'd been badly burned, and the veins beneath my skin were streaked with what appeared to be mild blood poisoning, indicating damage to the deep tissue.

But Sol's spider-shaped claim – and the blight that had accompanied it – was completely gone.

Zayn pressed his hand to his mouth, his wide eyes pooling with tears as they met mine.

"I'm…free?" I whispered.

He just stared at me wordlessly, frozen in place as though he still couldn't believe it.

"Zayn – I'm free!" I flung my arms around his neck with an ecstatic shriek, crushing my lips against his.

He hesitated for the span of a startled, disbelieving gasp, then pulled me into a tight embrace, one hand clutching my body against his chest, the other knotting in my hair. *"Jiyâné kalb'ímtha,"* he rasped against my lips, tears pooling in his eyes. "You came back to me."

I clutched the front of his vest, pulling him even closer. "I promised I'd never leave you."

He kissed me deeply, fiercely, his tears intermingling with my own.

Unfortunately, our beautiful moment was yet again interrupted by a shrill, tea-kettle-like whistle.

"TAL-YAAAAAAAAAA!" Biscuit screamed, having finally accepted that I was not, in fact, a zombie.

I let go of Zayn just in time for our familiar to dive-bomb my chest as though he'd been shot from a cannon, once again knocking me backward. While I lay splayed-out on the ground, trying to catch my breath, he and Mavros clambered all over me like hyperactive golden retrievers, letting out identical squawks of joy. A bright flash exploded in my periphery, from which two over-stimulated Chihuahuas burst into existence. Before I knew it, I was at the bottom of a literal dog pile, with the entire wolf pack howling and lapping at my cheeks.

"Hey, hey – take it easy!" I laughed, pressing my face into Ricky's soft black fur. As I did, a flashbulb memory burst in front of my eyes – one of a familiar figure sweeping me into a tight embrace, his white robes ensconced in brilliant blue light.

Give your mother the biggest hug from me when you get back.

I jerked upright with a sharp gasp, sending the menagerie scattering.

"What's wrong?" Mom demanded. She, Zayn, and Lamswyth knelt beside me, all three of them sporting varying expressions of concern.

I reached forward to pull her into a tight, one-armed hug, while my other hand blindly groped for Zayn's.

"Tal, what is it?" he asked. "What's—"

"I saw them," I breathed, squeezing his hand tightly. "Your family, Zayn – I saw them."

Mom pulled away from me with a start.

Zayn's grip around my fingers stiffened.

"Your mother, brother, sisters, aunt…your stepfather too…" I rubbed my temples, desperately trying to cling to the hazy images that were rapidly fading from my mind. "They all wanted you to know how sorry they are, and how much they love you. And… And…" I grimaced, squeezing my eyes shut. "*Ugh*, damnit! I think Dad said something about a…a tie box, maybe?"

My mom and Zayn exchanged stunned glances. "What?!"

Shaking the last of the fog from my head, I looked between the two of them, dumbfounded. "What?"

"What do you mean, *Dad told you?!*"

"Huh?" I gaped at my mother, completely lost. "What do you mean, what do I mean?"

She stared back at me, her eyes as wide as saucers before she whirled on Zayn. "Did you hear what she—"

"Yes," he answered hoarsely. "I heard."

"Your Highnesses!" Lam called from behind us. "I think it's high time you grace your valiant soldiers with a few much-needed reassurances."

"He's right," I said, interrupting whatever frantic, hushed conversation Mom and Zayn were in the middle of having.

"Yes – of course." Zayn cleared his throat. "Tal, think you can make it back down there? If not, I can carry you."

I hesitated, seriously considering his offer, then shook my head. "No, I can walk."

"I'll help you," he said, wrapping an arm around my waist.

"You have no idea how good it feels to be touched by you again." I sighed contentedly, resting my head on his shoulder.

He kissed the top of my head with trembling lips. "Believe me when I say I do."

Releasing echoing shrieks of jubilation, Biscuit and Mavros launched into the sky, soaring in wide, celebratory spirals. Glitter floated down from their contrails like fairy dust, catching the attention of the crowd below.

With Zayn's help, I staggered to my feet, eliciting an uproarious cheer from the elves.

Except, I quickly realized, it wasn't just the elves who were celebrating our victory; scattered among the intermingled elven clans were hundreds of banshees, harpies, tommyknockers, humans, and even—

Holy shit. I swallowed in disbelief, regarding the sizable gathering of incubi, succubi, and vampires, who stood apart and away from the main crowd. And yet, they were here…

With us.

I tightened my grip on Zayn's arm as we slowly descended the hill, marveling at the diversity standing before us. Hundreds – no, *thousands* – of fae from every corner of the continent had gathered in that pockmarked clearing, rejoicing in our collective, hard-fought victory. When we reached the bottom of the hill, they all crowded around us, raising a triumphant assortment of fists, daggers, and pickaxes in the air.

"Talia!" a familiar voice cried.

My head snapped up as Korinne and Safir burst through the front of the crowd. Safir was limping badly, and Korinne had a wide gash above her eyebrow – but they were alive.

"Ko-Ko!" I sobbed, reaching for her. When she hesitated, I pointed to my shoulder. "Look! The claim is gone!"

"Oh, thank the Creator!" She pulled me into a rib-cracking hug. Where have you *been?* We thought you were dead!"

"Not this one!" Safir beamed, ruffling my hair. "Our steadfast queen is unbreakable!"

"Wait a minute!" Korinne gasped, gripping me by the elbows. "All those mysterious fires, the attacks on the incarnates – was that *you* out there?!"

I felt a blush creeping into my cheeks. "Uh…yeah." I rubbed the back of my neck. "Some of that might have been me."

"*This* is our mysterious guardian!" Safir cried out in Elvish, clutching my wrist and hoisting my arm over my head. *"Tálya'mthá'ya, Paşéni'şah ve amát'işík!"*

"To our Talia!" Korinne repeated as she gripped my other hand. "Our Queen of Queens and Light of Hope!"

The roar that erupted from the crowd was so thunderous, my knees shook both from the force of it and from sheer mortification. But then I felt Zayn's steadying hand on my back. When I glanced at him over my shoulder, he was beaming down at me, his eyes glassy. Lam and my mother stood beside him, one daintily dabbing their eyes while the other was convulsing from happy sobs – though not in the order you'd expect.

"BE QUIET!" an angry voice thundered, cutting off the boisterous celebration like a record scratch.

Dozens of startled fae were forced to leap out of the way as Grog stomped his way through the crowd, bellowing, "FIRST GROG GET CHASED FROM HOME BY UGLY BANSHEE THING WITH BELL, THEN GROG TRY NAP UNDER TREE BUT STUPID TREE BURN, THEN GROG FINALLY FIND NICE DITCH TO NAP. BUT THEN SCREAMS START, AND THEN RAIN START, AND NOW GROG TIRED *AND* WET *AND* GROG'S EARS HURT!"

As the troll stomped closer, his every step sending shockwaves through the ground, Zayn pressed a hand to his forehead, muttering, "Oy vey."

"Who invited this *schmegegge?*" Mom demanded. "What are you—hey! Get out of there!" She batted my hand away, but I'd already stolen the headphones out of her purse and was busy drawing a Transformation Rune on them.

When Grog appeared in front of us a few moments later, his ham-sized fists raised in a head-squashing stance, I thrust a pair of fuzzy pink earmuffs in his direction. "Here. Take these."

He stared at me in confusion.

Sighing, I gestured for him to bend down so I could place them over his droopy ears. "Better?" I called up to him.

"WHAT?" he shouted back.

"I *said,* is that better?!"

"*WHAT?!*—OH!" A wide grin spread across Grog's face. Before anyone had time to react, he reached down, plucked me from the ground, and wrapped me in a back-cracking hug. "NASTY UGLY THING MAYBE NOT SO NASTY AFTER ALL!" he grinned, exposing a row of rotting green teeth, then quickly crinkled his wart-covered nose. "STILL UGLY THOUGH!"

Zayn and Korinne both reached forward and grabbed me the second my feet were back on the ground, yanking me away from the troll. But he was already sauntering away, humming an off-key song to himself, before settling in at the back of the crowd.

"YELLING OKAY NOW!" he hollered, flashing us a warty thumbs up.

"Fucking trolls," Zayn muttered, rubbing the bridge of his nose.

"You owe me a new pair of headphones," Mom grumbled.

Sighing, I turned back to the gathering of fae standing before me, my wide eyes roving across their familiar faces:

There was Boris, and his cousin Morris, who had apparently traveled all the way from the Obsidian Cliffs to help keep our palace standing; Lanmè, who stood in human form with several of her sisters at the edge of the lake, nodding her silent approval; Saoirse and the other banshees, who were shrouded in their usual veil of ice and fog and yet smiling for the first time; my grandmother, Xianis, who was beaming at me with unrestrained pride while her flock of harpies squawked in triumph… And, lurking at the edge of the crowd, not quite meeting my eyes, were several dozen of Sol's Unseelies – including a certain triumvirate of Chrises.

"Korinne, look," I whispered, pointing in their direction.

She stiffened, but after an encouraging nudge from me, she motioned them over.

Evans, Pine, and Hemsworth exchanged nervous glances before trudging across the field. The rest of the incubi and succubi begrudgingly followed, though the vampires hung back, lurking beneath the shade of a lone unburned tree.

Zayn's grip around my hand tightened as the three of them approached, but Korinne's face actually broke into a wide smile.

"Luther, Xander, Jeff—" she started.

I let out a loud snort. *"Jeff?"*

"—it's wonderful to see you all here," Korinne finished, flashing me a wayward wink.

"Yes." I cleared my throat. "Wonderful."

Zayn's eyes narrowed. Letting go of my hand, he strode right up to the three of them, who visibly recoiled as he approached. "Explain yourselves," he said, his voice as cool and sharp as a razor.

Evans, Pine, and Hemsworth, which would forever be their names as far as I was concerned, exchanged glances – scowls, really – while the rest of the in-succubi shifted anxiously behind them.

"Well?" Zayn demanded.

Finally, Hemsworth cleared his throat. "Look – Sol created safe spaces for us, places where we could feed safely. Where we didn't have to feel like pariahs or demons, you know? We could just…exist. And so, we were pretty happy to follow him wherever he made us feel like first-class citizens. But when he brought up the subject of war, which isn't exactly our thing—"

"Yeah, we're lovers, not fighters!" Pine chimed in, earning him a nudge from Evans.

"—we fought him over it."

"Which landed a dozen of us in the void," Pine muttered.

"And left a couple dozen more without heads." Evans grimaced.

"Not to mention all the poor, strung-out vamps he dragged out of the club mid-orgy," Hemsworth finished. "Those guys definitely got the worst of it."

Evans's grimace deepened as the three of them regarded the small cluster of surviving vampires, who were still cloistered together beneath the protective shade of their tree.

"As I was saying," Hemsworth continued, "we were more or less okay with Sol in his nightclub-owning capacity. But we didn't support…this."

He gestured bleakly to the smoking ruin surrounding us – scorched earth, razed trees, incarnate husks…and bodies. So many bodies. I swallowed tightly as I surveyed the final toll of war. There had to be at least two hundred vampire and striga bodies strewn across the clearing, their mangled corpses set ablaze by the rising sun. Scattered among them were several horse-sized, black reptiles – which Sol had dredged up from Fire Island, most likely against their will – as well as a dozen incubi and succubi. My eyes lingered on the line of at least fifty soldiers that several of the elves were carefully laying side by side, gently folding their arms over their chest and closing their eyelids.

Most were fallen elves – including Zayn's brother – but a handful of harpies, tommyknockers, banshees, and humans were resting among them.

All casualties of war.

My vision blurred as my eyes settled on Tanak, who was kneeling beside the body of his son, Éyrel, clutching his limp hand against his chest.

Tell my dad I said hi, okay? And that I'm going to be just fine.

The dream I'd been having when my heart stopped beating was long gone now. But I vividly remembered the portal that took me to the Third Realm when my body was on the verge of death, and seeing Laleh and Éyrel there. When all was finished here, I would help Tanak lay his son's body beneath the shade of the Great Phoenix Tree, and tell him what Éyrel said – that there's no pain on the other side, only light.

One of the succubi stepped forward, bringing my attention back to the immediate matter at hand. I recognized her as the willowy, lime-haired gal who used to stop by Flourish and Dots from time to time so Zayn could etch one of those "weird, expensive squiggles" on her body.

I exhaled softly. So much had happened since then – and all in the span of a couple of weeks.

"We don't want to hurt anybody," the succubus said, directing her words at me. "We just want to be able to exist without it being a crime."

I took Zayn's hand in mine as I gazed up at him. "I think you of all people can understand that, can't you?"

He pressed his mouth into a line, but didn't argue.

I turned back to the succubus, smiling. "In other words, I'm sure we can come up with something."

A murmur rippled through the gathering of in-succubi, who were all beginning to stand a little straighter.

"You're all right, Zaffre," Pine grinned, taking a step forward.

"You can call me Talia." I smiled, extending a hand in his direction.

A bolt of magenta lightning slammed into the patch of ground between us, knocking him hard on his ass while sending everyone else in the immediate vicinity into a frantic tizzy.

"What the hell was that?!" Mom screeched, clutching Lam against her bosom – not that he was complaining.

Carefully stepping around the partially molten ground at my feet, I crossed my arms and sighed. "Lanmè's right. Before those talks can happen, you have to promise that you'll decommission all of those horrible siren traps."

"L-Lanmè?" Pine stammered from the ground, his normally-perfect coif of hair standing on end, in every direction. "Wh-Who's that?"

"Oh, yeah…! Hey, everyone!" I called, raising my voice as I gestured toward the lake. "This is my close friend, Lanmè – Queen of the Eastern Seas."

While everyone else was exchanging stunned looks with one another, Korinne offered Lanmè a small wave, which the mermaid shyly returned.

"You can all thank her and her sisters for saving the humans," I continued, my eyes darting to the scantily-clad club-goers, who were still sort of aimlessly milling about in an entranced daze. "As well as the Great Phoenix Tree, which would have burned if it hadn't been for the rain she conjured."

Though that comment in particular elicited a number of shocked gasps and murmurs from the crowd, none of the bipedal fae made any move to acknowledge the mysterious creature who was bravely staring each of them down, despite being vastly outnumbered.

And then something truly miraculous happened.

Spurred by Boris and Morris, who moved first, the rest of the tommyknockers dropped to one knee, removed their hats, and bowed their heads. Seeing this, the elves eventually relented as well, pressing their hands to their chests in a show of thanks.

Lanmè's wide, silvery gaze darted to mine, but I merely smiled, pressing my own palm to my heart.

Thank you, I mouthed to her.

Squeezing my hand, Zayn took a step forward. "Thank you as well to our friends from the north, who came to our aid alongside their valiant king…my brother." His voice trembled on the last word, but he forged on. "Mikhæl saved my life today, along with countless others. His sacrifice – and your allegiance – will never be forgotten."

The white-cloaked elves of the north bowed their heads in acknowledgement, while many of their cousins from the south placed comforting hands on their shoulders.

"To the Winter King!" Lam cried.

"Zóbahâri' Padeşáh'ya!" the elves echoed.

When the cheers had quieted, I added, "To the banshees, the sirens, the harpies, and the tommyknockers, we'd also like to offer our sincere thanks for your help." I smiled at Boris and Morris, who were beaming up at me with twinkling eyes. "Truly, we could not have done it without you."

"We are at your service, my gilded blossom!" Morris swept into a very low bow as several hundred tommyknockers threw their hats in the air, triggering a jubilant cheer from everyone else. Many of the elves knelt to clasp the knockers' small hands in theirs. Some even mustered the courage to extend a hand to the banshees, though their faces visibly blanched as they did. Meanwhile, the harpies had forgone handshakes altogether, in favor of zealous, bare-breasted hugs.

I cleared my throat. "And to the succubi, incubi and vampires that remain, we welcome you…and look forward to the new friendship we hope to forge in these coming months."

A renewed hush fell over the crowd. Everyone's attention shifted to the vampires, who were still huddled beneath the protective shade of the surviving tree. The protracted moment of silence that followed soon became a solid minute of awkward shifting and shuffling feet.

Just as I was about to blurt out some stupid joke to break the silence, a lone, muffled clap sounded from the center of the group. The surrounding fae parted to expose Saoirse, who was staring right at me, a smile unfurling from her pale lips as she nodded her approval. One by one, the other banshees joined in, followed by my mother, and then Xianis. Eventually, the tommyknockers were all clapping as well, along with about half of the elves.

I reached into Zayn's cloak, where he'd carefully tucked his mother's grimoire in an inside pocket, whispering my thanks when it again opened to the exact page I'd mentally requested. Within moments, a dark cloud materialized just above the vampires, blocking the sun's rays from reaching them. After exchanging long, wary looks with one another, they timidly crept out from beneath their tree, mincing toward the parting crowd.

I held my breath as my mother casually strode toward them, shouting out some totally inappropriate joke about a Jew, a priest, and a vampire. Whatever the punchline was, the vampires ate it up. The closest one to her actually clasped her on the shoulder while he kicked his pale, hairless head back in a full-bellied laugh.

When they followed my mom to join the larger crowd, a lump appeared in my throat. There weren't many vampires left in that clearing, only a dozen or so. But in that moment, I knew: more would come. And when they did, we'd figure things out.

Together.

Lamswyth let out a triumphant bleat. "Not since the fall of Laman has such a diverse gathering of fae stood side by side in peace!" He pressed a hand to his scruffy chest, dropping to one knee. "And it is all thanks to Your Highnesses – our noble and magnanimous king and queen!"

As he swept into a deep bow, so too did the elves, tommyknockers, banshees, harpies, and – to my immense shock – more than half of the in-succubi.

Heat broiled in my cheeks. "Lam, please, you don't have to—"

"Long live King Zæynek!" he bellowed, his thunderous cry echoing across the smoking battlefield. "Long live Queen Talia!"

The others echoed his cheer with equal ferocity and then some – even Grog, who was standing at the back of the crowd, happily adjusting his fuzzy pink earmuffs.

"Long live King Zæynek!" Their collective chant rose higher and higher, until the ground itself was trembling from the force of it. *"Long live Queen Talia!"*

I literally wanted to crawl into a hole.

Zayn squeezed my hand tightly, flashing me that heart-melting, crooked smile of his. "How long should we let this go on before we tell them?"

"Tell them what?"

He just continued smiling at me, his beautiful emerald eyes catching in the early morning sunlight.

"I..." My breath caught as realization suddenly clicked into place – followed by an immense, overwhelming surge of relief. "Really?"

He nodded.

"I…but…" I shook my head in disbelief. "You're okay with this? Like, truly, genuinely, one-hundred-percent okay? Because if you're not, I completely—"

"I'm more than okay with it," Zayn interjected, pressing a finger to my lips. "Now…would you like to tell them, or should I?"

"Um…" I faltered, anxiously chewing on a hangnail. "My voice travels farther, I guess."

"At your leisure"—Zayn made a sweeping gesture with one hand, motioning me forward—"my queen."

"Oh, come on!" I protested.

He flashed me a wink. "Hey, I had to say it at least once."

Sighing, I turned back to the crowd, cupping my hands around my mouth. *"HEY EVERYONE!"*

Their mortifying chant came to an abrupt halt.

"She's a banshee after my own heart," Mom sniffled, pressing her hands against her chest.

"Oh, she's far more harpy than banshee," Xianis grinned from beside her.

"As if a harpy's voice could ever carry that far!"

I shot them both a look, then cleared my throat. "Um, Zæynek and I would once again like to thank all of you – not only for your loyalty and faith, but for fighting alongside us. We're forever in your d—"

Zayn nudged me. "Don't say the 'D-word' around fae," he muttered under his breath.

"—er, you have our everlasting gratitude," I quickly amended. "But that said…" I trailed off, casting Zayn one last questioning glance.

With a firm nod of support, he wrapped his arm around my shoulder tightly, bracing us both for what he knew would come next.

I waited until the crowd had gone completely silent, then took a deep breath.

"As of this moment, Zæynek and I are officially relinquishing our titles as King and Queen."

XXVI.
Fifty Shades of Gold

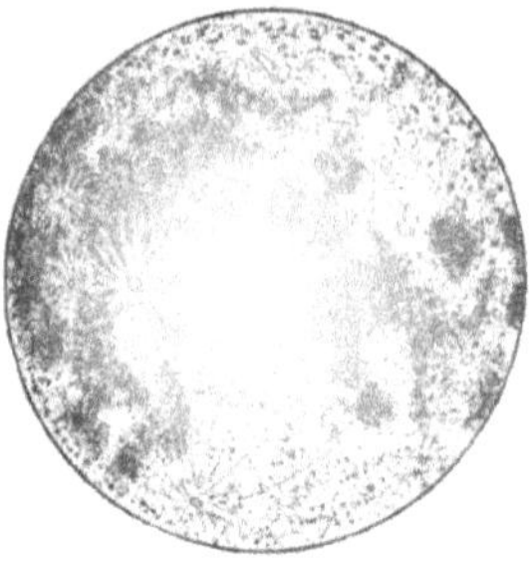

48 Hours Later

Zayn and I stumbled through the door of his Miami apartment at a quarter after midnight, clothes rumpled, hair in disarray, and with aubergine circles etched under our eyes. He dropped his bag to the ground, slumping against the door to close it, while I plopped face-first on his pristine white couch, Converse sneakers dangling over the side of the armrest.

"Is it possible to die from sleep deprivation?" I asked, my voice muffled from the couch cushion my face was smushed against.

"Yes." Zayn slumped down beside me. "Which means I am going to make you sleep for at least three days, because you're never allowed to die on me again – *ever*."

"Ever," I agreed, the word yet again smothered by the couch cushion. "But before I slip into a self-induced coma, can I at least take a shower?"

When Zayn didn't immediately answer, I craned my neck to look over at him. He nodded at me tiredly. "Help yourself –

but for the love of the Creator, please leave me more than three minutes of hot water this time."

I made a grunt of acknowledgement as I peeled myself off the couch and shuffled toward his bathroom, unbuttoning my grubby shirt before the door had even shut behind me. When all of my clothes had been removed and considerately placed in Zayn's empty hamper – unlike my own bathroom, which always looked like a semi-truck filled with women's clothing had crashed inside it – I opened the glass door of his lavish, marble-tiled shower and turned the polished brass knobs to get the water flowing.

While the shower warmed up, I regarded myself in the illuminated mirror above the sink, taking in the disaster that was my naked body with a tempered grimace. The Replenishing Rune Zayn had tattooed on me had worked wonders, as did the myriad of healing elixirs Korinne had brewed up back at the Summer Palace, where we'd hosted the first ever Convocation of Fae – a momentous first step in demolishing the long-standing elven monarchy and creating a democratic governing body in its place. The initial talks went about as expected, with an abundance of arguing, suspicious glances, and bureaucratic fluff. But between my mother's brisket and an impressive exhibition of diplomatic acrobatics on the parts of Zayn and myself, we actually managed to draft the rough concept of our proposed Fae Council: a parliament of sorts, with representation from every fae race.

Not a single delegate was particularly happy with the proposal, but hey, that's the mark of a good compromise, right?

Sighing, I continued my bodily survey in the rapidly-fogging bathroom mirror – paying particular attention to the raw, shiny skin of my left shoulder. Though Korinne's healing tonics had been nothing short of miraculous, the scars of Sol's mark would likely remain on my body forever. But I didn't mind –

they were a reminder of everything I'd fought for – and lived through.

My eyes drifted across the rest of my torso, which was no longer glowing gold – thanks to my Concealment Rune and the mundane sun of Earth's solar system. Most of my other tattoos had been used up, leaving my skin woefully bare. Even Biscuit was gone; he and Mavros were staying at Grandma's house for the evening so Zayn and I could get some sleep. And also because, according to my mother, her "poor babies" were looking "far too thin" and needed some fattening up (never mind the fact that familiars don't actually need food to live). Neither Biscuit nor Mavros had cast us a second glance as we dropped them off at Mom's house, where she was already busy teaching Lam how to make Earth-style Hollandaise sauce in her tiny kitchen.

I chuckled to myself, shaking my head. In a million years, I never would have expected to find a satyr – in a frilly lilac apron, no less – two Chihuahua familiars, a shape-shifting raven, and a sentient tattoo hanging out in my mother's Miami condo.

But hey, it wasn't the weirdest thing I'd seen that day.

Once Zayn's bathroom had been sufficiently sauna-fied, I plugged in my phone for the first time in two weeks, skipping right past the dozens of notifications I'd accumulated during that time to pull up the heavy metal playlist I'd specifically curated for bathroom ablutions. Then I helped myself to a fresh razor and a new toothbrush from Zayn's bathroom cabinet, stepped into the steaming shower, and shut the door behind me.

A protracted moan escaped my throat the moment the hot spray of water hit my body. I allowed myself to bask beneath the luxurious high-pressure showerhead for a solid three minutes, then used Zayn's fancy-shmancy Korean hair products to wash and condition my hair, lathered up my entire body, shaved my legs, and brushed my teeth right there in the shower – mostly because I couldn't bring myself to get out just yet. I'd never considered showers to be therapeutic, but the longer I was in there, and the harder I scrubbed, the lighter my shoulders grew.

When the door to the bathroom quietly opened and closed, I didn't notice; the music was loud and I was still rinsing residual suds from my eyes. However, when the shower door slid open and closed a moment later and two powerful arms gently wrapped around my waist, suffice it to say: I noticed.

"I had to get hot water somehow," Zayn murmured in my ear, sending a jolt of longing straight to my thighs.

I quickly finished rinsing the soap from my hair and face, then turned around to face him, biting my trembling lip. Every free moment of the last two days had been spent putting things back together: creating ad hoc governments, restoring burned-down forests, burying loved ones, and mending broken factions, crack by splintered crack.

Apart from the handful of solo naps I'd managed to sneak in, Zayn and I hadn't had a single moment of silence, let alone a second to ourselves.

His cupped hands slid down my arms, leaving a trail of goosebumps in their wake. I gazed up at him, into those deep emerald pools that were looking at me with such intensity, I momentarily forgot how to breathe.

"Turn around," I whispered.

His eyebrow arched in surprise, but he did as I asked.

After lathering up my palms, I began massaging soap into his tensed shoulders, beginning at the empty space between his shoulder blades that had once housed Sol's Dominion Rune. His head lolled back and he let out a low moan that turned my legs to rubber. With a tremendous amount of concentration on my part, my thumbs continued moving in slow, firm circles as I worked my way down his back, dutifully loosening every knotted muscle I found.

Zayn pressed his palm to the tiles, letting his head rest on his arm. "Fuck," he groaned. "How is it that you always know exactly how to touch me?"

I didn't answer. I was too entranced by the rivulets of soap and water that were snaking between his flexed muscles. Zayn's naked body truly was a work of art – carved as though from marble, adorned with masterfully-drawn tattoos that were so vivid and realistic, the thorns protruding from the flowers and vines that wove across his back looked as though they really might prick my finger.

Having kneaded his tensed muscles into submission, I wrapped my arms around his torso, pressing my cheek against his back. His hands clenched my wrists, pinning me against him. A moment later he gently removed my arms, turned around, and curled a finger beneath my chin to tilt my face toward his. Slowly, gently – as though he were still afraid of breaking me – he brought his lips to mine.

I instinctively rose on tip-toes, curling my fingers behind his neck to deepen the kiss. Zayn's hands slid down my waist, tightly gripping my hips as he pulled me against him, his arousal as rock-hard as I'd ever felt it. Throbbing warmth gathered between my thighs in anticipation of receiving him. But he didn't make any move to insert himself; he just kissed me tenderly, caressing my hips in small circles with his thumbs.

"I never knew I had the capacity to love anyone the way I love you," he murmured against my lips. "I've never felt so whole, so filled from the inside out."

"Me neither," I whispered.

He kissed me once more, then dropped his soft lips to my jaw, my neck, my collarbone… A low moan escaped my throat as his mouth found the hardened peak of my left breast, flicking it with his tongue while his cupped hand deftly massaged the right. When he gently pinched my nipple between his thumb and forefinger, I arched my back and gasped. His free hand snaked to the small of my back, supporting the curve of my spine, while my fingers twined into his dripping-wet hair. Zayn stayed there for a moment, swirling his tongue around the tightly beaded tip of one breast while massaging the other. But after giving my nipple one last gentle nibble – eliciting another sharp cry of pleasure from me – his lips traced down my stomach, leaving a trail of kisses in their wake as he knelt first to one knee, and then the other.

I let out a low whimper when his hands slid between my thighs, spreading them. When he dropped his mouth between my legs, and slid his tongue between my lower lips, my knees nearly buckled. I pressed my back and palms against the tiles for support as his tongue slid all the way up, and then all the way back down my center.

"Fuck," I gasped, knotting my fingers into his hair.

Fluent as he was in my body language, he slid his tongue deeper.

I arched my back, knees trembling and toes flexed, pushing myself against his mouth. His tongue once more found the tingling bundle of nerves above my opening, rubbing it in small circles before his lips closed around it entirely.

My jaw dropped open in a wordless cry as he sucked on my clit, simultaneously massaging it with the tip of his tongue. I didn't even have time to prepare myself; the orgasm that rocked my core was so powerful, my knees buckled from right underneath me. But Zayn was there to catch me, looping his arms beneath my thighs as he lifted me up, pressing my back against the tiles as he slid the entire length of his erection inside me. The muscles in my core were still spasming, sending buzzing currents of pleasure rippling between my thighs. I wrapped my legs around his hips, clenching him in every possible way as he rocked back and forth inside of me, prolonging the undulating waves of ecstasy coursing between my thighs.

The climax intensified, culminating in a second, even more powerful orgasm – something I never even knew my body was capable of. I buried my face against his neck, muffling the primal cry that tore from my throat as he thrust his hips against mine in perfect rhythm, plunging his entire length deep inside me.

When I collapsed against him as dead weight, he brushed his lips against mine, whispering, "Are you okay?"

"Better than okay," I choked out, then reached forward to cup his face in two hands, kissing him deeply.

A low rumble vibrated in his chest as he kissed me back passionately, his tongue dancing over mine as we drank from one another's wells. Without breaking our kiss, he clutched my ass harder, rocking his hips back and forth, slow and deep, grinding his shaft against my tingling clit until I squirmed and writhed.

"Fuck," I gasped. "You're gonna make me come again!"

"Good," he growled, biting the side of my neck.

His strokes became harder and faster as he sucked on my skin, gently nibbling it between his teeth.

I moaned his name as I dragged my fingertips across his shoulders. The quivering spring deep inside me was coiling again, tighter and tighter – so much so, I didn't know how much more I could take.

"Please—" I broke off in an uncontrolled moan.

"Please what?" Zayn's low, gravelly whisper brushed against my ear, sending a shiver down my spine.

"I need—" I gasped, yet again robbed of words as he swiveled his hips, bringing me closer and closer to the edge. "I-I need you…t-to come inside of me…*please!"* I cried out as he plunged himself even deeper, filling me to the hilt.

Zayn's entire body stiffened. He crushed his lips against mine as I roughly knotted my fingers into his hair, my thirst for him unquenchable. With a rumbling groan, his fingertips digging into my thighs hard enough to make me yelp in pained pleasure, he emptied himself inside of me.

My name burst through his lips in a euphoric moan as I ground myself against the base of his shaft, getting off on the sound of his pleasure. The coil inside me snapped, and the dam broke, sending pulsing waves of ecstasy cascading through my body. We both cried out as we finished together, clutching one another in feverish rapture. He buried his face in my breasts, his shoulders rising and falling from the exertion, while I lay my cheek atop his head, working to catch my breath.

After a moment, Zayn gently released my legs, wrapping his arms around me in a tight embrace as I slid from his hips. I could feel his lips pressing against the top of my head as I buried my face against his chest, using his strength for support.

"I could make love to you ten times a day and still never get enough of you."

"You read my mind," I murmured, desperately stifling a yawn.

He chuckled softly. "Let's get you to bed, *kalb'ímtha*."

I could only nod, too tired to move any other part of my body, while Zayn turned off the water, wrapped me in a towel, and scooped me into his arms. After carrying me to his bedroom, he pulled down the silk comforter of his bed with one hand and gently laid me beneath the sheets.

A few moments later, he sidled up next to me, pulling me against his chest.

"You feel like home," I mumbled, half asleep.

"Aza hame-şey'émtho ni." He pressed his lips to my forehead, running his gentle fingers through my hair. "You are my everything."

Tilting my head back, I kissed him with the last waning drop of energy I had, then drifted off into a deep, blissful sleep.

At some point during the night, my peaceful dreams were punctured by a nightmare. I was trapped in a place of shadows, inhabited by even darker shadows that were reaching for me with long, groping fingers.

Please don't leave me, a voice rasped from the darkness. *Please.*

I started awake with a gasp, clutching the sheets in two trembling fists.

The dark silhouette standing by the window whirled around, his green eyes faintly glowing in the moonlight. "Tal? What's wrong?"

My heart was beating too fast to answer.

Zayn climbed into bed, scooping me into his arms. "What did you see?" he asked softly.

"The Other," I panted. "H-He was there, begging me not to leave him."

"It's okay," Zayn murmured as he stroked my hair gently. "It was just a dream."

"No." I shook my head, pressing my face against the warmth of his bare chest. "I was *there*, Zayn. I was in the Other, with Sol – right before I was brought back to the Third Realm."

His hand stilled on the back of my head. "When you were brought *back* to the Third Realm?"

I nodded. "That's where I was for the two days you couldn't find me. I…felt something…calling to me. And before I knew it, I was deep in the forest, standing in front of the Great Phoenix

Tree. When I reached out to touch it, a portal opened in the base of the tree, and I…I fell through."

Zayn's entire body stiffened, but he said nothing.

"It's so beautiful there," I whispered. "I-I can see it when I sleep, clear as day. But the moment I wake up…the memories fade." My eyes filled with tears as they rose to meet Zayn's. "I wish I could make myself remember, so I could tell you everything."

"My Talia, the Realmwalker…" Zayn chuckled softly as he brushed a tear from my cheek. "No one ever comes back from the Third Realm – and yet, here you are, upset with yourself because you can't remember the journey in vivid detail."

"But—"

He pressed a finger to my lips. "The living aren't meant to remember that which came before life. If they did, there would be no point in living, would there?"

I considered his words for a long moment, then shook my head weakly. "No…I guess not."

Sighing, I looked over at the window, where the full moon was casting a column of pale blue light across the silk sheets. "*Ayi'şík emœ yem beşévi*," I whispered softly, holding out my hand to the moonlight.

The invisible Lunar Rune on my arm flickered to life, shimmering with magic. As a golden flush traveled from my fingers to my toes, I could feel Zayn's eyes roving across my naked body alongside it.

He let out a sharp intake of breath. "But…how? We're galaxies away from the Fae Realm…"

I just smiled at him, squeezing his hand until both of our bodies were awash in magic and moonlight. "Just goes to show you that magic can exist anywhere."

Zayn opened his mouth to reply, but whatever it was he was planning to say evaporated on his tongue the moment I pressed my lips to his. He leaned back against the headboard, opening his arms to me as I climbed on top of him, straddling his hips between my knees. Perhaps it was the fleeting memory of death, or the rush of magic coursing through my elven blood – whatever the reason, I needed Zayn more in that moment than I'd ever needed him before. With a small cry, I crushed my lips against his, consumed not just by desire, but by an overwhelming surge of gratitude.

I'd come so close to losing this.

To losing *him*.

Zayn's thumbs caressed my tear-stained cheeks as he curled his fingers into my hair, cupping my face. With effort, I managed to pull away from the intoxicating kiss, brushing kisses along his jaw, his throat, his chest… His hands knotted into my hair as I worked my way down, until I was kneeling between his legs on hands and knees, bringing my parted lips to the head of his erection.

His entire body tensed.

"Tal, are you sure—" His question ended in a sharp exhale as I slowly slid my tongue up and down the underside of his arousal, not once breaking eye contact with him as I did.

The muscles of his abdomen tensed and flexed in response, and I could taste his anticipation beading on the tip. Immensely aroused – and more than a little self-satisfied – by the reaction I was causing, I licked Zayn's hardening arousal from base to tip in controlled, leisurely movements, deftly swirling my tongue all along the extra-sensitive ridge before dropping back down again.

His arms spread across the headboard, clenched hands gripping the top of it. "Fuck, Talia," he gasped, tilting his head back. "How are you—oh, *fuck!*"

He slipped into Elvish after that, too preoccupied to bother with English.

Smiling to myself, I wrapped my lips around the engorged head of his cock, massaging the sensitive underside with my tongue as I took in as much of him as I could. Zayn's ensuing groan slicked my thighs with longing, but I continued lavishing him with pleasure until his entire body shuddered with an impending climax – at which point, I climbed on top of him, my knees tightening around his hips as I slid myself onto his rock-hard arousal.

Without missing a beat, Zayn reached forward and gripped my waist, plunging his full length inside of me. I bit my lip as I ground my pelvis against his, taking him as deep as I possibly could. Our bodies rocked and undulated, perfectly in sync, fusing together seamlessly.

Drunk with pleasure – and yet thirsty for more – I leaned down to kiss him, eliciting a low rumble from his chest that both chilled my spine and warmed my core. Zayn knotted his fingers into my hair, pulling me deeper – as though he too were trying to eradicate every last millimeter of space between our bodies.

"Talia," he groaned my name against my mouth, sending a jolt of electrified desire between my legs.

I cried out, my back arching as I propped my hands behind me, gripping the top of his thighs for support. His powerful hands clenched me by the hips while his thrusts became harder and deeper, filling me until it hurt – but God, it hurt so good. Head lolled back in ecstasy, I straddled that exhilarating line between pain and pleasure, reveling in the joy, the freedom, the *power* of my own autonomy. And not just mine; Zayn had spent half of his life as a slave, his body abused and his choices stolen.

But now, thanks to our hard-fought victory, his body was his, and my body was mine, allowing us to freely give ourselves to one another in a way we weren't able to do before. Every moment of intertwined pleasure we chose to share from that day forward would simultaneously be a celebration of life and freedom – something I, for one, would never take for granted ever again.

Sensing my mounting urgency, Zayn tightened his grip on my waist as he rocked his hips against mine, his fingers digging into my flesh hard enough to leave bruises. I rode him to the brink of mutual release, gathering my hair above my head as a sheen of sweat dotted my breasts. The moment my thighs began to tremble from exertion, Zayn flipped me over on my knees, one hand reaching across my stomach to pin my back against his chest, while the other gently wrapped around my throat.

"Do you like this?" he rumbled against my ear, positioning himself behind me.

I was so fucking turned on, all I could do was nod my feverish assent.

He slid himself inside me with ease, tightening his grip around my throat as he rocked his hips against my ass in perfect rhythm. I sank into his chest, gripping the crook of his arm for support. His other hand slid from my waist to the space between my thighs, until his fingertips found my throbbing bundle of nerves, gently rubbing it in small circles that made stars explode in front of my vision.

When his fingers eased through the wetness that had gathered at the junction of my thighs, my back arched reflexively. I slipped my hands behind his neck and leaned my head against his shoulder, panting. His mouth caught mine and I moaned into the kiss, my tongue rolling over his. Zayn kissed me back hungrily, gripping my throat with one hand while his other hand massaged the growing knot of pleasure forming between my legs. His fingertips worked in slow, tight circles, winding me tighter and tighter, while the head of his cock stroked the sensitive spot deep inside of me, bringing me to the brink yet again. The muscles in my core were both tightening and convulsing, creating a tension deep within me that was almost unbearable.

"Come for me, Talia," he whispered, his voice as rough as sandpaper. He was as close as I was – I could taste it on his breath. "*Mæthir ama'yla, Sevyá'mtha.*"

A primal cry tore from my throat as the knot within me quickly unraveled, sending wave after wave of pleasure coursing through my body like seismic tremors.

"Talia!" Zayn gasped, pinning me against his chest as he emptied himself inside of me.

I leaned against his arm like a rag doll, my knees too weak to hold me upright.

With a groan, Zayn sank against the headboard, his arm still wrapped around my waist as I collapsed against him. When he withdrew his hand from between my thighs, his fingertips were dripping with the pleasure he'd given me. He brought them to his lips, closing his eyes with a soft hum as he savored my taste.

"There is nothing in this realm or the next that tastes as good as you," he whispered, making my thrumming heart skip a beat. I twisted around to bring my trembling lips to his, while he held me tightly against him, lazily running his fingers up and down the trail of goosebumps he had left along my spine.

Several rapturous moments later, when I'd eventually mustered the strength to pull away, I was surprised to see streaks of dim morning light streaming through the window.

Zayn shook his head ruefully. "I'm a terrible lover."

"Come again?" I blinked, gawking at him.

"I told you I'd make you sleep for three days, and here I am making love to you until dawn."

"And yet I feel like I slept for twenty hours." I bit his lower lip playfully. "I swear, there must be some sort of mutual energy exchange when we make love, because I feel like I could run a marathon – metaphorically," I added quickly, lest he think I was possessed.

"Are you sure you don't have any succubus blood in the Kestenbaum family tree?" he murmured, kissing me again. "Because for the life of me, I cannot keep my hands off of you."

"Who knows?" I traced a finger along one of the vines that wove across his left pectoral muscle, surprised at the pang of longing that slithered through my core.

Zayn apparently felt it too, because his eyes lit up wickedly as I swung a leg over his, positioning myself millimeters above his stirring erection.

BANG! BANG! THUMP!

Zayn sat bolt-upright at the sound of the front door crashing open. "What the—"

"TALIA! ARE YOU IN THERE?"

I let out a shrill yelp as my mother's voice permeated the entire apartment, toppling off of Zayn just in time to wrap the sheet around my naked torso.

"Time to wake up, *kindelah*!" Mom called, covering her eyes as she burst through the door of Zayn's bedroom. "Are you both decent?"

"MOM!" I shrieked. "Are you CRAZY?! Why didn't you knock?!"

"We WERE knocking! For ten minutes!" She pulled her hand away from her eyes, waggling her eyebrows at our disheveled states. "But I'm beginning to see why you didn't hear us!"

Biscuit and Mavros soared into the room after her, landing on the headboard above us.

"Morning!" Mavros chirped, hanging her head upside down to greet me.

"Morning?!" I barked. "It's the middle of the night!"

"It's six a.m.!" Mom rolled her eyes, fingering her pendants.

Lucy and Ricky materialized in twin puffs of red smoke, bounding onto the bed with wagging tails and lolling tongues. I gathered the sheets higher on my chest while Zayn reached forward to scratch both dogs behind the ears, quietly muttering, "I *just* washed these sheets."

"Six a.m. *is* the middle of the night!" I blustered. "And how the *hell* did you get in here anyway? Zayn's apartment is warded!"

"Come now, you mustn't talk to your poor mother like that!" Sidling up beside her in the narrow doorway, Lam patted my "poor mother's" arm sympathetically.

Mom closed her eyes as though steeling herself against an impending heart attack, gripping the satyr's hand for emotional support. "You see what I have to put up with, Lambchop?"

"There, there," he comforted her. "She'll understand when she has lambkins of her own, won't she, my pet?"

She let out a woeful sniffle.

"Regarding the intrusion," Lamswyth continued, "the blame lies with me. When you didn't respond to our repeated 'tele-foam' calls and protracted knocking, Diedre became understandably distressed and made the very reasonable request that I break down the door to make certain you were both alive." He casually patted the panpipes resting atop his hairy belly, eliciting an exasperated groan from Zayn. "Now, as you both know, the next council meeting will be commencing soon, and the delegates are demanding their fearless leaders oversee this next round of voting."

"We're not their leaders!" I protested.

"Oh, but you are." Lam's eyes were twinkling. "So, it's time to get up, up, up!"

With that, he yanked the sheet off the bed in a gallant flourish.

"Nakie Tallie!" Biscuit screeched, flapping his wings.

"WHAT THE ACTUAL FUCK?!" I shrieked, leaping behind Zayn, who – in typical incubus form – made no move to cover himself up.

Meanwhile, my mother – in typical lusty, middle-aged woman form – let her gaze linger on his prodigious package just a little too long for it to have been an accident, while Lam blustered out a million apologies, covering his eyes in mortified horror.

"I'm so sorry – I hadn't realized you were lounging in the buff!"

"EVERYBODY GET OUT!" I screamed, jerking a finger at the hallway.

"Okay, *okay*! Sheesh, you don't have to wake up the entire neighborhood!" Mom griped as she and Lamswyth turned to leave. "But hurry up and get out of bed, would you? I brought all the ingredients to make cheese blintzes—c'mon *tatelehs*!" she whistled at the four familiars. "Breakfast time!"

The Chihuahuas leapt off the bed, their claws skittering across the tile floor as they tore between Mom's legs, while Biscuit and Mavros launched from the headboard, both of them screaming, "CHEEEEEESE!" at the top of their lungs.

"*For the last time,*" I screeched, leaping out of bed to slam the door behind them, "I'M LACTOSE INTOLERANT!"

As the door swung shut, shaking the walls from the force of it, Mom yelled back, "Blintzes don't have lactose!"

"I'm gonna kill her," I panted, storming to Zayn's closet to yank one of his long-sleeved shirts over my head. "I swear to God, I'm gonna do it this time." I whirled around to face him, expecting his unbridled support, or at the very least, his solemn promise to bail me out of jail after the deed was done.

Instead, he was just casually leaning against the headboard, fingers interlaced behind his head and ankles crossed, while his entire perfect, stupid, mouthwatering body shook with barely-contained laughter.

EPILOGUE

6 MONTHS LATER

The rotund, dimpled butt cheek jerked and wriggled beneath my fingers, eliciting an exasperated sigh from me, the stalwart curator of said derrière. It belonged to a squirming fifty-something-year-old gentleman whose leather motorcycle chaps had been bunched up just beneath the crease of his glutes so that I, his illustrious Runemaster, could add the final rune to his rattlesnake-cobra abomination, the tail of which ended right there on his exposed bottom.

As he let out another pitiful whimper, I was forced to look up from the impeccable line I was pulling. “You doing okay over there, Roy?”

“Uh-huh.” His arms were wrapped around the chair he was straddling as though he were clinging to a life raft. “Doing great. How’s Monty doing?”

"Almost…done…" I murmured, using my boss-turned-boyfriend's super-expensive, hand-crafted magical ink to pull the last line of the complex rune. When I was finished, I gently cleaned the area just above Roy's butt crack with *droka* ointment to both sanitize and seal in the magic, then released the breath I felt like I'd been holding for the last few minutes. "All set!" I beamed, marveling at my creation; of all the tattoos I'd designed over the last three years, that unruly butt cobra was by far my favorite.

"And you're *sure* he'll be just like before?" Roy asked, craning his head over his shoulder to take a look.

"Even better." I smiled. "Familiars are way more obedient than blood incarnates."

Biscuit let out a ridiculing squawk from the cozy nest of towels he and Mavros had made inside one of our now-empty ink cabinets.

"Correction," I amended. "Familiars are *usually* more obedient than incarnates – unless you spoil them rotten like these two."

"Almond?" Mavros cawed, carefully readjusting the sparkly black egg she and Biscuit were currently taking turns warming.

"For the third time, *no* – the two of you ate them all!"

She made an irritated grunt, as though *I* were the one who had devoured an entire pound of unshelled almonds the night before.

Roy made a similar grunt as he readjusted his jeans and leather chaps, then hoisted himself back into a seated position. "Alright, Monty boy, c'mon out and say hi to Daddy!" he coaxed over his shoulder.

Monty's red eyes glowed to life, and a moment later, a massive black cobra-slash-rattlesnake materialized beside Roy on the vinyl seat.

I breathed a sigh of relief – after all, this was the first familiar I'd ever made without Zayn's close supervision. And if I'd pulled even one slightly imperfect line during the long, meticulous process, this would've been a complete dis—

"Oh shit!" Roy yelped.

With a predatory hiss that turned my blood to slush, the cobra lunged for Roy's face, its two-inch venomous fangs aimed directly for the man's exposed jugular.

"ROY!" I screamed, freezing mid-lunge as the snake started *licking Roy's face* like a goddamn golden retriever.

"Oh hey – easy there, boy!" Roy laughed, hugging the lethal creature against his chest as though it were a stuffed teddy bear. Monty Python nuzzled up against his scruffy beard, letting out what can only be described as a cat-like purr of contentment.

I crossed my arms over my chest, suppressing a shudder. "To each his own," I muttered, just as Biscuit disappeared from the nesting cabinet in a bright magenta flash. "Hey – where'd he go?" I asked Mavros, who only shrugged. I looked down at my forearm, where both her and Biscuit's side-by-side portraits were empty – meaning Biscuit was probably hanging out with Zayn… Except Zayn was on a Costco shopping date with my mother, and there was no way he'd be comfortable schlepping our ostentatious, magical familiar around Miami on a random Wednesday night.

"Huh." I rubbed the back of my neck, then glanced at the clock – just past nine p.m. – and shrugged. "Well, Roy, do you have any questions about aftercare?" I asked, gathering up the used tattoo supplies so I could re-sanitize my station.

"Oh, yeah, sure do!" He pulled a crumpled-up list from his leather vest pocket, balancing his reading glasses on his nose – quite the contrast to his scraggly gray beard, exposed neck tattoos, and the tattered bandana wrapped around his forehead.

"Let's see…the wife wants to know what to feed 'im, and how big of a cage he'll need."

"Well, he shares a piece of your soul, so he'll probably like whatever you do—"

"…cornbread and smoked brisket…" he muttered, jotting down a note to himself.

"—but familiars don't technically need to eat, so don't let him trick you into thinking he's starving or anything." I stuck my tongue out at Mavros, who immediately stuck her tongue back out at me. "And he won't need a cage, nor would he likely tolerate one. When he's sleepy or bored or grumpy, he'll just go home – back to his tattoo form," I clarified, seeing Roy's confused expression. "You can try training him to 'go home' on command, but in my experience, that only works around forty percent of the time."

"Forty…percent…of time," Roy muttered, scrawling that down. "Okay. Will I need to come in for regular touch ups or anything? Also, Dottie wanted me to ask you how long familiars live for."

"No need for touch ups." I got to work spraying down my metal stand with MadaCide, then tossed the used paper towels in the trash alongside the used ink caps. "Your own magic will maintain the integrity of the ink, though sunscreen will help keep his colors vibrant. And he'll live as long as you do, so for his sake, you might want to start trading out Budweiser for broccoli… By the way, did you ever figure out who your mystery fae relative is?"

"Yup!" He grinned. "I just found out my long lost mee-maw is still alive and kickin' – and a banshee, at that! She's a Benefactor, just like me!"

"No kidding!" I gasped. "My *bubbe* was a banshee too! What's your grandma's name?"

"Sheer-shie!"

My jaw was practically grazing the floor. "Do you mean 'Saoirse'?"

"Yeah, that! Turns out I've got Irish banshee blood running through these here Texan veins!" He beamed, tapping the inside of his elbow.

"No fucking way! My great-grandmother's sister's name is Saoirse!" My eyes widened. "Is it possible it's the same banshee?"

Roy slapped his thigh. "If it is, that means you an' me are practically cousins!" He scooped me into one burly arm for a tight hug, where I came face to face with the grinning cobra he was squeezing in his other arm.

When the rocky-talkie in my pocket started to buzz, I let out a suffocated wheeze of relief.

"Hang on, Roy – that's probably Zayn!" I grunted. As I worked to wriggle free from his grasp, I couldn't help but wonder why Zayn would be calling me from the rocky-talkie instead of his cell phone.

"Hello?" I gasped upon extricating myself from Roy's death-grip.

"What's wrong?" Zayn's static-y voice greeted me from the other side of the glowing rock. *"Did everything go okay with Roy's familiar?"*

"Everything's fine," I reassured him. "Both Roy and Monty are doing great. Is Biscuit with you?"

"He's right here, yes. I would have used our link to call you, but Biscuit's a little, uh...preoccupied."

"Preoccupied?" I frowned. "And where exactly is 'here'?"

"Your mother and I had to make a quick stop in the Fae Realm for belæru *blossoms, and while we were here, I ended up getting pulled into some Council developments. Would you mind popping through the filing cabinet real quick?"*

"I mean, yeah, I could close up shop early, I guess..." I chewed on my lip, glancing between Roy, his butt snake, and the clock. "But I'm donating blood first thing tomorrow morning, so I can't be out too late."

"I'll have you home before midnight, I promise."

"Yeah...okay," I relented. "Let me just say goodbye to Roy and lock up."

"You should bring him along," Zayn said, keeping his tone carefully nonchalant.

I stared at the rock in my hand. "You want me to bring *Roy* to the Fae Realm...?"

"Yeah – his grandmother is here and wants to say hello."

"Mee-maw?!" Roy exclaimed.

"*Saoirse* is there?" I asked, frowning. "Why—"

"Sevyá'mtha," Zayn interjected, simultaneously making my heart skip several beats as it always did when he spoke in his mother tongue, *"amá'ye gúlvene. Trust me."*

"Okay," I sighed. "Yeah... I—er, *we'll* be there soon."

"Kalb'ímtha azá'ye dáşti."

Despite my annoyance at Zayn's evasiveness, I couldn't help but smile. "I love you too."

"Hot diggity!" Roy whooped as he pulled out his phone to fire off a quick message to Dottie. "The Fae Realm! I haven't been there since I was a tot! Which part are we goin' to?"

"Uh...the Assembly Building," I replied after locking up the front of the shop and turning the sign to CLOSED. "Formerly known as the Summer Palace."

"And what's this I hear about you donating blood?" He regarded the bouquet of tropical flowers adorning my arms, where a few dozen runes had been skillfully hidden among the colorful blossoms. "I mean, I knew you had gotten over your needle phobia enough to finally get inked, but I didn't realize you were going as far as getting them jabbed in your vei—"

"Uh-uh!" I waved a hand in his face, cutting him off. "Don't remind me!"

Suppressing a shudder, I walked over to the empty ink cabinet-slash-birdie casbah, where I extended an arm inside for Mavros to perch onto, then flipped on the warming lamp. The light made her and Biscuit's glittering egg sparkle like a disco ball, bringing an accompanying flare of warmth to my chest.

"You're okay leaving her for a couple of hours?" I asked.

Mavros nodded, shifting her eyes to the Sensor Rune Zayn had etched into the cabinet last week, which would immediately notify us of any egg-hatching activities in our absence.

"I can't wait to meet her," I whispered, kissing the top of Mavros's head. Then, clearing my throat, I turned back to Roy. "So, uh, as you know, my blood is kinda rare – well actually, it's insanely rare," I chuckled. "I have Rh-null blood – otherwise known as gold blood – which means my red blood cells lack all Rh antigens."

Roy nodded vigorously. "Oh, yeah, sure – antigens."

I coughed into my hand to stifle a laugh while unlocking the door to the office Zayn and I now shared. "All of that is just to say that my blood is highly valued in this realm as well, because it can be donated to anyone – even to other people with extremely rare blood types. And since there are only like eight active Rh-null blood donors in the entire world, the people at the blood bank always have, like, an extravagant spread of cookies waiting for me on donation days."

Roy let out a low whistle. "Cookies or no, for a gal who used to pass out at the sight of a needle, that's a pretty noble thing of you to do."

"If by 'used to,' you mean last Thursday…" I shivered, quickly pushing the unfortunate fainting incident from my mind. "Okay!" I rubbed my hands together vigorously. "So, this is the portal we'll be taking to the Fae Realm."

I activated the palace-bound Portal Rune with my palm, then yanked open the filing cabinet, bathing the room in blinding, kaleidoscopic light.

"Sweet baby Jesus!" Roy yelped, leaping backward.

"It's best to just, like, plug your nose and jump in," I grinned. "And keep your hands and arms tucked against your body, otherwise your limbs might end up going to a different place than the rest of you, which, from experience, isn't a pleasant sensation. Oh, and if you get nauseated, definitely try to wait until you're out of the wormhole before you puke, because you'll end up vomiting in like three different galaxies, which is not as cool of a flex as you'd think."

Roy openly gawked between me and the filing cabinet – most likely trying to decide if I was joking or not – then hastily made the sign of the cross before clutching Monty against his chest like a life jacket, plugging his nose, and leaping inside.

Mavros let out a husky croak – her version of laughing – before diving in after them.

After taking one last look at our office, with my eyes lingering on the cleared-off desk where Zayn had made sweet, toe-curling love to me just that morning, I plugged my own nose, then stepped into the drawer.

My feet landed on solid stone somewhere between two seconds and two millennia later – time gets kind of tricky when you're moving between dimensions. After popping a berry-flavored Tums in my mouth and then offering Roy – who was green-faced and panting – the same, I opened the door to the broom closet and stepped into the upstairs hallway of the east wing. Mavros casually shook out her feathers on my shoulder, while Roy vomited into a two-thousand-year-old elven vase.

"You get used to it," I said, patting him on the shoulder.

"Hey, Tal."

"Zayn!" I whirled around at the sound of his voice. Without warning, I leapt into his arms and wrapped my legs around his hips, planting several dozen kisses on his lips – you know, my usual casual greeting.

"Hot damn," Roy muttered, wiping the sickness from his mouth. "Is that how she always greets you after an hour apart?"

"No." Zayn grinned at him after gently setting me back down. "She usually takes off her clothes first."

I elbowed him in the side, not even remotely offended.

"Saoirse and the other banshees are downstairs in the banquet hall," Zayn said to Roy. "Mavros can show you the way. I just need to borrow Talia for a few minutes before we join you."

"I'll bet you do," he chuckled to himself as he turned to follow Mavros down the hallway.

"Hey, Roy?" I called after him. "You might want to have Monty go home before you head down there. I'm not sure the castle walls can withstand that many simultaneous banshee screams."

Blanching, Roy quickly ushered his snake back into his pants before skittering to the end of the hall, yelling, "Wait for me!" as Mavros soared out of sight.

Grinning, I turned back to Zayn. "So…what's all this about? Are the vampires causing trouble again?"

Without answering, he twined both hands in my freshly-dyed turquoise hair, bringing his lips to mine in a surprisingly tender kiss. When he pulled away a few moments later, I wavered in my spot, trying to catch both my balance and my breath.

When he and my mother had left for "Costco" earlier that evening, he'd been wearing designer jeans and a tight blue t-shirt that hugged every glorious dip and ripple of his upper body. But he'd changed his clothes since then, and was currently donning an emerald-green *tulúm* – an elven tunic made of fine silk and brass buttons – which he wore over formal black slacks.

"Did I miss a memo or something?" I glanced down at my own outfit – a pale blue summer dress I'd bought on sale at Kohl's last summer – letting out a small sigh of relief that I hadn't thrown on my usual pair of cutoff shorts and a tank top that morning.

"Would you come with me?" he asked softly, reaching for my hand. "I'll explain everything in just a moment."

Nodding, I took his hand and followed him down the hallway, all the way to the last door on the left, which opened into yet another hallway. And at the end of *that* hallway was a set of ornately-carved double doors. When Zayn pushed them open, I let out a gasp. Inside was a small, circular chamber. It housed two rows of wooden pews, a simple altar at the front, and dozens of lit candles that had been placed all around the room: on the floors, atop the jutted-out stones of the walls, and inside the window wells. But it was the windows themselves that stole the very breath from my lungs.

Each stained-glass pane depicted a different lunar cycle of the four fae moons, which were surrounded by hundreds of stars – each one a separate star-shaped piece of glass embedded inside the majestic eight-panel mosaic. I'd never seen a room like it, more painted glass than stone. Even the ceiling was made from a dome of clear glass, which allowed the light of all four moons to illuminate the chapel, awakening the Lunar Runes on both our bodies.

I turned to face Zayn, spellbound by the beauty of this hidden chamber. He was standing in front of the altar, his eyes glowing as brightly as the Lunar Runes I'd helped him tattoo on his body – part of his newfound effort to embrace his elven roots.

"Zayn?" I whispered, slowly approaching the altar. "What…" I swallowed, then tried again. "What is all this?"

He took my hands in his – to my surprise, they were shaking. "Talia, one of the greatest regrets of my life was not claiming you when I had the chance – and almost losing you as a consequence of my inaction."

I tried to take a deep breath, but for some reason my lungs had forgotten how to expand.

"But even after all of that, I can't bear the thought of putting another claim on your body." His fingers gently brushed the shiny pink skin on my left shoulder. "You're not my property – you're my equal in every way. Better, even, because every day I spend with you leaves me a far better man than I was the day before." As he brought my knuckles to his lips, I noticed the tears shining in his eyes. "But the more time I spend with you, the more I find myself desperately wishing there were some way to show the world that I belong to you, and you to me… And so, for the last few months, I've been working on a new rune." He reached into his pocket, where he pulled out a piece of paper adorned with a complex symbol unlike anything I'd ever seen before.

"This is…*stunning,*" I breathed, running my fingers across the delicate lines and writing. "You made this?"

"Yes." Zayn smiled. "With some help. Lamswyth helped Endow it with a special class of magic. Your mother provided me with the Hebrew translations, and Korinne was able to track down the lunar and planetary phases for your birthday and mine, in both realms."

"Oh my God," I whispered, pressing my hand to my open mouth. "That's my name written in Hebrew!"

"Yes – and that's mine in Elvish," he said, pointing to the writing in the lower left corner of the triangle. "This is the banshee word for 'heart'"—he tapped the symbol just underneath the sign of Saturn, the planet associated with my birthday—"and that character right there is how harpies write 'eternal.'" His finger moved across the design. "This script in the lower right quadrant is Infernal for 'soul' – that's the ancient language of incubi," he added, noting my momentary confusion.

I stared at him, completely and utterly speechless.

Zayn cleared his throat nervously. "Unlike traditional claims, this rune doesn't exert any sort of force or control over its bearer. And it only works properly when it's part of a pair; by attuning itself to the life force of its companion, it pulses in time with their heartbeat..." The Adam's apple in his throat bobbed. "I was thinking we could use this to claim each other, so to speak. Though you can absolutely say 'no' if you don't feel comfortable with the idea – a-and truly, it wouldn't change a single thing between us if you said—"

"Yes," I blurted out.

His eyes widened. "Yes?"

My face broke into a wide grin as I flung my arms around his neck. "Yes, of course!"

He caught my wrists between his hands, kissing me fiercely.

"It's absolutely perfect," I whispered against his lips. "Can we do it right now?"

"I thought – or rather, I was hoping – you would say that." He smiled, withdrawing a tin of *droka* ointment and a handheld tattoo machine from his pocket. "The cartridge is already filled with the proper ink. Would you like to do the honors first?"

I nodded eagerly. "Where would you like me to put yours?"

Zayn unfastened the top three buttons of his tunic, exposing the upper part of his chest. "Here," he whispered, pointing to an area of scar tissue just above his heart.

"That's…" A knot of emotion rose and caught in my throat. "That's where your Fulmination Rune used to be – the one you were going to use to…to…" My mouth had gone too dry to finish.

"To kill myself," he whispered, gently brushing the tears from my lashes with his thumb. "Yes. Back when I thought it was the only way to destroy Sol… That's why it seemed fitting to put your claim in its place. You saved my life that day, Talia – and have continued to save me every day since."

My fingers were trembling as I took the tattoo machine from him. After taking a few minutes to study his design and steady my hands, I carefully began to etch our shared claim just above Zayn's heart. I pressed my other hand to his chest as I worked, continually glancing between the rune I was drawing, the design he'd created, and his shining green eyes. When there was only one line left, I pressed the tip of the needle into my thumb, using my blood to seal the final stroke in his skin.

The tattoo immediately flared to life, radiating with bright golden light as it pulsed in time with my own thrumming heartbeat.

I exhaled softly. "That's incredible."

"Made even better by your hand." Zayn gently took the tattoo machine from me, kissing my fingertips as he did. "Where would you like yours?"

Without hesitating, I pointed to the space just above my own heart. "Right here."

He smiled, leaning down to brush his lips against the spot just beside my father's locket, then etched the rune one line at a time – gently, painstakingly, and with the unparalleled skill of a true Runemaster. When there was only one stroke left, he pressed the needle into his thumb as I had, augmenting the rune with his own blood. Just like the tattoo I'd placed on him, the freshly-embedded ink above my heart flared to life, palpitating with bright light – not gold, but silver, like the blood that ran through his veins. Wide-eyed, I pressed my hand to the side of Zayn's neck; the rune on my chest was pulsing in perfect sync with his heart, including the beat it skipped from the touch of my fingers.

Zayn took my right hand in his, then gently placed his other palm above the tattoo on my breast. *"Ama azá'ye dáşti, Talia Judith Kestenbaum…kalb'ímth'i-œlún."*

I did the same, whispering, "And I am yours, Zæynek al'Bâramahd…until my heart stops beating."

His face broke into a jubilant smile as he brought his lips to mine, kissing me with tender force. I entwined my hands behind his neck, standing on tip-toes to deepen the kiss.

With a small hum of effort, he pulled away a few moments later, pressing his forehead against mine to gaze deep into my eyes. "This rune is the only one of its kind, utterly unique – just like you."

I opened my mouth to reply; unfortunately, what was meant to be a poignant, tear-inducing declaration of my undying love for him came out as a shrill yelp as the entire floor shook with the combined force of at least a dozen banshee screams. "What the hell was that?!"

"I'm guessing that was Roy introducing his pet cobra to his 'mee-maw,'" Zayn sighed, rubbing the bridge of his nose with one hand while ushering me out the door with the other. "We'd better go – it'll be much harder to sign the final draft of the treaty alongside the other delegates if the entire castle collapses."

"The final draft is ready?" I gasped.

He nodded. "Ready and waiting for our signatures – if a certain butt cobra doesn't ruin six months of deliberations, that is."

At that, the two of us stopped in our tracks, exchanging a look of pure panic as we did, before simultaneously breaking into a full-on sprint.

"Monty Python, you get your scaly butt back here right now!" Roy was shouting as he chased his familiar through the densely crowded banquet hall. "I mean it, or there will be no cornbread for you tomorrow!"

The snake skittered to a halt, sending the nearest cluster of banshees into another shrieking fit.

"Please, I beg you!" Morris was imploring them. "The stones can't take the strain!"

I clapped a hand over my mouth, though my stifled grin immediately turned into a grimace as Zayn and I made our way through the completely packed chamber. Even now, six months later, I found myself wincing whenever someone brushed against me in a crowd – as though Sol's claim might reappear at any moment.

Inhaling deeply, I pressed a hand to the already-healed tattoo on my chest, comforted by the intermingling warmth of Zayn's heartbeat and mine.

There were so many people crammed into that massive hall, as though every surviving soldier from the battle had shown up with their spouse, children, next-door neighbors, and grandparents in tow. I smiled at a large group of female tommyknockers, who looked just like their husbands, but with slightly smaller noses, as well as a gaggle of satyrs who were bleating over some off-color joke. Even Grog had shown up, fuzzy earmuffs and all. The troll flashed me a green-toothed grin and a friendly wave as we passed.

In order to accommodate the sheer number of fae that had come to witness the historic signing, two of the three banquet tables had been removed from the dining hall, and the third was pushed horizontally against the far end of the chamber. There, ten chairs had been arranged for the ten fae delegates who had been selected to represent their constituents. Safir was seated on the far left, acting on behalf of the southern elves. Beside her sat Kløssen, who spoke for the elves of the north. Then came Lam, official envoy of the realm's surprisingly robust satyr population; Saoirse, on behalf of all the banshee covens; and Xianis, representing the harpies. Boris, the delegate for the tommyknocker clans, was standing on the chair beside her. Beside him sat Lanmè, who was decked out in colorful garlands of dried seaweed, iridescent seashells, and a shimmering blue dress for the occasion.

And then, of course, was my mother, who was advocating in an official capacity for the vampires because their presiding covens were still ironing out some residual kinks regarding acceptable snacking practices. Zayn took his seat beside her as the realm's official ambassador for the in-succubi, while I lowered myself into the last chair, right behind the placard that read: TALIA KESTENBAUM, EMISSARY FOR THE HUMANS AND THE VOICELESS.

I personally fought to add that last part to my title. After all, the realm was home to countless fae, many of whom either couldn't speak or simply chose not to: unicorns, smaller pixies, and dragons, to name a scant few. Hell, even fachans needed someone looking out for them – provided they didn't try to maim their own delegate in the process, of course.

"Here, *bubaleh*, you've got some *schmutz* on your cheek," Mom said, leaning toward Zayn. "Did you do it yet?" she whispered – which, in Jewish-mother terms, is a half-step below a shout.

"Not yet," he murmured.

"Do what?" I asked, raising a suspicious eyebrow.

"Order!" Lam bellowed, banging his palm on the table in lieu of a gavel, which "someone" had apparently forgotten to bring to the last few meetings.

And yes, that someone was me.

Zayn squeezed my hand beneath the table. "I'll tell you after."

I frowned. "But—"

"Order!" Lam tried again, though it didn't do much to dull the low roar of the thousands of Seelies and Unseelies who had gathered before us.

Luckily, Mom was ready with her patented two-finger whistle, which sliced through the air like a sharp knife through slow-cooked brisket, silencing the entire crowd.

"Thank you, plum-blossom!" Lam called over to her.

"No problem, Lamby-kins!"

After balancing a pair of thick glasses on the tip of his nose, Lam rose to his hooves, holding a scroll of rolled-up parchment aloft. "I hereby call to order the thirty-seventh session of the interim Fae Council, with the fervent hope that we may conclude this gathering as the inaugural assembly of the cooperative initiative that shall henceforth be known as the Governing Council of Fae."

The crowd broke into a robust smattering of applause that carried all the way through the massive double doors of the banquet hall, which had been propped open so that several hundred more spectators could flood into what used to be known as the throne room.

Out of the corner of my eye, I noticed the tattoo on my chest was fluttering rapidly; it took me a moment to register that it was mirroring Zayn's skyrocketing heart rate. A pang of sympathy knotted in my chest; the last time a large gathering of fae had convened within these walls, their peace treaty wound up unsigned and soaked in the blood of those who had penned it.

"Hey." I squeezed his hand tightly beneath the table. "I'm right here."

He flashed me a grateful smile.

"I want to thank not only our delegates, but their dedicated constituents as well, who arrived here within a mere candle or two following the announcement. It has taken nearly two seasons to finalize this treaty, given the many races of the continent – not to mention their accompanying considerations, which we've painstakingly taken into account. Upon reaching a consensus earlier this evening, we knew it would be necessary to act quickly. So, to those of you who portaled here from the far reaches of the continent – using properly-working Waypoints, thanks to the efforts of this council," he added proudly, "we both thank and welcome you. Today is a day for the history books – a day that shall be regaled by future generations not just with stories, but with murals and songs and theatrical reenact—"

Safir coughed – a not-so subtle hint for Lamswyth to speed things along.

"Ah, yes, well…" he blustered, taking a moment to recompose himself after skipping past what was most likely meant to be a two-hour speech. "Suffice it to say, it is a historic moment for our realm, and one I am honored to share with all who have gathered here." With a businesslike flourish, Lam unfurled the thirty-foot-long scroll, which rolled halfway down the table. "Delegates, please take out your quills, and remember: as is the case in *all* matters of this council, this motion must pass unanimously in order to be signed into law."

He, along with several others at that table, cleared their throats nervously.

Safir rose to her feet, quill in hand. "It is with great optimism and joy that I sign this historic treaty on behalf of the southern elves, who look forward to a new era of cooperation and equality among *all* fae."

The room erupted into cheers as she pressed her pen to the parchment. Korinne, who was standing at the very front of the crowd with a smile that spread from ear to ear, wiped a tear from her eye.

Kløssen took the parchment next. "The northern elves, as well, look forward to an age of peace and prosperity," he said, in a rather clipped, heavily-accented tone. But he too signed without hesitation, drawing an equally-fervent cheer from the crowd.

Next was Lam, who noted his signature without further preamble, followed by Saoirse, who likewise signed the treaty sans spectacle or drama, politely brushing away the ice before passing it along.

And then came Xianis.

My grandmother's bare breasts swung from her chest like two over-filled sand bags as she rose to her talons. Lam watched them, mesmerized, before roughly clearing his throat and shifting his gaze to the ceiling.

"It was not my wish to create a joint council of fae," Xianis called out, sending a sharp hush through the room. "On the contrary, I fervently espoused a reinstatement of the monarchy, which should have been ruled by my granddaughter, Talia"—she jerked a wing in my direction, making me slump halfway down my chair—"the gold-blooded daughter of my beloved son, Howard, who was the last-born son of the late King Saedis."

A collective gasp rose up from the crowd.

"Oh, fuck me," I groaned, scrubbing a hand across my face.

Mom's eyes shifted to scarlet as she bared her pointed incisors. "Xianis, if you don't shut up and sign that treaty right now—"

"Oh, go pluck a tail feather, Diedre," Xianis harrumphed, turning back to the visibly uncomfortable crowd. "*As I was saying,* I was in full support of the rightful ruler of this realm ascending to her Creator-given place… Unfortunately, my granddaughter is not as ambitious or as cunning as her grandmother."

I stared at Xianis through the slits of my fingers, horrified.

"No, she is neither ruthless nor power-hungry. In fact, Talia would sooner regurgitate the worm right out of her own empty gullet to feed the destitute and impoverished – yet another reason she would have made a wonderful queen. Luckily for all of you," she continued, her sneer softening into a wry smile, "she did something far more noble instead: she helped create this governing body."

I withdrew my hands from my eyes, jaw falling open.

"Regrettably, this historic treaty doesn't grant the harpies a single drop of precedence over the rest of you, despite my familial connection to the parliament's stalwart leader. It will merely protect our rights alongside everyone else's, ensuring an egalitarian society." Her wild blue eyes darted to me, her mouth curling into a mischievous grin. "Which, I suppose, will just have to be good enough."

With that, she gathered up her boobs from the parchment, brandishing her own, self-feathered quill, and signed it with an ostentatious flick of her wing.

The harpies erupted in a triumphant cacophony of screeches and squawks, while the rest of the hall broke into scattered, polite applause.

"And here you were worrying she would make a scene," Zayn muttered to my mom, eliciting a disdainful snort.

The treaty then arrived at Lanmè, who darted a quick glance in my direction before rising to her feet. The accompanying hush through the chamber was so profound, you could have heard a pin drop from fifty feet away.

"While the mermaids cannot promise we will *never* drown one of you," she began, her voice as clear and lovely as a windchime, "particularly if you were to tread too far into our waters, or if, for example, the saltwater fish population were to drop significantly—"

This time it was Zayn who buried his face in his hands, stifling a groan.

"—we are pleased to see the prohibition of siren traps included in this agreement, and therefore promise to do our very best to allow the majority of you safe passage through our waters."

She gracefully sat back down in her seat, signing her name in a delicate flourish.

There wasn't a ton of applause after that speech.

One by one, the rest of the delegates rose, each sharing a few brief words about their hope and excitement for the future before dutifully adding their own names to the growing list of signatures at the bottom of the treaty. When the parchment finally arrived at my mother, she rose to her feet, her marble-white skin flushing several shades of pink.

"Hi, everyone," she waved, then cleared her throat. "Uh, seeing as I'm only half-vampire, I'm just going to stay on the council until the rest of the vampires are ready to integrate back into fae society. Now, as you all hopefully know by now, the vampires had become completely dependent on The Sex Pervert Who Shall Not Be Named because the blood he was giving them was laced with an incredibly addictive drug. And for anyone who's ever worked with addicts, you know how hard it is to kick the habit, not to mention the lengths they'll go to for the next hit. However, I'm happy to report that the vampire soup kitchen is off to a great start. We've successfully rehabilitated over a hundred vampires, all of whom have pledged to stop by the kitchen for a steaming bowl of donated blood instead of maiming one of you."

Zayn and I exchanged glances as Mom went to sit down, then quickly stood back up. "Oh, and please help me give a big thank you to Korinne, whose herbal supplements have really helped with the withdrawal symptoms – thank you, *bubeleh!*"

The pointed tips of her ears turning pink, Korinne waved to the politely-clapping crowd while Mom signed off for the vampires, then passed the parchment to Zayn.

He gave my hand a quick squeeze before standing. "I want to thank all of the incubi and succubi who have gathered here today, who have nobly vowed to obtain consent from all potential sexual partners."

"Hooray for consent!" I cheered, clapping.

"I'm also happy to report that all of Sol's predatory nightclubs have been placed under new management. Thank you very much to Xander, Luther, and Jeff for overseeing that."

The applauding crowd parted for the triumvirate of Chrises, all three of whom were beaming from ear to ear.

"Who knows?" Zayn added. "With all of the positive changes occurring in the community, we might just see a chivalrous, sparkly incubus making an appearance in human mainstream media."

"We're way ahead of you!" Pine shouted.

"Yeah," Hemsworth added. "And Robert Pattinson's already on board!"

I let out a loud laugh, only to snap my mouth shut when no one else joined in. "Wait – Robert Pattinson's an incubus?"

Zayn nodded as he leaned forward to sign his name. "Yeah, nice guy too. I'll introduce you sometime."

I sat there for a long, rapidly-blinking minute before realizing everyone was waiting on me. I stood up nervously, grateful to feel Zayn's steadying hand on the small of my back as the room erupted in hushed whispers.

"Is that really Saedis's granddaughter?"

"Did you know she has gold blood?"

"I heard she's a queen in the human realm!"

"Um…" I started, my cheeks heating as I regarded the single line on the parchment without a signature. "I-I'm really sorry, but I don't think I can do this."

Lam's prodigious forehead plunked against the table, prompting Zayn, my mother, and every other delegate to stare at me in open-mouthed shock while the crowd exploded in salacious titters.

Frowning, I pulled a Sharpie out of my bra, uncapping the lid with my teeth. "Calm down, guys. All I was saying is that I don't think I can do it with a quill like the rest of you."

Korinne's snort was so loud, the rest of us gaped at her in surprise. "Teach your apprentice how to use a quill, Zæynek!"

"I've tried!"

"And I'm not his apprentice anymore!" I shouted, then quickly cleared my throat. "Um, anyway, there's not much else I can add, since the other delegates pretty much summed it all up." I glanced down the table, where nine fae emissaries were watching me with varying degrees of smiles. "But I would like to say how proud I am of everyone here, and to those hoping to join us in the future. Change is hard – I know that better than anyone. But I think trust is even harder, especially when you've been hurt so many times." My eyes darted to Zayn's, where they remained firmly glued. "And yet, here we are – each of us with our own unique scars and sorrows – *choosing* to set those fears aside so we can forge a better path forward…together. And I think that's a pretty big accomplishment in and of itself."

Zayn's brilliant green irises shone with pride.

"On behalf of my ancestors – human, Seelie, and Unseelie alike – as well as those fae who have yet to find a voice in this beautiful realm, I'm proud to sign my name as your tenth delegate," I said, scrawling my name on the final line of the parchment, simultaneously signing the new Governing Council of Fae into law.

The screams and applause that ensued were so loud, you'd have thought the entire room was filled with banshees. But no, it was just the collective cheer of a new, emboldened, peaceful generation of fae, all fiercely resolute in their pursuit of cooperation and peace. Biscuit and Mavros soared into the room like two brilliant fireballs, each alight in rainbow and gold flames that sent the crowd into an absolute tizzy. Korinne ran right up to Safir, throwing her arms around her in a celebratory embrace. Safir, in a rare momentary lapse of inhibition, swept Korinne into a passionate, open-mouthed kiss, which sent my heart leaping into my throat. Korinne took a stunned step backward, her eyes as wide as saucers, before throwing herself back into Safir's arms and kissing her fiercely.

"Atta girl," I whispered, grinning to myself. I turned to Zayn, preparing for us to do the same. But he wasn't standing.

He was kneeling.

"Lambchop!" my mother squealed. "He's doing it!"

"I'm coming!" Lamswyth shouted, practically leaping over the other delegates like a Billy goat.

Zayn pulled a small box from his pocket, flipping open the lid to reveal a diamond ring inside – but not just any diamond ring. My bulging eyes roved over the massive diamond and platinum band, where delicate filigree had been etched into a beautiful floral pattern.

"Is that…?" I choked out.

"The ring you designed for yourself was so beautiful, I knew I'd never be able to top it." The smile that stretched across Zayn's face was so wide – so genuine – it made my heart swell. "I found it sitting in my desk drawer, where you had left it and then promptly forgot about it six months ago. So, I've been carrying it around with me ever since, waiting for the right moment to ask you."

"To…ask me?" I stared at him, the edges of my vision turning white as my breaths started coming in short, shallow wheezes.

"Don't you dare faint!" Mom barked, thrusting my inhaler at me.

Zayn gazed up at me, his irises shining like two polished gems while Biscuit and Mavros circled above us, showering the two of us in falling glitter. "Talia, I love you more than I've ever loved anyone, with more fervor than I ever thought possible." He reached forward to take my hand in his, flashing me that same crooked smile that had made me fall in love with him to begin with. "Talia Judith Kestenbaum…will you make me the happiest man in all the realms by becoming my wife?"

"Yes," I whispered, more reflex than thought.

"Yes?" Zayn repeated, the word nearly lost to the swelling crescendo of cheers surrounding us.

"Yes!" I shrieked, dropping to my knees to throw my arms around his neck. "Yes, I'll marry you!"

"Oh, happy day!" Lam bleated.

"Tell her the other thing!" Mom gestured frantically.

"Oh, right!" Zayn reached into his pocket, withdrawing a second ring with a tiny princess-cut diamond set in yellow gold.

"That's the ring your father gave me when he proposed thirty years ago," Mom wept. "I searched for that thing for *two years*, only to realize it had fallen off when I was packing up a box of his old ties!"

The hairs on the back of my neck stood on end, and for the briefest moment, I could have sworn I smelled Dad's cologne.

"Anyway," she continued, simultaneously blowing her nose into Lam's soiled handkerchief. "I want you to wear this when you go to work, because you shouldn't wear such gaudy jewelry in that part of town – it's not safe!"

"Not safe for the lamentable creature who dares cross the most powerful Runemaster in all the realms!" Lam chortled.

Zayn slipped the platinum ring on my finger, then unclasped my necklace so I could thread my mother's ring through the chain. When I put the necklace back on, the gold ring settled beside my gold locket, gleaming as brightly as my gold blood.

"Beautiful," he whispered, pressing his lips to my forehead.

He helped me to my feet just in time for us both to be crushed by a veritable dog-pile of tearful embraces: Mom, Lam, Saoirse, Roy, Korinne, Safir, my grandmother…the list of well-wishers was as long as the treaty we'd just signed. It took several minutes before the crowd had thinned enough for Zayn and I to find our way back into each other's arms.

"Did you ever think you could be so happy?" I asked him, half-laughing, half-sobbing.

"No." He swept me into a tight embrace, kissing the tears from my eyes. "Not in a million lifetimes."

Several hours later, and well after midnight, Zayn and I finally crawled into my tiny twin bed inside my tiny studio apartment, winding down for the night.

"Goodnight, Mavros," Zayn whispered, gently scratching the ruffled feathers along her neck.

After taking a few moments to bask in his Grade-A head scratches, she hopped onto my wrist, peering up at me with wide, intelligent eyes.

"Goodnight, Mavvie," I said, kissing the top of her head. "Sweet dreams."

She nuzzled up against my cheek, then disappeared in a blaze of gold, reappearing as a matching tattoo on both Zayn's forearm and mine.

Once Biscuit had triple-checked their egg, which was perfectly swaddled in its pile of soft towels that had been painstakingly placed beneath a warm heating lamp, he perched atop the comforter on one foot, taking a moment to preen his vibrant rainbow feathers before bed.

"Head scratch?" he asked, sidling toward my hand.

"Always," I smiled.

"Did you tell him about the surprise that's coming tomorrow?" Zayn asked, joining in on the head-scratch fest.

"S'prise?" Biscuit asked, snapping to attention.

"Oh, you know, nothing special," I said, keeping my voice casual. "Just some supplies for when your little chicky arrives…feeding syringes, an extra perch for the shop…and eight pounds of marzipan."

"MAR-ZEE-PAN!" Biscuit screeched, flapping his wings. "S'prise come now?"

"Not now. Tomorrow."

"T'morrow come now?"

"No." Zayn laughed. "Tomorrow comes tomorrow. Now go to bed, you little degenerate. You'll need all the sleep you can get before that little chick has you up all night on feeding duty."

"Doody…" Biscuit sighed. "Okay. G'night." He gave us a little wave with his claw before disappearing in a colorful flash.

I ran my fingers over his tattoo, admiring how his rainbow flames faded perfectly into the golden fire from which Mavros's beautiful raven form emerged, her wings spread like a phoenix rising from gilded ashes.

"Will you miss this place?" Zayn asked as he pulled me tightly against his chest.

"Will I miss the cramped kitchen, not having a bathtub, and the fact that my recycling bin is right next to my clothes hamper?" I tapped my chin in mock thoughtfulness. "Hmm, let me think about that."

Zayn kissed my forehead, chuckling. "Did you hear your mom hocking me about grandchildren three minutes after I proposed to you? Jewish mothers really don't waste any time getting down to baby business, do they?"

"Oy vey," I groaned. "Did you tell her you're not even sure if you can have kids?"

"I would have, but I'm not ready to die yet."

"Smart move." I nodded, switching off the tiny lamp on my nightstand.

We held each other in the dark for a few moments before Zayn quietly asked, "And if I can't? If it turns out I'm sterile, like most incubi?"

I yawned as I nuzzled even closer to him, burying my face in his chest. "Then we'll remain a family of four – soon to be five – and I'll love you all the same."

"Oh, Tal," Zayn whispered, pressing his lips to my forehead. My eyes slowly began to close, only to flutter back open when he murmured, "And if we live to be hundreds of years old, having spent so much time in the other realm?" He forced out a chuckle. "For creatures like us, promising to love someone 'til death do us part' is a bit more of a commitment than it is for humans."

I abruptly reached out to flick the light back on. "Are you having second thoughts about getting married?" I asked, biting my lip.

Zayn's eyebrows drew together in genuine confusion. "No – I'm worried you might get sick of *me* after a century or two!"

I thought about that for a long moment, chewing on the inside of my cheek. "I guess I can't really promise to love you until death, can I?"

Shock flickered across Zayn's expression, though he pressed his lips into a tight smile to hide it. "No…No, I guess I could never ask you to make such a promise. I mean, most elves are strictly monogamous for the entirety of their lives, but…" He swallowed, his smile wavering. "But I suppose that's a pretty lofty standard."

"Yes," I agreed. "It's pretty unrealistic."

Zayn nodded again, the Adam's apple in his throat bobbing as he reached across the bed to turn off the light.

"It's unrealistic"—I put my hand on his arm, stopping him—"because I already died once…and even then, I never stopped loving you. Not for a single moment."

His eyes widened.

"So, in actuality, a more accurate vow would be something like, 'I'll love you forever, *refusing* to let death do us part.'"

Zayn cupped my face in his hands, crushing his lips against mine. The hot pang of longing that twisted through my core was so intense, I let out a soft whimper. As I hoisted myself onto his lap, pressing my hands to his chest, a low rumble vibrated beneath my palms.

"Tal, no," Zayn growled, shaking his head. "You have to wake up early."

He flicked off the light.

I leaned down to kiss him again, my lips curling into a mischievous grin as I turned the light back on. "Eh, I'll sleep when I'm dead."

I could feel Zayn's throbbing hot arousal pressing between my legs as his grip on my waist tightened. Without wasting another second, I tore off his shirt, then quickly yanked off my own—

And then the phone on my nightstand began to vibrate.

"What the…?" I muttered, reaching for it. "Oh, for fuck's sake – it's my mom."

"Answer it," Zayn urged. "It might be important."

Sighing, I tapped the vibrating green bubble. "Mom, what's wrong? It's one-thirty in the—"

"So, Lamby and I are out taking a walk on the boardwalk tonight, just minding our own business—"

"What?" I demanded, not bothering to switch to speakerphone because her voice was already permeating the entire room. "You can't just casually stroll around Miami with a *satyr!*"

"Oy, calm down! It was eleven p.m. on a Tuesday night – who's gonna see? Besides, I let him borrow one of my tracksuits so no one would notice. Anyway," she barreled on before I could interject again, *"so there we are, talking about all the grandbabies*

we're gonna have, when out of nowhere, I get a whiff of 'jiy-rows'—"

"Jiy-rows?" I repeated, dumbfounded.

"I think she means gyros," Zayn whispered.

"And as I'm breathing in this delicious, mouthwatering smell, it occurs to me that I haven't eaten all day. Suddenly, all I can think about are gyros! Before I know it, I'm flying through the air, with Lamby-kins shouting up at me from down below—"

"Whoa, whoa, whoa! What do you mean, *flying?!*"

"What do you mean, what do I mean? I mean flying! Anyway, the next thing I know, I'm flying through the open window of that little Greek bistro off Biscayne Boulevard – you know the one with the pistachio baklava that's to die for?"

"MA!" I shouted. "Go back to the part where you were flying!"

"Well, by then, I wasn't flying anymore!"

"That's true," Lam interjected. *"By the time I arrived at the establishment, she had already transformed from a bat and back into her human form—"*

"WHAT DO YOU MEAN *FROM A BAT?!*" I shrieked into the receiver.

"ANYWAY, this little old lady was sitting at the register counting money," Mom continued, *"and the moment she sees me, she starts screaming bloody murder like I'm Dracula himself! Of course, I can't understand a single word of it because, you know, it's all Greek to me. But then the* meshuggeneh yenta *starts chasing after me with a wooden cross, yelling something about 'Christós'!"*

Zayn clapped a hand over his mouth.

"So I finally turn to this old woman – who's still waving this crucifix at me like a Catholic priest at an exorcism, mind you – and I roll my eyes and say, "Oy, lady, have you got the wrong vampire!"

I stared at my phone in mute horror, unable to muster up a single syllable in response to the increasingly-incomprehensible words coming out of my mother's mouth.

"And anyhow, long story short, that's how Lambchop and I ended up getting three whole trays of baklava for FREE! Isn't that great? You and Zayn will have to come over tomorrow to help us eat it all! Talia? ...Hello?"

After a solid ten seconds of silence had passed, Zayn gently took the phone from my hand and turned the volume all the way down before speaking into the receiver. "That's great, Dee—er, Mom. We'll be sure to stop by for some baklava tomorrow... Mm-hmm, sure thing... Yes, I will remind her not to lose the ring you gave her... I agree, that would be terrible... Okay, we love you too... Goodnight."

Exhaling sharply, he switched my phone to silent and set it back on the nightstand to charge, turned off the light, then pulled me against his chest, where he began dutifully stroking my hair. "Do you, uh...want to talk about it?"

"Which part?" I moaned into his shoulder. "The part about my mom frolicking around Miami with a satyr, her turning into bat, or the fact that every Greek restaurant in the state is going to start keeping wooden Stars of David on hand for the next time some random Jewish vampire flies through the window looking for 'jiy-rows'?"

Zayn was quiet for a long moment. "You know...I didn't take you seriously before, but I think I finally understand now."

"Understand what?"

As he brushed a kiss against my forehead, I could feel his lips quivering from the laughter he was desperately trying to suppress. "In all the realms of the universe, there is no force greater – or more terrifying – than the love of a Jewish woman."

The End.

SOLOMON
JAÍNA
SAEDIS
XIANIS
MARÁNTHE
YENNA
MIKHÆL
ZÆYNEK
HOWARD
DIEDRE
TALIA
MARRIAGE
DALLIANCE
BANSHEE
ELF
INCUBUS
HUMAN
HARPY

NOTE FROM THE AUTHOR

I cannot believe it's been just over a year since *Inked* came out.

I remember March 2022 like it was yesterday, mostly because it was a pretty bleak time in my life. My mental health wasn't great for several reasons; chief amongst them, I believed I'd failed as a writer despite my best efforts, and was seriously considering throwing in the towel to pursue other, more lucrative (and far less fulfilling) endeavors.

But now here we are, one year later. And in that time, the Gilded Blood series has accumulated 2,000+ Amazon reviews, a 4-book audiobook deal, over 5 million KU pages read, tens of thousands of books sold, and #1 international urban fantasy bestseller tags from half a dozen countries.

To everyone who has supported this series, thank you from the bottom of my heart. You are, quite literally, a life saver, and I absolutely would not – could not – be doing this without you.

As for what's next, I suppose time will tell. But, with luck, and your support, I hope to remain on this extraordinary writing journey and continue sharing my stories with all of you. So, if you enjoyed this series, or any of my other books, please consider leaving a review! More than anything else, your words help indie authors get the exposure we need to create new stories to share with you, our beloved readers.

One final note: To anyone who might be thinking about throwing in the towel on their own dream, please take this as your sign to give yourself just one more wholehearted push. After all, you never know where you might be a year from now.

Rachel ♡

www.RachelRener.com
(You can order signed books here!)
www.facebook.com/thelightningconjurer
www.twitter.com/RachelRener
@AuthorRachelRener
@AuthorRachelRener

ואקוממוע

GLOSSARY FOR THE GOYIM

Used by Ashkenazic Jews, Yiddish is a language that is related to German (but also has many Slavic, Hebrew, and Aramaic loan words). Though originally written in Hebrew, the below definitions are an American hybrid of Yiddish and English called Yinglish.

Enjoy!

Boychik
(BOY-chick) n. | term of endearment for a young boy, or a young man, esp. one with whom you are familiar.

Bubaleh
(BUB-e-leh) n. | "little grandma"; a general term of endear-ment, esp. for children

Bubbe
(BUB-eh) n. | Grandmother/Grandma (Zayde is Grandfather)

Chalerya
(hal-AIR-re-ah) n. | a mean-spirited woman; a shrew; harpy.

Chutzpah
(HOOTZ-pah) n. | nerve; insolence; sass; confidence
var: **Chutzpahdik** *(HOOTZ-pah-dik)* adj. | Showing chutzpah

Farkakteh
(fuh-KOK-teh) adj. (vul.) | lousy, messed up, ridiculous; shitty, full of shit

Farshtinkener
(*fuh-SHTOONK-eh-neh*) n. | stinky person; smelly person; adj. smelly, stinky, rotten

Goyim
(GOY-im) n., pl. | non-Jewish persons, gentiles

Kasha varnishkes
(KASH-ah var-NISH-kehs) n. | traditional Jewish dish made with sautéed onions, cooked bowtie pasta, and buckwheat groats or kasha.

Kibitz
(KI-bitz) v. | to meddle; to make unwanted and intrusive comments; to needlessly interfere.
var: **Kibitzer** *(KIB-bit-zer)* n. | one who kibbitzes

Kindelah
(KIN-de-la) n. | Lit. "little children"; (as a term of address) "friends", "guys".

Kugel
(KUH-gl) n. | a baked pudding or casserole, usually made from lokshen or Jewish egg noodles

Kvetch
(kVETCH) v. | to gripe; complain; to bemoan one's fate.

Matzo
(MAHT-sa) n. | unleavened bread

L'chaim
(leh-HIGHM) phr. | a Jewish toast, literally "to Life!" in Hebrew

Meshuggeneh
(me-SHOO-ge-neh) n./adj. | Crazy; a crazy person.
var: **Meshugge** *(me-SHOOG-eh)* adj. | crazy; insane

Mensch
(MENSH) n. | a stand-up person of integrity and honor.

Mishegas
(MISH-eh-goss) n. | madness; craziness; insanity

Oy!
(OIY) excl. | a lament, a protest, a cry of dismay, a reflex of delight; *Oy!* is uttered in as many ways as the utterer's histrionic ability permits.

Oy gevalt!
(OIY ge-VALT) phr. | an exclamation of fear, panic, astonishment, etc. A cry for help, such as “Oh my God!” or “Good grief!” (Literally, “Oh, violence!”)

Oy gotenyu!
(OIY GOT-en-yoo) phr. | “God help us!” An exclamation of panic, pain, shock, or dismay.

Plotz
(PLAHTS) v. | to split, to burst, to explode; to pass out or faint [usually from excitement]

Schlep
(SHLEP) v./n. | to haul or carry (something heavy or awkward); a tedious or difficult journey

Schmaltz
(SHMALTS) n. | rendered chicken fat, often used to make latkes and matzo ball soup

Schmatta
(SHMAH-tah) n. | Old/ratty [comfortable] piece of clothing.

Schmegegge
(shmuh-GEH-ghee) n. | a contemptible person, an idiot

Schmuck
(SHMUCK) n. | slang, vulgar: one who is stupid or foolish; an obnoxious, detestable person. (Literally: penis)

Schmutz
(SHMUHTS) n. | dirt, stain, or filth.

Shreken
(SHREK-en) n. | “monsters” or “frights;” little known fact: the title of the 2001 film, *Shrek*, is based on the romanization of the Yiddish word for “monster”

Shabbos
(SHA-bus) n. | Ashkenazic term for Shabbat or the Sabbath; Judaism’s day of rest that starts just before sundown each Friday and ends at nightfall on Saturday.

Shiksa
(SHIK-sa) n. | a somewhat disparaging term for a non-Jewish female

Tateleh
(TAHT-e-leh) n. | a term of endearment for a boy or man; lit., “little father”

Tuchus
(TOO-kus) n. | rear end, bottom, backside, buttocks

Verklempt
(fer-KLEMT) adj. | overcome with emotion; choked up.

Yenta
(YEN-tah) n. | a blabbermouth, someone who can't keep a secret, a vulgar and ill-mannered woman, a shrew.

JÍNI KELÍMI'NAZ / ELVISH DICTIONARY
(TAL AL'BAŞÁ / SOUTHERN DIALECT)

– PRONUNCIATION –

VOWELS	PRONUNCIATION	CONSONANT DIFFERENCES
a / â / á	ah ("spa")	R = flipped
æ	eye ("my")	K̂ = ch like *challah*
ꜵ	ow ("wow")	Ş = sh like *shave*
e / é	ey ("hey")	V = softer, almost like W
i / í	ee ("see")	No Q, W, X or C (without -h)
o / ó	oh ("low")	
œ	uh ("sum")	^ = guttural
u / ú	ooh ("coo")	◌́ = emphasized

– PHRASES –

ELVISH	ENGLISH
Ama azá'ye dáşti, kalb'ímth'i-œlún.	I am yours until my heart stops.
Amá'ye gúlvene.	Trust me.
Amæ ka'selrána namstad, azæ'damír.	We've come in peace to warn you.
Anak'tho al'preyam(i).	May your harvest be bountiful.
Aşek ema/azæ muhávsi.	May the Creator protect her/you.
Aşek ema rahât edír.	May she rest in peace (lit: May the Creator bring her comfort.)
Aşeki'şík aza muhávsi.	May the light of the Creator protect you.
Aşek'ríhmi dothára præd'na! El'thanek fucking lo máreth íbna!	Loosely: "May the Creator damn it all! That [fucking] son of a bitch!"
Aşek'ye lénim edím…	I swear to the Creator…

Ayi'şík emæ yem beşévi, Aşeki'rûm emæ muhávsi, Væyéni'k̂aan emæ hafízi, Aşeyái'preyám'en emæ korsávi."	*Elvish prayer:* May the light of the moon nourish us, May the grace of the Creator protect us, May the blood of our veins preserve us, May the blessings of the Mother sustain us.
Aza hame-şey'émtho ni.	You are my everything.
Aza na-vaşí el sahíp ama'ye taş'en şálvar.	You do not have the right to question me.
Aza téşik'en edím.	Thank you.
Azæ ni al'Jíni'k̂aan ta? (Amæ ni al'Jíni'k̂aan.)	Are you both of elven blood? (We are both…)
Ema k̂aan krâliyet vaşía.	She is of royal blood.
Emæ (ni) œldurúş.	I'll kill them (both).
Evet / Na	Yes / No
İnát'tho niyé cham'ak ta?	What is your business here?
Kalb'ímtha azá'ye dáşti	I love you (lit: my heart belongs to you.)
Nyæ al'Jín-tal na-hâlmi ta?	Why is she not speaking Elvish?
Niya chamak Padeşáh'tho ta?	Where is your king?
Nyæ ka'selrána cham'ak ta?	Why have you come here?
Sevyán'the sivích'en váşi!	Fuck him! (lit: may his lover get venereal pustules!)
Seyúz Aşeya azæ'le hâlmir istía.	The great mother wants to speak with you.
Za'thol!	Get in here!
Zíman al'chamak!	Land ho!

– Glossary –

Elvish	**English**
'emtho/'imtha	My (m/f)
'ila / 'yla	For
'tho/'tha	Your (m/f)
'ye	At / to
Ama / Aza / Azæ / Amæ	I (me) / you / you (pl.) / we (us)
Amát	Hope

Anak	Crop
Arényi'dayen	Spider parrot
Aşek	Creator
Aşeya	Mother
Ay	Moon
Ay'aşéya	Moon Mother
Ayi'şík	Moonlight
Başá	South
Chamak / Al'chamak / Niya chamak	Here / There / Where
Damír	To warn
Daştír	To belong
Diká	Girl / Daughter
Edír	To give
El'/Al'	Of / That / To
Ema / Emo / Emæ	she (her) / he (him) / they (them)
Gulvenir	To trust
Hâlmir	To speak
Háme	Every / all
Háme-şey	Everything
İnát	Business/Purpose
İşík	Light / torch / candle
İstír	To want
Jín / Jíni / Jíni'tal	Elf / Elven / Elvish
Jiyâné kalb'ímtha	My betrothed (lit: life of my heart)
Ka'[verb]	Past tense modifier
K̂aan	Blood
Kalb	Heart
Kelími'naz	Dictionary (lit: word silo)
Kœrta	A long-sleeved, high-collar dress
Kórsavir	To sustain
Krâliyet / Krâliye	Royal / Crown
Lénim edír	To swear
Mæthir	To come/arrive
Muhávsir	To protect
Musáf	Advisor

Namstad	Peace
Nir	To be
Niya / Niyé / Niyæ	What / Who / Why
Nya / Nyé / Nyæ	What / Who / Why
Œldrur	To kill
Œlun	Death
Pádeşah / Paşahdî Şahéni'şah / Paşéni'şah	King / Queen King of Kings / Queen of Queens
Paş'aşéya	Queen's mother
Peşir	Son
Preyam	Bounty / blessing
Preyamír	To be blessed/bountiful
Rahât	Comfort
Rahât edír	To comfort (someone)
Rûm	Grace
Şahéni'musáf	King's advisor
Şazáde / Şazád'emtho	Prince / my prince
Şey	thing
Sahíp	Right / Privilege
Selránir	To come
Sevyá	Lover / Darling
Seyúz	Big/Great
-ta	Question / interrogative
Tal	Tongue/speech
Taş'en şályar	To question/doubt (lit: to cast stones)
Teşík'en (Edír)	(To give) Thanks
Tulúm	A man's tunic
Væyen	Veins
Váşir	To have
Ve / O	And (too) / Or
Yem beşévir	To feed
Za'thol!	Get in here!
Zíman	Land
Zóbahâr	Winter

Cheat Sheet for Aspiring Runemasters

Rune	*Appellation*	*Function*	*Target*
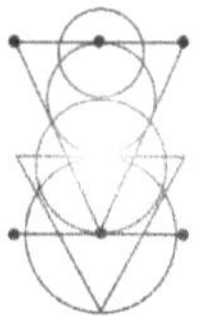	**Amplification Rune**	Used to Increase, Intensify, & Inspire	Any object producing auditory or visual output
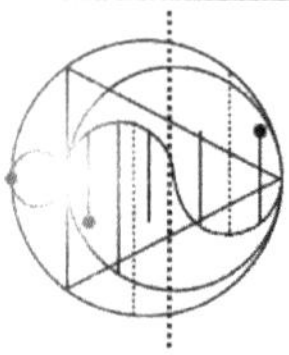	**Animalia Rune**	Used to Change into any Creature or Critter	Any living creature with a corporeal form
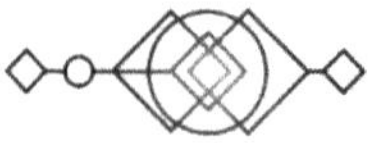	**Chaining Rune**	Used to Bind, Bolt, & Bond	Any tangible object or creature, up to 100 standard fae stone* *1,278.4 terran lbs
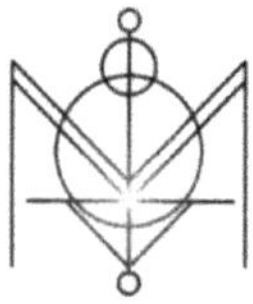	**Concealment Rune**	Used to Cover, Camouflage, & Conceal	Any object / creature with a minor magical signature
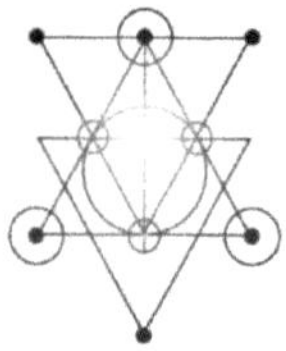	**Greater Concealment Rune**	Used to [Greatly] Conceal, Camouflage, & Cache	Any object / creature with a potent magical signature

	**Greater Counteraction Rune**	Used to Neutralize, Nullify, & Negate	Most curses, spells, jinxes, hexes, and magical afflictions
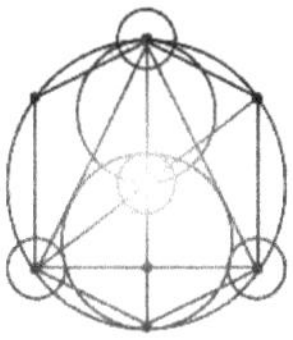	**Extinguishing Rune**	Used to Snuff, Smother, & Souse	Fire, sparks, and (depending on the ink used) unbridled sexual fervor* **Incubi, succubi, and satyrs excluded*
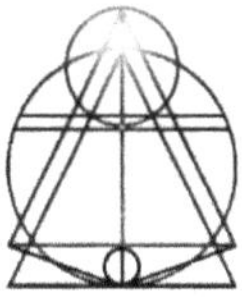	**Fulmen Rune**	Used to Electrocute, Electrify, & Eliminate	Any tangible object or creature *(Need access to sky and /or Greater Condensation Rune)*
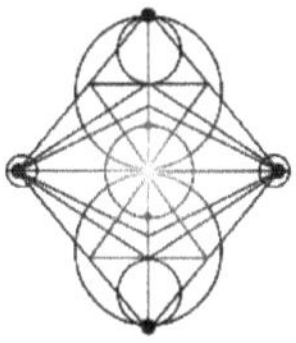	**Ignis Rune**	Used to Burn, Blister, and Set Ablaze	Any tangible object or creature
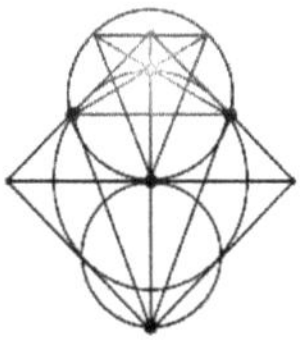	**Immolation Rune**	Used to Incinerate, Immolate, & Ignite	Any tangible object or creature

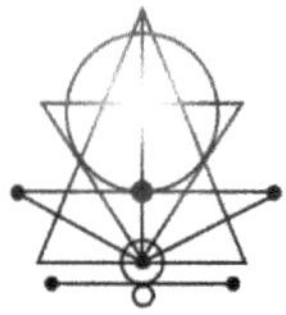	**Laundering Rune**	Used to Scrub, Scour, & Straighten	Any tangible, soiled object / creature
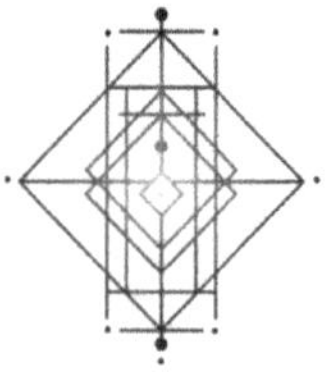	**Ligature Rune**	Used to Tether, Truss, & Tie	Any tangible object / creature
	**Protection Rune**	Used to Defend Against Malignant & Malevolent Miscreants	Any living creature with a corporeal form
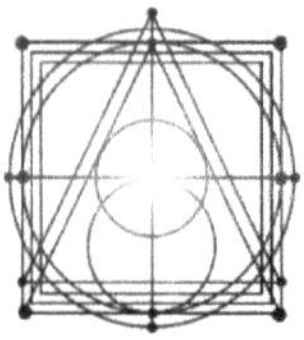	**Restoration Rune**	Used to Repair, Reinforce, & Renovate	Any dilapidated object *(Not to be used on living creatures due to risk of limb disarrangement)*
	**Resurgence Rune** (a.k.a. "Greater Revitalization" Rune)	Used to Revitalize, Recover, & Restore	Any dilapidated creature *(Not to be used on inanimate objects due to risk of inadvertent animation)*
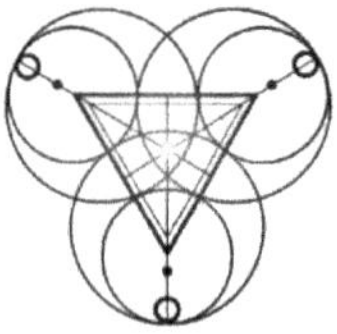	**Shield Rune**	Used to Shelter, Safeguard, & Secure	Any tangible object / creature

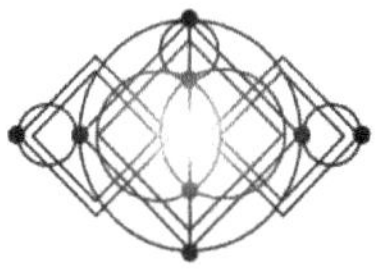	**Smokescreen Rune**	Used to Dissolve, Disperse, & Disappear	Self
	**Tesseract Rune**	Used to Teleport, Transport, & [Instantaneously] Travel	Any living creature with a corporeal form
	**Translation Rune**	Used to Transcribe, Transform, & Transliterate	Any living creature with some semblance of auditory processing
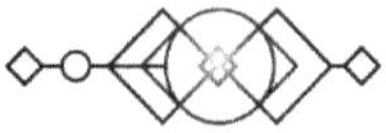	**Unchaining Rune**	Used to Unbind, Unclasp, & Unlock	Any bound object or creature* **Excluding iron binds*
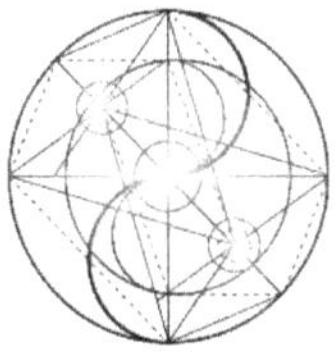	**Ventus Rune**	Uses Wind to Propel, Push, & Press Ahead	Any tangible object / creature

The Lightning Conjurer Series

Three years ago, I woke up in an abandoned cabin without a single memory – not even my own name. Since then, I've been doing my best to stay off the grid. But this week? Well, that's proving to be a problem.

From freak tornados to exploding fireplaces, strange things are happening all around me. Aiden, my new (and irritatingly attractive) college professor, says he knows "what" I am. A strange car is following me everywhere I go. And now an organization of people claiming to be "like me" are entreating me to join them. But the deeper I venture into this world, the more I wonder – is this organization a safe haven or a cult?

Whatever it may be, I can't turn back now. Because the only way to unearth my past, my name, and this growing power deep within me is to brave the lion's den...

Even if that means disclosing the one secret about me that will shake the very world to its core.

~ Read Now on Amazon ~

THE GIRL WHO TALKS TO ASHES

Things change around Lilah. Like actually change.
An apple disintegrates. People age.
Dogs transform into puppies.
Or bones.

These changes seem to be tied to her epileptic seizures which is why she has to take that daily little blue pill. In fact, the pill works so well that Lilah seems like any other normal teenager.

Until the day she chooses not to take the pill. That day changes everything and Lilah begins to wonder what could happen if she let the seizures happen. But can she control them or will they control her?

~ READ NOW ON AMAZON~

THE LITTLE MORSEL

Feral, a retired war hero with ancient bones and thinning scales, has been living in a dragon retirement home for several centuries. There, his daily routine is always the same: wake up with creaky joints, force down the stale protein bars from Bites of Knights, avoid the caterwauling old females on the shuffleboard court, and then return to bed to dream of flying.

But when a tiny stray human shows up at his front boulder, Feral's ho-hum world is turned upside down. Once a tentative agreement not to eat this strange little "morsel" is forged, the two of them embark on a journey for applesauce that ends with each of them saving the other's life – in more ways than one.

THE LITTLE MORSEL is a warm, lighthearted adventure that shines a delicate light on loneliness, neglect, found family, and purpose. Multifaceted and relatable, it is a story that can be enjoyed by children and adults alike.

~ READ NOW ON AMAZON ~

FROM THE SHADOWS

VILLAINOUS TALES OF DARK LORDS, DESPOTS, AND DEVILS

I thought I would be the hero. Instead, I became the villain.

They curse me, call me ruthless, insane, unhinged... a monster.

But is life so black and white?

What if they took the time to understand my motivations? Would they still condemn me if they recognized the same monster lurking inside themselves? There's a villain inside us all. Unhinge yourself from reality and walk with me into the darkness.

If you dare...

FROM THE SHADOWS is an anthology of twenty-one villainous stories brought to you by the authors of Indie Fantasy Addicts.

~ READ NOW ON AMAZON ~

ACKNOWLEDGEMENTS

Dear Aaron: It's *possible* that when the *Gilded Blood* series magically transformed from three books into four, I may have gotten a *teensy* bit more obsessive / hyper-focused / manic than usual. Luckily, I had my husband / best friend / life buddy to remind me to do things like eat, drink water, take vitamins, and unclench my shoulders from time to time. On behalf of my mental, emotional, and musculoskeletal health: thank you, I'm sorry, and I'll never do that again… Probably.

Mom – while we may have screamed at one another like full-blooded banshees back when I was a brilliant, infallible, perfectly-polite teenager, and you were a calm, level-headed, not-even-a-teensy-bit neurotic parent-of-a-teenager, I'm so grateful that we've been able to foster such a close and loving adult relationship. Thank you for being so incredibly supportive of me and of this series, even when I stuck Dee Dee in purple velour tracksuits and made her go a little "batty" at the end. I love you to the moon and back. ♥

To Terrance / Smegol the Seagull / my sweet Jungle Chicken, I know you can't read, but I nevertheless wanted to tell you that I love you even more than you love almonds. Biscuit never could have blazed to life if not for you. Thank you for being my floof, even when you try to eat the keys off my keyboard as you're doing right now. sdjkaghawe

To the rest of my family, both biological and found, thank you so much for your love, support, enthusiasm, and unwavering encouragement these past few years. Dad, I'm really glad we had the idea of getting you a PG-rated version of the series. Thanks for partaking in Talia and Zayn's story, albeit the far less interesting chaste version!

To my J-squad, Janice, Jenn and Jessica, thank you for keeping me sane, or at least pretending that I was sane, during the 30 or 40 meltdowns I had while writing this book. I am immensely and forever grateful for your friendship.

David Green, you are a gift and a treasure and I love you immensely. Thank you for absolutely everything you do for me (and everyone else)! I can't wait to write our first adventure together!

To my editor, Sara, who has been such a champion and earnest supporter of this series: thank you for getting me through ~~three~~ er, *four* realms and back safely, all while dealing with multiple languages, anatomical quandaries, and em-dashes galore. It's been a wonderful 360,728-word ride!

Ashlynn – "I've heard it said that people come into our lives for a reason, bringing something we must learn. And we are led to those who help us most to grow, if we let them, and we help them in return." I'm so glad books have brought us back together after all these years. Thank you for everything you've done for this series and for me

Being a pantster is hard. Being a pantster working on her 4th book in an unplotted series is even harder. But having alpha readers like Aaron K., David G., Katie C., Mel W., Jessica W., Janice A., and Jessica L. help make it feel far less stressful. Thank you all so, so much!

To my ARC team, many of whom have been here since my very first book, I cannot thank you enough for your enthusiasm, your reviews, your shares, your gentle bullying of all your bookish friends to pick up my books… I appreciate your loyalty and support more than you could ever know!

I must offer my profound gratitude to @kayliereads_alot, @miche_123a, and @bookofmatchesmedia for spotlighting this series and drawing readers and excitement in a way I never could. I am immensely, *immensely* grateful to you and am forever in your d—*er.* Wait. You three ladies aren't fae, are you? *squinty eye*

To all of my readers and friends over at Indie Fantasy Addicts, you are the greatest corner of the internet and one of my favorite places to hang. I love and appreciate you all so much!

Tara Novie, I'll never be able to thank you enough for the work and heart you've poured into this series, bringing Talia to life in the audiobooks in a way no one else could. You are amazing, and I'm so grateful to call you a friend.

And to my readers, who come last in my dedications only because my gratitude for you is so profound and overwhelming: thank you for picking up my books when there are a record-shattering number of published books to choose from. Thank you for sticking with me throughout this series, which I've poured my heart into in hopes that your lives will be a little brighter because of it. And thank you, from the bottom of my heart, for making it possible for me to tell stories such as this by means of your support and generosity. I couldn't do this without you, and not a single day goes by where I take that for granted. I love you all.

(Even you, Christopher, who left a 1-star review of *Inked* citing that women should never do gymnastics unless they are wearing appropriately-short skirts.)

ABOUT THE AUTHOR

Rachel Rener is a #1 International bestselling contemporary fantasy author who loves blurring the line between science and magic.

She graduated from the University of Colorado after focusing on Psychology and Neuroscience. Since then, she has lived on three continents and has traveled to more than 40 countries.

When she's not engrossed in writing or hanging out at Indie Fantasy Addicts, Rachel enjoys riding her motorcycle, reading fantasy books, going to rock shows (both musical and mineralogical), Vulcanology (the lava kind as well as the pointy-eared variety), and playing D&D on the coolest podcast around, Of Dice and Friends. She lives in Colorado along with her husband and a feisty umbrella cockatoo named Terrance (a.k.a. "Jungle Chicken") that hangs out on her shoulder as she writes – whether invited or not.

Ingram Content Group UK Ltd.
Milton Keynes UK
UKHW020637180523
421954UK00014B/377

9 781088 013793